Praise for
Christopher Moore

"Clearly the unhinged Hiaasen. He's *Daily Show*–funny and willing to subvert anything."

—Janet Maslin, *The New York Times*

"The funniest writer of comic fantasy novels working today."

—*Washington Post Book World*

"The careers of the writers with even a quarter as much wit and joie de vivre as Moore are always worth following."

—*USA Today*

"Few contemporary authors are as consistently bizarre, poignant, funny and wonderful as Christopher Moore."

—*Rocky Mountain News* (Denver)

"Christopher Moore is a very sick man, in the very best sense of the word."

—Carl Hiaasen

"The thinking man's Dave Barry or the impatient man's Tom Robbins."

—*The Onion*

"If there's a funnier writer out there, step forward."

—*Playboy*

"Christopher Moore is rapidly becoming the cult author of today, filling a post last held by Kurt Vonnegut."

—*The Denver Post*

Also by Christopher Moore

CHRISTOPHER MOORE

COYOTE BLUE

Simon & Schuster Paperbacks

New York   London   Toronto   Sydney

Simon & Schuster Paperbacks
A Division of Simon & Schuster, Inc.
1230 Avenue of the Americas
New York, NY 10020

This book is a work of fiction. Names, characters, places, and incidents either are products of the author's imagination or are used fictitiously. Any resemblance to actual events or locales or persons, living or dead, is entirely coincidental.

First Simon & Schuster trade paperback edition March 2008

SIMON & SCHUSTER PAPERBACKS and colophon are registered trademarks of Simon & Schuster, Inc.

For information about special discounts for bulk purchases, please contact Simon & Schuster Special Sales at 1-800-456-6798 or business@simonandschuster.com

Designed by Jill Putorti

Manufactured in the United States of America

20 19 18 17

Library of Congress Control No.: 93030469

ISBN-13: 978-1-4165-5847-7
ISBN-10:   1-4165-5847-0

This book is dedicated to the Crow people.

ACKNOWLEDGMENTS

The author would like to thank the following people who helped during the research and writing of Coyote Blue:

IN CAMBRIA, CALIFORNIA: Darren Westlund, Dee Dee Leichtfuss, Jean Brody, Kathy O'Brian, Mike Molnar, Allison Duncan, and Elizabeth Sarwas.

IN LIVINGSTON, MONTANA: Tim Cahill, Bev Sandberg, Marnie Gannon, Cal Sorensen, Scott McMillian, Steve Potenberg, Dana and David Latsch, and Libby Caldwell.

IN CROW COUNTRY: Larry Kindness, the Oliver and Elizabeth Hugs family, the Hartford Stops family, Dale Kindness, Clara Whitehip Nomee, Melody Birdin Ground, John Doyle, and Barbara Booher at the Custer Battlefield National Monument.

IN WASHINGTON: Kathe Frahm in Seattle, for letting me be sick on her couch for a month; Adeline Fredine, the Colville tribal historian; Deborah J. MacDonald; and Mike Robinson.

And Nick Ellison in New York, Paul Haas in Los Angeles, and Rachelle Stambal at my side. Thanks.

AUTHOR'S NOTE

The people in this book are all products of my imagination and any resemblance to persons living or dead is purely coincidental. While some of the places in this book do exist, I've changed them for my own purposes, and any resemblance to real places is just an oversight on my part. In short, the whole thing is a damnable lie and contains not a shred of truth.

PRONUNCIATION

NOUN
When the word *coyote* refers to a canine animal, it is pronounced KAI-YO-TEE.

PROPER NOUN
When *Coyote* refers to a character of human appearance, or in the name *Old Man Coyote*, it is pronounced KAI-YOTE.

ADJECTIVE
When *coyote* is used as a modifier, as in *coyote ugly* (if you wake up in bed with your arm under the head of someone who is *coyote ugly*, and you would gnaw it off rather than wake that person up), it is pronounced KAI-YO-TEE.

TITLE
The title of this book is pronounced KAI-YO-TEE BLEW. Readers who have a problem with pronunciation might want to read it silently the first time through. This is doubly important if you are reading this on an airplane.

COYOTE BLUE

PART ONE

EPIPHANY

CHAPTER ONE

LIFE WILL FIND YOU

SANTA BARBARA, CALIFORNIA

While magic powder was sprinkled on the sidewalk outside, Samuel Hunter moved around his office like a machine, firing out phone calls, checking computer printouts, and barking orders to his secretary. It was how he began every business day: running in machine mode until he left for his first sales appointment and put on the right persona for the prospect.

People who knew Sam found him hardworking, intelligent, and even likable, which is exactly what he wanted them to find. He was confident and successful in business, but he wore his success with a humility that put people at ease. He was tall, lean, and quick with a smile, and people said he was as comfortable in a Savile Row suit before a boardroom of businessmen as he was lounging in jeans at Santa Barbara's wharf, trading stories and lies with the fishermen. In fact, the apparent ease with which Sam mastered his environment was the single disturbing quality people noticed in him. How was it that a guy could play so many roles so well, and never seem uncomfortable or out of place? Something was missing. It wasn't that he was a bad guy, it was just that you could never get close to him, you never got a feel for who he really was, which is exactly how Sam wanted it. He thought a show of desire,

of passion, of anger even, would give him away, so he suppressed
these emotions until he no longer felt them. His life was steady,
level, and safe.

So it happened that on an autumn-soft sunny day, not two
weeks after his thirty-fifth birthday, some twenty years after he
had run away from home, Samuel Hunter stepped out of his office
onto the sidewalk and was poleaxed by desire.

He saw a girl loading groceries into an old Datsun Z that was
parked at the curb, and to the core of his being, Sam wanted her.

Later he would recall the details of her appearance—a line of
muscle on a tan thigh, cutoff jeans, the undercurve of a breast
showing below the half shirt, yellow hair tied up haphazardly, ten-
drils escaping to brush high cheekbones and wide brown eyes—
but her effect on him now was like a long, oily saxophone note
that started somewhere in that lizard part of the brain where the
libido resides and resonated down his body to the tendons in his
groin and back into his stomach to form a knot that nearly doubled him over.

"You want her?" The question came from beside him, a man's
voice that startled him a bit, but not enough for him to tear his
eyes from the girl.

The question came again. "You want her?"

Already off balance, Sam turned toward the voice, then stepped
back in surprise. A young Indian man dressed in black buckskins
fringed with red feathers sat on the sidewalk by the office door.
While Sam tried to regain mental ground, the Indian dazzled a
grin and pulled a long dagger from his belt.

"If you want her, go get her," he said. Then he flipped the dagger
across the sidewalk into the front tire of the girl's car. There was a
thud and a high squealing hiss as the air escaped the tire.

"What was that?" the girl said. She slammed the hatchback and
moved to the front of the car.

Sam, in a panic, looked for the Indian, who had disappeared,
and then for the knife, which had vanished as well. He turned and

looked through the glass door into his outer office, but the Indian wasn't there either.

"I can't believe I manifested this," the girl said, staring at the flattened tire. "I've done it again. I've manifested failure."

Sam's confusion blossomed. "What *are* you talking about?"

The girl turned and looked at him for the first time, studied him for a second, then said, "Every time I get a job I manifest some kind of tragedy that ruins my chances of keeping it."

"But it's just a flat tire . . . You can't manifest a flat tire. I saw the guy that did this. It was . . ." Sam stopped himself. The Indian in black had triggered his fears of being found out, of going to prison. He didn't want to relive the shock. "It was probably some glass you picked up. You can't avoid that sort of thing."

"Why would I manifest glass in my tire?" The question was in earnest; she searched Sam's face for an answer. If he had one, he lost it in her eyes. He couldn't get a grip on how to react to any of this.

He said, "The Indian—"

"Do you have a phone?" she interrupted. "I have to call work and tell them I'll be late. I don't have a spare."

"I can give you a ride," Sam said, feeling stupidly proud of himself for being able to speak at all. "I was just leaving for an appointment. My car's around the corner."

"Would you do that? I have to go all the way to upper State Street."

Sam looked at his watch, out of habit only; he'd have driven her to Alaska if she had asked. "No problem," he said. "Follow me."

The girl grabbed a bundle of clothes from the Datsun and Sam led her around the corner to his Mercedes. He opened the door for her and tried not to watch her get in. Whenever he looked at her his mind went blank and he had to thrash around looking for what to do next. As he got in the car he caught a glimpse of her brown legs against the black leather seat and forgot for a moment where the ignition slot was. He stared at the dashboard and tried to calm himself, even as he was thinking, *This is an accident waiting to happen.*

The girl said, "Do you think that the Germans make such good cars to atone for the Holocaust?"

"What?" He started to look at her, but instead turned his attention to the road. "No, I don't think so. Why do you ask?"

"It doesn't matter, I guess. I just thought it might bother them. I have a leather jacket that I can't wear anymore because when I have it on I have to drive miles out of my way to avoid going by cow pastures. Not that the cows would want it back—zippers are hard for them—but they have such beautiful eyes, it makes me feel bad. These seats are leather, aren't they?"

"Vinyl," Sam said. "A new kind of vinyl." He could smell her scent, a mix of jasmine and citrus, and it was making driving as difficult as following her conversation. He turned the air-conditioning on full and concentrated on timing the lights.

"I wish I had calf eyes—those long lashes." She pulled down the visor and looked in the vanity mirror, then bent over until her head was almost at the steering wheel and looked at Sam. He glanced at her and felt his breath catch in his throat as she smiled.

She said, "You have golden eyes. That's unusual for someone with such dark skin. Are you an Arab?"

"No, I'm . . . I don't know. I'm a mongrel, I guess."

"I never met a Mongrel before. I hear they were great horsemen, though. My mother used to read me that poem: 'In Xanadu did Kublai Khan a stately pleasure dome decree . . .' I don't remember the rest. Someone told me that the Mongrels were like the bikers of their time."

"Who told you that?"

"This person who's a biker."

"Person?" Sam knew there was some reality to grab on to somewhere, a position from which he could regain control, if only he could get a straight answer.

"Do you know where the Tangerine Tree Café is on upper State? That's where I work."

"Just tell me a block or so before we get to it."

Even after twenty years Sam found it impossible to distinguish one area of Santa Barbara from another. Everything was the same: white stucco with red tile roofs. The city had been partially destroyed by an earthquake in 1925, and since then the city planners had required all commercial buildings to be built in the Spanish-Moorish style—they even dictated the shade of white that buildings were painted. The result was a beautifully consistent city with almost no distinctive landmarks. Sam usually spotted his destination just as he passed it.

"That was it back there," the girl said.

Sam pulled the car to the curb. "I'll go around the block."

She opened the car door. "That's okay, I can jump out here."

"No! I don't mind, really." He didn't want her to go. Not yet. But she was out of the car in an instant. She bent back in and offered her hand to shake.

"Thanks a lot. I work until four. I'll need a ride back to my car. See ya." And she was gone, leaving Sam with his hand still extended and the image of her cleavage burned onto his retinas.

He sat for a moment, trying to catch his breath, feeling disoriented, grateful, and a little relieved, as if he had looked up just in time to slam on the brakes and avoid a collision. He took his cigarettes from his jacket and shook one out of the pack, but when he reached for the lighter he noticed the bundle of clothes still lying on the seat. He grabbed the clothes, got out of the car, and headed down the street to the café.

The doors to the café were the big, heavy, hand-carved, pseudo-Spanish iron-banded variety common to almost all Santa Barbara restaurants, but once through them the decor was strictly Fifties Diner. Sam approached a gray-haired woman in a waitress uniform who was manning the cash register at the head of the long counter. He didn't see the girl.

"Excuse me," he said. "The girl that just came in here—the blonde—she left these in my car."

The woman looked him up and down and seemed surprised at his appearance. "Calliope?" she said, incredulously.

Sam checked his tie for spots, his fly for altitude.

"I don't know her name. I just gave her a ride to work. She had a flat tire."

"Oh." The woman seemed relieved. "You didn't look like her type. She went to the back to change. I guess she won't get far without these." The woman took the clothes from him. "Did you want to speak to her?" she asked.

"No, I guess not. I guess I'll let her get to work."

"It's no problem, that other guy is waiting for her too." The woman nodded down the counter. Sam followed her gaze to where the Indian was sitting, smoking a cigarette and blowing the smoke in four directions with each drag. He looked up at Sam and grinned. Sam backed away from the counter and through the doors, tripping on the step down to the sidewalk, almost falling, but catching himself on the wrought-iron railing.

He leaned on the railing feeling as if he had just taken a hard shot to the jaw. He shook his head and tried to find some sort of order to what was happening. It could be some kind of setup; the girl and the Indian in it together. But how could they know who he was? How did the Indian get to the café so fast? And if it was blackmail, if they knew about the killing, then why be so sneaky about it?

As he climbed back into the Mercedes he tried to shake off the feeling of foreboding that was creeping over him like a night fog. He'd just met the most beautiful woman he had ever seen and shortly he would see her again. He had come to her rescue; what better first impression? Even if he hadn't planned it. The Indian was a coincidence. Life was good, right?

He started the car and put it into gear only to realize that he couldn't remember where he was going. There had been an appointment when he left the office. He drove several blocks trying to remember the appointment and who he was going to be when he got there. Finally he gave up and pressed the autodialer on his cellular phone. As the phone beeped through the numbers to his office it hit him: the source of his discomfort. The Indian had had golden eyes.

In the time it took for his secretary to answer, twenty years of his life, of denial and deception, was pulled away in a stinging black undertow, leaving him feeling helpless and afraid.

CHAPTER TWO

MONTANA MEDICINE DRUNK

CROW COUNTRY, MONTANA

Black Cloud Follows thundered across the dawn silence of a frost-glazed Little Bighorn basin, out of Crow Agency, under Highway 90, and into the gravel parking lot of Wiley's Food and Gas. A '77 ocher-colored Olds Cutlass rattletrap diesel, Black Cloud Follows stopped, coughed, belched, and engulfed itself in a greasy black cloud of exhaust. When the cloud moved on, wafting like a portable eclipse through the golden poplar and ash trees on the Little Bighorn's banks, Adeline Eats stood by the Cutlass twisting the baling wire that held the driver's door shut.

Adeline's blue-black hair was layered large and lacquered into a flip. A hot-pink parka over her flannel shirt and overalls added a Michelin Man concentric-circle symmetry to her oval shape. As the Cutlass chugged and bucked—the thing that refused to die—Adeline lit a Salem 100, took a deep drag, then delivered a vicious red Reebok kick to Black Cloud Follows's fender. "Stop it," she said.

Obediently, the car fell silent and Adeline gave the fender an affectionate pat. This old car had been indirectly responsible for getting her a husband, six children, and a job. She couldn't bring herself to be mean to it for long.

Walking around to unlock the back door, she noticed something lying in a tuft of frost-covered buffalo grass: something also frost covered, that looked very much like a body. *If he's dead,* she reasoned, *he can wait until I've made some coffee. If he ain't, he'll probably want some.*

She let herself into the store and waddled around turning on lights and unlocking doors, then started the coffee and went out to unlock the laundromat, another of the cinder-block buildings in the Wiley's Food and Gas complex, which also included an eight-room motel. Crunching back through the grass, she looked at the body again, which hadn't moved. But for the frost, Old Man Wiley would have been out at dawn setting gopher traps all over the grounds and would have taken care of the body problem. He would have also given Adeline no end of shit about Black Cloud Follows, which he had been doing for fifteen years.

It had been Wiley, a white man, who had named the car in the first place. It was not the Crow way to name cars or animals, but Wiley missed no chance to get in a dig at the people from whom he made his living. Maybe, Adeline thought, a morning of peace was worth dealing with a body.

When the coffee was finished, she filled two large Styrofoam cups (one for her and one for the body) and poured a generous amount of sugar in each. The body had long braids, so she assumed he was Crow and would probably take sugar if he was alive. If he was dead Adeline would drink his, and she definitely wanted sugar.

Back in the buffalo days, the Cheyenne prophet Sweet Medicine had seen a vision of men with hair on their faces who would come bringing a white sand that was poison to Indians. The prophecy had come true, the white sand was sugar, and Adeline blamed the white man for poisoning her right up to two hundred pounds.

She took the coffee, butt-bumped through the back door, and crunched through the grass to where the body lay. He was facedown and his Levi jacket and jeans were crystalline blue with frost. Adeline nudged him in the ribs with her foot. "You froze?" she asked.

"Nope," the body said into the ground; a little dust came up with the steam.

"You hurt?"

"Nope." More dust.

"Drunk?"

"Yep."

"You want coffee?" Adeline sat one of the cups by his head. The body—she was still thinking of him as the body—rolled over and she recognized him as Pokey Medicine Wing, the liar.

Creaking, Pokey sat up and tried to pick up the coffee, but couldn't seem to get his frozen hand to work. Adeline picked up the cup and handed it to him.

"I thought you was dead, Pokey."

"I might have been. Just had me a medicine dream." As he raised the cup to his lips the shakes set in and he had to bite the edge of the cup to steady it. "I died twice before, you know. . . ."

Adeline ignored the lie and pointed to one of his braids, which had fallen into his coffee cup.

Pokey pulled the braid out and wiped the beaded band around it on his jacket. "Good coffee," he said.

Adeline shook a Salem out of her pack and offered it to him.

"Thanks," he said. "You gotta offer a prayer after a medicine dream."

Adeline lit his cigarette with a Bic lighter. "I'm a Christian now," she said. She really hoped he wouldn't use the cigarette to carry a prayer. She'd only been a Christian for a few weeks and the old ways made her a little uncomfortable. Besides, Pokey was probably lying through his tooth—he had only one—about the medicine dream.

Pokey squinted up at her and grinned, but did not pray. "I saw my brother Frank's boy, the one with the yellow eyes who threw that cop off the dam. You remember?"

Adeline nodded. She really didn't want to hear this. "Maybe you should tell a medicine man."

"I *am* a medicine man," Pokey said. "Just no one believes me. I don't need no one else to tell me about my visions. I saw that boy with Old Man Coyote, and there was a shade with 'em that looked like Death."

"I got to go to work now," Adeline said.

"I need to find that boy and warn him," Pokey said.

"That boy's been gone for twenty years. He's probably dead. You was just dreaming." Pokey was a liar and Adeline knew that there was no reason that she should let his ravings bother her, but they did. "If you're okay, I got to go to work."

"You don't believe in medicine, then?"

"Mr. Wiley will be coming in soon. I got to open the store," Adeline said. She turned and started back toward the store.

"Is that a screech owl?" Pokey shouted after her.

Adeline dropped her coffee, fell into a crouch, and scanned the sky in a panic. In the old tradition the screech owl was the worst of omens; vengeful ghosts lived in screech owls; seeing or hearing one was like hearing the sound of your own death. Adeline was terrified.

Pokey grinned at her. "I guess not. It must just be a hawk."

Adeline recovered and stomped into the store, praying to Jesus to forgive Pokey for his sins, but adding to her prayer a request for Jesus to beat the shit out of Pokey if He had the time.

CHAPTER THREE

THE MACHINES OF IRONY BRING MEMORY

SANTA BARBARA

After Sam's secretary gave him the address of his appointment he hung up the cellular phone and punched the address into the navigation system he'd had installed in the Mercedes so he would always know where he was. Wherever Sam was, he was in touch. In addition to the cellular phone he wore a satellite beeper that could reach him anywhere in the world. He had fax machines and computers in his office and his home, as well as a notebook-sized computer with a modem that linked him with databases that could provide him with everything from demographic studies to news clippings about his clients. Three televisions with cable kept his home alive with news, weather, and sports and provided insipid entertainments to fill his idle hours and keep him abreast of what was hot and what was not, as well as any information he might need to construct a face to meet a face: to change his personality to dovetail with that of any prospective client. The bygone salesman out riding on a shoeshine and a smile had been replaced by a shape-shifting shark stalking the sale, and Sam, having buried long ago who he really was, was an excellent salesman.

Even as some of Sam's devices connected him to the world,

others protected him from its harshness. Alarm systems in his car and condo kept criminals at bay, while climate control kept the air comfortable and compact discs soothed away distracting noise. A monstrous multiarmed black machine he kept in his spare bedroom simulated the motions of running, cross-country skiing, stair climbing, and swimming, while monitoring his blood pressure and heart rate and making simulated ocean sounds that stimulated alpha waves in the brain. And all this without the risk of the shin splints, broken legs, drowning, or confusion that he might have experienced by actually going somewhere and doing something. Air bags and belts protected him when he was in the car and condoms when he was in women. (And there were women, for the same protean guile that served him as a salesman served him also as a seducer.) When the women left, protesting that he was charming but something was missing, there was a number that he could call where someone would be nice to him for $4.95 a minute. Sometimes, while he was getting his hair cut, sitting in the chair with his protections and personalities down, the hairdresser would run her hands down his neck, and that small human contact sent a lonesome shudder rumbling through him like a heartbreak.

"I'm here to see Mr. Cable," he said to the secretary, an attractive woman in her forties. "Sam Hunter, Aaron Assurance Associates. I have an appointment."

"Jim's expecting you," she said. Sam liked that she used her boss's first name; it confirmed the personality profile he had projected. Sam's machines had told him that James Cable was one of the two main partners who owned Motion Marine, Inc., an enormously successful company that manufactured helmets and equipment for industrial deep-sea diving. Cable had been an underwater welder on the rigs off Santa Barbara before he and his partner, an engineer named Frank Cochran, had invented a new fiberglass scuba helmet that allowed divers to stay in radio contact while regulating the high-pressure miasma of gases that they breathed. The two became millionaires within a year and now, ten years later, they were thinking of taking the company public. Cochran wanted to be sure that at least one of the partners could retain controlling interest in the company in the event that the other died. Sam was trying to write a multimillion-dollar policy that would provide buyout capital for the remaining partner.

It was a simple partnership deal, the sort that Sam had done a hundred times, and Cochran, the engineer, with his mathematical way of thinking, his need for precision and order, his need to have all the loose ends tied up, had been an easy sale. With an engineer Sam simply presented facts, carefully laid out in an equationlike manner that led to the desired answer, which was: "Where do I sign?" Engineers were predictable, consistent, and easy. But Cable, the diver, was going to be a pain in the ass.

Cable was a risk taker, a gambler. Any man who had spent ten years of his life working hundreds of feet underwater, breathing helium and working with explosive gas, had to have come to terms with fear, and fear was what Sam traded in.

In most cases the fear was easy to identify. It was not the fear of death that motivated Sam's clients to buy; it was the fear of dying unprepared. If he did his job right, the clients would feel that by turning down a policy they were somehow tempting fate to cause them to die untimely. (Sam had yet to hear of a death considered "timely.") In their minds they created a new superstition, and like all superstitions it was based on the fear of irony. So, the only lottery ticket you lose will be the winning one, the one time you leave your driver's license at home is the time you will be stopped for speeding, and when someone offers you an insurance policy that only pays you if you're dead, you better damn well buy it. Irony. It was a tacit message, but one that Sam delivered with every sales pitch.

He walked into Jim Cable's office with the unusual feeling of being totally unprepared. Maybe it was just the girl who had thrown him, or the Indian.

Cable was standing behind a long desk that had been fashioned from an old dinghy. He was tall, with the thin, athletic build of a runner, and completely bald. He extended his hand to Sam.

"Jim Cable. Frank told me you'd be coming, but I'm not sure I like this whole thing."

"Sam Hunter." Sam released his hand. "May I sit? This shouldn't take long." This was not a good start.

Cable gestured for Sam to sit across from him and sat down. Sam remained standing. He didn't want the desk to act as a barrier between them; it was too easy for Cable to defend.

"Do you mind if I move this chair over to your side of the desk? I have some materials I'd like you to see and I need to be beside you."

"You can just leave the materials, I'll look them over."

Technology had helped Sam over this barrier. "Well, actually it's not printed matter. I have it in my computer and I have to be on the same side of the screen as you."

"Okay, I guess that's fine, then." Cable rolled his chair to the side to allow Sam room on the same side of the desk.

That's one, Sam thought. He moved his chair, sat down beside Cable, and opened the notebook computer.

"Well, Mr. Cable, it looks like we can set this whole thing up without any more than a physical for you and Frank."

"Whoa!" Cable brought his hands up in protest. "We haven't agreed on this yet."

"Oh," Sam said. "Frank gave me the impression that the decision had been made—that this was just a meeting to confirm the tax status and pension benefits of the policy."

"I didn't know there were pension benefits."

"That's why I'm here," Sam said. It wasn't why he was there at all. "To explain them to you."

"Well, Frank and I haven't gotten down to any specifics on this. I'm not sure it's a good idea at all."

Sam needed misdirection. He launched into the presentation like a pit bull/Willy Loman crossbreed. As he spoke, the computer screen supported his statements with charts, graphs, and projections. Every five seconds a message flashed across the screen faster than the eye could see, but not so fast that it could not nibble on the lobes of the subconscious like a teasing lover. The message was: *BE SMART, BUY THIS.* Sam had designed the program him-self. The *BE SMART* part of the message could be modified for each client. The options were: *BE SEXY, BE YOUNG, BE BEAUTI-FUL, BE THIN, BE TALL,* and Sam's personal favorite, *BE GOD.* He'd come up with the idea one night while watching a commer-cial in which six heavily muscled guys got to run around on the beach impressing beautiful women presumably because they drank light beer. *BE A STUD, DRINK LIGHT.*

Sam finished his presentation and stopped talking abruptly, feeling that he had somehow forgotten something. He waited, let-ting the silence become uncomfortable, letting the conversation lay on the desk before them like a dead cat, letting the diver come to the correct conclusion. The first one to speak loses. Sam knew it. He sensed that Cable knew it.

Finally, Jim Cable said, "This is a great little computer you have. Would you consider selling it?"

Sam was thrown. "But what about the policy?"

"I don't think it's a good idea," Cable said. "But I really like this computer. I think it would be smart to buy it."

"Smart?" Sam said.

"Yeah, I just think it would be a smart thing to do."

So much for subliminal advertising. Sam made a mental note to change his message to: *BE SMART, BUY THE POLICY.* "Look, Jim, you can get a computer like this in a dozen stores in town, but this partnership policy is set up for right now. You are never going to be younger, you'll never be in better health, the premium will never be lower or the tax advantage better."

"But I don't need it. My family is taken care of and I don't care who takes control of the company after I'm dead. If Frank wants to take a policy out on me I'll take the physical, but I'm not bet-ting against myself on this."

There it was. Cable was not afraid and Sam knew no way to in-still the fear he needed. He had read that Cable had survived sev-eral diving accidents and even a helicopter crash while being shuttled to one of the offshore rigs. If he hadn't glimpsed his mortality before, then nothing Sam could say would put the Reaper in his shaving mirror. It was time to walk away and salvage half of the deal with Cable's partner.

Sam stood and closed the screen on the computer. "Well, Jim, I'll talk to Frank about the specifics of the policy and set up the appointment for the physical."

They shook hands and Sam left the office trying to analyze what had gone wrong. Again and again the fear factor came up. Why couldn't he find and touch that place in Jim Cable? Granted, his concentration had been shot by the morning's events. Really, he'd done a canned presentation to cover himself. But to cover what? This was a clean deal, cut and dried.

When he climbed back into the Mercedes there was a red feather lying on the seat. He brushed it out onto the street and slammed the door. He drove back to his office with the air conditioner on high. Still, when he arrived ten minutes later, his shirt was soaked with sweat.

CHAPTER FOUR

MOMENTS ARE OUR MENTORS

SANTA BARBARA

There are those days, those moments in life, when for no particular reason the senses are heightened and the commonplace becomes sublime. It was one of those days for Samuel Hunter.

The appearance of the girl, the wanting she had awakened in him, had started it. Then the Indian's presence had so confused him that he was fumbling through the day marveling at things that before had never merited a second look. Walking back into his outer office he spied his secretary, Gabriella Snow, and was awed for a moment by just how tremendously, how incredibly, how child-frighteningly ugly she was.

There are those who, deprived of physical beauty, develop a sincerity and beauty of spirit that seems to eclipse their appearance. They marry for love, stay married, and raise happy children who are quick to laugh and slow to judge. Gabriella was not one of those people. In fact, if not for her gruesome appearance, an unpleasant personality would have been her dominant feature. She *was* good on the phone, however, and Sam's clients were sometimes so relieved to be out of her office and into his that they bought policies out of gratitude, so he kept her on.

He'd hired her three years ago from the résumé she had mailed in. She was wildly overqualified for the position and Sam remembered wondering why she was applying for it in the first place. For three years Sam had breezed by her desk without really looking at her, but today, in his unbalanced state, her homeliness inspired him to poetry. *But what rhymed with Gabriella?*

She said, "Mr. Aaron is very anxious to talk to you, Mr. Hunter. He requested that you go right into his office as soon as you arrived."

"Gabriella, you've been here three years. You can call me Sam." Sam was still thinking about poetry. *Salmonella?*

"Thank you, Mr. Hunter, but I prefer to keep things business-like. Mr. Aaron was quite adamant about seeing you immediately."

Gabriella paused and checked a notepad on her desk, then read, "'Tell him to get his ass in my office as soon as he hits the door or I'll have him rat-fucked with a tire iron.'"

"What does that mean?" Sam asked.

"I would assume that he would like to see you right away, sir."

"I guessed that." Sam said. "I'm a little vague on the *rat-fucked* part. What do you think, Gabriella?"

> *Gabriella, Gabriella,*
> *As fair as salmonella.*

"I'm sure I don't know. You might ask him."

"Right," Sam said.

He walked down the hall to Aaron Aaron's outer office, composing the next line of his poem along the way.

> *It wouldn't surprise me in the least*
> *If you were mistaken for a beast.*

Aaron Aaron wasn't Aaron's real name: he had changed it so his insurance firm would be the first listed in the yellow pages. Sam didn't know Aaron's real name and he had never asked. Who was he to judge? Samuel Hunter wasn't his real name either, and it was certainly less desirable alphabetically.

Aaron's secretary, Julia, a willowy actress/model/dancer who typed, answered phones, and referred to hairdressers as geniuses, greeted Sam with a smile that evinced thousands in orthodontia and bonding. "Hi, Sam, he's really pissed. What did you do?"

"Do?"

"Yeah, on that Motion Marine deal. They called a few minutes ago and Aaron went off."

"I didn't do anything," Sam said. He started into Aaron's office, then turned to Julia. "Julia, do you know what *rat-fuck* means?"

"No, Aaron just said that he was going to do it to you for sucking the joy out of his new head."

"He got a new head? What's this one?"

"A wild boar he shot last year. The taxidermist delivered it this morning."

"Thanks, Julia, I'll be sure to notice it."

"Good luck." Julia smiled, then held the smile while she checked herself in the makeup mirror on her desk.

Walking into Aaron's office was like stepping into a nineteenth-century British hunt club: walnut paneling adorned with the stuffed heads of a score of game animals, numbered prints of ducks on the wing, leather wingback chairs, a cherrywood desk clear of anything that might indicate that a business was being conducted. Sam immediately spotted the boar's head.

"Aaron, it's beautiful." Sam stood in front of the head with his arms outstretched. "It's a masterpiece." He considered genuflecting to appeal to the latent Irish Catholic in Aaron, but decided that the insincerity would be spotted.

Aaron, short, fifty, balding, face shot with veins from drink, swiveled in his high-backed leather chair and put down the *Vogue* magazine he had been leafing through. Aaron had no interest in fashion; it was the models that interested him. Sam had spent many an afternoon listening to Aaron's forlorn daydreams of having a showpiece wife. "How was I to know that Katie would get fat and I would get successful? I was only twenty when we got married. I thought the idea of getting laid steadily was worth it. I need a woman that goes with my Jag. Not Katie. She's pure Rambler." Here he would point to an ad in *Vogue*. "Now, if I could only have a woman like that on my arm . . ."

"She'd have you surgically removed," Sam would say.

"Sure, be that way, Sam. You don't know what it's like to think that getting a little strange could cost you half of what you own. You single guys have it all."

"Stop romanticizing, Aaron. Haven't you heard? Sex kills."

"Sure, suck the joy out of my fantasies. You know, I used to look forward to sex because it was fifteen minutes when I didn't have to think about death and taxes."

"If you do think about death and taxes it lasts half an hour."

"That's what I mean, I can't even get distracted with Katie anymore. Do you know what someone with my income has to pay in taxes?" The question came up in every one of their conversations. They had worked together for almost twenty years and Aaron always treated Sam as if he were still fifteen years old.

"I know exactly what someone with your income is *supposed* to pay in taxes, about ten times what you actually pay."

"And you don't think that that weighs on me? The IRS could take all this."

Sam rather liked the vision of a team of IRS agents loading large dead animal heads into Aaron's Jag and driving off with antlers out every window while Katie stood by shouting, "Hey, half of those are mine!" No matter how much Aaron attained, he would never let go of his fear of losing it long enough to enjoy it. In his mind's eye, Sam imagined Aaron mournfully watching as they carried the wild boar head out by the tusks.

"This thing is gorgeous," Sam said. "I think I'm getting a woody just looking at it."

"I named it Gabriella," Aaron said proudly, forgetting for a moment that he was supposed to be angry. Then he remembered.

"What the fuck did you just pull over at Motion Marine? Frank Cochran is talking lawsuit."

"Over a little subliminal advertising? I don't think so."

"Subliminal advertising! Jim Cable fainted after that stunt you pulled. They don't even know what happened yet. It could be a heart attack. Are you out of your fucking mind? I could lose the agency over this."

Sam could see Aaron's blood pressure rising red on his scalp. "You thought it was a great idea last week when I showed it to you."

"Don't drag me into this, Sam, you're on your own with this one. I've pulled some shit in my time to push the fear factor, but I never had a client attacked by an Indian, for Christ's sake."

"Indian?" Sam almost choked. He lowered himself very gently into one of the leather wingbacks. "What Indian?"

"Don't bullshit me, Sam. I taught you everything you know about bullshitting. Right after you left his office Jim Cable walked out of the Motion Marine building and was attacked by a guy dressed up as an Indian. With a tomahawk. If they catch the guy and he tells that you hired him, it's over for both of us."

Sam tried to speak but could find no breath to drive his voice. Aaron had been his teacher, and in a twisted, competitive way, Aaron was his friend and confidant, but he had never trusted Aaron with his fears. He had two: Indians and cops. Indians because he was one, and if anyone found out it would lead to policemen, one of whom he had killed. Here they were, after twenty years, paralyzing him.

Aaron came around the desk and took Sam by the shoulders. "You're smarter than this, kid," he said, softening at Sam's obvious confusion. "I know this was a big deal, but you know better than to do something desperate like that. You can't let them see that you're hungry. That's the first rule I taught you, isn't it?"

Sam didn't answer. He was looking at the mule deer head mounted over Aaron's desk, but he was seeing the Indian sitting in the café grinning at him.

Aaron shook him. "Look, we're not totally screwed here. We can draw up an agreement signing all your interest in the agency over to me and backdate it to last week. Then you would be working as an independent contractor like the other guys. I could give you, say, thirty cents on the dollar for your shares under the table. You'd have enough to fight the good fight in court, and if they let you keep your license you'll always have a job to come back to. What do you say?"

Sam stared at the deer head, hearing Aaron's voice only as a distant murmur. Sam was twenty-six years and twelve hundred miles away on a hill outside of Crow Agency, Montana. The voice he was hearing was that of his first teacher, his mentor, his father's brother, his clan uncle: a single-toothed, self-proclaimed shaman named Pokey Medicine Wing.

CHAPTER FIVE

THE GIFT OF A DREAM

CROW COUNTRY—1967

Sam, then called Samson Hunts Alone, stood over the carcass of the mule deer he had just shot, cradling the heavy Winchester .30-30 in his arms.

"Did you thank the deer for giving its life up for you?" Pokey asked. As Samson's clan uncle, it was Pokey's job to teach the boy the ways of the Crow.

"I thanked him, Pokey."

"You know it is the Crow way to give your first deer away. Do you know who you will give it to?" Pokey grinned around the Salem he held between his lips.

"No, I didn't know. Who should I give it to?"

"It is a good gift for a clan uncle who has said many prayers for your success in finding a spirit helper on your vision quest."

"I should give it to you, then?"

"It is up to you, but a carton of cigarettes is a good gift too, if you have the money."

"I don't have any money. I will give you the deer." Samson Hunts Alone sat down on the ground by the deer carcass and hung his head. He sniffed to fight back tears.

Pokey kneeled beside him. "Are you sad for killing the deer?"

"No, I don't see why I have to give it away. Why can't I take it home and let Grandma cook it for all of us?" Pokey took the rifle from the boy, levered a cartridge into the chamber, then let out a war whoop and fired it into the air. Samson stared at him as if he'd lost his mind.

"You are a hunter now!" Pokey cried. "Samson Hunts Alone has killed his first deer!" he shouted to the sky. "Soon he will be a man!"

Pokey crouched down to the boy again. "You should be happy to give the deer away. You are Crow and it is the Crow way."

Sam looked up, his golden eyes shot with red and brimming with tears. "One of the boys at school says that the Crow are no more than thieves and scavengers. He said that the Crow are cowards because we never fought the white man."

"This boy is Cheyenne?" Pokey said.

"Yes."

"Then he is jealous because he is not Crow. The Crow gave the Cheyenne and the Lakota and the Blackfoot a reason to get up in the morning. They outnumbered us ten to one and we held our land against them for two hundred years before the white man came. Tell this boy that his people should thank the Crow for being such good enemies. Then kick his ass."

"But he is bigger than me."

"If your medicine is strong, you will beat him. When you go on your fast next week, pray for warrior medicine."

Samson didn't know what to say. He would go to the Wolf Mountains next week for his first vision quest. He would fast and pray and hope to find a spirit helper to give him medicine, but he wasn't sure he believed, and he didn't know how to tell Pokey.

"Pokey," the boy said finally, very quietly, his voice barely audible over the hot breeze whistling through the prairie grass, "a lot of people say that you don't have no medicine at all, that you are just a crazy drunk."

Pokey put his face so close to Samson's that the boy could smell the cigarette-and-liquor smell coming off him. Then, softly, in a gentle, musical rasp he said, "They're right, I am a crazy drunk. The others are afraid of me 'cause I'm so crazy. You know why?"

Sam sniffed, "Nope."

Pokey reached into his pocket and pulled out a small buckskin bundle tied with a thong. He untied the thong and unfolded the buckskin on the ground before the boy. In it lay an array of sharp teeth, claws, a tuft of tan fur, some loose tobacco, sweet grass, and sage. The largest object was a wooden carving of a coyote about two inches tall. "Do you know what this is, Samson?" Pokey asked.

"Looks like a medicine bundle. Ain't you supposed to sing a song when you open it?"

"Don't have to with this one. Nobody ever had medicine like this. I ain't never showed it to anyone before."

"What are those teeth?"

"Coyote teeth. Coyote claws, coyote fur. I don't tell people about it anymore because they all say I'm crazy, but my spirit helper is Old Man Coyote."

"He's just in stories," Sam said. There isn't any Old Man Coyote."

"That's what you think," Pokey said. "He came to me on my first fast, when I was about your age. I didn't know it was him. I thought it would be a bear, or an otter, because I was praying for war medicine. But on the fourth day of my fast I looked up and there was this young brave standing there dressed in black buckskins with red woodpecker feathers down his leggings and sleeves. He was wearing a coyote skin as a headdress."

"How did you know it wasn't just somebody from the res?"

"I didn't. I told him to go away and he said that he had been away long enough. He said that when he gave the Crows so many enemies he promised that he would always be with them so they could steal many horses and be fierce warriors. He said it was almost time to come back."

"But where is he?" Samson asked. "That was a long time ago and no one has seen him. If he was here they wouldn't say you were crazy."

"Old Man Coyote is the trickster. I think he gave me this medicine to make me crazy and make me want to drink. Pretty Eagle, who was a powerful medicine man then, told me how to make this bundle and he told me that if I was smart I would give it to someone else or throw it in the river, but I didn't do it."

"But if it is bad medicine, if he is your spirit helper and doesn't help you . . ."

"Does the sun rise just for you, Samson Hunts Alone?"

"No, it rises all over the world."

"But it passes you and makes you part of its circle, doesn't it?"

"Yeah, I guess so."

"Well maybe this medicine is bigger than me. Maybe I am just part of the circle. If it makes me unhappy then at least I know why I am unhappy. Do you know why you are unhappy?"

"My deer . . ."

"There will be other deer. You have your family, you are good in school, you have food to eat, you have water to drink. You can even speak Crow. When I was a boy they sent me off to a BIA school where they beat us if we spoke Crow. Next week, if your heart is pure, you will get a spirit helper and have strong medicine. You can be a great warrior, a chief."

"There aren't any chiefs anymore."

"It will be a long time before you are old enough to be a chief. You are too little to be unhappy about the future."

"But I am. I don't want to be Crow. I don't want to be like you."

"Then be like you." Pokey turned away from the boy and lit another cigarette. "You make me angry. Give me your knife and I will show you how to dress this deer. We will throw the entrails in the river as a gift to the Earth and the water monsters." Pokey looked at Samson, as if waiting for the boy to doubt him.

"I'm sorry, Pokey." The boy unsnapped the sheath on his belt and drew a wickedly curved skinning knife. He held it out to the man, who took the knife and began to field-dress the deer.

As he drew the blade down the deer's stomach he said, "I am going to give you a dream, Samson."

Samson looked away from the deer into Pokey's face. There

were always gifts among the Crow—gifts for names, Sun Dance ceremony gifts, powwow gifts at Crow Fair, naming ceremony gifts, gifts for medicine, gifts to clan uncles and aunts, gifts for prayers: tobacco and sweet grass and shirts and blankets, horses and trucks—so many gifts that no one could ever really be poor and no one ever really got rich. But the gift of a dream was very pure, very special, and could never be repaid. Samson had never heard anyone give a dream before.

"I dreamed that Old Man Coyote came to me and he said, 'Pokey, when everything is right with you, but you are so afraid that something *might* go wrong that it ruins your balance, then you are Coyote Blue. At these times I will bring you back into balance.' This dream that I dreamed I give to you, Samson."

"What does that mean, Uncle Pokey?"

"I don't know, but it is a very important dream." Pokey wiped the knife on his pants and handed it to Samson, then hoisted the deer up on his shoulders. "Now, who are you going to give this deer to?"

CHAPTER SIX

A MALADY OF MEDICINE

"Look, Sam," Aaron said. "I can see that you're not thrilled about the buyout. So be it. I understand that you've put a lot into this agency. I can give you forty cents on the dollar, but you'll have to take a note. I'm a little cash poor since Katie made me put that trophy room on the house."

Sam looked down from the deer head. "Aaron, I didn't hire an Indian to attack Jim Cable. I still had half of the deal wrapped up with Cochran, which would have put me in the door at any time in the future to close Cable. I wouldn't have jeopardized that."

Aaron took two hand mirrors out of his desk drawer and began to juxtapose them to get a glimpse of the back of his head. Sam was used to this—it was Aaron's hourly balding check. "Cochran's secretary saw the Indian get out of your car," Aaron said matter-of-factly. Then, looking back to the mirrors, he said, "I've been mixing Minoxidil with a little Retin A and that stuff the Man from U.N.C.L.E. sells on TV. Do you think it's working?"

Sam thought of the feather on the car seat. He was sure he'd locked the car; there was no way the Indian could get in without setting off the alarm. "I don't care what anyone saw, I didn't hire the fucking Indian to attack Cable and I can't believe you bought their story without asking me." The anger felt good. It cleared his head a little.

Aaron put the mirrors down on the desk and smiled. "I didn't buy it, Sam. But if it was true you can't blame me for taking a shot at your shares."

"You greedy little fuck."

"Sam." Aaron lowered his voice and took his "fatherly" tone. "Samuel." A little wink. "Sammy, hasn't my greed always been in your best interest? I'm just trying to keep you sharp, son. Would you have had any respect for me if I hadn't tried to make the best of a bad situation? That's the first thing I taught you."

"I don't know any Indian. It didn't happen, Aaron."

"If you say it didn't, it didn't. You've always been straight with me. I don't even remember the time you cut all the cords off those smoke alarms we were selling because that lady wanted cordless models."

"You told me to do that! I was only seventeen years old."

"Right, well, how was I to know she smoked in bed?"

"Look, Aaron, I'll find out what happened at Motion Marine and take care of it first thing in the morning. If they call back while I'm out, try not to sign a confession for me, okay? I've had an incredibly shitty day and I've got to meet someone on upper State Street in a few minutes, so if that's all . . ."

"You really like the new head?"

Normally Sam would have lied, but with so many questions filling his head his highly developed lying center seemed to have shut down. "It sucks, Aaron. It sucks and I think you should sue the Man from U.N.C.L.E." He walked out as Aaron was snatching up his hand mirrors.

Gabriella was just hanging up the phone when Sam walked in. "That was the security director from your condominium association, Mr. Hunter. He'd like to talk to you right away. The association is holding an emergency meeting tonight to discuss what they are going to do about your dog."

"I don't have a dog."

"He was very upset. I have his number, but he insisted upon seeing you in person before the"—she checked her notepad—" 'lynch mob gets hold of you.'"

"Call him back and tell him that I don't have a dog. Dogs aren't allowed in the complex."

"He mentioned that, sir. That seems to be the problem. He said that your dog was on your back patio howling and refused to let anyone get near it and if you didn't get up there he would have to call the police."

All Sam could think was *Not today.* He said, "All right, call them and tell them I'm on my way. And call the garage down the street and have them come up and fix the flat tire on that orange Datsun out front. Have them bill it to my card."

"You have a three o'clock appointment with Mrs. Wittingham."

"Cancel it." Sam started out of the office.

"Mr. Hunter, this is a death claim. Mr. Wittingham passed away last week and she wants you to help fill out the papers."

"Gabriella, let me clue you in on something: once the client is dead we can afford to be a little lax on the service. The chance of repeat business is, well, unlikely. So reschedule the appointment or handle it yourself."

"But sir, I've never done a death claim before."

"It's easy: feel for a pulse; if there isn't one, give them the money."

"I am not amused, Mr. Hunter. I try to maintain a businesslike manner around here and you continually undermine me."

"Handle it, Gabriella. Call the garage. I have to go."

It was only five minutes from Sam's office to his condo in the Cliffs, a three-hundred-unit complex on Santa Barbara's mesa. From Sam's back deck he could look across the city to the Santa Lucia Mountains and from his bedroom window he could see the ocean. Sam had once rented the apartment, but when the Cliffs went condo ten years before he optioned to buy it. Since then the value of his apartment had increased six hundred percent. The complex offered three swimming pools, saunas, a weight room, and tennis courts. It was restricted to adults without children or dogs, but cats were allowed. When Sam first moved in, the Cliffs had a reputation as a swinging singles complex, a party mecca. Now, after the rise in real estate prices and the death of the middle class, most of the residents were retirees or wealthy professional couples, and the cooperative agreement they all signed set strict limitations on noise and numbers of visitors. A team of security guards patrolled the complex in golf carts twenty-four hours a day under the supervision of a hard-nosed ex-burglar named Josh Spagnola.

Sam parked the Mercedes by Spagnola's office in the back of the Cliffs' clubhouse, which, with its terra-cotta courtyards, stucco arches, and wrought-iron gates, looked more like the *casa grande* of a Spanish hacienda than a meeting place for condo dwellers. The door to the office was open and Sam walked in to find Spagnola shouting into the phone. Sam had never heard the wiry security chief shout. This was a bad sign.

"No, I can't just shoot the damn dog! The owner is on the way, but I'm not going into his townhouse and shooting his dog, rules or no rules."

Sam noticed that even in anger Spagnola remembered to use the word *townhouse* to refer to the apartment. No one wanted to pay a half-million dollars for an apartment; a townhouse was another thing. People were touchy about how one referred to their homes. When Sam was selling to people who lived in trailers he always referred to them as *mobile estates.* The term added a certain structural integrity; you never heard on the news of a tornado touching down and ripping the shit out of a park full of mobile estates.

"I *am* listening, Dr. Epstein," Spagnola continued. "But you don't seem to understand my position on you missing your nap. I don't give a desiccated damn. I don't give a reconstituted damn. I don't give a creamed damn on toast. I don't give a damn. I'm not entering Mr. Hunter's home until he arrives."

Spagnola looked up and gestured for Sam to sit. Then he grinned, mimed a mimic of the caller he was listening to, looked bored, feigned falling asleep, gestured the international sign language for being jerked off, then said, "Is that so, Doctor? Well, as far as I know I have no superiors since the Crucifixion, so give it your best shot." He slammed down the phone.

Sam said, "Got something on Dr. Epstein?"

Spagnola smiled. "He's porking the Cliffs' highly ethical Monday-Wednesday-Friday masseuse."

"Everybody's porking her."

"No, everybody's porking the Tuesday-Thursday-Saturday masseuse. Monday-Wednesday-Friday is very exclusive."

"And highly ethical."

"Says so in the brochure." Spagnola grinned, then casually picked up a legal pad from his desk and looked it over. "Samuel, my friend, your puppy has kept me on the phone with charming folks like Epstein all day. Shall I read you the log?"

"I don't know what you're talking about, Josh. I don't have a dog."

"Then you will want to notify security about the large canine that is currently on your back deck disturbing Dr. Epstein's nap."

"I'm not kidding, Josh. If there's a dog on my deck I don't know anything about it." Sam suddenly remembered that he'd left the sliding door to the deck open. "Christ!"

"Yes, the door is open. I've told you about that before, it's an invitation to burglars."

"That deck is twenty feet off the ground. How did a dog get up there? How did it get in my apartment without setting off the alarm?"

"I was wondering that same thing. If it isn't your dog, how did it get up there? It looks bad. The other association members are having an emergency meeting tonight to discuss the problem."

"There isn't a problem. Let's just go get the damn dog and take it to the pound."

"Yes, let's. I'll read the log to you while we walk over." Spagnola rose, picked up the legal pad, and led Sam out the door, then paused, locked the office, and set the alarm. "Can't trust anyone," he said.

They walked brick paths shaded with arbors of pink and red bougainvillea while Spagnola read. "Nine a.m.: Mrs. Feldstein calls to report that a wolf has just urinated on her wisterias. I ignored that one. Nine oh-five: Mrs. Feldstein reports that the wolf is forc-ibly having sex with her Persian cat. I went on that call myself, just to see it. Nine ten: Mrs. Feldstein reports that the wolf ate the Per-sian after having his way with it. There was some blood and fur on her walk when I got there, but no wolf."

"Is this thing a wolf?" Sam asked.

"I don't think so. I've only seen it from below your deck. It has the right coloring for a coyote, but it's too damn big. Naw, it can't be a wolf. You sure you didn't bring home some babe last night who forgot to tell you that she had a furry friend in the car?"

"Please, Josh."

"Okay. Ten fourteen: Mrs. Narada reports that her cat has been attacked by a large dog. Now I send all the boys out look-ing, but they don't find anything until eleven. Then one of them calls in that a big dog has just bitten holes in the tires on his golf cart and run off. Eleven thirty: Dr. Epstein makes his first lost-nap call—dog howling. Eleven thirty-five: Mrs. Norcross is put-ting the kids out on the deck for some burgers when a big dog jumps over the rail, eats the burgers, growls at the kids, runs off. First mention of lawsuit."

"Kids? We've got her right there," Sam said. "Kids aren't allowed."

"Her grandkids are visiting from Michigan. She filed the proper papers." Spagnola took a deep breath and started into the log again. "Eleven forty-one: large dog craps in Dr. Yamata's Aston Martin. Twelve oh-three: dog eats two, count 'em, two of Mrs. Wittingham's Siamese cats. She just lost her husband last week; this sort of put her over the edge. We had to call Dr. Yamata in off the putting green to give her a sedative. The personal-injury lawyer in the unit next to hers was home for lunch and he came over to help. He was talking class action then, and we didn't even know who owned the dog yet."

"You still don't."

Spagnola ignored Sam. "From twelve thirty to one we had mass sightings and frequent urinations—I won't bore you with de-tails—then one of my guys spotted the dog and followed it to your building, where it disappeared for a minute and reappeared on your deck."

"Disappeared? Josh, aren't you screening these guards for drug use?"

"I think he meant that he lost sight of it. Anyway, it's been on your deck for a couple of hours and all the residents are convinced that it's your dog. They want to boot you out of the complex."

"They can't do that. I own the place."

"Technically, Sam, they can. You own shares in the whole complex, and in the event of a two-thirds vote by the residents they can force you to sell your shares for what you paid for them. It's in the agreement you signed. I looked it up."

They were about a hundred yards from Sam's building and Sam could now hear the howling. "That apartment's worth five times what I paid for it."

"It is on the open market, but not to the other residents. Don't worry about it, Sam. It's not your dog, right?"

"Right."

Outside Sam's front door thirty of his neighbors were waiting, talking in heated tones, and glancing around. "There he is!" one shouted, pointing toward Sam and Spagnola. For a moment Sam was grateful that Spagnola was at his side, and at Spagnola's side was a .38 special.

The ex-burglar leaned to Sam and whispered, "Don't say anything. Not a word. This could get ugly—I see at least two lawyers in that bunch."

Spagnola raised his hands and walked toward the crowd. "Folks, I know you're angry, but we need Mr. Hunter alive if we're going to deal with the problem."

"Thanks," Sam said under his breath.

"No charge," Spagnola said. "It never occurred to them to kill you. Now they'll be embarrassed and go home. Lynchings are so politically incorrect, you know." Spagnola stopped and waited. Sam stayed beside him. As if the security chief had choreographed it, the people in front of Sam's door began to look around, avoiding eye contact with one another, then shuffled off, heads down, in different directions.

"You're amazing," Sam said to Spagnola.

"Nope, it's just that for a lot of years my living depended on the predictability of the professional class. Now it depends on the predictability of the criminal class. Same skills, less risk. You want me to go in first?"

"You have the gun."

"Okay, you wait here." Spagnola unlocked the door and palmed it open slowly. When the door was open just enough for him to pass, the thin security guard snaked through the opening and closed the door behind him.

Sam noticed that the howling had stopped. He put his ear to the door and listened, forgetting for a moment that he had installed a soundproof fire door. A few minutes passed before the latch clicked and Spagnola poked his head out.

"Well?" Sam said.

"How attached are you to that leather sofa?"

"It's insured," Sam said. "Why, did he tear it up? Is he in there?"

"He's in here, but I was wondering if you had some sort of—well—sentimental attachment to the sofa."

"No. Why? What's going on?"

Spagnola threw the door open and stepped out of the way. Sam looked through the foyer into the sunken living room, where a large tan dog had his teeth dug into the arm of the leather sofa and was humping away on it like a furry jackhammer.

"Josh, shoot that animal."

"Sam, I know how you feel. You go through life thinking that you're the only one, then you walk in on something like this—it's a blow to the ego."

"Just shoot the damn dog, Josh."

"Can't do it. California law clearly states that a firearm may only be discharged in city limits in cases of imminent physical danger. Doesn't say a word about protecting the honor of someone's couch."

Sam ran down the steps into the living room, but as he approached the dog turned and growled at him. The dog laid its ears back against its head, narrowed its golden eyes, and, still growling, began to back Sam into the corner of the living room.

"Josh! Does this qualify as imminent physical danger? Please say yes."

"Getting there," Spagnola said, very calmly, as he drew his weapon. "Don't let him see you're afraid, Sam. Dogs can sense fear."

"This isn't a dog, this is a coyote. This is a wild animal, Josh." Sam was flattened against the fifty-two-inch screen of his television and was still pushing so that the television was tilting back, ready to fall. He could smell a foul, musky odor coming off the animal. "Shoot it, please. Now, please."

"Quiet, Sam. I'm aiming. You can't shoot them in the head. They need that to see if it's rabid. Coyotes aren't normally aggressive. I saw it on PBS."

"This one didn't see the program, Josh. Shoot him."

"It might take two shots to drop him. If he leaps, cover your throat until I get the second one into him."

Spagnola fired and the TV shattered behind Sam. The coyote stood its ground unaffected. Sam backpedaled over the destroyed television as Spagnola fired again, taking out a vase on the mantel. The coyote looked at Spagnola quizzically. The third shot shattered the sliding glass door, the fourth and fifth punctured a stereo speaker, and the sixth ricocheted off the fireplace and out over the city.

When Spagnola's revolver clicked on an empty chamber he turned and bolted out the front door. Sam climbed off the broken television and braced for the coyote's attack. His ears rang with residual gunfire but he could hear laughing from across the room. The coyote was gone, but sitting on his couch, dressed in black buckskins trimmed with red feathers, was the Indian, his head thrown back in laughter.

"Hey!" Sam shouted. "What are you doing?"

In an instant the Indian leapt up and ran through the shattered glass door onto the deck. He looked over his shoulder and grinned at Sam before vaulting over the railing and dropping out of sight.

Sam ran to the deck and looked over the rail. The Indian was gone, but he could hear his cackling laugh echoing down the canyon into town.

Sam stumbled back from the rail and into the house, where he sat down on the couch and cradled his head in his hands. There had to be an explanation. Someone was screwing with his life. He riffled through his past as far as he would allow himself, looking for enemies he might have made. They were there—competing salesmen, angry customers, angrier women—dotting his life like dandelions on a lawn, but none would have gone to such elaborate measures to cause him trouble. In an honest assessment of himself he realized that he had never really been passionate enough about anything to really make that big a difference to anyone, good or bad. Since he'd run from the reservation he couldn't afford the high profile of passionate behavior. Still, there had to be an answer somewhere.

Sam thought about prayer, then faith, then remembered something that lay tucked away in the back of his sock drawer. He ran up the stairs to his bedroom and threw open the drawer. He removed a small buckskin bundle and untied the thong that held it together. Objects he had not seen in twenty years—teeth, claws, fur, and sweet grass braids—spilled out on the dresser. Among them lay a red feather that he had never seen before.

Sam looked at the coyote medicine and began to tremble.

COYOTE MAKES THE WORLD

A long time ago there was water everywhere. Old Man Coyote looked around and said, "Hey, we need some land." It was his gift from the Great Spirit that he could command all of the animals, which were called the Without Fires Clan, so he called four ducks to help him find land. He ordered each of the ducks to dive under the water and find some mud. The first three returned with nothing, but the fourth duck, because four is the sacred number and that is the way things go in these stories, returned with some mud from the bottom.

"Swell," said Old Man Coyote. "Now I will make some land." He made the mountains and the rivers, the prairies and the deserts, the plants and the animals. Then he said, "Guess I'll make some people now, so there will be someone to tell stories about me."

From the mud he made some tall and beautiful people. Old Man Coyote liked them very much. "I will call them Absarokee, which means 'Children of the Large-Beaked Bird.' Someday some dumb white guys will come here and get the translation all wrong and call them Crow."

"What are they going to eat?" one of the ducks asked.

"They have no feathers or fur. What will they cover themselves with?" asked a second duck.

"Yes," said a third duck. "They're pretty, but they won't be able to stay out in the weather."

Old Man Coyote thought for a while about how much he disliked ducks, then he took some more mud and made a strange-looking animal with a thick coat and horns. "Here," he said. "They can get everything they need from this animal. I'll call it a buffalo."

The fourth duck had been standing by watching all this and smoking a cigarette. "It's a big animal. Your people won't be able to catch it," he said, blowing a long stream of blue smoke in Old Man Coyote's face.

"Okay, so here's another animal that they can ride so they can catch the buffalo."

"And how will they catch that one?" asked the fourth.

"Look, duck, do I have to work out everything? I made the world and these people and I've given them everything they need, so just back off."

"But if they have everything they need, what will they do? Just sit around telling stories about you?"

"That would be good."

"Boring," said the duck.

"I'll make them a bunch of enemies. They'll be hopelessly outnumbered and have to fight all the time and do all kinds of war rituals. How's that?"

"They'll get wiped out."

"No, I'll stay with them. The Children of the Large-Beaked Bird will be my favorites, although some of their enemies can tell stories about me too."

"But what if the buffalo animals all get killed?"

"Won't happen. There's too many of them."

"But what if they do?"

"Then I guess the people are fucked. I'm tired and dirty and cold from standing in all that water. I'm going to invent the sweat bath and warm up."

So Old Man Coyote built a sweat lodge out of willow branches and buffalo skins. He heated the rocks in a fire and put them in a pit in the middle of the sweat lodge, then he and the ducks crawled inside and closed the door, making it completely dark inside.

"Hey, put out that cigarette!" Old Man Coyote said to the fourth duck.

The duck threw the cigarette on the hot rocks and smoke filled the lodge. "That smells pretty good," Old Man Coyote said. "Let's throw some other stuff on the fire and see how it goes." He threw on some cedar needles and they smelled pretty good too, then he threw on some sweet grass and some sage. "This stuff will be part of the sweat ceremony too. And some water—we need some water so it will really get hot and miserable in here."

"And we can get truly purified and clean?" asked the third duck.

"Right," said Old Man Coyote. "First I'll pour four dippers of water on the rocks for the four directions."

"And the four ducks."

"Right," said Old Man Coyote. "Now I'll pour on seven dippers for the seven stars of the Big Dipper. Then ten more because ten is a nice even number."

He handed each of the ducks a willow switch to beat their backs with. "Here, wail on yourself with these."

"What for?" asked the second duck.

"Tenderize ... er ... I mean ... it brings up the sweat and purifies you."

Then, when the ducks were beating their backs with the willow branches, Old Man Coyote said, "Okay, now I'm going to pour a whole bunch of dippers on the rocks. I'm not even going to count, but we are going to be really hot and really clean and pure." Then he poured and poured until it was so hot in the lodge that he could not stand it and he slipped out the door, leaving the ducks inside.

Later, after he had plunged into the river to cool off, he ate a big meal and laid down to rest. "That was plumb swell," he said to himself. "I think I'll give the sweat to my new people. It can be their church and sacrament and they can think of me whenever they go in. It is my gift to them. I guess no one really needs to know about the ducks." Then Old Man Coyote picked up a willow twig and picked a bit of duck meat from between his teeth. "The sage gives them a nice flavor, though."

CHAPTER SEVEN

THE CHILDREN OF THE LARGE-BEAKED BIRD

CROW COUNTRY—1967

Samson Hunts Alone sat on a bench by the sweat lodge behind his grandma's house, watching as Pokey carried the hot rocks with a pitchfork from the fire to the pit in the sweat lodge. Samson was supposed to be paying attention to the ritual that Pokey was performing and preparing himself to pray to the Great Spirit to bring him good medicine on his fast, but more than anything he wanted to be inside with the little kids and the women watching *Bonanza* on television. Grandma had cooked up a big batch of fry bread for the meal after the sweat and Samson's stomach growled when he thought about it.

Pokey, straining under a pitchfork full of red-hot rocks, said, "Can't nobody cross my path between the fire and the sweat during the first four trips."

Uncle Harlan, who was sitting next to Samson, let out a sarcastic snicker. Pokey looked up at him, his brow lowered in reproach.

"The boys have to learn, Harlan," Pokey said.

Harlan nodded. On the other side of Samson sat his two older cousins, Harry and Festus, thirteen and fourteen, who had been through the sweat for purification and prayer for their success on

the basketball court at Hardin Junior High School. They had come
the fifteen miles down to Crow Agency with Harlan, their father,
to participate in Samson's sweat.

Uncle Harlan didn't believe in the old ways. He often said that
he didn't want his boys to grow up with their heads full of ideas
that didn't work in the modern world. Still, because of the obliga-
tions he felt to his family he often drove down for sweats, partici-
pated in ritual gift giving, and never missed the Sun Dance in
June. He lived in Hardin, north of the reservation, where he re-
built truck engines during the day and drank hard in the bars at
night. He fought often and lost seldom. When he was drinking
with Uncle Pokey, the two of them lying on the bed of Pokey's
pickup staring into the limitless stars of Montana's big sky, passing
a bottle of Dickel Sour Mash between them, Harlan would talk of
his time in Vietnam, of the two brothers he lost there, and of the
warrior blood that was part of the Hunts Alone family. Pokey
would answer Harlan's painful pride with parables and mystical
references until Harlan could stand it no longer.

"Damn it, Pokey, can your medicine fix a Cummins diesel? Can
it fill out a tax form? Can it get you a job? Fuck medicine. Fuck
fasting. Fuck the Sun Dance. If I thought I could do it, I'd take
Joan and the kids and go a thousand miles from here."

"You'd be back," Pokey would say. Then the two of them would
lie there drinking in silence for long minutes before one of them
would bring up basketball, hunting, or truck engines—some topic
safe and far away from Harlan's anger.

Some of those nights Samson would crawl out of his cot, sneak
past the six cousins that slept in his room and out into the yard,
where he would lie by the wheel of the old truck and listen to the
two men talk.

Harlan was the only adult Samson knew who would talk about
the dead, so the boy would lie there with his face against the cold
grass hoping to hear something about his father or his mother,
but mostly he heard about his two uncles, dead in the jungles, or
his grandfather, who died piece by piece in a white hospital of dia-

betes. His father had died too young to leave many stories or a strong ghost. Not that Harlan would admit to believing in ghosts. "If I'm haunted," he would tell Pokey, "it's not by my unrevenged brothers, it's by you and your back-assward ways."

After time and hangovers passed, Samson would ask Pokey about Harlan and always get the same answer. "Poor Harlan, he is out of balance. I should dance for him at the Sun Dance." It was no answer. Samson remained confused.

Samson watched as Harlan rose from the bench and undressed for the sweat. He was tall and lean, his skin deep red-brown in the firelight, his eyes and hair black as an obsidian arrowhead: pure Crow brave. But as Samson undressed he wondered why his uncle seemed so unhappy with his heritage. He treated his Crow blood like a curse, while Pokey seemed to see it as a blessing. They were half brothers, sharing the same mother, belonging to her clan, growing up in the same house; why were they so different? Why did neither one seem to be able to live comfortably in his own skin?

Naked, they all entered the low dome of the sweat lodge and sat in a circle around its perimeter. Pokey placed a bucket of water by the fire pit, then he pulled down the door flap. He added sweet grass and cedar to the hot rocks and fragrant smoke filled the lodge as he sang a prayer song. His prayers were in English, which Samson knew embarrassed him some. Pokey, like Grandma, had gone to a boarding school run by the BIA where Indians were forbidden to speak or learn their own language or religion. In this way the BIA hoped that the Native American culture would disappear into the larger white culture, assimilated. Harlan, on the other hand, was ten years younger than Pokey and, like Samson, had been taught Crow in school as part of the BIA's move to preserve Indian culture.

Pokey poured four dippers of water onto the rocks and Samson lowered his face to avoid the steam. As Pokey sang, Samson let his mind wander to the Ponderosa. He would like to live on that big ranch in that big house and have his own room and two guns like

Little Joe Cartwright. Until Grandma had taken all their per capita money a year ago and bought the big black-and-white television at the Kmart in Billings, Samson thought that everyone lived in a small house with twenty cousins and five or six aunts and uncles and their grandma. Everyone on the reservation seemed to. Before the television arrived Samson did not know he was poor. Now he spent every evening piled in the front room with his family watching people he did not know do things he did not understand in places he could not fathom, while the commercials told him that he should be just like those people. None of those people ever took a sweat.

Pokey had poured the seven dippers and the sweat lodge was so hot that Samson's mind went white. He lay down on the floor to breathe some cooler air. Someone lifted his head and asked him if he was okay. He answered yes and passed out.

Water was being splashed on his face. Samson came to and realized that he was being held in Harlan's strong arms.

"We did a naming ceremony for you, Samson," Harlan said. "From now on you shall be called Squats Behind the Bush. And you owe each of us a carton of cigarettes and a new Ford truck."

Samson saw that Harlan was grinning at him and he smiled back. "If I don't take the name, do I have to give you the gifts?"

Harlan laughed and set the boy on his feet by a fifty-five-gallon drum where Harry and Festus were pouring dippers of water over their heads.

After they were dried off and redressed Pokey moved the rocks out of the pit and replaced them with hot ones from the fire so the women could take their sweat.

Pokey finished and led them into the house, which was surprisingly quiet. The little kids were in bed and the women filed out to the sweat silently as soon as the men entered. The cheap Formica table was set with five plastic bowls around a big pot of venison-and-cabbage stew and a basket of fry bread. Harlan poured them all coffee from a big black urn on the counter while Pokey dished up the stew. Samson attacked a piece of fry bread and was tearing away at its stretchy, donutlike crust when Harlan sat down next to him and said, "So, Squats Behind the Bush, what are you gonna do tomorrow if you see Old Man Coyote in your vision like your Uncle Pokey did?"

Festus and Harry giggled. Samson answered the sarcasm in earnest. "Pokey's the only one with Coyote medicine. Pretty Eagle said so."

"Good thing too," Harlan said. "Some of us have to live in the real world."

"Harlan!" Pokey shouted. "Let it go."

"It's gone," Harlan said. "It's as gone as can be, Pokey."

They finished their meal in silence, Samson wondering what Harlan meant by "It's gone." Later, as he fell asleep listening to the soft breathing of his cousins, he imagined himself living on the Ponderosa; sleeping in his own room, herding cattle on his own black horse, carrying two shiny six-guns, practicing his fast-draw, and always staying on the lookout for Indians.

CHAPTER EIGHT

✦

MEET THE MUSE, MR. LIZARD KING

SANTA BARBARA

Calliope Kincaid waited on the steps of the Tangerine Tree Café thinking about the past lives of lizards. A small, brown alligator lizard was sunning himself on the planter box by the steps and his lidless eyes, glazed but seeing, reminded Calliope of a picture of Jimi Hendrix that her mother had kept next to the bed when she was growing up. She wondered if this lizard really could be an incarnation of Jimi, and what he must feel like living in the planter box in front of a café, eating bugs and hiding, after being a rock star.

Between the ages of seven and nine Calliope had been raised a Hindu, and during that time she had developed an acute empathy for other creatures, never sure what bird or beast might just be Daddy or Grandma working off some karma. She had taken the concept almost to the point of agoraphobia—she was afraid to go out of the house for fear that she might crush some relative doing time as a stinkbug—when her mother moved into NSA Buddhism and Calliope s spiritual focus was changed to sitting before a gong with her mother, the two of them chanting for prosperity until the apartment's heater ducts began to vibrate. Evicted for disturbing other tenants, Calliope's mother turned to goddess worship, which Calliope liked because she didn't have to wear clothes to the rituals and there were always lots of flowers. When Calliope blossomed at thirteen and began to attract too much attention from neo-pagan males, her mother turned to Islam, changed her daughter's name to Akeema Mohammed Kincaid, and equipped her with a veil. Calliope, who had easily grasped the concepts of karma and reincarnation, of transcendentalism and oneness, of harmony with nature and the goddess within, was completely thrown by the concepts of guilt, self-flagellation, and modesty set down in Islam. She promptly shaved one side of her head, dyed the remainder of her waist-length blond hair hot pink, and began taking hallucinogenic drugs and sleeping with awkward, pimpled tough-boys with mohawks. Men replaced religion, and Calliope accepted their seductive lies with the same open wonder she had given the gods.

In an attempt to pull her daughter out of a spiritual tailspin, Mom turned Unitarian, but Calliope had already slashed the ecumenical apron strings and Mom was left to hopscotching religions on her own. Currently she lived in an ashram in Oregon where she acted as the spirit channel for a four-thousand-year-old, superenlightened entity named Babar (no relation to the elephant).

As a child exposed to so many religions, Calliope had developed a malleability of faith that stayed with her into adulthood. Through the assimilation of many spiritual beliefs, without science or cynicism to balance them, Calliope was able to define everything in her world, accept the highs and lows of life with resolve, and never be burdened by the need to understand. Why understand when you can believe? For Calliope, every event was mystical and every moment magical; a flat tire could be a manifestation of karma, or a lizard might be Jimi Hendrix. If she fell in love too easily and got hurt too often it wasn't bad judgment, it was just faith.

She was humming "Castles Made of Sand" to the lizard when Sam's Mercedes pulled up to the curb. She looked up and smiled at him, not the least bit concerned that he was thirty minutes late. It had never occurred to her that he might not show. No man had ever stood her up.

She ran to the car and tapped on the passenger window. Sam pushed the button and it whirred down. "Hang on a second, I have to do something," she said.

She went around to the front of the car and searched the grille until she found a moth that had met its end with minimal damage. She plucked the moth from the grille, took it to the planter box, and wiggled it in front of the lizard while singing a few bars of Hendrix's "Little Wing." The lizard snapped at the moth halfheartedly and slithered away under the geraniums to sulk. Calliope had been correct in guessing that this particular lizard had, indeed, been a rock star in a previous life, and if she had sung a chorus of "L.A. Woman" or "Light My Fire" the lizard would have been delighted, but how could she have known?

She dropped the moth into the planter box and returned to the car.

"Sorry I'm late," Sam said.

"It's only time," she said. "I'm always late."

"I had them fix your car." He was trying not to look at her. He'd just gotten enough control of his nerves to drive and he wasn't ready to be rattled by the girl again, but he wouldn't have thought of not picking her up. During the whole debacle at the condo, the urgency to see her again had hovered in the background of his mind and finally snapped him out of his confusion over the Coyote medicine. Was she connected to the Indian?

"That's sweet of you," she said. "Did you look at the car?"

"Look at it? No. I just had the garage come down."

"It's a great car," Calliope said. "It has over three hundred horsepower, a six-pack of Weber carburetors, competition suspension and gearing—it'll do over a hundred and eighty on a straightaway. I can blow most Porsches off the road."

Sam didn't know what to say, so he said, "That's nice."

"I know that women aren't supposed to care about things like that. My mother says that I'm obsessed with vehicles because I was conceived in the back of a VW microbus and spent most of my childhood in one. We moved around a lot."

"Where does she live?" Sam asked. He would ask her about the Indian, really, when the time was right.

"Oregon. I didn't build the car myself. I used to live with this sculptor in Sedona, Arizona, who built it for midnight drives in the desert. One day I was telling him that I thought that cars had replaced guns as phallic symbols for American men, and I thought it was interesting that he had one that was so small and fast. The next day he gave me the Datsun and went out and bought a Lincoln. It was very sweet."

"Very sweet," Sam echoed. Now or never, he thought. "Calliope—that is your name, right?"

"Yes," the girl said.

Sam put on his salesman's *this is a serious matter* voice. "Calliope, do you know who the—"

"My name wasn't always Calliope," she interrupted. "Sherman—he was the sculptor—started calling me Calliope, after the Greek muse of epic poetry. He said that I inspired men to art and madness. I liked the way it sounded so I took it as my real name. My mom even calls me Calliope now."

Sam had brought thousands of sales interviews back into control when the client tried to wander, he wouldn't let this girl sidetrack him. "Calliope, who was the Indian—"

"You know, the Indians used to change their names as they grew up and their personalities changed or when they did certain things, like Walks Across the Desert and stuff like that. Did you know that?"

"No I didn't," Sam lied. "But I really need to know—"

"Oh, there's my car!"

Sam slowed and pulled the Mercedes in behind the Z. "Calliope, before you go—"

"We can't have sex tonight," she said. "I have some things to do, but I can cook you dinner tomorrow if you want."

Sam turned to her, his mouth hanging open. She was smiling at him, waiting for his answer with her eyes wide, as if she'd just been surprised. He realized that every time he had looked at her she'd worn that same expression of wonderment, and each time it had thrown him. Dammit, he wouldn't be distracted. She was sharp, but he was sharper. He was in control here.

"Okay," he said.

"Terrific. I live at seventeen and a half Anapamu Street—that's upstairs. Whatever you do, don't go to the downstairs door. Six o'clock, okay?" Without waiting for his answer, she was out of the car and away.

Sam rolled down the window and shouted after her. "My name is Sam."

She looked back at him and smiled, then got into the Datsun and fired it up. Sam watched the little sports car tilt with the torque of the engine as she revved it. She burned off the back tires, filling the air with squeals and blue smoke as she pulled away.

⊛

CHAPTER NINE

QUITTING NOW GREATLY REDUCES THE CHANCE OF VISIONS

CROW COUNTRY—1967

It was well before dawn and no lights burned in the houses and shops of Crow Agency as Pokey piloted his old truck through town, a sleepy-eyed Samson wobbling on the seat next to him.

"How far is it to the fasting place?" Samson asked.

"About two hours, but only fifty or so miles as the Crow drives. Get it, as the Crow drives?" Pokey grinned at Samson and took a swig from a pint bottle of whiskey. He and Harlan had talked and drunk all night after Samson's sweat. Now he was using the road like a buttered harlot—he was all over the place while trying to stay in the middle—and scaring Samson, whose head whacked the window when Pokey got too much shoulder and had to yank the truck's retreads back onto the asphalt.

"Could we slow down, Pokey?"

"We're not going that fast."

Samson peeked at the speedometer, which registered zero, as did all the broken gauges in the truck. Pokey caught Samson looking and grinned again.

"I ain't in any danger at all, you know. I seen my death in a medicine dream. I get shot, and it ain't nowhere near this old truck. Nope, I'm plumb safe in this truck, no matter what I do."

"What about me?" Samson asked.

"Don't know? What's your death dream?"

"I didn't have one."

Pokey looked down at Samson with a worried expression. "You didn't?"

"Nope," Samson said with a gulp.

"Well then, if I wreck you could be plumb fucked." He began to weave more radically, leaning hard into Samson as the truck slipped off the shoulder again. "Oh, shit! These tires are bald too! Don't worry, son, I'll dance for your ghost at the Sun Dance!"

"Pokey, stop it!" Samson had begun to giggle as his uncle leaned into him.

"Quick, go to sleep fast, and dream of dying on top of a pretty woman, Samson. It's your only chance."

"Pokey!" Samson was doubled over with laughter now as Pokey fishtailed the truck back and forth in the road while pumping the brakes and the clutch, causing Samson's head to jerk around like a rag doll's.

Pokey shouted, "Blacken your face, Samson Hunts Alone, this is a good day to die." Then he slammed on the brakes and brought the truck to a skidding stop in the middle of the road. Samson was thrown to the floor of the truck among a collection of old beer cans and soda bottles. Still giggling, he climbed back up onto the seat and began pounding on Pokey's shoulder. Pokey grabbed his hands and shushed him.

"Look," Pokey said, nodding to the front of the truck. Samson turned to see a huge buffalo bull crossing the road in front of them.

"Where did he come from?" Samson asked as he watched the bull lumber out of the headlights.

"Must of wandered off the Yellowtail's place. They got a few head of buffalo."

"Good thing you saw him in time."

"I didn't see him. Them things are so dark they just eat up your headlights. I was just fooling with you when I stopped."

"We were lucky," Samson said gravely.

"Nope, I told you we was safe. Now you quit being afraid of things that ain't happened yet. That's why I gave you that dream."

Pokey geared up the truck and they rode in silence for a while, listening to the rattling grind of the old Ford's engine. The sky was just getting light and Samson could see the new leaves coming on the trees and the blossoms on the cottonwoods. He was glad his fast was to be in the time of the first grass. The days would be mild and warm, but not hot.

"Pokey," Samson said. "What do I do when I get thirsty?"

Pokey took a long pull on the pint before he answered. "You must pray that your suffering is accepted and you are given a spirit helper."

"But what do I do? What if I die?"

"You won't die. When your suffering is too much you must go to the Spirit World. You must see yourself traveling into a hole in the ground and down a long tunnel. You will come out into the light and you will be in the Spirit World. There you will not be hungry or thirsty. Wait there and your spirit helper will come to you."

"What if my spirit helper doesn't come?"

"You must go back down the tunnel again and again, looking for him. In the buffalo days you had to have a spirit helper to go into battle or people thought you were a Crazy Dog Wishing to Die."

"What's that?"

"A warrior who is so crazy, or so full of sadness, that he rides against the enemy just so they will kill him."

"Was my dad a Crazy Dog Wishing to Die?"

Pokey smiled and looked wistfully ahead. "It is bad luck to speak of it, but no, he did not wish to die. He just got too drunk and drove too fast after his basketball games."

They drove south through Lodge Grass, where the only activity was that of a few dogs trying to clear their throats for the day's barking and a few ranchers cadging free coffee at the feed and grain store. Once through town, Pokey turned east on a dirt road into the rising sun to the Wolf Mountains. In the foothills the road became deeply rutted and washed out in places. Pokey shifted into low and the truck ground down to a crawl. After a half hour of kidney-jarring bumps and vertiginous cutbacks, Pokey stopped the truck on a high ridge between the peaks of two mountains.

From here Samson could see all the way to Lodge Grass to the west, and across the green prairies of the Northern Cheyenne Reservation to the east. Lodgepole pines lined the mountain on both sides, as thick as feathers on a bird, thinning here, near the peak, where the ground was arid, strewn with giant boulders, and barren but for a few yucca plants and the odd tuft of buffalo grass or sage.

"There." Pokey pointed east to a group of car-sized boulders about fifty yards from the road. "That is the place where you will fast. I'll wait for you on this side of the road if you need me, but you must only come up here if you have a vision or if you are in trouble." Pokey grabbed a bag from the floor of the truck and handed it to Samson through the window. "There's a blanket in there and some mint leaves to chew when you get thirsty. Go now. I will pray for your success."

As he walked down the hill toward the boulders, Samson felt a lump rising in his throat. What good is medicine if you die of thirst? What good is medicine, anyway? He'd rather be in school. This was no fun, this was scary. Why did Pokey have to be so strange? Why couldn't he be more like Harlan, or Ben Cartwright?

Once on the downhill side of the boulders Samson could see the place where he would sit through his fast: a small stone fire ring under the overhang of one of the boulders. Samson sat down facing the sun, which was now a great orange ball on the eastern horizon.

He thought of Grandma at home. She would be pouring Lucky

Charms in everyone's bowls about now, getting his little cousin Alice's insulin out of the refrigerator and filling the syringe, making sure everyone was dressed and ready for school. Uncle Harlan would be sitting in the living room drinking coffee and telling all the kids to be quiet because of his hangover. Samson's aunts would be pulling the blankets off the sweat lodge and loading them into the back of Harlan's truck so they could take them to the laundromat. Normally, Samson would be trading punches in the arm with Harry and Festus and lying to Grandma about having his homework done. He wanted to be at home with everyone else, not sitting by himself up here on a mountain. He had never been by himself before. He decided he didn't like it. For the first time in his life he was lonely.

He tried to think of the Spirit World. Maybe he could go there really fast, find a spirit helper and go back up to the truck so Pokey could take him to Lodge Grass and get a Coke: thirty minutes, tops. Get in, get out, and nobody gets hurt, as Uncle Harlan always said, something he picked up in Vietnam.

Samson tried to imagine the hole he would enter the Spirit World through. He couldn't do it. Maybe a prayer.

"O Great Spirit and Great Mother," Samson prayed in Crow. "Hear my prayer. Please let me find my spirit helper so I can go home."

He waited a moment. Okay, that didn't work, back to the hole in the ground.

After two hours he grew bored and his mind wandered to the Ponderosa, then to school, home, the planet Krypton, the snack bar in Crow Agency, the McDonald's in Billings, the damp basement of Lodge Grass High School, where Harlan had taken him and shown him old black-and-white films of his father playing basketball. He wondered what his father had been like. Then wondered about his mother, who had died when he was only two. Her liver quit, Harlan said. No one else would talk about the dead. He tried to remember her, but could remember only Grandma and his aunts. The new feeling of loneliness was getting worse.

Maybe he could make up a vision. He could go tell Pokey that he had a vision and found his spirit helper and Pokey would tell him how to make his medicine bundle and he could go home. That would work. He thought for a moment about what animal he should pick for his spirit helper and decided on a hawk. He didn't know what hawk medicine was, but it was probably pretty good for you unless you raised chickens or something.

Samson ran up the hill and just as he was cresting the ridge he began to shout. "Pokey! Pokey! I had my vision! I saw my spirit helper!" When he reached the road the truck was nowhere in sight. He looked up and down the road, then crossed it and looked down the other side of the ridge. Pokey was gone.

Samson felt his lip begin to quiver and water fill his eyes. He sat down in the dirt as the first series of chest-wrenching sobs escaped him and echoed down the ridge. He buried his face in his knees and cried until his throat hurt. When finally he found the bottom of his sadness he looked up and wiped his eyes on his forearm.

Why would Pokey just leave him? Maybe he just went to buy some beer. Maybe he would bring back a Coke. Samson suddenly realized that he really was thirsty. The sun was moving higher in the sky and it was starting to get hot. He stood and looked around for a shady place to wait, but the closest shade was down by the boulders, and from there he wouldn't be able to see the truck coming. He sat on a small rock by the road in the full sun.

During the next two hours Samson chewed all his mint leaves and took to sucking pebbles to keep his mouth from getting dry while he drew pictures in the dust with a stick. He heard a car engine and looked up to see a cloud of dust coming off the road about two miles away. That would be Pokey.

Samson stood on the rock to see if he could make out the truck. As the cloud approached, however, he noticed that it wasn't Pokey's truck at all, but a big powder-blue car unlike any he had seen before. He sat back down on the rock and was fighting back another fit of sobs when the car skidded to a stop beside him, bringing with it a choking cloud of dust. There was a whirring sound and the car window slid down, revealing the big, round face of the driver, a white man, who seemed to have four or five spare chins under his first one.

"Excuse me, son." The driver smiled. "I seem to have gotten myself turned around here. Would you know the way to get to Highway Ninety?"

"It's a long way," Samson said. "You have to go down the mountain into Lodge Grass, then go to Crow Agency. That's where the highway is." The white man wasn't really white, he was more of a bright pink, and he smiled with his voice, like Samson was his best friend.

"You lost me, son. Lodge Grass?"

"You have to stay on this road down the mountain, then you have to turn."

"I got you there, son, but which way did you say I should turn?"

Samson pointed down the mountain and the driver's eyes followed his finger, then he turned back to Samson looking confused. "I don't suppose you are heading that way, are you, son?"

Samson thought for a minute before he answered. If this man would take him to the highway in Crow Agency he could walk home from there. Never trust a white man who wants to give you something, Pokey had said. Soon as you think you got it he will take it away and take everything you got along with it. But Samson couldn't figure out how the driver would take away a ride, and all he really owned was his hunting knife. If the white man tried to take that, Samson would cut his gizzard out. "I'm going to Crow Agency," the boy said. "I can show you the way."

"Well, jump in quick, partner. It's hotter than blazes out here and it's gettin' in the car."

Samson walked around the back of the car, remembering what Pokey had told him about not trusting white men. It was the biggest, bluest car he had ever seen. Maybe it was the heat, but it seemed to take a long time to walk around it. When he opened the door a blast of cold air hit him that instantly brought goose bumps to his arms and back. He jumped into the car and stared in amazement at the vents in the dashboard where the cold was coming from. He'd never experienced air-conditioning before.

"Close the door, son. You want to bake us?"

Samson closed the door as the car started moving. "It's cool in here, and it smells good."

The driver, still smiling, looked down at Samson and tipped the straw skimmer he was wearing. He was the fattest man Samson had ever seen and he was wearing a powder-blue suit the same shade as the car; he filled the driver's seat like a bagful of sky. Up close Samson could see that the man's skin was pink from little veins that ran through it like road maps.

"Thank you kindly, son. Name's Commerce. Lloyd Commerce, purveyor of the world's finest cleaning apparatus, the Miracle."

He held out a fat hand to Samson. Samson shook two of the giant fingers with his right hand. He let his left drop near the handle of his hunting knife. "I don't know what that is," Samson said. "I'm Samson Hunts Alone."

"You don't know about the Miracle? Well, Samson Hunts Alone, let me tell you: in a few years the Miracle will be the standard by which all vacuum cleaners will die. In a few years, if you don't have a Miracle in your broom closet you might as well just hang a sign outside your house saying 'We live in filth.' The Miracle is just the most advanced machine for the elimination of household dirt, dust, and disease that the world has ever known!"

Samson was amazed at how excited Lloyd was—it seemed that the more Lloyd talked, the pinker he got. Even if it was rude, Samson thought he should interrupt before Lloyd hurt himself. "I know what a miracle is. One of my aunts is a Christian. I don't know what a purveyor is."

Lloyd took a deep breath and shot a smile at Samson. "I am a salesman, son, one of the last truly free individuals on this planet. I sell miracles, son. Not just vacuum cleaners. I sell real loaves-and-fishes miracles." He paused for a moment and waited. Samson was hugging the car door, his hand on his knife thinking that this was the craziest talk he had ever heard from anyone besides Pokey.

"I know what you're thinking," Lloyd continued. "You're thinking, *Lloyd, what kind of miracle do you perform?* Am I right?"

"Nope," Samson said. "I was thinking about a Coke."

"There's some in a cooler in the backseat," Lloyd tossed off, trying to get back to his point. "Grab me one too, would you, son?"

Samson scrambled over the seat and dug into a cooler where a dozen Cokes lay in the ice around a fifth of rum. He grabbed two and slithered back over the seat. Lloyd took the Cokes and opened them. He handed one to Samson, who drank half the bottle in one pull.

"Miracles," Lloyd said.

Samson didn't care how crazy Lloyd was—life was fine. The car was cool and quiet and smelled like spices. He wasn't thirsty and he was going home. Even on the rough mountain road the car rode like a cloud. He closed one eye and rested, keeping the other eye on Lloyd. "Miracles?" Samson said.

"That's right! I can make dreams out of nothing, wants out of dreams, needs out of wants, and leave a dream in your hand. You know how I do it?"

Samson shook his head. This man was just like Pokey: if he wanted to tell you something he would tell you even if you dropped dead and rotted right before his eyes.

"Well, son, it all starts with a smile at the door. When you hit that door people ain't been sitting there waiting for you. They been sitting around thinking about how miserable they are. They got nothing to hang on to, nothing to go on for. When they answer that door they're as sour as green oranges, but I don't give it back to 'em. I give a smile of pure honey, and words just as sweet. I tell them what they want to hear. If they're ugly, I tell 'em they're looking fine. If they're a failure, I marvel at their success. Before they got the latch off the screen door I'm the best friend they ever had. And why? Because I see them as what they would like to be, not what they are. For once in their life they are living their dream, only because I make them think they are.

"But then they look around and get a little uncomfortable. If they got what they wanted, how come they ain't feeling it? How come they still feel empty? Well, son, between you and me, there ain't no contentment, no satisfaction, this side of the grave. You ain't never going to be as pretty or as rich as you want to be. No one ever has, no one ever will. Folks don't know that, though. Folks think that there's an answer to that scary feeling that keeps riding them no matter what they do."

"Coyote Blue," Samson said.

"Don't talk nonsense, boy, I'm trying to teach you something. Where was I? Oh, yeah, they think that there's an answer. So I give it to them. I watch their eyes while I'm telling them how damn good they're doing, and when they get right to the edge of panic 'cause they can't see it, I tell them about the Miracle.

"Suddenly a clean rug is all that stands between them and all they could ever be. I take out my machine, and I vacuum up their beds into a little black bag. Then I have them boil that bag on the stove until the whole house smells like a sun-ripe battlefield. You see, all that dead skin that falls off you in your sleep is in the mattress; when you boil it the smell is disgusting. There is filth in these folks' houses. How the hell you gonna be beautiful and successful with filth all around? You can't. Filth is the problem and the Miracle is the solution. Now they want it.

"So we talk some more and I make like I'm gonna leave, but they want the machine. I understand that, but they already got a vacuum cleaner. They don't need my machine. I guess a little filth never hurt no one. But they *do* need it, they say. They need it. And why do they need it? Because now it's all they got standing between them and their dream. So I write them up. I take their money and I leave them holding that dream in their hand while I drive away. Wants, to needs, to dreams—usually in forty-five minutes or less. Now that's a damn miracle, son."

"So you trick them," Samson said.

"They want to be tricked. I just provide a service. It ain't no different than going to the movies or seeing a magician. You don't
want to see that the pirates are using rubber swords, do you? You
don't want to see the secret pockets up the magician's sleeves, do
you? You want to believe in something that you know ain't true,
just for a while. People spend a lot of money and time to get
tricked. And I get to drive a nice car, stay in good motels, eat in
restaurants, and see the country in style."

Samson thought about that for a while. Driving around in a
big, cool, good-smelling car would be almost as good as living
on the Ponderosa. Maybe better. Nobody on the reservation
drove a car like this, and they hardly ever ate in restaurants,
except the burger stand in Crow Agency. Maybe tricking people
was the way to go. It sure sounded better than baling hay or
fixing truck engines.

"Do you think I could sell miracles?" Samson asked.

Lloyd laughed. "You got some growing to do first. Besides, it
takes a man of character to handle freedom. Do you have character, Samson?"

"Is that like medicine?"

"It's better than medicine. You get yourself some character and
come see me in a few years. Then we'll see."

That settled it. Samson was going to get himself some character
and sell himself some miracles. He lay back on the seat and closed
his eyes. Lloyd started talking again. The words were soft and
rhythmic and soon Samson Hunts Alone, full of Coca-Cola and
miracles, fell asleep.

"Samson, wake up."

Someone was shaking his shoulders. He opened his eyes and
saw Pokey holding him at arm's length.

"What are you doing up here by the road?" Pokey asked.

"What?" Samson looked around. He was on the ridge where he
had sat down before the big blue car had come along. "Where's
Lloyd?"

"Who's Lloyd?" Pokey asked. "I've only been gone a couple of hours. Why did you come up here? Did you have your vision?"

"No, I went for a ride. I took a ride home with a man who sold Miracles."

"Samson," Pokey said. "I don't think you took a ride anywhere. I think you better tell me what the man said to you."

Samson told Pokey about Lloyd Commerce, about the car as long as a house, about selling miracles and tricking people and living the good life. When he was finished Pokey sat staring at the boy for a long time before he spoke. "Samson, you had your vision. I'm sorry."

"Why are you sorry, Pokey? Because I didn't find my spirit helper?"

"I wish you saw a squirrel or a flicker, Samson, but you saw a vacuum cleaner salesman," Pokey said forlornly.

"But he was just a fat white man."

"He only looked like a white man. I think you saw Old Man Coyote."

CHAPTER TEN

OVER EASY, POLITICALLY CORRECT

SANTA BARBARA

Sam spent most of the night cleaning up the debris from Josh Spagnola's shooting exhibition. Exhausted from the overall strangeness of his day, he went to bed early, but lay awake until well after midnight, first worrying, then trying to understand what was happening to him, and finally fantasizing about the girl. Amid the misery he retained hope, although he could not logically figure out why. She was, after all, just a girl—the goofiest girl he had ever met. Still, the thought of seeing her again made him smile, and he was able to escape into dreamless sleep.

When he awoke the next morning, the world seemed a much kinder place, as if during the night the calamities of the previous day had become distant and harmless. Order had returned. At one time he might have met such a day by looking to the rising sun and thanking the Great Spirit for returning his harmony with the world, as Pokey had taught him. He would have looked for rain clouds, felt the promise of the day's winds, smelled the dew and the sage, listened for the call of an eagle, the best of good-luck signs, and in that short time he would have confirmed that he and the world were of one spirit, balanced.

Today he missed the rising sun by three hours. He met his day in the shower, washing his hair with shampoo that was guaranteed to have never been put in a bunny's eyes and from which ten percent of the profits went to save the whales. He lathered his face with shaving cream free of chlorofluorocarbons, thereby saving the ozone layer. He breakfasted on fertile eggs laid by sexually satisfied chickens that were allowed to range while listening to Brahms, and muffins made with pesticide-free grain, so no eagle-egg shells were weakened by his thoughtless consumption. He scrambled the eggs in margarine free of tropical oils, thus preserving the rain forest, and he added milk from a carton made of recycled paper and shipped from a small family farm. By the time he finished his second cup of coffee, which would presumably help to educate the children of a poor peasant farmer named Juan Valdez, Sam was on the verge of congratulating himself for single-handedly saving the planet just by getting up in the morning. He would have been surprised, however, if someone had told him that it had been two years since he had set foot on unpaved ground.

He was writing a note to himself to put a new subliminal message on his computer, SAVE THE WORLD, BUY THIS POLICY, when Josh Spagnola called.

"Sam, did you hear what happened at the association meeting last night?"

"No, Josh, I've been cleaning up my place."

"*The* place, Sam. I think this will be an easier transition if you start referring to it as *the* place."

"You mean they voted to buy me out? Without even asking me? I can't believe it."

"I was actually very surprised myself. People seem to dislike you in the extreme, Sam. I think the dog was just their excuse for a general fuck-over."

"You told them it wasn't my dog, didn't you?"

"I told them, but it didn't matter. They hate you, Sam. The doctors and lawyers hate you because you make enough money to live here. The married guys hate you because you're single. The married women hate you because you remind their husbands that they aren't single. The old people hate you because you're young, and the rest just hate you because you aren't Japanese. Oh, yeah, one bald guy hates you because you have hair. For a guy that maintains a low profile, you've built quite a little snowball of resentment."

Sam had never given his neighbors a second thought, never even spoken to most of them, so now the realization that they hated him enough to take away his home was a shock. "I've never done anything to hurt anybody in this complex."

"I wouldn't take it personally, Sam. Nothing brings people together like hate for profit. You didn't have a chance against the clay tennis courts."

"What does that mean? We don't have clay tennis courts."

"No, but when they buy your townhouse for what you paid for it, then sell it to someone more suitable at the market rate, the association will have enough profit to build clay tennis courts. We'll be the only complex in Santa Barbara with clay courts. Should raise the value of the property at least ten percent. Sorry, Sam."

"Isn't there anything I can do? Can't I bring legal action or something?"

"This isn't an official call, Sam. I am calling as your friend and not on behalf of the association, so let me give you my best advice on taking legal action: it's suicide. Half the guys that voted you out are lawyers. In six months you'd be broke and they'd be drinking your blood over backgammon. The time for legal advice was eight years ago when you signed that agreement."

"Great. Where were you then?"

"I was stealing your Rolex."

"You stole my Rolex? That was you? My gold Rolex? You dick!"

"I didn't know you then, Sam. It was a professional thing. Besides, the statute of limitations has run out. It's time to forgive and forget."

"Fuck you, Josh. You'll get a bill for the damage you caused."

"Sam, do you know how concerned I am about your bill? I don't give a decaying damn, I don't—"

Sam hung up on the security guard. The phone immediately rang and Sam stared at it for a minute. Should he let Josh get the satisfaction of the last word? He looked at the shattered remains of his television, picked up the phone, and shouted, "Look, you wormy little fuck, you're lucky I don't come down there and pop your head like a pimple!"

"Sam, this is Julia, down at the office. I have Aaron on the line for you."

"Sorry, Julia, I was expecting someone else. Hang on a second." He sat down on the couch and held the receiver to his chest while he tried to regain his composure. Too much change, too fast. He couldn't let Aaron catch him with his guard down. His good friend Aaron, his partner, his mentor. And Josh Spagnola was supposed to be his friend too. What was the deal with Josh? He'd turned on Sam overnight. Why?

Sam lit a cigarette and took a long drag, then blew the smoke out in a slow stream before speaking into the phone. "Julia, you caught me in the shower. Tell Aaron I'll be in the office in an hour. We'll talk then." He hung up before she could respond. He dialed the number of the Cliffs' security office. Josh Spagnola answered.

"Josh, this is Sam Hunter."

"Very rude, Sam. Hanging up when I am telling you how little I care is very rude."

"That's why I'm calling, Josh. I've heard your little speeches before. I want to know what you've got on me."

"Then you haven't seen the paper this morning?"

"I told you before, I've been patching holes all fucking morning. What goes?"

"Seems that Jim Cable, the diving mogul, was attacked by an Indian outside of his office and had a heart attack. They said he had just finished an appointment with an insurance agent."

"So, what's your point, Josh?"

"The point is, Sam, that after I ran out of your place yesterday, I

went through the apartment next door and ran out on the deck. I
thought I could come in from behind the dog and get a shot at it.
But when I got there I saw an Indian vaulting over the rail of your
deck. The Indian was wearing black, just like the one they described in the paper. Interesting coincidence, huh?"

Sam didn't know what to say. Spagnola had half the complex
under his thumb for one reason or another, but Sam didn't know
how the burglar used his information other than as a license to be
rude. Sam didn't want to bring up blackmail when Spagnola
might just be in this to watch him squirm. Sam had watched a
thousand clients squirm under his own manipulation, but he
wasn't sure how to go about it himself. He decided to take a direct
approach. "Okay, Josh," he said. "I'm squirming. Now what?"

"Sammy, I love you, kid. You and I are like peas in a pod. You,
me, and that Aaron guy at your office."

"You know Aaron?"

"Just spoke to him this morning when I called your office. Your
secretary said that you were no longer with the firm and Mr.
Aaron was taking all your calls from now on. Aaron and I had a
long talk."

"Did you tell him about the Indian?"

"No, he told me. Strange thing, Sam, he seems to want you out
of the business pretty badly, but not just for the profit. I think he's
afraid of the attention you're going to get if it turns out that you're
associated with the Indian who attacked Cable. Who do you think
has more to lose: you or Aaron?"

"Neither of us is losing anything, Josh. This whole thing is a
mistake. I don't care what you saw, I don't know anything about
any Indian, and I resent the veiled threat."

"No threat, Sam. Just information. It's the cleanest commodity,
you know? No fingerprints, no fibers, no serial numbers. It's kind
of ethereal—religious in a way. People will pay for something that
they can't smell, or taste, or touch. It's fucking glorious, isn't it? I
should have been a spy."

Sam listened to Spagnola sigh, then to the breathing over the line. Here it was again, the standoff. How many times had he backed down over the years? How many times had fear of discovery caused him to lie low and play the role of the victim? Too damn many. He always seemed to be running from the past and avoiding the future, but the future came anyway.

Very softly, barely speaking over a whisper, Sam said, "Josh, before you become too enraptured, remember the information you don't have."

"What's that, old buddy?"

"You have no idea who I am or what I'm capable of."

There was a silence on the line, as if Spagnola was considering what Sam had said. "Good-bye, Josh," Sam whispered.

He hung up the phone, grabbed his car keys, and headed out the door to the Mercedes. As he disarmed the alarm and climbed in the car he realized that he also had no idea who he was or what he was capable of, and for the first time in his life it didn't frighten him. In fact, it felt good.

COYOTE GETS HIS POWERS

One day, a long time ago, before there were any men or televisions, and only animal people walked the Earth, Great Spirit, the first worker, decided that he would give everyone a new name. He told the animal people to come to his lodge at sunrise and he would give each one a new name with all the powers that went with it. "To be fair," Great Spirit said, "names will be given on a first-come, first-served basis." The Earth was a pretty fair place in those days as long as you showed up on time.

Coyote had a problem with this method, however. He liked to sleep until lunchtime and lie around thinking up tricks until late afternoon, so getting up at sunrise was a problem, but he really wanted to get a good name. "'Eagle' would be good," he thought. "I would be swift and strong. Or if I take the name of 'Bear' I will never be defeated by my enemies. Yep, I got to get me a good name even if I have to stay up all night."

When the sun went down Coyote looked all over for a good espresso bar, but even in those days they were full of pretentious pseudointellectual animal people who sat around in open-toed moccasins and whined about how unfair the world was, which it wasn't. "I don't have the stomach for that," said Coyote. "I think I'll just score some magic wake-up powder and stay wired that way."

Coyote went to see Raven. It was well known among the animal people that Raven had a connection with a green bird from South America and was always good for some wake-up powder.

"I'm sorry Coyote, my friend, but I cannot extend you any credit. I'll need three prairie dogs, up front, if you want the product. And remember, I like my prairie dogs squashed real flat." Raven was a greasy little prick who thought he was cool because he wore sunglasses all the time, even at night. Who was he to act so high and mighty? Coyote was insulted.

"Look, man, I'll have a new name tomorrow. I'm going to go for 'Eagle.' Just advance me the gram now and I'll give you six prairie dogs in the morning."

Raven shook his head. Coyote slunk away.

"I can stay awake without magic," Coyote said. "I just have to concentrate."

Coyote tried to stay awake, but by the time the moon was high in the sky he started to doze off. "This isn't working," he said. "I can't keep my eyes open." Talking to himself often gave Coyote ideas, which was a good thing, because hardly anyone else would talk to him. He broke a couple of thorns from a cactus and used them to prop his eyes open. "I'm a genius," he said. Then he fell asleep anyway.

When Coyote finally awoke the sun was directly overhead. He rushed to Great Spirit's lodge and burst through the door flap. "'Eagle'! I want 'Eagle,'" he said.

His eyes were dry and cracked from being propped open and his fur was matted with blood where the thorns had pierced his eyelids.

"'Eagle' was the first to go," Great Spirit said. "What happened to you? You look like hammered shit."

"Bad night," Coyote said. "What's left? 'Bear'? 'Bear' would be good."

"There's only one name left," Great Spirit said. "Nobody wanted it."

"What is it?"

"'Coyote.'"

"You're shitting me."

"Great Spirit is not a shitter."

Coyote ran outside where the other animal people were laughing and talking about their new names and powers. He tried to get them to trade names, but even Dung Beetle told him to get lost. Great Spirit watched Coyote from his lodge and felt sorry for him.

"Come here, kid," Great Spirit said. "Look, you're stuck with a lousy name, but maybe I can make up for it. You have to keep the name, but from now on you are Chief of the Without Fires. And from now on you can take on any shape that you choose and wear it as long as you wish."

Coyote thought about it for a minute. It was a pretty good gift; maybe he should work this pity angle more often. "So that means that everyone has to do what I say?"

"Sometimes," Great Spirit said.

"Sometimes?" Coyote asked. Great Spirit nodded and Coyote figured he'd better leave before Great Spirit changed his mind. "Thanks, G.S., I'm outta here. Got to see someone about some sunglasses." Coyote loped off.

CHAPTER ELEVEN

THE GOD, THE BAD, AND THE UGLY

SANTA BARBARA

During the short drive to his office Sam decided that if Gabriella gave him the least little bit of shit he would fire her on the spot. If his life was going to fall apart before his eyes there was no reason to suffer the slings and arrows of ungrateful employees. There were also twenty younger agents who worked under him, and as long as he held partnership in the agency he held the power to hire and fire. *Let one of them mouth off,* he thought. *Let one of them look sideways at me and they're going to be a distant memory, taillights on the horizon, gone, out, shit-canned, pink-slipped, instantly unemployed.*

He walked into his office with his temper locked, loaded, and ready to fire, but was immediately disarmed when he saw Gabriella tilted back in her chair, skirt thrown up around her waist, her legs spread wide and high heels alternately pumping in the air and digging into the back of the naked Indian, who was on his knees in front of her, wheeling her chair back and forth, thrusting into her with greedy abandon and yipping with each stroke as counterpoint to the monkey noises that escaped Gabriella in rhythmic bursts.

"Hey!" Sam shouted.

Gabriella looked over the Indian's shoulder at Sam and held one finger in the air as if marking a point, then pointed to the message pad on the desk. "One call," she gasped. The Indian pulled her to him in a particularly violent thrust and Gabriella grabbed his shoulder with both hands, popping her press-on nails off and across the room like tiddlywinks.

Sam shook off his shock, ran forward, and caught the Indian around the neck in a choke hold. The Indian pumped wildly in the air as Sam dragged him off Gabriella and across the outer office. He fell over backward into his office with the Indian still squirming in his grasp and it occurred to him that unless things turned quickly to his advantage he was in serious danger of being humped. He rolled the Indian over on the carpet and pinned him, facedown, while he looked around for a weapon. The only thing in reach was the big multiline phone on his desk. Sam released the choke hold and lunged for the phone, catching it by the cord. He swung around with it just in time to hit the Indian in the face as he was rising to his hands and knees. The phone exploded into a spray of electronic shrapnel and the Indian fell forward onto his face, unconscious but twitching against the carpet in petit-mal afterhumps.

Sam looked at the broom of colored wires at the end of the cord where the phone used to be, then dropped it and staggered to his feet. Gabriella was standing by the door, smoothing her skirt down. Her lipstick was smeared across her face and her hair was spiked into a fright wig of hair spray and sweat. She started to speak, then noticed that one of her breasts was still peeking out of her dress. "Excuse me." She turned and tucked herself in, then turned back to Sam. "I'll hold your calls," she said officiously, then she pulled the door closed, leaving Sam alone in the office with the unconscious, naked Indian.

"You're fired," Sam whispered to the closed door. He looked down at the Indian and saw a bloodstain spreading around his head on the carpet. He didn't seem to be breathing. Sam fell to his knees and felt the Indian's neck for a pulse. Nothing.

"Fuck, not again!" Sam paced around the desk four times before he fell back in his leather executive chair and clamped his hands on his temples as if trying to squeeze out a solution. Instead he thought of police and prison and felt hope running through his fingers like liquid light, leaving him dark with despair.

A growling noise from the floor. Sam looked over the desk to see the body of the Indian moving. He started to breathe a sigh of relief when he realized that the body wasn't moving at all, it was changing. His eyes went wide with terror as the arms and legs shortened and grew fur, the face grew into a whiskered muzzle, and the spinal column lengthened and grew into a bushy tail. Before Sam could catch his breath again he was looking at the body of a huge black coyote.

The coyote got to its feet and shook its head as if clearing its ears of water, then it leapt on the desk and growled at Sam, who rolled his chair back until it hit the wall behind his desk.

Sam pushed himself up by the chair arms until he was almost standing against the wall, desperately trying to put even a millimeter more between himself and the snarling muzzle of the coyote. The coyote crawled forward on the desk until its face was only inches from Sam's. Sam could feel the coyote's moist breath on his face. It smelled of something familiar, something burnt. He wanted to turn his head away and close his eyes until the horror went away, but his gaze remained locked on the coyote's golden eyes. He wanted to scream but there was no breath for it and he found his jaw was moving but no sound was coming out.

The coyote backed away and sat on the desk, then raised its lowered ears and tilted its head to the side as if perplexed. Sam felt himself take a breath and the strange urge to say "Good doggie" came over him, but he remained rigid and quiet. The coyote began to shake and Sam thought it would attack, but instead it threw back its head as if to howl. The skin on the coyote's neck began to undulate and surge and took on the shape of a human face. The fur receded from the face, then away from the front legs, which became arms, then down the back legs, which lengthened into crouching human legs. As the fur peeled it lost its black color, turning the burnt tan of a normal coyote. It was as if a human was literally crawling out of a cocoon of coyote skin, the black color becoming black buckskins trimmed with red feathers. A minute passed in what seemed a year as the transformation took place. When it was finished the Indian was crouched on Sam's desk wearing a coyote-skin headdress that had once been his own skin.

"Fuck," Sam said, falling back into the chair, his eyes trained now on the golden eyes of the Indian.

"Woof," the Indian said with a grin.

Sam shook his head, trying to get the image to go away. His mind was still rattling around in chaos trying to put this into some sort of meaningful context, but all he could do was wish that he would pass out and that his kneecaps would stop jumping with adrenaline.

"Woof," the Indian repeated. He jumped from the desk, adjusted the headdress that moments ago had been his skin, then sat in the chair opposite Sam. "Got a smoke?" he said.

Sam felt his mind lock on to the request. Yes, he understood that. Yes, he could do that. A smoke. He reached into his shirt pocket for his cigarettes and lighter and fumbled them out, lost his grip, and sent them skittering across the desk. He was scrambling for them when the Indian reached out and patted his hand. Sam screamed, the high-pitched wail of a little girl, and jumped back into his chair, which rolled back until his head snapped against the wall.

The Indian turned his head to the side quizzically, the same way the coyote had, then took the cigarettes from the desk and lit two with the lighter. He held one out to Sam, who remained pushed back in the chair. The Indian nodded for Sam to take the cigarette, then waited while Sam inched forward, snatched it out of his hand, and quickly retreated to his position by the back wall.

The Indian took a deep drag on the cigarette, then turned his head and blew the smoke out in rings that crept across the desk like ghosts.

Sam had curled into the fetal position in his chair and looked up only to cast a sideways glance at the Indian when he took a drag from his own cigarette. It occurred to him that he should feel silly, but he didn't. He was still too frightened to feel silly. When his cigarette was half gone he started to calm down. His fear was draining away, being replaced with indignant anger. The Indian sat calmly, smoking and looking around the office.

Sam put his feet on the floor, scooted the chair back under the desk, and set what he hoped was a hard gaze on the Indian. "Who are you?" he asked.

The Indian smiled and his eyes lit up like an excited child's. "I am the stink in your shoe, the buzz in your ear, the wind through the trees. I am the—"

"Who are you?" Sam interrupted. "What is your name?"

The Indian continued to grin while smoke trickled between his teeth. He said, "The Cheyenne call me *Wihio*, the Sioux, *Iktome*. The Blackfeet call me Napi Old Man. The Cree call me *Saultaux*, the Micmac, *Glooscap*. I am the Great Hare on the East Coast and Raven on the West. You know me, Samson Hunts Alone, I am your spirit helper."

Sam gulped. "Coyote?"

"Yep."

"You're a myth."

"A legend," the Indian said.

"You are just a bunch of stories to teach children."

"True stories."

"No, just stories. Old Man Coyote is just a fairy tale."

"Should I change shapes again? You liked that."

"No! No, don't do that." Sam had guessed the Indian's identity the day before when he'd opened the medicine bundle, but he had hoped it would all go away and he would find himself the victim of a childhood superstition. Religion was supposed to be a matter of faith. Gods were not supposed to jump on your desk and snarl at you. They weren't supposed to sit in your office smoking cigarettes. Gods didn't do anything. They were supposed to ignore you and let you suffer and die having never known whether your religion was a waste of time. Faith.

Sure, the gods were a badly behaving lot in stories—jealous, impatient, selfish, vengeful, smiting whole races of people, raping virgins, sending plagues and pestilence—and even as gods went, Coyote was a particularly bad example, but they were supposed to stay in the damn stories, not show up and hump your homely secretary until she made monkey noises.

"What are you doing here?" Sam asked.

"I'm here to help you."

"Help? You ruined my business and got me kicked out of my home."

"You wanted to scare the diver so I scared him. You wanted the girl so I gave her to you."

"Well what about all the cats at my condo complex? What about my secretary? How did that help me?"

"If I was not meant to have ugly women and cats they would not be so easy to catch."

It was the kind of backward, perverse logic that had irritated Sam as a child. Pokey Medicine Wing had been a master at it. It seemed to Sam at times as if the entire Crow Nation was trying to define a silicon-chip world with a Stone Age worldview. Sam thought he had escaped it.

"Why me? Why not someone who believes?"

"This is more fun."

Sam resisted the urge to leap over the desk and choke the Indian. It was still "the Indian" in his head. He hadn't yet accepted that he was talking to Coyote, Chief of the Without Fires. Even with the overwhelming evidence of the supernatural, he searched for a natural explanation for what was happening. A lifetime of disbelief is not easily shed. He tried to find some parallel experience that would put things in order, something he'd read or seen on PBS. Nothing was forthcoming, so he speculated.

How would Aaron react if faced with this situation? Aaron didn't acknowledge his Irish heritage any more than Sam admitted his own Crow roots. What if a leprechaun suddenly appeared on Aaron's desk? He'd affect a brogue and try to talk the little fucker into putting his pot o' gold into tax-deferred annuities. No, Aaron was not the person to think of in a spiritual emergency.

Coyote smiled as if he had read Sam's thoughts. "What do you want, Samson Hunts Alone?"

Sam didn't even hesitate to think. "I want my old life back to the way it was before you fucked it up."

"Why?"

Now Sam was forced to think. Why indeed? Every time Sam hired a new agent he glorified his and Aaron's lifestyles. He would take a bright, hungry young man for a ride in the Mercedes, buy him lunch at the Biltmore or another of Santa Barbara's finer restaurants, flash cash and gold cards and expensive suits—plant the *seed of greed*, as Aaron called it—then give the kid a means to pursue his germinating dream of material bliss while Sam collected ten percent on everything he sold. It was part of the show, one of the many roles he played, and the car, the clothes, the condo, and the clout were merely props. Without the props the show could not go on.

"Why do you want your life back?" Coyote asked, as if Sam had forgotten the question.

"It's safe," Sam blurted out.

"So safe," Coyote said, "that you can lose it in a day? To be safe is to be afraid. Is that what you want: to be afraid?"

"I'm not afraid."

"Then why do you lie? You want the girl."

"Yes."

"I will help you get her."

"I don't need your help. I need you gone."

"I am very good with women."

"Like you're good with cats and couches?"

"Great heroes have great horniness. You should feel what it is like to pleasure a falcon. You lock talons with her in the sky and do it while you both are falling like meteors. You would like it; they never complain if you come too fast."

"Get out of here."

"I will go, but I will be with you." Coyote rose and walked to the door. As he opened it he said, "Don't be afraid." He stepped out of his office and closed the door. Suddenly, Sam leapt to his feet and headed after him. "Stay off my secretary!" he shouted. He ripped open the door and looked into the outer office where Gabriella, her composure regained, was typing up a claim form. Coyote was gone.

Gabriella looked up and raised a disapproving eyebrow. "Is there a problem, Mr. Hunter?"

"No," Sam said. "No problem."

"You sounded frightened."

"I'm not frightened, goddammit!" Sam slammed the door and went to the desk for a cigarette. His cigarettes and lighter were gone. He stood there for a moment, feeling a flush of anger rise in him until he thought he would scream, then he fell back into his chair and smiled as he remembered something Pokey Medicine Wing had once told him: "Anger is the spirits telling you that you are alive."

CHAPTER TWELVE

CRUELLY TURN THE STEEL-BELTED RADIALS OF DESTINY

CROW COUNTRY—1973

In the six years since his vision quest Samson had endured almost daily interpretations of the vision by Pokey Medicine Wing. Again and again Samson insisted that it wasn't important, and again and again Pokey forced the boy to recall his experience on the mountain in detail. It was Pokey's responsibility as a self-proclaimed medicine man to bring meaning to the symbols in the vision. Over the years, as Pokey read new meanings, he tried to change his and Samson's lives to fit the message of the medicine dream.

"Maybe Old Man Coyote was trying to tell us that we should turn our dreams into money," Pokey said.

With this interpretation, Pokey dragged Samson into a series of entrepreneurial ventures that ultimately served no purpose except to confirm to the people of Crow Country that Pokey had finally gone full-bore batshit.

The first foray into the world of business was a worm ranch. Pokey presented the idea to Samson with the same blind faith with which he told Old Man Coyote stories, and Samson, like so many before him, was captivated with the idea of turning religion into money.

Pokey's eyes were lit up with liquor and firelight as he spoke. "They are building that dam up on the Bighorn River. They tell us that we will prosper from all the people who will come to the reservation to fish and water-ski on the new lake. That's what they told us when they put the Custer Monument here, but whites opened stores and took all the money. This time we will get our share. We'll grow worms and sell them for fishing."

They had no lumber to build the worm beds, so Pokey and Samson went to the Rosebud Mountains and cut lodgepole pines, which they brought down by the pickup load. Through a whole summer they hauled and built until the Hunts Alones' five acres was nearly covered with empty worm beds. Pokey, convinced that their success depended on getting a jump on other prospective worm ranchers, instructed Samson to tell everyone who asked that they were building corrals to hold tiny horses that they were raising for the Little People that lived in the mountains. "It's easier to keep a secret if people think you're crazy," Pokey said.

With the beds finished, they were faced with the problem of filling them. "Worms like cow shit," Pokey said. "We can get that for free." Indeed, had Pokey asked any of the ranchers in the area, they would have let him haul away all the manure he needed, but because most of the ranchers were white and Pokey did not trust them, he decided, instead, that he and Samson would steal the cow pies in the dead of night.

So it began: sunset, Samson and Pokey driving the old pickup into a pasture, Pokey driving slowly along while Samson followed on foot with a shovel, scooping piles into the bed of the truck, then the two of them stealing away with their reeking load to dump it in the worm beds, then out again. "The Crow have always been the best horse thieves, Samson," Pokey said. "Old Man Coyote would be proud of the trick we have played on the ranchers."

Pokey's enthusiasm mystified Samson, who couldn't muster the same self-satisfaction at stealing something that nobody wanted. Nevertheless, after a month of pasture raids the beds were full and they drove to the bait store in Hardin to buy their breeding stock: night crawlers and red worms, five hundred each.

Pokey burnt sage and sweet grass and prayed over the beds and they released the worms into the beds of manure. Then they waited.

"We shouldn't disturb them until spring," Pokey said, but many nights Samson spotted him sneaking out to one of the beds with a trowel, turning over a patch, then skulking away. One night Samson was sneaking out with his own trowel when he saw Pokey on his knees with his face pressed to a bed. He stood up when he sensed the boy behind him.

"You know what I was doing?" Pokey asked.

"No," Samson said, hiding his trowel behind his back.

"I was listening to the sound of money."

"You have shit on your ear, Pokey."

From that time forward they were both more careful about their nocturnal progress checks, but neither found worm one. They waited through the cold Montana winter, sure that come spring they would be waist deep in worms and money. Never mind the fact that Yellowtail Dam wouldn't be completed for two more years.

After the thaw they marched to the beds together, shovels in hand, to turn over their squirming horn of plenty, but shovel after shovel turned up empty. Into the third bed they began to panic and were wildly slinging shit in the air when Harlan pulled up.

"Digging for horses?" he asked.

"Worms," Pokey shouted, lifting the veil of secrecy with a single word.

"Where did you get the manure?"

"Around," Pokey said.

"Around where?"

"The ranches on the res."

Harlan began to laugh and Samson was afraid for a moment

that Pokey would brain him with the shovel. "You were trying to grow worms?"

"Old Man Coyote told us to," Samson said defensively. "We let go a thousand worms in here to breed so we could sell 'em to fishermen."

"I guess Old Man Coyote didn't tell you that cattle ranchers put a wormer in their cattle feed, huh?"

"Wormer?" Pokey said.

"That manure was poison to your worms. They were probably dead ten minutes after you put them in there."

Samson and Pokey looked at each other forlornly, the boy's lower lip swelling with disappointment, the man's temples throbbing with pain.

Some people believe that hard work is its own reward and a job well done is a tribute to a man's character; fortunately, none of those people were around or they would have been ducking shovel blows. Pokey and Samson decided to get drunk. Harlan stayed on to coach the boy through his first hangover and run interference with Grandma, who would have skinned the two men had she known they were giving liquor to a twelve-year-old.

It was the end of summer, a summer spent in sulking and speculating, before Pokey brought home the goats. He'd obtained the pair, a male and a female, from a dubious source in a Hardin bar by winning a bet that had something to do with a pineapple, a throwing knife, and a waitress named Debbie. Samson had difficulty putting the story together from Pokey's drunken ravings, but he gathered that because Debbie had survived, and the pineapple had not, Pokey had two goats on his hands.

"We could breed 'em and sell 'em for meat," Pokey said. "But I got a better idea. Them lawyers and doctors are flying into Montana from the city and paying a thousand bucks a head to shoot bighorn sheep. I say we go to the airport in Billings and wait for one of them to get off a plane, then tell 'em they can come to the res and shoot one for two–three hundred. I can be the faithful Indian guide and lead them all over hell and back, and you can take the goats up into the mountains and tie them up where they can shoot 'em."

Despite Samson's objections that even a city lawyer might know the difference between a bighorn sheep and a nanny goat, Pokey insisted that come morning they would be on the road to riches. Come morning, however, when Samson went outside to look at the goats he found them lying on their backs, legs shot stiff to the sky with rigor mortis, dead as stones. In his excitement Pokey had tied the goats next to a patch of hemlock, and the goats, perhaps sensing what was planned for them, munched their last meal and joined the ranks of Socrates.

Not all of Pokey's quests for spiritual capitalism were complete failures. He and Samson made a little money with the "authentic" Indian fry-bread taco stand they set up outside of the Custer Battlefield National Monument, until the health department objected to the presence of marmot and raccoon meat in their *all-beef* tacos. And they did make forty dollars selling eagle feathers to tourists (actually the feathers of two buzzards that had dined on tainted goat carcass), which they used to buy marijuana seeds that produced a respectable crop of grape-sized casaba melons. (Harlan referred to this as the magic beans incident.) And finally, while Samson was busy with school and basketball and a developing obsession with girls, Pokey turned to prostitution and made five bucks from the owner of the Hardin 7-Eleven who paid the shaman to take his sandwich sign and go stand somewhere else.

Samson was fifteen by the time Pokey decided that perhaps they were not meant to turn their dreams into money. Once again he sat the boy down in the kitchen to recount the vision.

"Pokey, I don't even remember much of the vision, and besides, how important could it be? I was only nine." Samson's friend Billy Two Irons was waiting outside to drive them to a "forty-nine" party at the Yellowtail Dam and Samson was not in the mood to be cross-examined about an event that he was trying desperately to leave behind, along with the rest of the trappings of childhood.

"Do you know why the Crow never fought the white man?" Pokey asked gravely.

"Oh, fuck, Pokey, not now. I've got to get going."

"Do you know why?"

"No. Why?"

"Because of the vision of a nine-year-old boy. That's why."

As much as Samson wanted to leave, he had spent too many years listening to the Cheyenne and Lakota call his people cowards to walk out now. "What boy?" he asked.

"Our last great chief, Plenty Coups. When he was nine he went on his first fast, just like you. He cut pieces from his skin and suffered greatly. Finally, his vision came, and he saw the buffalo gone and then he saw the white man's cattle covering the plains. He saw white men everywhere, but he saw none of our people. The medicine chiefs heard his vision and said that it was a message. The Lakota and the Cheyenne had fought the white men and lost their lands. The vision meant that if we fought the white men we would lose our land and be wiped out. Our chiefs decided not to fight and the Crow survived. We are here because of the vision of a nine-year-old boy."

"That's great, Pokey," Samson said, having gained nothing useful from the story. He was not going to quell any ridicule from non-Crows by telling them that his people had changed their way of life over a mystical vision. It was hard enough trying to live down the reputation of his crazy uncle as it was. "I have to go now."

He grabbed the drum that Pokey had made him and took off through the living room, high-stepping over his eight younger cousins, who were sprawled on the floor watching cartoons on televsion. " 'Bye, Grandma," he tossed over his shoulder to his grandmother, who sat in a tattered easy chair among the kids, adding the final touches to a beaded belt she was making for him.

In front of the Hunts Alone house a tall, acne-speckled Billy Two Irons was pouring a jug of water into the radiator of a twenty-year-old Ford Fairlane. Most of the water was draining out of the bottom of the engine onto the ground at his feet.

"That thing going to make it up to Yellowtail?" Samson called.

"No problem, bro," Billy said without looking up. "I got twenty milk jugs of water in the backseat for the trip up. Coming home's downhill most of the way."

"You fix the exhaust leak?"

"Yep, tomato can and a hose clamp. Works fine as long as you keep the windows down."

"How about the brakes?" Samson was staring over Billy's shoulder into the greasy cavern of the engine compartment.

Billy capped the radiator and slammed the hood before he answered. "You let it coast down to about ten miles an hour and throw it in reverse it'll stop on a dime."

"Then let's do it." Samson jumped into the car. Billy threw the empty milk jug into the backseat, climbed in, and began cranking the engine. Samson looked back to the house and saw Pokey coming out the front door waving at them.

"Hit it, man," Samson said. "Let's go."

The car finally fired up just as Pokey reached the window. He shouted to be heard over the din of the damaged muffler. "You boys watch out for Enos, now."

"We will, Pokey," Samson said as they pulled away. Then he turned to Billy Two Irons. "Is Anus working nights again?" *Anus* was the name they used for Enos Windtree, a fat, meanspirited half-breed BIA cop who liked nothing better than to terrorize kids partying at some remote spot on the res. Once, at a forty-nine party near Lodge Grass, Samson and Billy and nearly twenty others were drinking and singing with the drums when Samson heard a distinct, sickening series of mechanical clicks right by his ear: the sound of a twelve-gauge shell being jacked into a riot gun. When he turned to the noise Enos hit him in the chest with the butt of the gun, knocking him to the ground. Then Enos shot the lights and windshields out of two cars before sending everyone on their way. When Samson told the story, people just said he was just lucky Enos hadn't hit him in the face, or shot somebody. There were rumors that it had happened before. And people *were*

dying on the Lakota reservation at Pine Ridge, killed by the tribal
police in what amounted to a civil war.

"Enos works whenever he can find someone to fuck with," Billy
said. "I'd like to hang that fat fuck's scalp from my lodgepole."

"Oooooo, brave warrior, heap big pissed off," Samson chided in
pidgin—*speaking Tonto,* they called it.

"You telling me you wouldn't want to see Anus's head through
a rifle scope?"

"Yeah, if I thought I could get away with it. But a rifle would be
too quick."

For an hour and a half, between stops to add water to the radiator, they theorized on the best way to do away with Enos Windtree.
When they finally arrived at the party it had been decided that
Enos should have his entire body abraded with a belt sander and a
two-inch hole saw slowly driven through his skull with a drill
press. (Samson and Billy had just finished with their first year of
shop class and were still fascinated by the macabre potential of
every power tool they had used; this fascination, of course, was fed
by their shop teacher, a seven-fingered white man who described
in detail every accident that had mangled, mutilated, or murdered
some careless shop student since the turn of the century. The
teacher had been so successful in instilling *respect for the tools* in
the boys that Billy Two Irons had taken to skipping two classes
after shop to mellow out and would have had a nervous break-
down had Samson not finished building his friend's birdhouse for
him.)

Billy pulled the Fairlane slowly onto the dam and up to a dozen
cars that were parked haphazardly on the three-hundred-foot
structure. He threw the car into reverse and gunned the engine
until the transmission screamed in protest and the car stopped in
a jerking, squealing mechanical seizure.

Samson was out of the car in an instant and a warm wind
coming off the newly formed reservoir washed over him with the
scent of sage. Twenty people were gathered at the rail of the dam,
beating drums and singing a song of heartbreak and betrayal in

Crow. Samson scanned the faces in the moonlight, recognizing and dismissing each until he spotted Ellen Black Feather, and smiled. She was wearing jeans and a T-shirt. Her long hair was blowing in a black comet tail behind her, her shirt was wrapped tight around her in the wind, and Samson noticed, to his delight, that she was braless. She saw Samson and returned his smile.

It was perfect. Just as he had envisioned it on a dozen nights while he lay in the dark with his cousins sleeping around him. They would sing and drink for a while, maybe smoke a joint if somebody had one, then he and Ellen would finish the evening in the backseat of the Fairlane. He walked to Ellen and sat beside her on the rail of the dam, oblivious to the three-hundred-foot drop behind him. As he started to beat his drum and sing he looked back to the car to see Billy adding water to the radiator. It suddenly occurred to him that if he were going to enjoy the favors of Ellen Black Feather in the back of Billy's car, it would be a good idea to move the twenty jugs of water first. He excused himself with a pat on her knee and returned to the car.

"Billy, help me get these jugs into the trunk."

"They're all empty, don't worry about them."

"I'm going to need the space. Just open the trunk, okay?"

Billy handed him the car keys. "Hunts Alone, you are a hopeless horndog."

Samson grinned, then took the keys and ran around to the back of the car. He was loading his first armload of jugs into the trunk when he heard a car pass by and the singing abruptly stopped. Samson looked up to see the green tribal police car stopping in the middle of the partiers, some thirty yards away.

"Fuck. It's Anus," Billy said. "Let's get out of here."

"No, not yet." Samson eased the trunk lid down and joined Billy at the front of the car. They watched Enos Windtree climb out of the car and reach back in for his nightstick. The partiers stood stock-still, as if they were standing near a rattlesnake that would strike at the first movement, but their eyes were darting around looking for possible lanes of escape. All except for Ernest

Bulltail, the biggest and meanest of the group, who met Enos's gaze straight on.

"This is an illegal gathering," Enos rasped as he swaggered up to Ernest. "You all know it, and I know it. The fine is two hundred dollars, payable right now. Cough it up." Enos punctuated his demand by driving the end of his nightstick into Ernest's solar plexus, doubling the big man over. Ernest made an effort to straighten up and Enos hit him across the face with the nightstick. One of the other men stepped forward but froze when Enos dropped his hand to the Magnum strapped to his hip.

"Now for my fine," Enos said.

"Fuck you, Anus!" someone screamed, and Samson's heart sank as he realized that it was Ellen. Enos turned from Ernest and started for the girl.

"I know how you're going to pay up," Enos said to Ellen with a leer.

Samson knew he had to do something, but he wasn't sure what. Billy was tugging on his sleeve, trying to get him to go, but he was fixated on Enos and Ellen. Why hadn't they brought a weapon? He moved to the back of the car and opened the trunk.

"What are you doing?" Billy whispered.

"Looking for a weapon."

"I don't have a gun in the car."

"This," Samson said, holding up a tire iron.

"Against a three fifty-seven? Are you nuts?" Billy grabbed the tire iron and wrenched it out of Samson's hand.

Samson was almost in tears now with frustration. He looked back up the dam to see Enos, his gun at Ellen's head, putting his free hand under her shirt.

Samson pushed Billy aside, then reached into the trunk and pulled out the spare tire. He began creeping up the dam, cradling the heavy spare in his arms. The others watched him, eyes wide with fear. Ten yards away from Enos he started running, the tire held out in front of him.

"Enos!" Samson shouted. The fat policeman pulled away from

Ellen and was bringing up his gun to fire when the tire hit him in the chest and drove him back over the railing. Samson followed, tumbling halfway over the rail before someone caught the back of his shirt and tugged him back. He didn't turn to see who it was, he just stared over the railing at the dam wall that disappeared into the darkness two hundred feet below.

The others joined him at the rail and several minutes passed before the stunned silence was broken by Billy Two Irons. "I just had that spare fixed," he said.

PART TWO

THE CALL TO ACTION

CHAPTER THIRTEEN

FORGET WHAT YOU KNOW

CROW COUNTRY—1973

Of all the people who had seen Enos go over the side of the dam, only Billy Two Irons seemed to have avoided a state of stunned silence. While the others were still staring over the edge into the darkness, Billy was already formulating a plan to save his friend.

"Samson, come here."

Samson looked back at Billy. He was beginning to shiver with unused adrenaline; a look of dreamy confusion had come over him. Billy put his arm around Samson's shoulders and led him away from the railing.

"Look, Samson, you're going to have to run."

A moment passed and Samson did not answer until Billy jostled him. "Run?"

"You have to get off the res and not come back for a long time, maybe never. Everyone here is going to think that they're going to keep this a secret, but when the cops start kicking ass, your name is going to come out. You've got to go, man."

"Where will I go?"

"I don't know, but you have to. Now go get in the car. I'm going to try and raise some money."

Grateful that someone was thinking for him, and because he didn't know what else to do, Samson followed Billy's instructions. He sat in the car and watched his friend going from person to person on the dam collecting money. He closed his eyes and tried to think, but found that there was a movie running on the back of his eyelids: a slow-motion loop of a fat cop with a spare tire in his face going backward over a rail. He snapped his eyes open and stared, unblinking, until they filled with tears. A few minutes later Billy threw a handful of bills on the front seat and climbed in the car.

"I told them you were going to hide out in the mountains and I was getting money for supplies. You should be able to get a long way before the cops figure out that you're not on the res. There's about a hundred bucks here."

Billy started the car and drove off the dam toward Fort Smith.

"Where are we going?" Samson asked.

"First we have to stop and fill up these jugs with water. I'll take you to Sheridan and you can catch a bus there. I don't trust this car to go any farther. If we break down in the middle of nowhere, you're fucked."

Samson was amazed at his friend's ability to think and act so quickly. Left to himself he knew he would still be staring over the dam wondering what had happened. Instead he was on his way to Wyoming.

"I should go home and tell Grandma that I'm going."

"You can't. I'll tell them tomorrow. And once you're gone you can't call or write either. That's how the cops will find you."

"How do you know that?"

"That's how they caught my brother," Billy said. "He wrote a letter from New Mexico. The FBI had him in two days after that."

"But . . ."

"Look, Samson, you killed a cop. I know you didn't mean to, but that won't matter. If they catch you they'll shoot you before you get a chance to tell what happened."

"But everyone saw."

"Everyone there was Crow, Samson. They won't believe a bunch of fucking Indians."

"But Enos was Crow—part Crow, anyway."

"He was an apple, only red on the outside."

Samson started to protest again but Billy shushed him. "Start thinking about where you're going to go."

"Where do you think I should go?"

"I don't know. You just need to disappear. Don't tell me where you're going when you figure it out, either. I don't want to know. You could try and pass for white. With those light eyes you might pull it off. Change your name, dye your hair."

"I don't know how to be white."

"How hard can it be?" Billy said.

Samson wanted to talk to someone besides Billy Two Irons, someone who didn't make as much sense: Pokey. He realized that for all his craziness, all his ravings, all his drinking and ritual mumbo jumbo, Pokey was the person he most trusted in the world. But Billy was right: going home would be a mistake. Instead he tried to imagine what Pokey would say about escaping into the white world. Well, first, Samson thought, he would never admit that there was a white world. According to Pokey there was only the world of the Crow—of family and clans and medicine and balance and Old Man Coyote. The white man was simply a disease that had put the Crow world out of balance.

Samson tried to look into the future to see where he would go, what he would do, but any plans he had ever made—and there hadn't been many—were no longer valid, and the future was a thick, white fog that would allow him to see only as far as the bus station in Sheridan, Wyoming. He felt a panic rising in his chest like a scream, then it came to him: this was just a different type of Coyote Blue. He was trying to look into the future too far and it was ruining his balance. He needed to focus on right now, and eventually he would learn what he needed to know when the future got to him. What did Pokey always say? "If you are going to learn, you need to forget what you know."

"Don't use all your money for the bus ticket," Billy said. "Once you get out of the area you can hitchhike."

"Did you learn all this when your brother got in trouble?"

"Yeah, he writes me letters from prison about what he did wrong."

"He put a bomb in a BIA office. How many letters can that take?"

"Not that. What he did wrong to get caught."

"Oh," Samson said.

Two hours later Samson was climbing on a bus headed for Elko, Nevada, carrying with him everything he owned: twenty-three dollars, a pocketknife, and a small buckskin bundle. He took a window seat in the back of the bus and stared out over the dark countryside, really seeing nothing, as he tried to imagine where he would end up. His fear of getting away was almost greater than his fear of being caught. At least if he were caught his fate would be in someone else's hands.

After an hour or so on the road Samson sensed that the bus was slowing down. He looked around for a reaction from the other passengers, but except for an old lady in the front who was engrossed in a romance novel, they were all asleep. The driver downshifted and Samson felt the big diesel at his back roar as the bus pulled into the passing lane. Out his window he saw the back of a long, powder-blue car. As the bus moved up Samson watched the big car glide below him, seeming to go on forever. He saw the back of the driver's head, then his face. It was the fat salesman from his vision. Samson twisted in his seat, trying to get a better look as they passed. The salesman seemed to see him through the blackout windows of the bus and raised a bottle of Coke as if toasting Samson.

"Did you see that?" Samson cried to the old lady. "Did you see that car?"

The old lady turned to him and shook her head, and a cowboy in the next seat groaned. "Did you see who was in that car?" Samson asked the bus driver, who snickered and shook his head.

The cowboy in the next seat was awake now and he pushed his

hat from over his eyes. "Well, son, now that you got me wetting myself in suspense, who was in the car?"

"It was the salesman," Samson said.

The cowboy stared at him for a second in angry disbelief, then pushed his hat back over his eyes and slid back down in his seat. "I hate fucking Mexicans," he said.

CHAPTER FOURTEEN

LIES HAVE LIVES OF
THEIR OWN

It took just six weeks for Samson Hunts Alone, the Crow Indian, to become Samuel Hunter, the shape-shifter. The transformation began with the cowboy on the bus mistaking Samson for a Mexican. When Samson left the bus in Elko, Nevada, and caught a ride with a racist trucker, he became white for the first time. He expected, from listening to Pokey all those years, that upon turning white he would immediately have the urge to go out and find some Indians and take their land, but the urge didn't come, so he sat by nodding as the trucker talked. By the time he got out at Sacramento, California, Samson had memorized the trucker's litany of white supremacy and was just getting into the rhythm of racism when he caught a ride with a black trucker who took amphetamines and waxed poetic about oppression, injustice, and the violent overthrow of the U.S. government by either the Black Panthers, the Teamsters, or the Temptations. Samson wasn't sure which.

Samson was booted out of the truck in Santa Barbara when he suggested that perhaps killing all the whites should be put off at least until they told where they had hidden all the money. Actually, Samson was somewhat relieved to be put out; he'd only been

white for a few hours and wasn't sure that he liked it well enough
to die for it. His immediate concern was to get something to drink.
He bought a Coke at a nearby convenience store and walked
across the street to a park, where, under the boughs of a massive
fig tree, amid a dozen sleeping bums, he sat down to consider his
next move. Samson was just summoning up an obese case of
hopelessness when a nearby bundle of rags spoke to him.

"Any booze in that cup?"

Samson had to stare at the oblong rag pile for a few seconds
before he noticed there was a hairy face at one end. A single
bloodshot eye, sparkling with hope, the only break in the gray
dinge, gave the face away. "No, just Coke," Samson said. Hope
dimmed and the eye became as empty as the socket next to it.

"You got any money?" the bum asked.

Samson shook his head. He had only twelve dollars left; he
didn't want to share it with the rag pile.

"You're new here?"

Samson nodded.

"You a wet?"

"Excuse me?" Samson said.

"Are you Mexican?"

Samson thought for a moment, then nodded.

"You're lucky," the bum said. "You can get work. A guy stops
near here every morning with a truck—picks up guys to do yard
work, but he only takes Mexicans. Says whites are too lazy."

"Are they?" Samson asked. He figured that after persecuting
blacks, hiding money, stealing land, breaking treaties, and keeping
themselves pure, maybe the whites were just tired. He was glad he
was Mexican.

"You speak pretty good English for a wet."

"Where does the guy with the truck stop? Has he been by
today?"

"I'm not lazy," the bum said. "I earned a degree in philosophy."

"I'll give you a dollar," Samson said.

"I'm having trouble finding work in my field."

Samson dug a dollar out of his pocket and held it out to the bum, who snatched it and quickly secreted it among his rags. "He stops about a block from here, in front of the all-night diner." The bum pointed down the street. "I haven't seen him go by today, but I was sleeping."

"Thanks." Samson rose and started down the street.

The bum called after him, "Hey, kid, come back tonight. I'll guard your back while you sleep if you buy a jug."

Samson waved over his shoulder. He wouldn't be back if he could avoid it. A block away he joined a group of men who were waiting at the corner when a large gate-sided truck pulled up, the back already half full of Mexicans.

The man who drove the truck got out and walked around to where the men were waiting. He was short and brown and wore a straw Stetson, cowboy boots, and thick black mustache over the sly grin of a chicken thief. The men who worked for him called him *patrón*, but ironically, the common term for his profession was *coyote*.

He scanned the group of men and made his choices with a nod and the crook of his finger. The men chosen, all Hispanic, jumped onto the back of the truck. The Coyote approached Samson and grabbed him by the upper arm, testing the muscle. He said something in Spanish. Samson panicked and answered him in Crow: "I'm on the lam, looking for a one-armed man that killed my wife." To Samson's surprise, this seemed to satisfy the Coyote.

The Coyote had been smuggling illegal aliens into the country for five years, and from time to time he encountered an Indian from the South, Guatemala or Honduras, who could not speak Spanish. Not being able to tell one Indian language from another, he assumed that Samson was one of these. *All the better,* he thought, *it will take longer for him to find out.*

After the Coyote brought his men over the border, he gave them a place to live (two apartments in which they slept ten to a room), food (beans, tortillas, and rice), and three dollars an hour (for backbreaking work that most gringos would never consider doing). He charged his customers eight dollars per man-hour and pocketed the difference. At the end of each week he paid his men in cash, after deducting a healthy amount for food and lodging, then drove them all to the post office, where he helped them buy money orders to send home to their families, leaving them nothing for themselves. In this way the Coyote could keep a crew under his thumb for three or four months before they found out that they could make more money working at menial jobs in restaurants or hotels. Then he would have to go back to Mexico for another load. Lately, however, he had been augmenting his crew with Mexicans who had found their own way over the border, and this allowed him to stretch his time between border runs.

The work was the hardest Samson had ever done, and at the end of the first day, back knotted and hands bloodied from swinging a pickax, he slept in the back of the truck until the *patrón* slapped him awake and led him into the apartment to show him his cot. Sleeping in a room with nine other people was nothing new to Samson, and the food, although spicy, was plentiful and good. He fell asleep listening to the sad Spanish love songs of his coworkers and feeling very much alone.

As the weeks passed he would hear the other men in the room whispering in the dark and this made him feel, even more, that he was the only person in a world of one. He had no way of knowing that they were talking about him, about how they never saw him send any money home, and about how they could take his money and no one would know because he was a dumb Indian and couldn't speak Spanish. Samson listened and imagined that they were talking about their homes and missing their families. He knew nothing of the Latin quality of machismo, which tacitly forbade the admission of a man's melancholy except in song.

The plan was to wait until the boy was taking a shower, then go through his pants and take the money. If he protested, they would cut his throat and bury him on the large estate where they were terracing hills into formal gardens. Whether they would have really killed the boy was doubtful; they were good men at heart and had only turned their minds to murder because it made them feel worldly and tough. When the boy was gone their nocturnal whispers turned back to boasts of the women they would have, the cars they would buy, and the land they would own when they returned to Mexico.

Samson was saved on a hot afternoon when the owner of the estate approached the Coyote while the crew was taking a break, eating cold burritos in the shade of a eucalyptus tree.

"Immigration took one of the busboys in my restaurant," the rich man said. "Do any of your guys speak English? I'll pay you to let him go."

The Coyote was shaking his head when Samson spoke up: "I speak English." The Coyote's chicken-stealing grin dropped like a rock. He had thought that he would be able to hold on to the Indian boy for a long time, and here he had gone and learned English in his spare time. The boy was worthless now. Better to cut the loss and see what he could get.

To quell their curiosity and dampen their ambition, the Coyote told the rest of the crew that the rich American had bought the boy for sexual purposes, and they all grinned knowingly as they watched Samson ride away in the long white Lincoln.

Samson found that it was easier to be Mexican while working in the restaurant. The work, although fast paced, was not heavy, and he was given a cot in the storeroom to sleep on until he found a place of his own. The owner was content with speaking a pidgin English peppered with Spanish words and Samson answered him by speaking a modified version of Tonto-speak. By this time Samson had also picked up a few essential Spanish phrases ("Where are the spoons?" "We need more plates." "Your sister fucks donkeys in Tijuana") which helped him make friends with the Mexican dishwashers and cooks.

From the moment he had arrived in Santa Barbara, a grinding homesickness began to settle in Samson's heart. When he lay in the dark storeroom at night, waiting to fall asleep, it would rise up and wash over him like a black tide, carrying with it a slithering blind predator that gnashed at the last shreds of his hope. "Forget what you know," Pokey had told him. With this in mind he set to do battle with his rising hopelessness. He refused to think of his family, his home, or his heritage. Instead he concentrated on the conversations he overheard in the restaurant as he cleared tables and poured coffee. Because he was Mexican, and a menial laborer, he was invisible to the affluent Santa Barbara customers, who spoke openly about the most intimate details of their lives, oblivious to the Spanish fly on the wall. . . .

"You know, Ashley has been having an affair with her plastic surgeon for six months and . . ."

"If I can get my legal ducks in a row, I should be able to push the convention center through the city council and . . ."

"I want the bathroom Southwestern, but Bob likes Art Nouveau, so I called our attorney and I said . . ."

"I know the offshore drilling is ruining the coast, but my Exxon shares have split twice in two years, so I said to my analyst . . ."

"Susan and the kids went to Tahoe, so I thought it was the perfect chance to show Marie the house. The bitch spilled a whole bottle of massage oil in the hot tub and . . ."

"I don't give a damn whether they needed it or not. If you do your job right you can sell air conditioners to Eskimos; need has nothing to do with it. Remember the three *m*'s: *mesmerize, motivate,* and *manipulate.* You're not selling a need, you're selling . . ."

"Dreams," Samson said, coming out of his shell to finish the sentence of a young insurance sales manager who had taken his agents to lunch so he could chew their ass. Samson surprised even himself by speaking up, but the man at the table seemed to be giving the same speech that he had heard from the powder-blue dream salesman. He couldn't resist.

"Come here, kid," the man said. He was wearing a wash-and-wear suit, as were the other five men at the table. A half-dozen acrid aftershaves clashed among them. "What's your name?"

Samson looked around the table at the men's faces. They were

all white. He decided at that moment to use a new name, not the
Mexican name he had taken, Jose Cuervo. "Sam," Samson said.
"Sam Hunter."

"Well, Sam"—he extended his hand—"my name is Aaron
Aaron. And I'll bet with some training you could outsell every
man at this table." He put his arm around Samson's shoulders and
spoke to the rest of the group. "What do you say, guys? I'll bet you
each a hundred bucks that I can take a busboy with the right attitude and turn him into a better salesman than any of you hotshots
inside of a month."

"That's bullshit, Aaron, the kid's not even old enough to get a
license."

"He can work on my license. I'll sign his applications. C'mon,
hotshots, do I have a bet?"

The men fidgeted in their seats, laughing nervously and trying
to avoid Aaron's gaze, knowing from Aaron's training that the first
one to speak would lose. Finally one of them broke. "All right, a
hundred bucks, but the kid has to do his own selling."

Aaron looked at Samson. "So, kid, are you ready to start a new
job?"

Samson tried to imagine himself wearing a suit and smelling of
aftershave, and the idea appealed to him. "I don't have a place to
stay," he said. "I've been saving so I can get an apartment."

"I've got it covered," Aaron said. "Welcome aboard."

"I guess I could give my notice."

"Fuck giving notice. You only give notice if you're planning to
come back. You're not planning on moving backwards, are you,
Sam?"

"I guess not," Samson said.

At twenty-five, Aaron Aaron had already accumulated fifteen
years of experience in the art of deception. From the time he
skimped on the sugar at his first lemonade stand to the time he
doubled the profits on his paper route by canceling his customers'
subscriptions, then stealing the papers out of a vending machine
to continue the deliveries, Aaron showed a near-genius ability for

working in the gray areas between business and crime. And by balancing dark desires with white lies he was able to sidestep the plague of Catholic conscience that kept him from pursuing an honest career as a pirate, which would have been his first choice. Aaron Aaron was a salesman.

At first, Aaron's only interest in Samson was to use the boy as an instrument of embarrassment to the other salesmen, but once he dressed the boy in a suit and had him trailing along on sales calls like a dutiful native gun bearer, Aaron found that he actually enjoyed the boy's company. The boy's curiosity seemed boundless, and answering his questions as they drove between calls allowed Aaron to bask in the sound of his own voice while extolling the brilliance of his last successful presentation. And too, the rejection of a slammed door or a pointed "no" seemed softened in the sharing. Teaching the boy made him feel good, and with this improvement in attitude he worked more, sold more, and allowed the boy to share in the prosperity, buying him clothes and food, finding him an apartment, and cosigning for a loan on a used Volvo.

For Samson, working under the tutelage of Aaron was perfect. Aaron's assumption that no one beside himself had the foggiest idea of how the universe worked allowed Samson the opportunity to hear lectures on even the most minuscule details of society, information he used to build himself into the image that Aaron wanted to see. Samson delighted in Aaron's self-obsession, for while the older man waxed eloquent on the virtues of being Aaron, it never occurred to him to ask Samson about his past, and the boy was able to surround himself in a chrysalis of questions and cheap suits until he was ready to emerge as a full-grown salesman.

As the years passed and his memories of home were stowed and forgotten, learning to sell became Samson's paramount interest. And Aaron, fascinated with seeing his own image mirrored and his own words repeated, failed to notice that Samson had become a better salesman than himself until other companies began approaching the boy with offers. Only then did Aaron realize that most of his income was coming from the override commission on Sam's sales, and that for five years Sam had trained all the new salesmen. To avoid losing his golden goose, Aaron offered Sam a fifty-fifty partnership in the agency, and with this added security, the business became Sam's shelter.

Now, after twenty years with the business as his only security, Sam was going to Aaron to sell his shares. As he entered Aaron's office he felt a deep soul-sickness that he had not felt since he had left the reservation.

"Aaron, I'll take forty cents on the dollar for my shares. And I keep my office."

Aaron turned slowly in the big executive chair and faced Sam. "You know I couldn't come up with that kind of cash, Sam. It's a good move, though. I'd have to keep paying you out of override, and with interest you wouldn't even take a cut in pay. I don't think you're in a position to negotiate, though. In fact, after the call I got this morning, I think twenty cents on the dollar would be more than fair."

Sam resisted the urge to dive over the desk and slap his partner's bare scalp until it bled. He had to take his fallback position sooner than he wanted to. "You're thinking that because Spagnola can put me with the Indian I have to sell, right?"

Aaron nodded.

"But just imagine that I ride this through, Aaron. Imagine that I don't sign off, that the insurance commission suspends my license, that criminal charges are filed and my name is in the paper every day. Guess whose name is going to be right next to mine? And what happens if I maintain my association with the agency and the insurance commission starts looking into your files? How many signatures have you traced over the years, Aaron? How many people thought they were buying one policy, only to find out that their signature showed up on a different one—one that paid you a higher commission?"

A sheen of sweat was appearing on Aaron's forehead. "You've done that as often as I have. You'd be hanging yourself."

"That's the point, Aaron. When I walked in here you were convinced that I was hung anyway. I'm just making room for you on the gallows."

"You ungrateful prick. I took you in when you—"

"I know, Aaron. That's why I'm giving you a chance to stay clean. Actually, you've got more to lose than I do. Once your files are open, then your income is going to become public knowledge."

"Oh!" Aaron stood and paced around to the front of the desk.

"Oh!" He waved a finger under Sam's nose, then turned and walked to the water cooler.

"Oh!" He kicked the cooler, then returned to his chair, sat down, then stood up again.

"Oh!" he said. It was as if the single syllable had stuck in his mouth. He looked as if he were going to launch into a tirade; blood rose in his face and veins bulged on his forehead.

"Oh!" he said. He fell back in the chair and stared at the ceiling as if his brain had pushed the hold button on reality.

"That's right, Aaron," Sam said after a moment. "The IRS." With that Sam moved to the office door. "Take your time, Aaron. Think about it. Talk it over with your buddy Spagnola; he can probably give you the current exchange rate of cigarettes for sodomy in prison."

Aaron slowly broke his stare on the ceiling and turned to watch Sam walk out.

In the outer office Julia looked up from applying lacquer to her nails to see Sam grinning, his hand still on the doorknob.

"What's with all the 'ohs,' Sam?" Julia asked. "It sounded like you guys were having sex or something."

"Something like that," Sam said, his grin widening. "Hey, watch this." He opened the door quickly and stuck his head back in Aaron's office. "Hey, Aaron! IRS!" he said. Then he pulled the door shut, muffling Aaron's scream of pain.

"What was that?" Julia asked.

"That," Sam said, "was my teacher giving me the grade on my final exam."

"I don't get it."

"You will, honey. I don't have time to explain right now. I've got a date."

Sam left the office walking light and smiling, feeling strangely as if the pieces of his life, rather than fitting back together, were jingling in his pocket like sleigh bells warning of Christmas.

CHAPTER FIFTEEN

○

LIKE GOD'S OWN CHOCOLATE, I'D LICK HER SHADOW OFF A HOT SIDEWALK

SANTA BARBARA

In spite of the fact that he was losing his home and his business, and was precariously close to having his greatest secret discovered by the police because of an Indian god, Sam was not the least bit worried. Not with the prospect of an evening with Calliope to occupy his thoughts. No, for once Sam Hunter was voting the eager ticket over the anxious, taking anticipation over dread.

Calliope lived upstairs in a cheese-mold-green cinder-block duplex that stood in a row of a dozen identical structures where the last of Santa Barbara's working middle class were making their descent into poverty. Calliope's Datsun was parked in the driveway next to a rusty VW station wagon and an ominous-looking Harley-Davidson chopper with a naked blond woman airbrushed on the gas tank. Sam paused by the Harley before mounting the stairs. The airbrushed woman looked familiar, but before he could get a closer look Calliope appeared on the deck above him.

"Hi," she said. She was barefoot, wearing a white muslin dress loosely laced in the front. A wreath of gardenia was woven into her hair. "You're just in time, we need your help. Come on up."

Sam took the stairs two at a time and stopped on the landing, where Calliope was wrestling with the latch on a rickety screen-door frame that was devoid of screening but had redwood lattice nailed across its lower half, presumably to keep out the really large insects. "I'm having trouble with the dinner," she said. "I hope you can fix it."

The screen door finally let loose with the jattering noise one as-sociates with the impact of Elmer Fudd's face on a rake handle. Calliope led Sam into a kitchen done in the Fabulous Fifties motif of mint enamel over pink linoleum. A haze of foul-smelling smoke hung about the ceiling, and through it Sam could make out the figure of a half-naked man sitting in the lotus position on the counter, drinking from a quart bottle of beer.

"That's Yiffer," Calliope said over her shoulder as she headed to the stove. "He's with Nina."

Yiffer vaulted off the counter, on one arm, fully eight feet across the kitchen to land lightly on his feet in front of Sam, where he engaged a complex handshake that left Sam feeling as if his fingers had been braided together. "Dude," Yiffer said, shaking out his wild tangle of straw-colored hair as if the word had been stuck there.

Feeling like a chameleon that has been dropped into a coffee can and is risking hemorrhage by trying to turn silver, Sam searched for the appropriate greeting and ended up echoing, "Dude."

In jeans, a sport shirt, and boating moccasins with no socks, Sam felt grossly overdressed next to Yiffer, who wore only a pair of orange surf shorts and layer upon layer of tan muscle.

"Calliope biffed the grub, dude," Yiffer said.

Sam joined Calliope at the stove, where she was frantically biff-ing the grub. "I can't get the spaghetti to cook," she said, plunging a wooden spoon into a large saucepan from which the smoke was emanating. "The instructions said to boil for eight minutes, but as soon as it starts to boil the smoke comes out."

Sam waved the smoke from the pan. "Aren't you supposed to cook the noodles separately?"

"Not in the sauce?"

Sam shook his head.

"Whoops," Calliope said. "I'm not a very good cook. Sorry."

"Well, maybe we can salvage something." Sam removed the pan from the heat and peered in at the bubbling black magma. "Then again, maybe starting over would be a good idea."

He put the pan in the sink, where a trail of ants was invading a used bowl of cereal. Sam turned on the water and started to swivel the faucet to wash the intruders away when Calliope grabbed his hand.

"No," she said. "They're okay."

"They'll get into your food," Sam said.

"I know. They've always been here. I call them my kitchen pals."

"Kitchen pals?" Sam tried to adjust his thinking. She was right—you couldn't just wash your kitchen pals down the drain like they were ants. He felt like he'd been saved from committing genocide. "So, I guess we should start some more spaghetti?"

"She only bought one box, dude," Yiffer said.

"I guess we can eat salad and bread," Calliope said. "Excuse me." She kissed Sam on the cheek and walked out of the kitchen while he stared at the ghost of her bottom through the thin dress.

"So, what do you do?" Yiffer asked with a toss of his head.

"I'm an insurance broker. And you?"

"I surf."

"And?"

"And what?" Yiffer said.

Sam thought he could hear the sound of the ocean whistling through Yiffer's ears as if through a seashell. "Never mind," he said. He was distracted by the sound of a baby screaming in the next room.

"That's Grubb," Yiffer said. "Sounds like he's pissed off."

Unable to see the second *b*, Sam was confused. "I thought grub was biffed?"

"No, *Grubb* is Calliope's rugrat. Go on in and meet him. Nina's in there with J. Nigel Yiffworth, Esquire." Yiffer beamed with pride. "He's mine."

"Your attorney?"

"My son," Yiffer said indignantly.

"Oh," Sam said. He resisted the urge to sit down on the floor and wait for his confusion to clear. Instead he walked into the living room, where he found Calliope sitting on an ancient sofa next to an attractive brunette who was breastfeeding an infant. The sofa was lumpy enough to have had a body sewed into it; stuffing spilled out of the arms where the victim had tried to escape. On the floor nearby, a somewhat older child was slung inside a blue plastic donut on wheels, which he was gaily ramming into everything in the room. Sam gasped as the child ran a wheel up over his bare ankle on a kamikaze rush to destroy the coffee table.

Calliope said, "Sam, this is Nina." Nina looked up and smiled. "And J. Nigel Yiffworth, Esquire." Nina pulled the baby from her breast long enough to puppet-master a nod of greeting from it, which Sam missed for some reason. "And that," Calliope continued, pointing to the drunk driver in the blue donut, "that's Grubb."

"Your son?" Sam asked.

She nodded. "He's just learning to walk."

"Interesting name."

"I named him after Jane Goodall's son. She let him grow up with baboons—very natural. I was going to name him Buddha, but I was afraid that when he got older if someone met him on the road they might kill him."

"Right. Good thinking," Sam said, pretending that he had the slightest idea of what she was talking about and that he wasn't wondering in the least who or where Grubb's father was.

"Nina moved in when we were both pregnant," Calliope said. "We were each other's Lamaze coaches. I was further along, though."

"What about Yiffer?"

"Scum," Nina said.

"He seems like a nice guy," Sam said, and Nina shot him an acid look. "As scum goes," he quickly added.

"He only lives here sometimes," Calliope said. "Mostly when he doesn't have gas money for his van."

Nina said, "We're having a yard sale day after tomorrow to raise some money to get him out of here. You might want to look at the stuff down in storage before the sale, pick up a bargain before it gets picked over."

Yiffer entered the living room munching on a loaf of French bread. He stood next to Sam and thrust the bread under Sam's chin. "Bite?"

"No, thanks," Sam said.

"Yiffer!" Calliope said. "That bread was for all of us."

"Truth," Yiffer said. He held the loaf out to Calliope. "Bite?"

"You ruined their dinner," Nina said, letting J. Nigel's head drop and wobble.

Yiffer grinned around a mouthful of bread and gestured toward Nina's exposed breast with his beer hand. "Looking good, babe."

Nina reattached J. Nigel and said to Sam, "I'm sorry, he's only like this when he's awake." To Yiffer she said, "Take some money out of my purse and go down to the corner and get a pizza."

Sam reached for his wallet. "Let me."

"No," Calliope and Nina said in unison.

"Cool!" Yiffer exclaimed, sandblasting Sam with a spray of bread crumbs.

"Go!" Nina commanded, and Yiffer turned and bounded out of the room. In a moment Sam heard the screen door open and footfalls on the steps.

"Sit down," Calliope said. "Relax."

Sam took a seat on the couch next to the two women and for the next forty minutes they exchanged pleasantries between the screaming demands of the babies until Nina handed a damp J. Nigel to Sam and left the room. Like most bachelors, Sam held a baby as if it were radioactive.

"That fucking asshole!" Nina shrieked from the other room, frightening Grubb, who screamed like an air-raid siren. J. Nigel was following suit when Nina returned to the living room, her purse in hand. "He took my rent money. The asshole took all my rent money. Can you guys watch J. Nigel for a minute? I've got to go find him and kill him."

"Sure," Calliope said. Sam nodded, adjusting J. Nigel for long-term holding.

Nina left. Calliope turned to Sam and over the din of screaming infants said, "Alone at last."

"I think J. Nigel needs changing," Sam said.

"So does Grubb. Let's take them into Nina's room."

Sam had slipped into the personality he referred to as "tough and adaptable," one he reserved for the more chaotic and bizarre situations he had encountered in his career. "I can do this," he said with a grin.

He hadn't changed a baby since the days on the reservation when he used to help with his cousins, but when he opened J. Nigel's diaper the memory came back on him like a fetid whirlwind, and he had to fight to keep from gagging. The adhesive strips on disposable diapers were a completely new adventure and he found after a few minutes that he had diapered his left hand perfectly while a squirming J. Nigel remained naked to the world. After changing Grubb and returning him to his plastic donut, Calliope liberated Sam from the diaper and started on J. Nigel, who giggled and peed like an excited puppy at her touch. Sam sympathized.

"Don't feel bad," she said. "The last time we let Yiffer babysit he duct-taped J. Nigel's diaper on and we had to use nail-polish remover to get the adhesive off."

"I haven't had much practice," Sam said.

"You don't have any kids?"

"No, I've never met anyone I wanted to have kids with." Sam

wanted to smack himself for saying it. *Remember, tough and adaptable.*

"Me either," Calliope said. "But Grubb is the best thing that ever happened to me. I used to drink and do a lot of drugs, but as soon as I found out I was pregnant I stopped."

Sam looked for an opening to ask about Grubb's father, but none came and the silence was becoming awkward. "That's great," he said. "I had my own battle with the bottle." Actually it hadn't been much of a battle. Aaron had insisted that social drinking was part of the job, but each time Sam had gotten drunk he was haunted by the stereotype of the drunken Indian that he thought he had left behind. It had been ten years since he'd had a drink.

"I'm going to put these guys down," Calliope said. "Why don't you go in the living room and put some music on."

In the living room Sam found a briefcase full of loose cassette tapes. Most of the tapes were New Age releases with enigmatic titles like *Tree Frog Whale Song Selections* by artists with names like Yanni Volvofinder. With further digging he found one called *The Language of Love* by a female jazz singer he liked, but when he opened the box he found that the tape had been replaced with one called *Catbox Nightmare* by a band called Satan's Smegma, obviously a Yifferesque selection. Finally he found *The Language of Love* languishing boxless in the bottom of the case and popped it into a portable stereo on a bricks-and-boards bookshelf.

Calliope returned to the living room just as the first song was rising in the speakers. "Oh, I love this tape," she said. "I've always wanted to make love to this tape. I'll be right back." She left the room again and returned in a moment with an armload of pillows and blankets, which she dropped in the middle of the floor. "Grubb sleeps in my room and he won't be asleep for a while." She began to spread the blankets out over the floor.

Sam stood by, trying to fight the objections that were rising in his mind about the speed at which things were progressing. She just assumed that he would say yes; it made him feel like—well—a slut. Then again, if this beautiful girl wanted to make love with him, who was he to object? Okay, so he was a slut; he was a tough and adaptable slut. Still, there was one thing that bothered him. "What if Yiffer and Nina come home with the pizza?"

"Oh, I don't think they'll be home that soon. This first time will be pretty fast."

"Hey." Sam thought he might have just been insulted, but on second thought he realized that the girl had just voiced something that he had really been worrying about, without even admitting it to himself. On second thought, she had relieved the pressure on him to perform.

Calliope finished fluffing the pillows, then unlaced her dress and let it drop to the floor. She stepped out of it and went to the stereo, where she turned up the volume, then she crawled naked under the top blanket and pulled it up to her neck. "Okay," she said.

Sam sat on the couch, stunned. She *was* stunning. But where was the seduction, the deception, the sweet lies and tender posturing? Where was the hunt, the cat-and-mouse game? Sam just stared at her and thought, *This is entirely too honest.*

"Are you okay?" she asked.

"Yes, it's just kind of . . ."

"You want me and I want you. Right?"

Who did she think she was? You can't just go around blurting out the truth like a prophet with Tourette's syndrome. He said, "Well, I guess. Yeah, that's right."

"Well?" She threw the covers back to make room for him.

Sam leapt off the couch and fought his way out of his clothes. He was under the covers, taking her into his arms, before his shirt settled to the floor. At the touch of her skin, her warmth, he felt every muscle in his body tense, then melt against her. He kissed her for a long time with none of the fumbling or awkwardness that he expected. He entered her and they began to move together in slow rhythm to the music. Calliope let out a long, low moan and dug her fingers into the muscles of his back. He joined her in the moan and pushed deeper, losing suddenly any thoughts or images or reservations, damn near losing consciousness to the warm, dark rhythm. A door slammed, violently shaking the windows of the apartment.

Sam pushed up on his arms. "What was that?"

"Nothing," she said, pulling him down.

Another door slammed, louder than the first. Sam pushed up again. "They're home."

"No, that's downstairs. Please." She wrapped her legs around his back and pulled him tight.

Distracted, Sam began to move again and Calliope moaned. A door slammed, glass shattered, and J. Nigel began crying in the front bedroom.

"What in the hell was that?"

"Nothing. Not now. Make love to me, Sam."

The house shook with the impact of a slamming door, then another, and Grubb began to cry as well. Sam winced, and came completely without pleasure. "Sorry," he said as he rolled over onto his back. Calliope stared at the ceiling for a moment as if she was bracing for the next impact. When it came she leapt to her feet and stormed naked out onto the balcony.

She bent over the railing and shouted, "Why are you doing this?"

Sam turned down the stereo and listened. Another door slammed, shaking the house, then a pathetic male voice came from below. "You've got someone up there. You slut."

"Don't talk to me that way. I don't act this way when you have someone down there."

Sam wanted to join her on the balcony, come to her defense ("Hey, buddy, she's not the slut here!"), but he couldn't seem to locate his pants.

"You whore!" the male voice said. "I'm taking my son."

"No, you're not!"

"You'll see," the voice said. Another door slam. Sam flinched. He was getting a little shell-shocked trying to put the pieces of this mystery together between slams.

"Jerk!" Calliope screamed. She stormed inside, slammed the door, and breezed by Sam on her way to tend to Grubb and J. Nigel. Sam sat naked on the floor wishing for a cigarette, or a clue, and repeating his new mantra in his head, *tough and adaptable tough and adaptable . . .*

In a few minutes, after the door slams had dwindled to one every few minutes, as if the guy downstairs was calming down, then losing his temper in spurts, Calliope appeared in the doorway, still naked.

"We need to talk," she said.

Sam was dressed now, desperately yearning for a cigarette, but he'd left them in the car and he wasn't about to pass the maniac downstairs without more information. "That would be good," he said.

Calliope picked up her dress and slipped it on, then sat down on the couch. "You're probably wondering who that is downstairs."

For the first time she seemed really uncomfortable, and Sam felt for her. "It's okay. I've had some trouble with my neighbors recently. It happens."

She smiled. "I used to be with him. He's Grubb's father."

"I gathered that."

"I was doing a lot of drugs then. He was exciting: riding his Harley, tattoos, guns."

"Guns?"

"I left him when I found out I was pregnant. He didn't want me to have the baby and he didn't want me to quit getting high."

"But why move upstairs?"

"I didn't. He moved in downstairs. You're the first man that I've had over since the split. I didn't know he'd act this way."

"Why don't you move?"

"You know how Santa Barbara is. I couldn't even pay rent here if it weren't for Nina, let alone come up with first, last, and a cleaning deposit."

Sam could see that she was still embarrassed. "You could ask the landlord to remove his doors. It would be quieter."

"I'm sorry. I really wanted it to be nice."

"Maybe I should go." Despite the weirdness, he didn't want to leave.

"I wish you would stay. When Grubb goes to sleep we can go in my room. If we're quiet . . ."

"I'll stay," Sam said. "He won't come up here and shoot us, will he?"

"No, I don't think so. He keeps talking about getting custody of Grubb. Killing us would look bad with the judge."

"Right," Sam said. So what if she had been involved with a psycho. At least it was a psycho who thought ahead.

Calliope led Sam down a hallway to her room at the back of the apartment. "I'll get us some salad," she said, leaving Sam to sit on the twin bed next to the crib where Grubb was drowsily gnawing a pacifier. The room looked like it had been decorated by a Buddhist monk from *Sesame Street*. On top of the dresser sat effigies of Buddha, Shiva, Bert, Ernie, and Cookie Monster, as well as an incense burner, a small gong, and a box of Pampers. A stuffed Mickey Mouse on the dressing chair wore a necklace of quartz crystal and a rawhide ring that Sam recognized as a Navaho dream catcher. The walls were hung with pictures of the Dalai Lama, Kali the Destroyer, and the Smurfs.

Looking around, Sam felt tempted to construct an excuse and bolt. Now that he'd had a moment to think about it, his tough and adaptable veneer was feeling pretty thin. If he could just get back to normal for a while he'd be okay. Then it hit him: there was no normal to return to. The controlled status quo that had been his life was no longer there; it had been shattered by Coyote, and Coyote was out there somewhere. Calliope, and all the chaos around her, had made him forget. Even with Smurfs, psychos, and kitchen pals, the forgetting was worth staying for.

CHAPTER SIXTEEN

LIVE, VIA THE SPIRIT WORLD SATELLITE NETWORK

SANTA BARBARA

Lonnie Ray Inman was sitting in a worn leather easy chair listening for noises to sift down from upstairs. He had loaded and unloaded his Colt Python .357 Magnum four times, nervously fumbling its deadly weight as he alternately entertained fantasies of vengeance and prison. Every few minutes he would rise and go to the window to see if the black Mercedes was still parked out front, then he would pause at the front closet, where he opened and slammed the door until the violence in his heart subsided enough for him to sit again. He was short and dark and muscles stood out on his bare arms like cables. The front of his black tank top was soaked with blood where he had ripped the skin of his chest with his fingernails, trying to destroy the tattoo of a naked woman, the same woman whose picture was airbrushed on the tank of his Harley, the same woman who had turned his thoughts to murder. Lonnie Ray Inman dropped six cartridges into the cylinder of the Python and snapped it shut, determined this time to make it out the door and up the stairs, where he would burst through the door and kill Calliope's new lover.

Fuck prison.

• • •

A thousand miles away, ten thousand feet up in the Bighorn Mountains, Pokey Medicine Wing watched Lonnie loading the gun. Pokey was into the second day of his fast and had been searching the Spirit World for clues to the whereabouts of his favorite nephew, Samson Hunts Alone. He had called for his spirit helper, Old Man Coyote, to help him, but the trickster had not appeared. Instead he was seeing a white city, with red roofs and palm trees, and a man who wanted to murder Samson.

Pokey's body sat, dangerously close to death, in the middle of a two-hundred-foot stone medicine wheel, the holiest of the Crow fasting places, just west of Sheridan, Wyoming. Pokey had been under the hoof of a bull-moose hangover when he began the fast, and now the dry mountain wind was sucking the last life-water from his body. Alone in the Spirit World, Pokey was unaware of his heart struggling to pump his thickening blood. He looked for a way to warn Samson, and called out for Old Man Coyote to help.

Coyote was in the locker room of the Santa Barbara YWCA when he heard Pokey's call. He had entered as a horsefly, and after watching the women in the showers for a while had changed himself into a baby hedgehog and was rolled into a ball in the soap dish, imitating a loofah. Lazy by nature, Coyote had given his medicine to only three people since time began—Pokey, Samson, and a warrior named Burnt Face, who had built the ancient medicine wheel—so it took him a while to realize that he was being called. Reluctantly, he left the hedgehog body in the capable hands of a soapy aerobics instructor and went to the Spirit World, where he found Pokey waiting.

"What?" Coyote said.

"Old Man Coyote, I need your help."

"I know," Coyote said. "You are dying."

"No, I need to find my nephew, Samson."

"But you *are* dying."

"I am? Shit!"

"You should end this fast now, old man."

"But what about Samson?"

"I've been helping Samson. Don't worry."

"But he has an enemy who is going to kill him. I saw him, but I don't know where he is."

"I know he has enemies. I am Coyote. I know everything. What's this guy look like?"

"He's white. He has a gun."

"That narrows it down."

"He has a tattoo of a woman on his chest—it's bleeding. He looks out a window and sees a motorcycle and a black car. That's all I know."

"Do you have any water on the mountain where your body is?"

"No. There's a little snow."

"I will help you," Coyote said. "Go now."

Suddenly Pokey was back in his body, sitting on the mountain. In his lap he found a package of dry Kool-Aid that had not been there before. He looked down at it and smiled, then fell forward into the dirt.

In the shower of the YWCA a naked aerobics instructor screamed and ran into the locker room when the loofah she was using turned into a raven. The bird circled the locker room twice and nipped her on the bottom with its beak before flying down the hall, into the lobby, and out an open skylight.

Across town, Calliope took the empty salad bowl from Sam and set it on the dresser next to a statue of Buddha. "More?" she asked.

"No, I'm full," Sam whispered. Grubb had fallen asleep in his crib and Sam didn't want to risk waking him. "Calliope," he said, "is this guy dangerous?"

"Lonnie? No. He thinks he's tough because he's in a biker club, but I don't think he's dangerous. His friends are a little scary, though. They take a lot of PCP and it makes them spiritually dense."

"I hate that," Sam said, proud because he was spiritually dense without the aid of drugs.

"I'm going to take the dishes out and check on J. Nigel. Why don't you light some candles? I don't think we should turn on the stereo, though. It might irritate Lonnie."

"We wouldn't want that," Sam said.

Outside, a raven landed on the hood of Sam's car. Lonnie Ray saw it from his window. "Shit on it. Shit on it," he said, but as he watched the raven seemed to disappear. Lonnie slammed the closet door until the doorframe splintered.

Coyote was a mosquito making his way through the air vents of the Mercedes. He flew out of the defroster vent and settled on the driver's seat, where he became a man. Sam's Rolodex was on the passenger seat next to his pack of cigarettes. Coyote lit a cigarette and flipped through the Rolodex until he found the card he was looking for. He removed it and tucked it into the waist of his buckskins.

Lonnie Ray was rattling through the kitchen cabinets, looking for liquor, when he heard the pounding at his front door. On his way through the living room he snatched the Python off the easy chair and shoved it in his jeans at the small of his back. He threw open the door and was nearly knocked down by the Indian who brushed him aside on the way into the room.

The Indian looked around the room and wheeled on Lonnie Ray. "Where is he? Where's the bastard hiding?"

Lonnie Ray recovered his balance and dropped his right hand to the grip of the Colt. "Who the fuck are you?"

"Don't worry about it. Where's the guy that drives that Mercedes?"

In spite of his own anger, Lonnie Ray was intrigued. "What do you want him for?"

"That's my business, but if he owes you money, you'd better get it back before I find him."

"You going to kill him?" Lonnie asked.

"If he's lucky," the Indian said.

"You got a gun?"

"I don't need a gun. Now where is he?"

"Chill, man, I might be able to help you out."

"I don't have time for this," the Indian said. "I'll just catch him at his house."

"You know where he lives?" Lonnie Ray asked. This was like a gift from heaven. He could send the Indian up to Calliope's to do the dirty work: no risk, no prison. If it didn't work, he and the boys could surprise the guy at his house tomorrow, no witnesses. Lonnie Ray hadn't really relished the idea of having to shoot Calliope, anyway.

"Yeah, I know where the bastard lives," the Indian said. "But he ain't there. He's somewhere around here."

"You give me his address, I'll tell you where he is."

"Fuck that," the Indian said, shoving Lonnie against the wall. "You'll tell me now."

Lonnie brought the barrel of the Python up under the Indian's chin. "I don't think so."

The Indian froze. "It's on a card in my pants."

Lonnie Ray held out his free hand. "Don't ever tell someone you don't have a gun, dipshit."

The Indian lifted his buckskin shirt, pulled a card from his waistband, and handed it to Lonnie Ray, who glanced at it and spun the Indian around by one shoulder, pointing him out the door.

Lonnie ground the barrel of the Python into the Indian's spine, stood on his toes, and whispered threateningly into the Indian's ear. "You didn't come here and you didn't see me. You understand?"

The Indian nodded.

"He's upstairs," Lonnie whispered. "Now go!" He shoved the Indian out the door. "And never, never fuck with a brother of the Guild." Lonnie closed the door. "Fucking A," he said with a giggle.

Upstairs, Calliope said, "Tell me what you know, Sam."

"About what?"

"About anything." She sat down next to him on the bed and brushed his hair back with her fingers. "Tell me what you know."

The silence that followed would have been awkward except Calliope seemed to expect it. She stroked his hair while he tried to think of what to say. He sorted through facts and figures and histories and strategies. Clever retorts, meaningless jokes, sophistries and non sequiturs rose in his mind and fell unspoken. She rubbed his neck and found a knot in the muscle that she worked her fingertips into.

"That feels good," Sam said.

"That's what you know?"

A smile rose to Sam's lips. "Yes," he said.

"What do you want?" she asked.

He shot her a sideways glance and saw the candlelight gleaming in her eyes. She was serious, waiting for an answer. "Is this a test?"

"No. What do you want?"

"Why don't you ask me what I do for a living? Where I live? Where I'm from? How old I am? You don't even know my last name."

"Would that stuff tell me who you are?"

Sam turned to face her and took her hand from his neck. He still had a niggling mistrust of her and he wanted to let it go. "The truth now—Calliope, are you part of something he cooked up? Some trick?"

"No. Who's he?"

"Never mind." Sam turned away from her again, stared at a candle flame on the dresser, and tried to think. She really didn't know about Coyote. What now?

"Well, what do you want?" she asked again.

He snapped, "Dammit, I don't know."

She didn't recoil or seem hurt, but began rubbing his neck again. "You came here because you wanted me, didn't you?"

"No. Yes, I guess I did." It wasn't bad enough that she had to keep telling the truth; now she was expecting it back, and he was out of practice.

"We've had sex. Do you want to go now?"

Christ, she was like some gorgeous New Age district attorney. "No, I . . ."

"Do you want a bowl of chocolate marshmallow ice cream?"

"That would be great!" Sam said. Off the hook, no further questions, Your Honor.

"See, it's not that hard to figure out what you want." She got up and left the room, heading for the kitchen again.

Sam sat back and waited, realizing that it had been some time since a door had slammed downstairs. Suddenly he was very uncomfortable with the silence. When he heard footfalls on the stairs outside he leapt to his feet and ran to the kitchen.

CHAPTER SEVENTEEN

A WHITE PICKET FENCE AROUND CHAOS

SANTA BARBARA

Sam hit the kitchen just as Yiffer stepped through the screenless section of the screen door.

"Cool! Ice cream!" Yiffer said, staggering to Calliope's side at the counter.

"Keep it down, Yiffer. I just got Grubb and J. Nigel down." Calliope picked up two full bowls of ice cream and nodded to the carton on the counter. "You can have the rest."

"Bitchin'." Yiffer grabbed a serving spoon from the empty salad bowl and dug into the ice cream, shoveling a baseball-sized clump into his mouth. Sam watched in amazement as Yiffer mouthed the ice cream until he got his jaws closed around it, then swallowed the whole clump, dipping his head snakelike to facilitate the passage. "Oh, shit, man," Yiffer said as he dropped the spoon and bent over, grabbing the bridge of his nose. "Major ice cream headache. Ouch!"

Sam heard footsteps on the stairs outside, ran to the door, and popped his head out to see who was coming, ready to duck back inside should it be the crazed biker from downstairs. To his relief, Nina was trudging up the steps, obviously a little drunk herself. "Did Yiffer come home?"

Sam said, "He's punishing himself with ice cream as we speak."

"I'll kill him." She ran the rest of the way up the steps and Sam helped her wrestle the door open, then he stepped out of harm's way as she stormed by him to Yiffer, who was still bent over, now holding his temples.

"You jerk!" Nina shrieked. "Who was that woman at the bar? And where the hell is my money?"

"Babe, I'm in pain here, I'm suffering."

Nina raised her fist as if to hammer Yiffer's back, then she spotted the serving spoon, picked it up, and began whacking the surfer unmercifully on the head with it. "You want pain (whack!), I'll give you pain (whack! whack! whack!). Suffering? (whack!) You wouldn't (whack!) know (whack!) suffering (whack!) if (whack!) . . ."

"Well," Calliope said. "I guess you guys need a little space. C'mon, Sam." She led Sam out of the kitchen and back to her bedroom. They sat eating and listening to Yiffer whining under Nina's attack. After a few minutes she was losing momentum and Yiffer's whines turned to moans. Soon Nina was moaning with him rhythmically. Sam stared at the candle on the dresser as if he hadn't noticed.

"They do this all the time," Calliope offered, "I think Nina gets in touch with that male energy that equates violence and sex."

"Excuse me?"

"Hitting Yiffer makes her horny."

"Oh," Sam said. He flinched at the sound of breaking dishes from the kitchen. Nina screamed, "Oh, yes, you asshole! Yes!" Yiffer groaned. The house shook with the sound of a door slamming downstairs and J. Nigel joined the din with a wail of his own.

"Lonnie must think that we're doing it," Calliope said.

"Do you think he'll give us time to explain before he shoots us?"

"Don't think about it," Calliope stood and stepped out of her dress, then gestured for Sam to take off his shirt. The moaning in the kitchen was rising in intensity and J. Nigel was wailing like a siren. The windows rattled with a salvo of door slams.

Sam looked at her and thought, *A bowl of ice cream, a load of loonies, and thou . . .* "Now?" he said. "Are you sure?"

Calliope nodded. She pulled his shirt off, then pushed him back on the bed and took off his shoes. Sam let her undress him as he tried to put the noise out of his mind. As she pulled the sheet over him and crawled in beside him, he imagined the two of them being shot in the act. When she kissed him he barely felt it.

In the crib next to them Grubb began to stir, and with the next series of door slams and a crash from the kitchen he came awake crying. Despite Calliope's soft warmth against him and the smell of jasmine on her hair, Sam was unable to respond.

"He'll be okay," Calliope said. She stroked Sam's cheek and kissed him gently on the forehead.

"I'll be back in a second," Sam said

He got up and wrapped his shirt around his hips, then, checking the hallway, he darted out of the room and into the bathroom. He closed the door behind him and leaned against it, staring blankly at the ceiling. The sex sounds from the kitchen reached a crescendo with a piercing scream from Nina, then stopped, leaving only the sounds of crying babies and slamming doors. Sam took a deep breath. "I can't do this," he said to himself. "This is too weird. Too fucking weird." He lowered the lid of the toilet and sat facing the shower stall, assuming the posture of Rodin's *Thinker*. For once in his life, it really seemed to matter that the sex be good, but this was like a combat zone. "I can't do this," he said.

"Sure you can," a voice said from behind the shower curtain. Sam screamed and jumped to the top of the toilet tank. Coyote stepped out of the shower holding a beaded leather pouch.

"What in the hell are you doing here?" Sam asked.

"I'm here to help." Coyote said.

"Well, get out of here. I don't need your help."

"You are wasting that woman."

"Do you have any idea what is going on around here? Listen." Another door slammed and Nina resumed shouting at Yiffer. From what Sam could make out it had something to do with the yard sale.

"You must leave here, then," Coyote said. "You must find a place on the woman's body and live there. Hear only her breath, smell only her scent."

"If you don't get out of here I won't even have a chance. What if she sees you? How could I explain your being here?" Thinking about it, Sam realized that if he told Calliope that there was an ancient trickster god in her bathroom she would accept it without question—would probably ask for an introduction.

Coyote held out the beaded pouch. "Put this on your member."

"What is it?" Sam asked, taking the pouch.

"Passion powder. It will make you as strong and stiff as a lance."

Sam shook the contents of the pouch—a fine brown powder— into the palm of his hand. He sniffed it. "What is it?"

"Corn pollen, cedar, sweet grass, sage, powdered elk semen—it is an old and powerful recipe. Try it."

"No way."

"You want the woman to think you are not a man?"

"If I try it will you go?"

Coyote grinned. "Put just a pinch on your member and you will pleasure the woman to tears."

"And you'll go?"

Coyote nodded. Sam tentatively took a pinch of the powder and began to sprinkle it on his penis.

Calliope opened the bathroom door, catching Sam in mid-sprinkle. "You won't need that, honey," she said. "I'm on the pill."

"But . . ." Sam looked around for Coyote, but the trickster was gone. "I was just . . ."

"Being responsible," Calliope said. "Thank you. Now come to bed." She took his hand and led him out of the bathroom. Sam submitted, glancing over his shoulder for signs of Coyote.

Yiffer and Nina had taken the fight to their bedroom. Nina was calling Yiffer an idiot and going on about a newspaper ad being misplaced. A door slammed downstairs and Yiffer stormed out of the bedroom. "I'm going to kick his ass!" he shouted. In the hall he looked up at Calliope and Sam as he passed. "Hi, kids," he said, then he proceeded down the hall. Sam could hear the kitchen screen door ripping off the hinges as Yiffer went through. "You're history, biker boy!"

Calliope pulled Sam into the bedroom and closed the door.

"Shouldn't we call the police or something?" Sam asked.

"No, he'll be okay. Lonnie's afraid of Yiffer. He won't fight him and he's afraid to shoot him because of jail."

"Oh, everything's fine, then," Sam said.

"Come to bed," Calliope said. Sam shot a glance to Grubb, who was lying quietly on his side staring suspiciously at Sam over the edge of a pacifier, as if saying, "What are you doing with my mom?"

"Can we blow out the candles?" Sam asked.

Without a word Calliope blew out the candles and pulled Sam down on top of her on the bed. Outside, the sounds of Nina screaming down from the top of the stairs, Yiffer pounding on Lonnie's door, and J. Nigel crying for attention faded into white noise.

You must find a place on the woman's body and live there." In the dark, the noise far away, Sam ran his hands over Calliope's body and the world of work and worry seemed to move away.

He found two depressions at the bottom of her back where sunlight collected, and he lived there, out of the wind and the noise. He grew old there, died, and ascended to the Great Spirit, found heaven in her cheek on his chest, the warm wind of her breath across his stomach carried sweet grass and sage, and . . .

In another lifetime he lived on the soft skin under her right breast, his lips riding light over the ridge and valley of every rib, shuffling through downy, dew-damp hairs like a child dancing through autumn leaves. On the mountain of her breast, he fasted at the medicine wheel of her aureole, received a vision that he and she were steam people, mingled wet with no skin separating them. And there he lived, happy. And for the first time in years he felt that he was home. She followed, traveled, lived with him and in him as he was in her. They lived lifetimes and slept and dreamed together.

It was swell.

CHAPTER EIGHTEEN

SHADOWPHOBIA

Saturday morning Josh Spagnola was sleeping in and dreaming of putting shampoo into bunnies' eyes when the Harley-Davidson crashed through his front door carrying a 270-pound, pissed-off, speed-crazed biker named Tinker. With the crash and thunder of the bike in his living room, Spagnola sat up in his nest of satin sheets thinking earthquake, listening for the sounds of his burglar alarms, which did not come. Spagnola's house was wired six ways to stop an elegant picklock or spry cutpurse from entering by stealth, sneak, or cat's-paw; he had, in fact, protected himself against someone exactly like himself. That anyone would break in on a battering ram of Milwaukee iron, in broad daylight, had never occurred to him.

Tinker, on the other hand, took the words *breaking and entering* quite literally, and found entering a rather empty experience without substantial breaking. He carried on his belt a policeman's riot baton, a blackjack, two hunting knives, and a set of brass knuckles. In a rare moment of sanity he had left his guns at home. His lawyer had advised against guns while on probation.

Tinker had received an early-morning call from Lonnie Ray, one of his brothers in the Guild.

"You want him dead?" Tinker had asked Lonnie.

"No, just fuck him up. And don't wear your colors. I don't want any connection to me."

"Is he big?" Tinker had a deep-seated fear of someday meeting someone as large and violent as himself.

"I don't know. Just wait until I call. You'll see the black Mercedes."

"You got it, bro," Tinker said, and hung up.

Tinker tried to wait for Lonnie's call, but he'd been up all night cooking up a batch of methedrine in the Guild's lab, and had lost his patience after sampling the product in order to take the edge off the case of beer he'd drunk. At daybreak his bloodlust got the better of him and he left.

In the bedroom, hearing a Harley do burnouts on his Berber carpet, Spagnola finally realized that something was seriously wrong. He leapt from bed and began searching through a trail of clothes he had left last night on the way to bed with the Tuesday-Thursday-Saturday masseuse from the Cliffs. He remembered kicking his gun belt away from the bedroom door when he sent her home at midnight and scrambled to the door. He was bending to unholster the gun when Tinker kicked the door open, catching Spagnola square in the forehead, knocking him cold.

Tinker looked down at the naked, unconscious little man and let out a sigh. The absence of terror was wildly unsatisfying for him. As a gesture of brotherhood to Lonnie he pulled the baton from his belt and with two vicious blows broke both of Spagnola's legs, then he sulked out of the bedroom, mounted his bike, and rode to the Guild's clubhouse to watch Saturday-morning cartoons.

Sam awoke to Yiffer yelling, "Get down! Don't let them see you!"

Sam looked around the room. Calliope and Grubb were gone. He got up and reached for his watch on the dresser while shouts and whispers continued from the living room. Six in the morning. It must have gone on all night: the shouting, the pounding, the babies crying. He was lucky to have slept at all. He dressed and walked into the living room.

"Get down," Yiffer said. "Don't let them see you." Sam dropped to a crouch in the doorway. Nina and Calliope were huddled under the front windows holding the babies. Yiffer was crouched by the door that led to the balcony. He rose up to peek out the window, then instantly dropped to cover.

"What is it?" Sam said. "Is someone shooting?"

Nina said, "No, it's the garage sale people. Stay down."

"Good morning," Calliope said. "Did you sleep well?"

"Fine. Who are the garage sale people?"

"They're fucking predators," Yiffer said. "They keep circling like sharks. Look." Yiffer gestured to the window.

Sam duck-walked to the window and peeked over the edge. Dodge Darts and Ford Escorts were cruising slowly by, stopping in front of the house, then moving slowly on.

Nina said, "Yiffer put the ad in the paper for our yard sale with the wrong date. They're all looking for us."

"Five of them have been to the door already," Yiffer said. "Whatever you do, don't answer it. They'll tear us apart."

"Probably ten of them went to Lonnie's door and left when he didn't answer," Calliope said.

"What happened with Lonnie?" Sam said.

Yiffer rose up and peeked out the window. "Christ! There's a whole van full of them outside." He dropped to a sitting position, his back to the door. To Sam he said, "Lonnie didn't answer when I went down there last night. As soon as he heard me come back upstairs he got on his bike and left."

Nina said, "How long are they going to circle? I have to go to work today."

"They're never going to leave," Yiffer wailed hopelessly. "They're going to just wait and pick us off one by one. We're doomed. We're doomed."

Nina slapped Yiffer across the face. "Get a grip."

Sam could think of only one thing, the cigarettes on the seat of his car. He had gone sixteen hours without a smoke and was feeling as if he would snap like Yiffer in a few minutes if he didn't get some nicotine into his system. "I'm going out there," he said. He felt like John Wayne—before the lung cancer.

"No, dude. Don't do it," Yiffer pleaded.

"I'm going." Sam stood up and Yiffer covered his head as if expecting an explosion. Sam picked up Grubb's plastic donut on wheels. "Can I borrow this?"

"Sure," Calliope said. "Are you coming back?"

Sam paused for a minute, then smiled and took her hand. "Definitely," he said. "I just need to take a shower and handle a few things. I'll call you, okay?" Calliope nodded.

"You'll never see him alive again," Yiffer whined.

Nina looked up apologetically. "He had a lot to drink last night. I'm sorry if our fighting disturbed you."

"No problem," Sam said. "Nice meeting you both." He turned and walked through the kitchen and out the door.

As he went down the steps, the van that Yiffer had spotted screeched to a halt in front of the duplex and a dozen gray-haired ladies piled out and rushed him. They met at the bottom of the steps.

"Where's the sale?" one said.

"This *is* the right address. We checked it twice."

"Where's the bargains? The ad said bargains."

Sam held the plastic donut up before them. "This is it, ladies. I'm sorry, but everything was gone but this when I got here. We were all too late. The quick and the dead, you know."

A collective moan came from the mob, then one shouted, "I'll give you ten bucks for it!"

"Twelve!" another shouted.

"Twelve fifty."

Sam gestured for them to be quiet. "No, I need this," he said solemnly. He hugged the donut to his chest.

Their purpose gone, they milled around for a moment, then gradually wandered back to the van. Sam stood for a moment watching them. The other garage sale people who had been circling the block saw them leaving, and Sam could almost feel the disappointment settling into their collective consciousness as they broke pattern and drove off.

"Great night," Coyote said.

Sam's nerves had been so worn from the night and morning that he didn't even jump at the voice by his ear. He looked over his shoulder to see Coyote in his black buckskins and a huge, white ten-gallon cowboy hat. "Nice hat," Sam said.

"I'm in disguise."

"Swell," Sam said. "I can't get rid of you, can I?"

"Can you wipe off your shadow?"

"That's what I thought," Sam said. "Let's go."

The shogun of the Big Sky Samurai Golf Course and Hot Springs was worried. His name was Kiro Yashamoto. He was driving his wife and two children in a rented Jeep station wagon up a winding mountain road to look at an ancient Indian medicine wheel. The day before, Kiro had purchased two thousand acres of land (with hot springs and trout stream) near Livingston, Montana, for roughly the price he would have paid for a studio apartment in Tokyo. The deal did not worry him; after the golf course and health club were built he would recoup his investment in a year from the droves of Japanese tourists who would come there. His children worried him.

During this trip Kiro's son, Tommy, who was fourteen, and his daughter, Michiko, who was twelve, had both decided that they wanted to attend American universities and live in the United States. Tommy wanted to run General Motors and Michiko wanted to be a patent attorney. As he drove, Kiro listened to his children discussing their plans in English; they paused only when Kiro pointed out some natural wonder, at which time they would dutifully acknowledge the interruption before returning to their conversation. It had been the same at the Custer Battlefield, the Grand Canyon, and even Disneyland, where the children marveled at the machinations of commerce and missed those of magic.

My children are monsters, Kiro thought. *And I am responsible. Perhaps if I had read them the haikus of Bashō when they were little instead of that American manifesto of high-pressure sales,* Green Eggs and Ham . . .

Kiro steered the jeep around a long gradual curve that rounded the peak of the mountain and the medicine wheel came into view: huge stones formed spokes almost two hundred feet long. In the center of the wheel a tattered figure lay prostrate in the dirt.

"Look, father," Michiko said. "They have hired an Indian to take tickets and he has fallen asleep on the job."

Kiro got out of the Jeep and walked cautiously toward the center of the wheel. He'd learned a lesson in caution when Tommy had nearly been trampled in Yellowstone National Park while trying to videotape a herd of buffalo. Tommy and Michiko ran to their father's side while Mrs. Yashamoto stayed in the car and checked off the medicine wheel on the itinerary and maps.

Tommy panned the camcorder as he walked. "It's just rocks, Father."

"So is the Zen garden at Kyoto just rocks."

"But you could make a wheel of rocks at your golf course and people wouldn't have to drive up here to see them. You could hire a Japanese to take tickets so you wouldn't lose revenue."

They reached the Indian and Tommy put the camcorder on the macro setting for a close-up. "Look, he has fallen asleep with his face on the ground."

Kiro bent and felt the Indian's neck for a pulse. "Michiko, bring water from the Jeep. Tommy, put down that camera and help me turn this man over. He is sick."

They turned the Indian over and cradled his head on Kiro's rolled-up jacket. He found a beaded wallet in the Indian's overalls and handed it to Tommy. "Look for medical information."

Michiko returned with a bottle of Evian water and handed it to her father. "Mother says that we should leave him here and go get help. She is worried about a lawsuit for improper care."

Kiro waved his daughter away and held the water to the Indian's lips. "This man will not live if we leave him now."

Tommy pulled a square of paper from the beaded wallet. He unfolded it and his face lit up. "Father, this Indian has a personal letter from Lee Iacocca, the president of Chrysler."

"Tommy, please look for medical information."

"His name is Pokey Medicine Wing. Listen:

Dear Mr. Medicine Wing:

Thank you for your recent suggestion for the naming of our new line of light trucks. It is true that we have had great success with our Dakota line of trucks, as well as the Cherokee, Comanche, and Apache lines of our Jeep/Eagle division, but after investigation by our marketing department we have found that the word *Crow* has a negative connotation with the car-buying public. We also found that the word *Absarokee* was too difficult to pronounce and *Children of the Large-Beaked Bird* was too long and somewhat inappropriate for the name of a truck.

In answer to your question, we are not aware of any royalties paid to the Navaho tribe by the Mazda Corporation for the use of their name, and we do not pay royalties to the Comanche, Cherokee, or Apache tribes, as these words are registered trademarks of the Jeep Corporation.

While your proposed boycott of Chrysler products by the Crow tribe and other Native Americans saddens us deeply, research has determined that they do not represent a large enough demographic to affect our profits.

Please accept the enclosed blanket in thanks for bringing this matter to our attention.

Sincerely, Lee Iacocca
CEO, Chrysler Corporation

Kiro said, "Tommy, put down the letter and help me sit him up so he can drink."

Tommy said, "If he knows Lee Iacocca he will be good to have as a contact, Father."

"Not if he dies."

"Oh, right." Tommy dropped to his knees and helped Kiro lift Pokey to a sitting position. Kiro held the bottle to Pokey's lips and the old man's eyes opened as he drank. After a few swallows he pushed the bottle away and looked up at Tommy. "I burned the blanket," he said. "Smallpox." Then he passed out.

CHAPTER NINETEEN

FIVE FACES OF COYOTE BLUE

Ever since the morning Adeline Eats had found the frost-covered liar in the grass behind Wiley's Food and Gas there had been a screech owl sitting atop the power pole in front of her house, sitting there like feathered trouble. In addition, Black Cloud Follows had blown a water pump, all of her kids were coming down with the flu, her husband, Milo, had gone off to a peyote ceremony, and she was trying desperately to stay out of Hell. It was unfair, she thought, that her new faith was being tested before the paint was even dry.

She wanted the owl to go away and take her bad luck with it. But to a good Christian, an owl was just an owl. Only a traditional Crow believed in the bad luck of owls. A good Christian would just go out there and shoo that old owl away. Of course, it wouldn't bother a good Christian.

Adeline had come to Christianity the same way she had come to sex and smoking: through peer pressure. Thinking about her six kids and her smoker's hack, she wondered if perhaps peer pressure didn't always lead to the best habits. Her sisters had all converted and they had referred to her as the heathen of the family until she caved in and accepted Christ. Now, only three weeks after

being washed in the blood of the Lamb, she was already backslid-
ing like a dog surprised down a skunk hole. The owl.

Adeline looked out the front window to check on the owl; he
was still there. Had he winked at her? She had pinned up her hair
and was wearing sunglasses and a pair of Milo's overalls, hoping
the owl wouldn't recognize her until she figured out what to do.
She was tempted to pray to Jesus to make the owl go away, but if
she did that, she would be admitting that she believed in the old
ways and she'd go to Hell. There was no Hell in the old ways. Then
again, she could load up Milo's shotgun, walk out in the yard, and
turn that old owl into pink mist. She couldn't see herself doing
that either—no telling what kind of trouble that would unleash.
And she couldn't wait for Milo and ask him for help: not after
weeks of working on him to leave the Native American Church
and trade in his peyote buttons for wafers and wine.

She ducked away from the window. One of the kids coughed in
the other room. Eventually she was going to have to take them
down to the clinic for treatment. But she was afraid to pass by the
owl. According to the priest, God knew everything. The sunglasses
and hairdo wouldn't fool God. God knew she was afraid, so He
knew she still had faith in the old ways, so she was going to Hell as
sure as if she'd been out all morning worshiping golden calves and
graven images.

"I got bad medicine from being Crow," she thought. "And I'm
going to Hell for being Christian. I should have let that old liar
Pokey freeze to death." She slapped herself on the forehead.
"Damn! Another Hell thought."

A nun with an Uzi popped up on the parapet of Nôtre Dame like
a ninja penguin. Coyote shot from the hip, winging her before she
could fire. She tumbled over the side, bounced off a gargoyle, and
splattered on the sidewalk below. A synthesized Gregorian chant
began to play as her spirit rose to heaven, a steel ruler in hand.
Coyote strafed a stained-glass window and took out a bazooka-
wielding bishop for two thousand penance points.

Sam walked into the bedroom, hair wet, a towel wrapped around his hips. "Nice shot," Sam said.

Coyote glanced up from the video game. "The red ones have killed me three times."

"Those are cardinals. You have to hit them twice to kill them. Wait until you get to the Vatican level. The pope has guilt-beam vision."

Before Coyote could look back to the screen the cathedral doors flew open and St. Patrick fired a wiggling salvo of heat-seeking vipers.

"Hit your smart bomb," Sam said.

Coyote fumbled with the control, but was too late. A snake latched onto his leg and exploded. The screen flashed *GAME OVER*, and a synthesized voice instructed Coyote to "go to confession."

Coyote dropped the control onto the bed with a sigh.

Sam said, "You did good. Gunning for Nuns is a hard game for beginners."

"I should have brought some cheating medicine. My cheating medicine never fails."

"This isn't like the hand game. This is a game of skill."

"Who needs skill when you can have luck?"

Sam shook his head and turned to go back to the bathroom. During the night something inside him had changed. Each time he thought things had reached a plateau of weirdness, something even weirder had happened. The result, he realized, was that he was now accepting anything that happened, no matter how weird, without resistance. Chaos was the new order in his life.

The phone rang and Sam, hoping it was Calliope, grabbed the receiver off the vanity. "Samuel Hunter," he said.

"You low-life, scum-sucking shithead!"

"Good morning to you too, Josh."

"You win, dickhead. There'll be a meeting of the co-op association tonight. They'll vote you back in. You can keep your apartment, but I want your guarantee that this is over."

"Okay."

"I hope you know I've lost all respect for you as a professional, Sam. The doctor says I'm going to walk with a limp for the rest of my life."

"There was a crooked man who had a crooked—"

"You broke my legs! My house is destroyed."

Sam peeked into the bedroom where Coyote was attacking the Sistine Chapel with a helicopter gunship. "Josh, I don't know what you're talking about, but I'm glad you came to your senses."

"Fuck you. I'm using up years of collected dirt to get your apartment back."

"*Townhouse,*" Sam corrected. "Not *apartment.*"

"Don't fuck with me, Sam. I'm in a cast up to my nipples and a sadistic nurse has been force-feeding me green Jell-O for an hour. Just tell me it's over."

"It's over," Sam said.

The phone clicked. Sam walked back into the bedroom. "What did you do to Spagnola?"

Coyote was rolling on the bed in exaggerated body English to tilt the gunship. "These birds are eating my tail rotor. I can't control it."

"Uh-oh, St. Francis released the doves of death. You're dead meat." Sam took a cigarette from the pack on the dresser and offered one to Coyote. "What did you do to Spagnola?"

"You said you wanted your old life back."

"So you broke Spagnola's legs?"

"It was a trick."

"You can't just go around breaking people's legs like some Mafioso fairy godmother."

The gunship spun out of control and crashed on the mezzanine. Coyote threw the joystick at the screen and turned to Sam. "How can I win if you keep talking to me? You whine like an old woman. I got you your house back!"

"I wouldn't have lost it if you had left me alone. Be logical."

"What gods do you know that are logical? Name two."

"Never mind," Sam said. He went to the closet and pulled his clothing out for the day.

Coyote said, "Do you have a light?"

"No."

"No? After I stole fire from the sun and gave it to your people?"

"Why, Coyote? Why did you do that?" Sam turned to point out the lighter on the dresser, but the trickster was gone.

Calliope's upbringing in the Eastern religions, with their emphasis on living in the now—of acting, not thinking—had left her totally unprepared to do battle with the future. She'd tried to ignore it, even after Grubb was born, but it had become more and more difficult to function on karmic autopilot. Now Sam had entered her life and she felt like she had something to lose. The future had a name. She wondered what she had done to manifest the curse of a nice guy.

"It feels wonderful, but I want more," Calliope said.

"I don't get it," Nina said. They were cleaning up the kitchen. Grubb was scooting around on the linoleum at their feet, tasting the baseboards, a table leg, a slow-moving bug.

"I've always felt separate from men, even during sex. It's like there's this part of me that watches them and I'm not really involved. But it wasn't that way with Sam. It was like we were really together, no barriers. I wasn't watching him, I was with him. When we were finished I lay there watching the pulse on his neck, and it was like we had gone to some other world together. I wanted more."

"So you're saying you're a hosebeast."

"Not like that. It was just that I want to feel that way all the time. I want my whole life to feel—complete."

"I'm sorry, Calliope, I don't get it. I'm happy if Yiffer doesn't pass out before we finish."

"I guess it's not a sexual thing. It's a spiritual thing. Like there's a part of life that I can touch but I can't live in."

"Maybe we just need to find a house where your ex doesn't live downstairs."

"That was pretty awful. I couldn't believe Sam didn't just leave."

Nina threw a dish towel at Calliope and missed. "You had a little good luck for a change, accept it. Not every guy has to be a creep like Lonnie."

"I'm a little afraid to leave Grubb with him when I go to work today."

"Lonnie won't hurt Grubb. He was just pissed that you were with someone else. Men are like that. Even when they don't want you, they don't want anyone else to have you."

"Nina, do you think there's something wrong with me?"

"No, you're just not very good at worrying. You'll get the hang of it."

"I've got to get back to the house," Lonnie said to Cheryl, who was pouring peroxide on his damaged chest. She wiped away the foam with a tissue, then poked the wound with a broken black fingernail.

"Ouch! What are you doing, bitch?"

Cheryl got up from the bed and pulled on a pair of leather pants. Lonnie could see her hipbones and shoulder blades pushing against her pale skin as if they would poke through any second.

"You're always thinking of her. Never me. What the hell is wrong with me?"

She turned to face him and he stared at her breasts lying like flaps against her ribs. She pulled back her lips in a snarl and Lonnie knew his face had betrayed him. "Fucking asshole," she said, pulling on a black Harley-Davidson T-shirt.

"It's not her, it's the kid. He's my kid. I have to watch him when she goes to work."

"Bullshit. Then why won't you fuck me?" She tossed her head and her long black hair fell into her face like seaweed on the drowned.

Because you look like you just escaped from fucking Auschwitz, Lonnie thought. He'd been with Cheryl for three months and had never seen her eat. As far as he could figure she lived on speed, come, and Pepsi. He said, "I worry about the kid."

"Then get custody. I can take care of him. I'd make a good mother."

"Right."

"You don't think so? You think that vegetarian bitch is a better mother than me?"

"No . . ."

"You start treating me right or I'm gone." Cheryl took a purse from the floor and began digging in it. "Where the fuck is my stash?" She threw the purse aside and stormed out of the room.

Lonnie followed her, carrying the denim vest sporting the Guild's colors. "I've got to go," he said.

Cheryl was dumping a bindle of white powder into a can of Pepsi. "Bring back some crank," she said.

As Lonnie walked out she added, "Tink called while you were sleeping. He said to tell you he took care of things."

Outside, Lonnie fired up his Harley and pulled out into the street. Tinker's news should have cheered him up, but it didn't. He felt empty, like he needed to get fucked up. He always felt that way lately. At one time being a brother in the Guild, being accepted for who he was, had been enough. Having all the women and drugs and money and power he needed had been enough. But since Grubb was born he felt like he was supposed to be doing something, and he didn't know what it was.

Maybe the bitch is right, he thought. As long as the kid tied him to Calliope he was going to feel shitty. It was time to feel good again.

Frank Cochran, the cofounder of Motion Marine, Inc., had spent most of the morning in his office milling over the bane of his existence: the human factor. Frank loved organization, routine, and predictability. He liked his life to be linear, moving forward from event to event without the nasty backtracking caused by surprises. *The human factor* was his name for the variable of unpredictability that was added to the equation of life by human beings. Today, the human factor was represented by his partner, Jim Cable, who was in the hospital after being attacked by an Indian.

Frank's thinking went thus: *If Jim dies there'll be insurance hassles, legal battles with the family, and someone will have to comfort Jim's mistress. But if Jim lives—maybe Jim's mistress should be comforted anyway....*

His train of thought was broken by the buzz of the intercom on his desk. "Mr. Cochran," his secretary said, "there's a man from NARC here to see you."

"I don't have any appointments until after lunch, do I?"

The office door burst open and Cochran looked up to see an Indian in black buckskins striding toward him. His secretary was shouting protests from her desk.

Cochran spoke into the intercom, "Stella, do I have an appointment with this man?"

"Native American Reform Coalition," Coyote said. "I understand that some insurance agent is taking credit for what happened to your partner."

Cochran had a very bad feeling about this. "Look, I don't know who you are, but I don't like surprises."

"Then this is going to be a very bad day for you." Coyote slammed the door behind him. "A very bad day." The trickster extended his right hand. "Nice to meet you."

Cochran watched in horror as the Indian's hand began to sprout fur and claws.

CHAPTER TWENTY

NEVERMORE

SANTA BARBARA

When Sam walked into his office Gabriella met him with a cup of coffee. "Mr. Hunter, I'd like to apologize for my behavior yesterday. I don't know what came over me."

"That's okay. I do."

"I hope you were able to resolve the difficulties at the Cliffs."

Sam wasn't prepared for civility from Gabriella; it was like encountering a polite scorpion. Life was changing before his eyes. "Everything's fine. Any calls?"

"Just Mr. Aaron." She checked her message pad. "He would like you to stop into his office if it wouldn't be too much trouble."

"Exact words?"

"Yes, sir."

"My my, has the Sugarplum Fairy been through here today?"

Gabriella checked the pad. "No message, sir."

Sam smiled and walked away. Down the hall Julia told Sam to go right in.

Aaron stood and smiled when Sam entered the office. "Sammy boy, have a seat. We need to talk."

Sam said, "Forty cents on the dollar, plus interest. You keep the office. I want out. That's it. You talk."

Aaron dismissed Sam's comment with a wave. "That's all

behind us, buddy. Cochran's lawyer called. There isn't going to be any lawsuit. You and I are square."

"What happened?" Sam knew he should be elated at the news, but instead he felt dread. For a moment he had relished the idea of giving up all the pretending. Now what?

"No explanation. They just backed off. They apologized for the mistake. You'll get a formal apology in the mail tomorrow. I never doubted you, kid. Not for a minute."

"Aaron, did you talk to Spagnola today?"

"Just briefly. Just a social call. He was pretty heavily medicated. I'm not sure I trust him, Sam. You want to watch your back around that guy. He's unstable."

Sam felt his ears heat up with anger. Aaron expected him to act like the betrayal had never happened. There was a time when he would have, but not now. "Forty cents on the dollar, plus interest."

Aaron lost his friendly-guy salesman's smile. "But that's behind us."

"I don't think so. You're a shit, Aaron. That doesn't surprise me. But it does surprise me that you went after me when I was down. I thought we were friends."

"We are, Sammy."

"Good. Then you won't mind having the papers on my desk by midweek. And you can pay the attorney fees. They're tax deductible, you know. And if you're late, you *will* need the write-off." Sam got up and started out of the office.

Aaron called after him. "We don't have to do this now."

Without turning Sam said, "Yes we do. I do."

Sam nodded to Julia as he passed but he couldn't muster a smile. *What have I done?* he thought.

In his outer office Gabriella was kicked back in her chair with her skirt up around her armpits. She seemed to be hyperventilating and her eyes were rolled back in her head.

"Gabriella! Again?"

She pointed to his office door. Sam threw the door open, banging it against the wall and disturbing a raven that was perched in the brass hat rack just inside. Sam stormed over to the bird, barely resisting the urge to grab it and rip its feathers out.

"Goddammit, I told you to stay off my secretary!" Sam shook his fist at the bird. "And what kind of bullshit did you pull over at Motion Marine to get them to drop the lawsuit? Can't you just leave me alone?"

"Why are you yelling at the bird?" The voice came from behind him. Sam looked around, his fist still threatening the raven.

Coyote was standing in the opposite corner of the office by the fax machine. Sam's anger turned to confusion. He looked at the bird, then Coyote, then the bird. "Who's this?"

"A raven?" Coyote speculated. He turned back to the fax machine. "Hey, what is this button that says 'network'?"

Sam was still looking at the bird. "It sends simultaneously to the home offices of all the companies we represent."

Coyote pushed the button. "Like smoke signals."

"What?" Sam dropped his fist, ran to the fax machine, and hit the cancel button a second too late. The display showed the transmission had gone out. Sam pulled the paper from the machine and stared at it in disbelief. Coyote had obviously lain on the copy machine to get the image.

"You faxed your penis? That machine prints my name at the top of each transmission."

"The girls in the home office will think highly of you, then. Of course, they will be disappointed if they ever see you naked."

The raven squawked and Gabriella appeared at the open door. "Mr. Hunter, a gentleman is here to see you from the police department."

Coyote held the Xerox up to Gabriella. "A picture of your friend," he offered.

A sharp-featured Hispanic man in a tweed sport jacket pushed his way past Gabriella into the office. "Mr. Hunter, I'm Detective Alphonse Rivera, Santa Barbara PD, narcotics division. I'd like to ask you a few questions." He held out a business card embossed with a gold shield, but did not offer to shake hands.

"Narcotics?" Sam looked to Coyote, thinking he would have disappeared, but the trickster had stood his ground by the fax machine. On the hat rack, the raven cawed.

"Nice bird," Rivera said. "I understand they can be trained to talk." Rivera walked to the bird and studied it.

"Pig," the raven said.

"He's not mine," Sam said quickly. "He belongs to—" Sam looked around and Gabriella was gone from the doorway. "He belongs to this gentleman." Sam pointed to Coyote.

"And you are?" Rivera eyed Coyote suspiciously.

"Coyote."

Rivera raised an eyebrow and took a notebook from his inside jacket pocket. "Mr. Hunter, I have a few questions about what went on at Motion Marine a couple of days ago. Would you prefer to talk in private?"

"Yes." Sam looked at Coyote. "Go away. Take the bird with you."

"Nazi scum," the raven cawed.

"I'll stay," Coyote said.

Sam was on the verge of screaming. Sweat was beading on his forehead. He composed himself and turned to Rivera. "We can talk in front of Mr. Coyote."

"Just a few questions," Rivera said. "You had an appointment with James Cable at ten. Is that correct?"

"I was there for about an hour."

"I was there too," Coyote said.

Rivera turned his attention to the trickster. "Why were you there, Mr. Coyote?"

"I was raising funds for NARC."

"Narc!" the raven said.

"Narc?"

"Native American Reform Coalition."

Rivera scribbled on a pad.

Sam said, "I don't understand. What does this have to do with narcotics?"

"We think someone put hallucinogens in the coffee over at Motion Marine. Two days ago James Cable claims he was attacked by someone fitting Mr. Coyote's description. He had a heart attack."

"I just asked him if his company would make a donation," Coyote said. "He said no and I went away." He had taken the Xerox of his penis from the desk and fitted it back into the fax machine. He searched the buttons. "'Insurance commissioner,'" he read as he pushed the button.

"No!" Sam dove over the desk for the cancel button. Too late. He turned to Rivera. "That document wasn't signed." He grinned and tried to move the conversation away from his panic. "You know, I was thinking—we've got an Indian, a policeman, and an insurance broker. We're only a construction worker away from the Village People."

Rivera ignored the comment. "Did you have any coffee while you were at Motion Marine, Mr. Hunter?"

"Coffee? No."

"And you didn't drink from the watercooler?"

"No. I don't understand."

"Today, three people at Motion Marine, including Frank Cochran, claim that they saw a polar bear in the offices."

Sam looked at Coyote. "A polar bear?"

"We think that someone slipped them some LSD. We're testing the water and the coffee now. We just wanted to talk to anyone who has been in the building in the last two days. You didn't see anyone strange hanging around while you were in the building?"

"I only saw Cable's secretary and Cable," Sam said.

Rivera flipped the notebook closed. "Well, thanks for your time. If you have any strange reactions or see anything strange, could you give me a call?" Rivera handed a card to Coyote. "And you too, if you would."

"*Cabrón*," the raven said.

"He speaks Spanish too," Rivera said. "Amazing." The detective left the office.

"'*Santa Barbara News-Press* advertising,'" Coyote read as he pushed the button. The fax machine whirred.

Sam started to go for the machine, then stopped and sat down in his chair. He sat for a minute rubbing his temples. "If that cop runs a background check on me, I'm going to jail. You know that, don't you?"

"You wanted your old life back."

"But a fucking polar bear?"

"Well, you have your old life back, whether you want it or not."

"I was wrong." It felt good saying it, the honesty in it. He wanted a new life. "I just want you to go away."

"I'm gone," Coyote said. "The girl is gone too."

"What does that mean?"

The feathers on Coyote's shirt turned black and his fingers changed to flight feathers. In an instant Coyote was a raven. He flew out the office door followed by the raven from the hat rack.

CHAPTER TWENTY-ONE

ALL HAPPY FAMILIES

SANTA BARBARA

Calliope stood in the driveway, holding Grubb, waiting for Lonnie to return. Nina had been right: she wasn't very good at worrying, but she was giving it a good effort. She was sure that Lonnie wouldn't hurt her or Grubb, but then again, Lonnie had never acted the way he had the night before. She wished that she could have asked Sam to stay with her and help her with a decision, but it would have been too much to ask so soon. She wished too that there were phones at the ashram and that she could call her mother for advice. And she couldn't just jump in the car and drive to see her mother as she always had before. She had her job, her house, and there was Sam now.

She was trying to push the dark specter of the unknown to the back of her mind when she heard the Harley approaching. She looked up to see Lonnie rounding the corner a block away, his new girlfriend clinging to him like a leech. Lonnie pulled into the driveway next to her and killed the engine.

"I'm late for work," Calliope said, wiping a trail of drool from Grubb's face with her finger.

The woman behind Lonnie glared at her and Calliope nodded to her and said, "Hi."

Lonnie reached for Grubb without getting off the bike. Calliope hugged Grubb close. She said, "I don't want him riding on the bike with you."

Lonnie laughed. "The way you drive? He's a hell of a lot safer on the bike."

"Please, Lonnie."

The woman reached out and took Grubb from Calliope. The baby began to cry. "He'll be fine," Cheryl hissed.

"Why can't you just stay at home with him?" Calliope asked.

"Places to go, people to meet," Lonnie said.

"I could get Yiffer to watch him." Calliope felt her breath coming hard. She didn't like the look of this hard woman holding her Grubb.

Lonnie said, "You tell Yiffer to watch his ass or I'll shoot it off."

"Lonnie, I have to go. Can't you just stay here? I'm only working the lunch shift today."

Lonnie grinned. "Aren't you going to stop by the hospital on your way home?"

"Hospital? No. Why?"

Lonnie fired up the Harley. "No reason." He laughed and coaxed the big bike around in the driveway.

As he gunned the engine and pulled into the street Cheryl shouted, "Don't worry, bitch, we'll put a dollar on black for you."

Over the roar of the Harley, Calliope could hear the woman grunt as Lonnie elbowed her in the ribs.

Calliope saw Grubb looking at her as they rounded the corner. Panic tore at her chest as what the woman had said sunk in. She turned and ran back up the steps.

By late afternoon the contractors had replaced Sam's sliding glass door and patched the bullet holes in the walls. Sam canceled the week's appointments, which gave him time alone with his thoughts. He soon found, however, that his thoughts, like monkeys in church, were bad company.

He tried reading to distract himself, but he found that he was simply looking at the pages. He tried napping, but as soon as he closed his eyes, images of Coyote and the police filled his head. When the worry became too much for him he thought of Calliope, which set off a whole new set of worries. What had Coyote meant, "The girl is gone"? Did it matter?

She was trouble. Too young, too goofy, probably too attractive. And the kid—he didn't need a kid in his life either. Trouble. If she had gone somewhere he probably was better off. He didn't need the hassles. That thought still bouncing through his mind, he grabbed the phone and dialed her number. No answer. He called information and got the number for the Tangerine Tree Café. She hadn't shown up for work today.

Where in the hell is she? Where in the hell is Coyote? The fucker knew where she went and he wouldn't tell. What had started as a niggling irritation turned to dread. *Why in the hell does it matter?* he thought.

Terrifying and black, a word rose in his mind that matched his feeling. He recoiled from it, but it struck him again and again like an angry viper. *Love:* the sickest of Irony's sick jokes. The place where logic and order go to die. Then again, maybe not. It was only bad if you were hiding, pretending to be something that you were not. Maybe the hiding could end.

Sam got up and headed out the door in what he knew was a ridiculous effort to find Calliope. He drove to the café and confirmed what they had told him on the phone. Then he drove to Calliope's house and found Yiffer and Nina getting out of the van as he pulled up.

Nina said, "I don't know where she is, Sam. She left a note saying that Lonnie had taken Grubb and she was going after him."

"Nothing about where she was going?"

"Any note at all is a big step for her. She used to disappear for days at a time with no note at all."

"Fuck." Sam started to get back in the car.

"Sam," Nina called. He paused. "The note said to tell you she was sorry."

"For what?"

"That's all it said."

"Thanks, Nina. Call me if she shows up." Sam gunned the Mercedes out of the driveway, having no idea where he was going.

He needed help. All his machines and access to information wouldn't help. He needed a place to start. Twenty-four hours ago he would have given anything to get rid of Coyote. Now he would welcome the trickster's cryptic, smart-assed answers—at least they were answers.

He drove around town, looking for Calliope's Z, feeling hope rise each time he spotted an orange car, and feeling it fall when it turned out not to be Calliope's. After an hour he returned home, where he sat on his sofa, smoking and thinking. Everything had changed and nothing had changed. His life was back to normal, and normal wasn't enough anymore. He wanted real.

At the Guild's clubhouse Tinker was digging at a flea bite on his leg, trying to pull his grimy jeans up over heavy boots to get at the tiny invader. "Fucking fleas," he said.

The Guild's president, Bonner Newton, let out a raucous snort. "You know what they say, bro," Newton said. "Lie down with dogs . . ." A din of harsh laughter rose in the room from the other Guild members.

"Fuck you guys," Tinker said, feigning anger while enjoying the attention. It wasn't that he liked ugly chicks, but who else would have him?

Nineteen of the twenty full members of the Guild were draped over furniture and sprawled on the floor, smoking joints and cigarettes, drinking beers and feeling at the few old ladies present. Outside, two strikers, members who had not earned their full colors, sat on the front porch watching for the law.

The house was a ramshackle stucco bungalow that had been built in the 1930s as part of a housing tract, before the term *housing tract* was part of the language. The walls were stained with blood, beer, and vomit. The carpet was matted with motor oil; the furniture was minimal and distressed. Only Tinker actually lived at the clubhouse. The rest of the club used it for meeting and partying.

The Guild had paid a hundred thousand dollars in cash for the house. The deed was registered under Newton's married sister's name, as was the ranch house the Guild owned in the Santa Lucia Mountains above Santa Barbara, which housed the lab that provided their income. Ironically, the ranch's nearest neighbor was a wobbly-headed ex-president who had declared a war on drugs, and who, from time to time, would stand on the veranda of his palatial ranch house sniffing the odor of cooking crank and calling, "Mommy, there's a funny smell trickling down out here."

The lab produced enough income to support all of the Guild's members and ensure that none of them had to work except to man the counter of the Harley-Davidson shop that Bonner Newton used to launder drug money.

Newton held an M.B.A. from Stanford. In an earlier time, before he fell from grace for smuggling cocaine, he had stalked the glass-cube buildings of Silicon Valley, wearing Italian suits and commanding crews of brilliant computer designers who could define the universe in terms of two digits, explain the chaos theory in twenty-five words or less, and build machines that emulated human intelligence—but who thought a vulva was a Swedish automobile. Newton's experience in coddling these genius misfits served him well as president of the Guild, for the members of the Guild were nothing more than nerds without brains: fat, ugly, or awkward men who found no acceptance in the outside world and so escaped into the security and belonging of an outlaw biker club. A Harley-Davidson and blind loyalty were the only requirements for membership.

"Listen up, you fucks," Newton said, calling the meeting to order. "Bitches outside." He paused and lit a cigarette while the women filed out the door, glaring at him over their shoulders. He was not a large or imposing man compared to the other members, but his authority was not to be questioned.

"Lonnie's not here yet," Tinker said.

"Lonnie's running an errand for us," Newton said. "We're going to take an impromptu road trip. A little business and a little pleasure."

"Fuckin' A," someone yelled. Newton gestured for quiet.

"Seems like someone forgot to tell me that we were running low on ether up at the facility." Newton always referred to the crank lab as "the facility." Tinker stopped scratching his leg and hung his head.

"Tink, you fucking idiot," someone said.

"Anyway," Newton continued, "I wasn't able to arrange a delivery, so we have to go get it. There's a rally in South Dakota in a couple of days. At Sturgis. The Chicago chapter is going to meet us there with a couple of barrels. I want three fifty-five-gallon drums rigged with false tops so if we get stopped by the law it looks like we're hauling motor oil. Tinker, you'll drive the pickup."

"Aw, come on, Newt," Tinker whined.

"Warren," Newton said. A thin biker with curly red hair looked up. "You fix one of the barrels for weapons, and make sure no one is packing. I don't want any weapons on anyone while we're riding."

A series of snorts, moans, and "Oh, fucks" passed around the room. Newton dismissed them with a wave. "Advice from the Gator," he said. Gator was short for the litigator, the Guild's attorney, Melvin Gold, who handled all their criminal cases free of charge in exchange for the assurance that he could also handle their personal injury suits. Bikers got run over a lot.

"Look," Newton insisted, "half of you are on probation. We don't need some rookie pig looking for glory to fuck us on a concealed-weapons charge. Are we clear?" Newton paused until someone answered, "We're clear."

"All right, then. Lonnie's making a run to Vegas with his old lady to get the money to pay for the ether. He'll meet us in South D. We're out of here at nine tomorrow morning, so don't get too fucked up tonight. Bring your camping shit. Let your bitches carry your stash." Newton dropped his cigarette and ground it out on the carpet. "That's all," he said.

The room filled with conversations about the trip. A few of the members got up to leave. When they opened the door a single flea hopped out with them. Once past the steps the flea changed into a horsefly and took flight. A block away the horsefly changed into a raven and headed toward the mesa and the Cliffs condominium complex.

CHAPTER TWENTY-TWO

SPRINKLING THE SON OF THE MORNING STAR

SANTA BARBARA

After almost twenty years as a salesman, Sam found that when he was confused his head filled with homilies that pertained to the profession. *Win an argument, lose a sale. If you look hungry, you will be. You can't sell if you don't pitch.* There were hundreds of them. He'd been running them through his mind for hours, trying to find some clue as to what he should do. The one that kept returning was *Never confuse motion with progress.*

To leave the house in search of Calliope without a clue as to where she might be would be movement for the sake of movement. Progress would be actually finding a clue to her whereabouts. He had no idea where to start looking for clues, so he lay on his bed and smoked, and tried to convince himself that he didn't want her.

She's probably found some other guy, he thought. *Losing the kid is just an excuse, a cowardly Dear John letter. It was just a one-night stand and I refuse to let it mean more to me than it meant to her. I've got my life back, intact, and there's no room for a young girl and a child. Nope. I'll rest up today and get back to work tomorrow. After I close a couple of deals, this week will just seem like a bad dream. It* was a good rationalization. Unfortunately, he didn't believe a word of it; he was worried about her.

Sam closed his eyes and tried to imagine the pages of his appointment book. It was a visualization he used to relax, a salesman's version of counting sheep. He saw the days and weeks spread out in front of him, and he filled in the blanks with lunches and prospects. By each of the names he made mental notes on how he would approach the pitch. Before long he was lost in a world of presentations and objections; the image of the girl faded away.

As he started to doze off he heard the sound of heavy breathing. He rolled on his side and steamy hot dog breath hit him in the face. He didn't open his eyes. There was no need to. He knew Coyote had returned. Perhaps if he feigned sleep the trickster would go away, so he lived there in the land of dog breath. A wet nose prodded his ear. At least he hoped it was a nose. With Coyote's sexual habits it could be. . . . No, he still smelled the breath. It was the nose.

I'm asleep, go away. I'm asleep, go away, he thought. He'd seen opossums try the same method to fool oncoming semi trucks, and it was working about as well for him. He felt the coyote climb onto the bed. Then he felt a paw on each of his shoulders. He groaned as he thought a truly sleeping guy might groan. Coyote whimpered and Sam could feel the canine nose press against his own.

Dog breath, Sam mused, *seems to have no distinction to it, yet it is distinctly dog breath. You could be at the cologne counter at Bloomingdale's, and someone could mist your wrist with an atomizer, and a single whiff would reveal the elusive scent to be dog breath as surely as if it had been squozen straight from the dog. Yet, what a wide spectrum of foulness dog breath can span, both in odor and humidity. This particular version of dog breath,* he felt, *is especially steamy, and carries a top note of stale cigarettes and coffee, as well as the usual fetid meat and butthole smells found in more common dog breath. This,* he thought, *is supernatural dog breath. I'm not likely*

*to be breathed upon by another dog in my lifetime that has recently
enjoyed a Marlboro over a cup of java.*

Despite his effort to distract himself with dog breath aesthetics,
Sam's tolerance was wearing out and he thought he might sneeze
or throw up any second. Coyote licked him on the mouth.

"Yuck!" Sam sat upright and wiped his mouth on his arm.
"Ack!" He shivered involuntarily and looked at the big coyote, who
grinned at him from the end of the bed. "There was no need for
that," Sam said.

Coyote whimpered and rolled over on his back in submission.

Sam got up from the bed and grabbed his cigarettes from the
nightstand. "Why are you back? You said you were gone for
good."

Coyote began to change into his human form. No longer afraid,
Sam watched the transformation with fascination. In a few seconds Coyote sat on the bed in his black buckskins wearing the
coyote-skin headdress. "Got a smoke?" he asked.

Sam shook one out of the pack and lit it for the trickster. Sam
took a small plastic box from his shirt pocket and held it out to
Coyote. "Breath mint?"

"No."

"I insist," Sam said.

Coyote took the box and shook out a mint, popped it in his
mouth, and handed the box back to Sam. "The girl is going to Las
Vegas."

"I don't care." The lie tasted foul in his mouth.

"If she tries to take her child from the biker she will be hurt."

"It's not my problem. Besides, she'll probably find another guy
to help her out." Sam felt both righteous and cowardly for saying
it. This role he was playing no longer fit. Quickly he added, "I
don't need the trouble."

"In the buffalo days your people used to say that a wife stolen
and returned was twice the wife she had been."

"They aren't my people and she's not my wife."

"You can be afraid, just don't act like it."

"What does that mean? You're worse than Pokey with your fucking riddles."

"You lost Pokey. You lost your family. You lost your name. All you have left is your fear, white man." Coyote flipped his cigarette at Sam. It hit him in the chest and hot ashes showered on the bed.

Sam patted out the embers and brushed himself off. "I didn't ask for you to come here. I don't owe the girl anything." But he did owe her. He wasn't sure what for yet, except that she had cut something loose in him. Why couldn't he cut loose the habit of fear?

Coyote went to the bedroom window and stared out. Without turning he said, "Do you know about the Crows who scouted for General Custer?"

Sam didn't answer.

"When they told Custer that ten thousand Lakota and Cheyenne warriors were waiting for him at the Little Bighorn he called them liars and rode on. The Crow scouts didn't *owe* Custer anything, but they painted their faces black and said, 'Today is a good day to die.'"

"The point?" Sam bristled.

"The point is that you will never know what they knew—that courage is its own reward."

Sam sat down on the edge of the bed and stared at Coyote's back. The red feathers across the buckskin shirt seemed to move on the black surface of Coyote's shirt. Sam wondered if he might not be light-headed from prolonged dog breath inhalation, but then the feathers drew a scene, and in a whirl of images and feathers, Sam was back on the reservation again.

There were three of them: boys hiding in the sagebrush by the road that led into the Custer Battlefield National Monument. Two were Crow, one Cheyenne. They were there on a dare that had started in ninth-grade gym class. The largest boy, the Cheyenne, was from the Broken Tooth family—descendants of a warrior who fought with Crazy Horse and Red Cloud on this very land.

"You going to do it?" said Eli Broken Tooth. "Or are you full of shit like all Crows?"

"I said I'd do it," Samson said. "But I'm not going to be stupid about it."

"What about you, breed?" Eli asked Billy Two Irons. "You a chickenshit?" Broken Tooth had been taunting Billy about his mixed blood for the whole school year and citing his own "pure Indian" lineage. The fact was that in buffalo days the mortality rate had been so high for young plains warriors that a woman might have three or four husbands in her lifetime, and have children by them all. Sometimes one of the husbands was a white man, yet since they all traced their kinship through their mother's line, the white ancestor could easily be forgotten.

Billy said, "I'll bet you got a few whiteys in your wigwam you don't even know about, Broken Dick."

Samson laughed and the others shushed him. The security guard was making a pass by the monument's high wrought-iron gate. They ducked their heads. A flashlight beam passed over them, paused, and moved on as the guard turned to walk up the hill toward the Custer burial site.

"You going to do it?" Eli asked.

"Once he's past the grave he has to go check on the Reno site. He'll take the jeep for that. When we hear the jeep, we'll go."

"Sure you will," said Eli.

"You coming?" Samson asked. He was more than a little afraid. The monument was federal land, and this was a time when an Indian causing trouble on federal land was something the government was going to great lengths to discourage after the Alcatraz takeover and the killings at Pine Ridge.

"I don't have to go," Broken Tooth said. "My people put him there. I'll just sit here and twist up a doobie while you girls do your thing." He grinned.

"The gate will be the bitch," Billy said. They looked at the fifteen-foot iron spears suspended between two stone pillars. There were only two cross members they could use as footholds.

They watched the guard amble the hundred yards down the hill to the visitor center. When they heard the jeep fire up, Samson and Billy took off. They hit the gate at the same time. The gate swung with the impact and clanged against the chains and padlock that held it closed. They scrambled up the bars, then hung over spearpoints and dropped to the asphalt. As they let go the chain sent a loud clang ringing down the valley. They both landed on their butts.

Samson looked to Billy. "You okay?"

Billy jumped to his feet and dusted off his jeans. "How come the Indians in the movies can do this shit in complete stealth?"

"Vocational training," Samson said. He started running up the hill toward the monument. Billy followed.

"Snake ahead," Samson said as he ran.

"What?"

"Snake," Sam repeated breathlessly. He leapt into the air over the big diamondback rattler that was lying in the road, warming itself on the asphalt. Billy saw the snake in time to pull up and slide on some loose gravel within striking distance.

When he heard Billy's shoes sliding he stopped and turned.

Billy said, "You were saying 'Snake,' right?"

"Back away and go around, Billy." Samson was so out of breath he could hardly talk. The rattler coiled.

"I thought you were saying 'Steak.' I was wondering, *Why is he yelling 'Steak' at me?*"

"Back away and go around."

"'Snake.' Well, I guess this explains it." Billy backed slowly away, then once out of striking distance ran a wide arc around the snake and up the hill.

Samson fell in beside him. The monument was still a hundred yards away. "Pace yourself," he said.

"Did you say 'Snake' again?" Billy said between pants.

Rather than answer, Samson fell into a trot.

The monument was a twenty-foot granite obelisk set on a ten-foot base at the top of a hill that overlooked the entire Little Big-horn basin.

"Let's do it," Samson said, heaving in breaths. The hill had been longer and steeper than he'd thought.

Billy unzipped his pants and stood beside Samson, who had already bared his weapon. "You know," Billy said, "it would have been easier to gang up on Eli and beat the shit out of him."

"I think I hear the jeep coming back," Samson said.

A long yellow stream arced out of Billy and splashed the side of the monument. "Then you better get going."

Samson strained. "I can't."

Billy grunted, trying to force his urine to run faster. "Go, man. That's headlights."

"I can't."

Billy finished and zipped up, then turned to face Samson. "Think rivers, think waterfalls."

"It won't come."

"Come on, Samson. He's coming. Relax."

"Relax? How can—"

"Okay, relax in a hurry."

Samson pushed until his eyes bugged. He felt a trickle, then a stream coming.

"Push it, Samson. He's coming." Billy began to back down the hill. "Push it, man."

The jeep's headlights broke over the hill and descended toward the monument. "Duck!" Billy said.

Samson squatted by the base of the monument and managed to stream urine down both pant legs before he got himself reaimed. Billy dove for cover next to Samson.

"Did you say 'Duck'?" Samson whispered.

"Shut up," Billy snapped.

Despite his fear, the adrenaline had made Samson giddy. He grinned at Billy. "I thought you were saying 'Truck,' which would have made more sense, but—"

"Would you shut up?" Billy risked a peek at the road. The jeep was coming toward them, rather than returning to the visitor center where it had started. As the jeep approached the monu-ment, they worked their way around its base, keeping the obelisk between themselves and the guard. "He won't stop, will he?" Billy said.

Samson could hear the jeep slowing as it passed the monument on the other side of them, not twenty feet away. They held their crouch until the jeep descended the hill and stopped halfway to the gate.

"He sees footprints," Billy said.

"On asphalt?"

"He saw us. I'm going to end up in jail like my brother."

"No, look, it's the fucking snake. He's waiting for it to get out of the road."

Indeed, the guard was inching the jeep forward slowly enough for the rattler to slither off into the grass. When the snake was gone the jeep revved up and continued down the hill, by the iron gate, and back around to the back of the visitor center.

"Let's go," Billy said. They ran down the road, Samson almost falling while trying to zip his pants and run at the same time. As they reached the gate Samson grabbed Billy's shoulder and pulled him back.

"What the fuck?" Billy said. Samson pointed to the chain. Billy nodded in understanding. The clanging.

Samson went to the center of the gate and grasped it. "Go," he said. "When you get over, hold it for me."

Without hesitation Billy leapt to the gate and climbed over, sliding down the opposite side instead of dropping as before. He held the gate and Samson started over.

As Samson reached the top of the gate and was working his feet between the spearpoints, he heard Eli's laughing from down the road and he looked up. A second later he heard a metal fire door slam at the visitor center. The quick turn took his balance and he tried to jump, but one of the spearpoints caught his jeans leg and he was slammed upside down into the gate. Billy held the chain, but there was a dull clank as Samson's forehead hit the bars.

It took Samson a second to realize that he was still hanging from the gate, his head still eight feet off the ground. "Unhook your leg," Billy said. "I'll catch you."

In this position Samson was facing the visitor center. He could see some lights going on inside. He struggled to push himself up on the bar, but the spearpoint was barbed. "I can't get it."

"Shit," Billy said. He held the gate with one hand and drew a flick knife from his back pocket with the other. "I'll come up and cut you down."

"No, don't let go of the gate," Samson said.

"Fuck it," Billy said. He let go of the gate and it clanged with Samson's swinging weight. Billy jumped on the bars and as he climbed Samson could hear the fire door open and slam again, then footsteps. Billy stood at the top of the stone pillar and put the knife to Samson's pant leg. "When I cut, keep hold of the bars."

Billy pulled the knife blade through the denim and Samson flipped over and slammed the bars again, this time right side up. The gate clanged again. Samson heard the jeep starting and saw the beams of the headlights come out from behind the visitor center. He looked to Billy. "Jump!"

Billy leapt from the fifteen-foot pillar. As he hit the pavement he yowled and crumpled. "My ankle."

Samson looked to the visitor center, where the jeep was pulling out. He grabbed Billy under the armpits and dragged him down into the ditch. They waited, breathlessly, as the jeep stopped and the guard, gun drawn, checked the lock and chain once again.

After the guard left they crawled down the ditch toward Eli. When he came into view, Samson helped Billy to his feet and supported him while he limped up to the big Cheyenne, who was taking a deep hit on a joint.

"Want a hit?" he croaked, holding the joint out to Billy.

Billy took the joint, sat down in the grass, and took a hit.

Eli let out a cloud of smoke and laughed. "That was the funniest fucking thing I've ever seen in my life." Then he spotted the wet streaks on Samson's pants. "What happened, Hunts Alone? I thought you were going to piss on Custer's grave. You get so scared you wet yourself?" He threw back his head to laugh and Samson wound up and tagged him on the jaw with a vicious roundhouse punch. Eli dropped to the ground and didn't move. Samson looked at his damaged fist, then at Eli, then at Billy Two Irons. He grinned.

Billy said, "You couldn't have done that twenty minutes ago and saved us all this trouble, could you?"

"You're right," Samson said. "I couldn't have done that twenty minutes ago. Let's get out of here before he comes to."

Samson helped Billy to his feet, then out of the ditch onto the road. As they headed toward Crow Agency it seemed to get darker as they walked, then darker still, until there was no light at all and Sam was in his bedroom staring at the back of a black buckskin shirt trimmed with red woodpecker feathers.

"It was a stupid thing to do," Sam said.

"It was brave," Coyote said. "It would have been stupid if you had failed."

"We found out later that Custer wasn't even buried there. His body was taken to West Point, so it was all for nothing."

"And what about the night on the dam? Was that all for nothing?"

"How do you know about that?"

Coyote turned and stared at Sam with his arms crossed, his golden eyes shining with delight.

"That was nothing but trouble," Sam said finally.

"Would you do it again?"

"Yes," Sam said without thinking.

"And the girl is nothing but trouble?" Coyote said.

Sam heard the words echoing in his mind. Going after the girl was the right thing to do. After all the years of doing the safe thing, it was time to do the right thing. He said, "You really piss me off sometimes, you know that?"

"Anger is the gods' way of letting you know you are alive."

Sam got up and stood face-to-face with the trickster, trying to read something in his eyes. He moved forward until their noses almost touched. "All you know is that she's going to Las Vegas? No address or anything?"

"Not so far. But if she misses them there, the biker is going on to South Dakota. She'll follow. I'll tell you the rest on the way."

"I don't suppose you could change into a Learjet or something practical."

Coyote shook his head. "Just living things: animals, bugs, rocks."

Sam reached into his shirt pocket, pulled out the box of breath mints, and handed them to Coyote. The trickster raised his eyebrows in query.

Sam said, "Eat those. I can't handle dog breath through an eight-hour drive."

PART THREE

QUEST

CHAPTER TWENTY-THREE

PAVLOV'S DOGS AND THE RHINESTONE TURD

LAS VEGAS

The only distractions from the noise of his own mind were desert-dried roadkills, thrown retreads, and road signs reflecting desolation. Sam drove, smoked, and fought drowsiness by worrying about how he would find the girl. The trickster slept in the passenger seat.

Sam had been to Las Vegas three times before—with Aaron—to see championship boxing at Caesar's Palace. Two hundred dollars bought them seats at nosebleed altitude, closer to the moon than the ring, but Aaron insisted that there was nothing like *being there*. Without binoculars, following the progress of the fight was like tracking down a rumor. Sam usually watched the women and did his best to keep Aaron calmed down.

As soon as they walked into a casino Aaron started. "This is my town! The lights, the excitement, the women—I was born for this place." Then Aaron would drop a couple thousand at the tables and suck free gin and tonics until he staggered. In the morning Sam would drag Aaron out of a tangle of satin sheets and hookers, throw him in the shower, and listen to his long lament of remorse and hangover as he lay in the backseat of the car with a jacket over his head, whining the whole way home about how he would never return. Aaron never failed to fuel the greed machine and was always dumbfounded when it juiced him of his hope.

It was the machine that fascinated Sam. While Aaron ground himself through the velvet gears, Sam watched the workings of the most elaborate Skinner box on the face of the Earth. Drop the coin, hear the bell, see the lights, eat the food, see the women, hear the bell, see the lights, drop the coin again. The ostentation of the casinos did not create desire for money; it made money meaningless. There were no mortgages in a casino, no children needing food, no car needing repairs, no work, no time, no day, no night; those things—the context of money—were someplace else. A place where people returned before they realized that a turd rolled in rhinestones is a turd nonetheless.

Sam saw the glow from Las Vegas rising over the desert from thirty miles out. He poked Coyote in the leg and the trickster woke up.

"Hold the wheel," Sam said.

"Let me drive. You can sleep."

"You're not driving my car. Just hold the wheel."

Coyote held the wheel while Sam punched buttons on the console. The screen of the navigation system flickered on. Sam punched a few more buttons and a street map of Las Vegas lit up green on the screen. A blip representing the Mercedes blinked along Highway 15 toward the city.

"Okay," Sam said, taking the wheel again.

Coyote studied the screen. "How do you win?"

"It's not a game, it's a map. The blip is us."

"The car knows where it is going, like a horse?"

"It doesn't know, it just tells us where we are."

"Like looking out the window?"

"Look, I'm going to have to sleep when we get to Vegas. I don't even know where to start looking for Calliope."

"Why don't you ask the car?"

Sam ignored the question. "I'm going to get us a room." He

dialed information on the cellular phone, got the number of a casino hotel, then called and reserved a room.

The exits off the highway were marked by names of casinos they led to, not by the names of streets or roads. Sam took the exit marked CAMELOT. He followed the signs down the surface streets lined with pawnshops, convenience stores, and low-slung cinder-block buildings under neon signs that proclaimed, CASH FOR YOUR CAR, CHECKS CASHED HERE, MARRIAGES AND DI-VORCES—TWENTY-FOUR-HOUR DRIVE-THRU WINDOW.

Coyote said, "What are these places?"

Sam tried to think of a quick explanation, but was too weary from lack of sleep to tackle the concept of Las Vegas in twenty-five words or less. Finally he said, "These are places where you go if you want to fuck up your life and you don't have a lot of time to do it in."

"Are we going to stop?"

"No, I seem to be fucking up at a fine rate of speed, thank you." Sam spotted the pseudomedieval towers of Camelot rising above the strip, multicolored pennons flying from standards tipped with aircraft warning lights. He wondered what the real King Arthur (if there was a King Arthur, and who was he to question the truth behind myth?) would have thought about the casino named after his legendary city. Would he recognize anything? Would he cower in fear at the sight of his first electric light? Flush toilet? Automobile? Would he be reduced to a pathetic Quixote attacking this place where chivalry was a quaint marketing idea? Or would the Once and Future King lay eyes on a leggy keno girl and raise another lance to lead the knights of the Round Table in a charge? The women, Sam decided, would be Arthur's touchstone, and his downfall.

He shot a glance at Coyote. "When we get there you're going to see a lot of women without a lot of clothes on. Stay away from them."

Coyote looked surprised. "I never touch a woman who does not want it—"

"Don't touch!" Sam interrupted.

Coyote slouched in his seat. "Or need it," he whispered.

Sam drove the Mercedes over a giant drawbridge and stopped at the valet parking station where a dozen young men dressed like squires were scrambling around unloading cars, filling out slips, and driving cars away.

"This is it," Sam said. He popped the trunk and got out, leaving the engine running. A warm desert wind washed over him at the same time a young man ran around the car and held out a numbered slip of paper. "Your ticket, milord."

Sam dug in his pocket for a bill to tip the kid, but found nothing. "I'm sorry," he said. "I don't have any cash on me. I'll get your name and leave a tip at the desk."

The kid tried to force a smile and failed. "Very good, milord." He jumped in the car and slammed the door. Sam cringed and tapped on the window. The window whirred down; the kid waited.

Sam leaned in and read the kid's plastic badge. "Look, uh, Squire Tom, I really will leave a tip at the desk for you. We left in a hurry and I forgot to get cash."

The kid waited, gunning the engine.

"There's an alarm remote on the keys. Could you turn it on after you park it? One chirp is armed."

Squire Tom nodded and pulled away. Sam heard him say, "The pox on you, Moorish pig," over the squeal of the tires. *How authentic,* Sam thought. He watched the Mercedes disappear around the corner and wondered why valet parking always made him feel as if he had seen his car for the last time.

Coyote stood across the lane waving to the car. He looked over. "Moorish pig?"

"The dark skin, I guess," said Sam. He led Coyote past a half-dozen squires and an overweight guy in a purple-and-yellow jester's outfit with a radio on his belt and a badge that read, *Lord Larry,* over another drawbridge, and into the casino.

Trumpets played a fanfare as they crossed the threshold under a brace of huge broadswords. A jolly electronic voice welcomed them to Camelot. Sam spotted a woman in a peasant dress by a sign reading, *Ye Olde Information.* The badge she wore, next to a magnificent display of cleavage, read, *Lusty Wench Wendy.* Sam pulled Coyote back and approached the girl.

"Excuse me, er, Wendy. I have a room reserved and I need to find a cash machine."

The girl spoke in a whining fake-English-over-true-Brooklyn accent. "Well"—she threw out a hip, struck a pose—"if milords proceed through the casino to the left to the second arch, ye will find the registration desk. There's cash machines by every arch, milord."

"Thanks," Sam said. He started to walk away, then turned back to the girl. "Excuse me, but I've been here before and I thought everyone was a lord or a lady. Lusty wench is a new one."

The English accent had overheated and failed. "Yeah. About three months ago they said it was getting sorta confusing. You know, six Lord Steves, ten Lady Debbies. They use a bunch of other medieval titles now. The bellboys are serfs. Lusty wenches, alchemists, stuff like that."

"Oh, thanks," Sam said as if he understood. He led Coyote into the chaos of the casino, looking for a cash machine while trying to move quickly. Coyote's appearance was attracting attention, and when people looked up from a slot machine or blackjack table, Sam knew they were truly distracted. As they passed a carousel of slot machines, a middle-aged woman who was pumping quarters into a machine by the handful leaned so far back to get a look at the trickster that she nearly toppled off her stool. Sam caught her and steadied her. "He works at the Frontier, up the strip," Sam said.

Coyote peeked over Sam's shoulder, winked at the woman, then licked his eyebrows. The woman's jaw dropped.

"Exotic dancer," Sam explained. The woman nodded, a little stunned, and returned her attention to the slot machine.

"I wish you wouldn't do that," Sam said to Coyote. "And don't you have any other clothes? Something a little more conservative?"

"Wool?" Coyote made an incredibly realistic sheep noise. A pit boss at the blackjack tables raised an eyebrow and two security jesters fell in behind Sam and Coyote.

"Be cool," Sam said. He turned under a hanging tapestry of a unicorn and stopped by a cash machine, checking over his shoulder for the security jesters. They waited and watched, standing a few feet away, while Sam took a deck of credit cards from his wallet and shuffled through them. When he inserted one of the cards in the machine and punched his identification number the jesters moved off.

"They're gone," Coyote said.

"Yeah, as long as it looks like you're going to spend money I guess it doesn't matter what you look like."

Coyote watched as the cash machine spit a stack of twenties into the tray. "You win," he said. "You picked the right numbers the first time."

"Yeah, I'm lucky that way."

"Try again, see if you win."

Sam grinned. "I'm very good at this game." He put a different card into the machine and punched the same PIN number while Coyote watched. The machine whirred and another stack of twenties shot into the tray.

"You won! Play again."

"No. We need to check in." Sam picked up the money and walked to a registration desk that was long enough to land planes on. At this hour of the morning there were only two people on the desk, a lusty wench named Chantel and a very tall, thin, very black man in a business suit and wraparound sunglasses who stood back from the desk and watched, unmoving.

"Hunter, Samuel," Sam said. "I have a reservation." He placed a credit card on the desk. The girl typed for a second. The computer beeped and the girl looked over her shoulder at the black man, who moved like liquid to her side. He consulted the screen for a moment. *What now?* Sam thought.

The black man looked down at Sam and a crescent moon of a

smile appeared on the night sky of his face. He picked up Sam's credit card and handed it back. "Mr. Hunter, thank you for joining us again. The room's on Camelot, sir. And if there's anything I can get you, please don't hesitate to call down and ask."

Sam was dumbfounded. Then he remembered. The last time he had stayed here Aaron had lost almost twenty thousand dollars and billed it to their suite of rooms. The suite had been registered in Sam's name. Vegas loves a loser.

"Thank you"—Sam read the man's nameplate, which was pinned at Sam's eye level—"M.F." No *Lord*, no *Squire*, no title at all—just M.F.

"The second elevator on your left, Mr. Hunter," the lusty wench said. "Twenty-seventh floor."

"Thanks," Sam said. Coyote grinned at the girl and Sam dragged him away to the elevator, where the trickster immediately punched in four floor numbers and stood back. "This time, I will win."

"It's a fucking elevator," Sam said. "Just push twenty-seven."

"But that is not the lucky number."

Sam sighed and pushed the floor number, then waited while they stopped at all the floors Coyote had pushed on their way to twenty-seven.

Once in the room, Sam stripped to his shorts and fell onto one of the king-size beds. "Get some sleep if you can. I'll try and figure out how to find Calliope in the morning. I'm too tired to think now."

"You sleep," Coyote said. "I will think of a plan."

Sam didn't answer. He was already asleep.

COYOTE LOSES HIS ASS

Coyote and his friend Beaver had been hunting all day, but neither had found any game. After a while they sat down on some rocks and began talking.

"This is your fault," Coyote said. "I can always find game."

"I don't think so," Beaver said. "If you are such a good hunter, why is your wife so skinny?"

Coyote thought about his skinny wife and Beaver's fat little wife and he was jealous. "Well, how about a bet?" he said. "Tomorrow we will each go out hunting. If you get more rabbits, you can come to my lodge and sleep with my wife so you can see that my skinny wife is better. But if I get more rabbits, I get to sleep with your wife."

"Sounds fair," Beaver said.

The next day, after the hunt, Coyote came to Beaver's lodge carrying his one scrawny rabbit. "Oh, Mrs. Beaver," he called. "I've come to collect on my bet."

Mrs. Beaver called from inside the lodge. "Oh, Coyote, you are a great hunter. Mr. Beaver just stopped by with twenty rabbits on his way to your lodge. You better go stop him and tell him that you got more."

"Right," Coyote said. "I'll be right back." He slunk off to his lodge dragging his rabbit.

His wife was waiting outside. "Nice rabbit," she said. "Beaver is inside. I'll see you in the morning." Coyote's wife went into the lodge and pulled down the door flap.

All night Coyote sat outside his lodge shivering and listening. At one point he heard his wife cry out.

"Beaver!" Coyote shouted. "Don't you hurt my wife."

"He's not hurting me," Mrs. Coyote said. "I like it!"

"Swell," Coyote said.

The next morning Beaver came out of Coyote's lodge singing and grinning. "No hard feelings, right?"

"A bet is a bet," Coyote said.

Mrs. Coyote peeked out and said, "Maybe this will teach you not to gamble."

"Right," Coyote said. Then he called to Beaver, "Hey, how about playing the hand game with me—double or nothing?"

"Sounds good," Beaver said. "Let's go down to the river."

At the river Coyote said, "This is for a night with your wife." Then he picked the wrong hand.

"You really shouldn't gamble," Beaver said.

"I'll bet you my best horse for a night with your wife," Coyote said.

After a while, Coyote had lost all his horses, his lodge, his wife, and his clothes. "One more time," he said.

"But you don't have anything left," Beaver said.

"I'll bet you my ass against everything else."

"I don't want your ass," Beaver said.

"I thought you were my friend."

"Okay," Beaver said. He hid the stone behind his back. Coyote picked the wrong hand.

"Can I borrow your knife?" Coyote said.

"I don't want your ass," Beaver said.

"A bet is a bet," Coyote said. He took Beaver's knife and cut off his ass. "Boy, that stings."

"I've got to go," Beaver said. "I'll tell your wife she can come and sleep in my lodge if she wants to." He picked up all of Coyote's things and went home.

When Coyote got home his wife was waiting. "Beaver took the lodge," she said.

"Yep," Coyote said.

"Where's your ass?" she asked.

"Beaver got that too."

"You know," she said, "there's a twelve-step program for gambling. You should look into it."

"Twelve steps." Coyote laughed. "I'll bet I can do it in six."

CHAPTER TWENTY-FOUR

COYOTE IN TRICKSTER TOWN

LAS VEGAS

Coyote had been a long time in the Spirit World, where everyone knew him, so no one would gamble with him. Now that he was in Trickster Town, he wanted to make up for lost time. He waited for Sam to fall asleep, then he took the salesman's wallet and went down the elevator to the casino.

Coyote saw hundreds of shiny machines blinking, and ringing, and clanking big coins into hollow metal bowls. He saw green tables where people traded money for colorful chips and a woman in a cage who paid money for the chips. He saw a wheel with a ball that went around and around. When the ball stopped a man took everyone's chips. *The key to that one,* Coyote thought, *is to grab your chips when you see the ball slowing down.*

At one green table, a shaman with a stick chanted while players threw bones. There was much shouting and moaning after each throw and the shaman took many chips from the players. *That is a game of magic,* Coyote thought. *I will be very good at that one. But first I must use Sam's cheating medicine on this machine.*

The trickster stood by a machine that he had seen Sam win

from two times. He took one of the gold cards from Sam's wallet and slipped it into the machine, then he pressed the number that he had seen Sam use. The machine beeped and spit the card out.

"Panther piss!" Coyote swore. "I've lost." He pounded on the machine, then stepped back and drew another card from Sam's wallet. He put it in the machine and pressed the number. The machine beeped and spit out the card. "Balls!" Coyote said. "This cheating medicine is no good."

A round woman in pink stretch pants who was standing behind Coyote cleared her throat and made an impatient humphing noise. Coyote turned to her. "Get your own machine. This one is mine."

The woman glared at the trickster and tapped her foot.

"Go, go, go," Coyote said, waving her away. "There are many machines to play on. I was here first. Go away."

He put another card into the machine and hunched over the keyboard so the woman would not steal his cheating medicine. He looked back over his shoulder. She was trying to see what he was doing. "Go away, woman. My cheating medicine will not help you. Even if you win you will still be ugly."

The woman wrapped the strap of her pocketbook around her wrist and wound up to swing it at Coyote. Coyote was going to turn into a flea and disappear into the carpet, but he would have had to drop Sam's wallet to do it, so he hesitated and the woman let fly.

Coyote ducked and covered his head, but the blow didn't come. Instead he heard a solid thud above his head and looked up to see a huge black hand holding the pocketbook in the air, the woman dangling from the strap at the other end. Coyote looked up further, craning his neck, until he saw a dazzling crescent moon of a smile in the face like night sky.

"Is there a problem?" said the crescent moon in a soft, calm, deep voice. The giant lowered the woman, who stood stunned, staring up at what looked like a living late-afternoon shadow in sunglasses. The giant was used to shocking people—white people anyway; a seven-foot black man anywhere off a basketball court nonplussed most. He squeezed the woman's shoulder gently to bring her back to her senses. "Are you all right, ma'am?" Again the smile.

"Fine. I'm fine," the woman said, and she tottered off into the casino to tell her husband that, by God, they would spend their next vacation in Hawaii where natives and giants—if they were there at all—were part of the entertainment.

The giant turned his attention to Coyote. "And you, sir, can I help you with anything?"

"You look like Raven," Coyote said. "Do you always wear sunglasses?"

"Always, sir," the giant said with a slight bow. He pointed to the brass nameplate on his black suit jacket. "I'm M.F., customer service, at your service, sir."

"What's the M.F. stand for?" Coyote asked.

"Just M.F., sir. I am the youngest of nine children. I suppose my mother was too tired to come up with a full name."

This was not entirely true, nor entirely false. The giant's mother had, indeed, been weary by the time he was born, but she had also developed an unnatural obsession with dental hygiene as a child, after she was chosen to be one of the first students ever to participate in a Crest toothpaste test. It had been her single moment of glory, her fifteen minutes of fame (and her best checkup ever). When she grew up she married a navy man named Nathan Fresh, and as she bore her children she christened them in remembrance of her day in the dental sun. The first of the Fresh children, a boy, was named Fluoristat. Then came three more boys: Tartar, Plaque, and Molar. Then two girls: Gingivitis and Flossie (the latter after the famous dental hygiene cow). After normal deliveries of two more sons, Bicuspid and Incisor, she had a long, difficult labor with her largest and last son, Minty. Later, Mother Fresh swore that had the child taken one more minute to come into the world, she would have named him Mr. Tooth Decay out of spite—a fact that gave little solace to the man named Minty Fresh.

Coyote said, "People think that it stands for *motherfucker*, don't they?"

"No," Minty said. "No one has ever mentioned it."

"Oh," Coyote said. "Can you fix this machine? When I give it the cheating number it just beeps."

Minty Fresh looked at the cash machine, which was still blinking the message INSTRUCTIONS IN ENGLISH, SPANISH, OR JAPANESE. CHOOSE ONE. "You'll need to choose a language, sir." He reached down and pushed the English button. "It should be fine now."

Coyote inserted a card and punched two numbers on the keyboard, then looked at Minty. "This is my secret number."

"Yes," Minty said. "If you need anything at all, please ask for me personally." He turned and walked away.

Coyote finished punching the PIN number. When the machine prompted him for an amount he punched in $9999.99, the maximum allowed by the six-figure field. The machine whirred and spit five hundred dollars into the tray, then flashed a message saying that this was the card's transaction limit. Coyote tried the card again and got another five hundred. The third time the machine refused the transaction so Coyote tried another card. After running all of Sam's cards to their limit he walked away from the machine with twenty thousand dollars in cash.

Coyote went to the roulette table and held the four-inch brick of twenties out to the croupier, a slight Oriental woman in a red-and-purple silk doublet with a name badge that read, *Lady Lihn*. The croupier said, "On the table." She gestured for Coyote to put the money down. She nodded to a pit boss. "Watch count, please," she said mechanically. The pit boss, a sharp-faced, slick-haired Italian man wearing a polyester suit and a ten-thousand-dollar Rolex, moved to her side and watched as she counted the bills out on the table.

"Changing twenty thousand," Lady Lihn said. "How would you like this, sir?"

"Red ones," Coyote said. The pit boss raised an eyebrow and smirked. Lady Lihn looked irritated.

"Red is five dollar. No room on table."

The pit boss addressed Coyote. "Perhaps you'd like two hundred in fives and the rest in hundreds, sir."

"What color are the hundreds?" Coyote said.

"Black," Lady Lihn said.

"Yellows," Coyote said.

"Yellows are two dollars."

"You pick," Coyote said.

Lady Lihn counted out racks of chips and pushed them in front of Coyote. The pit boss nodded to a cocktail waitress, then to the stack of chips in front of Coyote, which the cocktail waitress interpreted as "Take the order." The cocktail waitress would bring strong drinks until Coyote started to get drunk, then she would bring watered drinks until he looked tired, when she would offer coffee and disappear until the caffeine kicked in.

"Can I bring you something to drink?"

Coyote turned to the cocktail waitress and stared into her cleavage. "Yes," he said.

The waitress held a pen ready over a cocktail napkin. "What can I bring you?"

Coyote shot a glance to a woman at the table who was drinking a mai tai, resplendent with paper parasols and sword-skewered tropical fruit. He grabbed the woman's drink and downed half of it, nearly taking his eye out with the plastic broadsword. "One of these," Coyote said. He replaced the drink in front of the woman, who didn't seem to notice that it had been missing. She'd been riding the alcohol-and-caffeine roller coaster for hours and was absorbed in winning back her children's college fund.

"Bets down," Lady Lihn said. Coyote put a single red chip on black and the ball was dropped. Coyote watched the ball race around the outside of the wheel. When it slowed and dropped to the numbers he reached for his bet.

"No touch bet," Lady Lihn snapped. In an instant the pit boss, the cocktail waitress, and two security jesters in steel-toed elf shoes were at Coyote's side. The trickster pulled his hand back. *It will be hard to trick these people*, Coyote thought. *They talk like wolves, all twitches and gestures and smells.*

The ball dropped into a red slot and Lady Lihn placed another red chip next to Coyote's. "I win, I win, I win," Coyote chanted. He did a skipping dance around the table and sang a victory song.

Above the casino, in a mirrored dome, a video camera picked up Coyote's dancing image and sent it to a deck of monitors where three men watched and, in turn, watched each other watch. One pressed a button and picked up a telephone. "M.F.," he said. "This is God. Customer service on table fifty-nine. The Indian you were talking to a few minutes ago. Watch him."

"I'm on it," Minty Fresh said. He turned to the girl who was working behind the computer. "God wants me on the floor."

The girl nodded. As Minty walked by her she sang softly, "He knows when you are sleeping. He knows when you're awake. . . ."

Minty Fresh smiled. He really didn't mind being watched. Because of his size, people had always watched him. He had never blended into any background, never entered a room unnoticed, never been able to sneak up on someone. Attracting attention was as natural to him as being. And for every original-thinking dolt who asked him how the weather was up there, there was a woman who wanted to research the wives' tale of proportional hand-foot-penis size. (A tale, Minty thought, dreamed up by the unsatisfied wives of small-footed men.)

Minty spotted the Indian at the roulette table. The two security jesters had moved off a few feet but were still watching, as was the pit boss. When Minty came to the table they nodded in acknowledgment and moved off. The croupier looked at Minty and immediately looked back to the bets on the table. Minty Fresh put her on edge. It wasn't his size that rattled her, but the fact that no one was exactly sure what his job was, only that when there was a problem, he was there. He handled things.

Lady Lihn dropped the ball into the wheel. It raced, then rattled into a slot, and she raked all the bets off the table. Coyote cursed and let out a howl. The woman playing next to him staggered back and wandered away, carrying visions of her children wearing paper hats and saying, "I was going to go to college, but my mother went to Vegas instead. Would you like fries with that?"

Coyote looked at Minty Fresh. "She was bad luck. I lost half of my chips because of her."

"Perhaps you should move to a different table," Minty said. "We can open a private table just for you."

Coyote grinned at Minty. "You think you have a table where you can trick me?"

"No, sir," Minty said, a little embarrassed. "We don't wish to trick you."

"There's nothing wrong with tricking people. They pay you to be tricked."

"We like to think of it as entertainment."

Coyote laughed. "Like movie stars and magicians? Tricksters. People want to be tricked. But you know that, don't you?" He picked up his chips and walked to a crap table.

Minty thought for a moment before following the Indian. He prided himself on being able to handle any situation with complete calm, but he found dealing with this Indian made him nervous, and a little afraid. But of what? Something in the eyes. He moved in behind Coyote, who was throwing chips on the crap table.

"You can't bet the numbers until the point has been made, sir," said the stickman, a thin, balding man in his forties. He pushed Coyote's chips back across the table. The stickman looked over Coyote's head and nodded to Minty Fresh before pushing the dice to the shooter. "Place your bets," he said, and the dealers working at either end of the table checked the bets on the felt. "New shooter coming out," the stickman said.

A blond woman in a business suit and perfect newswoman

makeup picked up the dice and blew on them. "Come on, seven," she said. "Baby needs new shoes."

Coyote twisted his neck to look at Minty Fresh. "Does talking to them work?"

Minty nodded to the table as the woman let fly with the dice, rolling a two.

"Snake eyes!" the croupier said.

"Lizard dick!" Coyote shouted back.

The blond woman cursed and walked away from the table. The stickman shot a glance to Minty, then continued. "Two. Craps. No pass. No come. Place your bets. New shooter coming out." He pushed the dice to Coyote, who threw a handful of black chips on the table and picked up the dice.

"You are small, but I am your friend," Coyote said to the dice. "You have beautiful spots." He pulled the rawhide pouch from his belt and poured a fine powder on the dice.

"You can't do that, sir," the stickman said.

Minty Fresh gently took the dice from Coyote and handed them to the boxman, who sat across from the stickman watching an enormous rack of chips that was the table's bank. He inspected the dice, then gave them to the stickman, who dropped them in his tray and pushed a fresh pair to the trickster.

"What is this, shade?" Coyote said. "The shaman gets to use his power stick but I can't use my cheating powder?"

"I'm afraid not," Minty said.

Coyote picked up the new dice and chucked them to the end of the table.

"Eight! Easy," the stickman said.

"Did I win?" Coyote asked Minty.

"No, now you have to roll another eight before you roll a seven or eleven."

Coyote rolled again. The dice showed a pair of fours.

"Eight. Winner. Hard way," the stickman chanted. The dealer placed a stack of black chips next to Coyote's bet.

"Ha," Coyote said, taunting Minty Fresh. "See, I am good at this game."

"Very good," Minty said with a smile. "You roll again."

Coyote placed the remainder of his chips on the table. The dealer immediately shot a glance to the boxman, who looked to Minty Fresh. Minty nodded. The boxman nodded. The dealer counted Coyote's chips and stacked them on the pass line. "Playing twenty-one thousand."

Coyote threw the dice.

"Two!" the stickman said. The dealer raked in Coyote's chips and handed them to the boxman, who stacked the racks in the table bank.

"I lost?" Coyote said incredulously.

"Sorry," Minty said. "But you didn't crap out. You can shoot again."

"I'll be back," Coyote said. He walked away and Minty followed him through the casino, into the lobby, and out the door. Coyote handed the valet ticket to a kid named Squire Jeff, then turned to Minty, who stood by the valet counter.

"I'll be back with more money."

"We'll hold a place for you, sir," Minty said, relieved that the Indian was leaving.

"I was just learning your game, shade. You didn't trick me."

"Of course not, sir."

Squire Jeff pulled up in the Mercedes, got out, and waited with his hand out. Coyote started to get into the car, then stopped and looked at the valet. He took the pouch from his belt and poured a bit of powder into the kid's hand, then got in the car and drove away.

Minty felt a wave of relief wash over him as he watched the Mercedes cross the drawbridge. Squire Jeff, still holding his palm out, turned to Minty Fresh.

"What am I supposed to do with this?"

"You could snort it."

Squire Jeff sniffed at the powder, then wrinkled his nose and brushed the powder from his hand. "Fucking Indian. You work inside, right?"

Minty nodded.

Squire Jeff looked Minty up and down. "You play any ball?"

"One year, UNLV."

"Injury?"

"Attitude," Minty said. He walked back into the casino.

CHAPTER TWENTY-FIVE

WHEELS, DEALS, AND THE PERSISTENCE OF VISIONS

LAS VEGAS

Calliope sat in her car shivering and watching. She was parked up the street from a Vegas Harley-Davidson shop where she had once gone with Lonnie on a delivery for the Guild. The street was deserted, and dark except for the odd glow of neon in the window of a closed pawnshop. Litter danced in dust devils of desert wind that had grown cold through the night. Calliope curled up in the driver's seat and tried to cover herself with one of Grubb's blankets. The smell that came off the blanket, a mix of sour milk and sweet baby, made her sad, and even though she had stopped breastfeeding months ago, her breasts ached for her son.

She caught some motion out of the corner of her eye: two figures coming out of an alley onto the sidewalk: men. They were walking toward the car. Calliope slid down in the driver's seat. The mother instinct, the feeling of righteous invincibility that had filled her when she had come here, was leaking away. Right now she was not protecting her child; she was afraid for herself.

As the men approached she saw that they were young toughs, swaggering with their own willingness to violence, even as they staggered from the effect of some drink or drug. She slid further down in the seat, and when their shadows fell across the car's hood she twisted down and covered herself with Grubb's blanket. She heard their footsteps scrape and stop at the car, heard their voices above her.

"Check out this motherfucker."

"Some tall dollars here—there's a grand in tires on this thing."

"Pop the hood."

Calliope heard someone trying to open the door.

"Locked."

"Hang on a minute, I saw a brick back a ways."

Footsteps away. The car rocked with the continued yanking at the door handle. Calliope could hear the keys swinging in the ignition. The second man was coming back. Her breath caught. She waited for the crash. Sweat trickled down her forehead and dripped onto the gearshift knob.

"No man, not the windshield. You can't drive it with a broken windshield."

"Oh, right."

Calliope braced herself for the impact of the brick, then something in her mind screamed NO! Her feet were still on the pedals. She pushed the clutch and gas to the floor, reached out from under the blanket, and turned the key.

The Z roared to life, thundered, then screamed as she kept the gas to the floor. She sat up and glanced at the two startled men, who were cowering a few feet away. Instantly their surprise turned to anger and the taller of the two raised the brick. Calliope popped the clutch and fought to keep the car straight as the tires burned off on the asphalt. She heard a loud crack behind her and felt splinters of glass hit her from behind.

She power-shifted through three gears, turning over the tires and kicking the car sideways with each slam of the shifter. By the time she backed off the gas the speedometer was threatening 110. There was a thumping coming from the engine and a high-pitched wailing coming from somewhere. She looked into the rearview mirror to see the hole in the back window and, behind it, flashing red and blue police lights.

She hesitated only long enough to throw Grubb's blanket off her shoulders, then slammed the Z into third, floored it, and said a quick prayer to Kali the Destroyer.

If Lonnie Ray Inman had ever made the connection that whenever he read the words *American Standard,* spelled out in cornflower blue against white porcelain, he felt a sudden urge to urinate, he might have understood why Grubb, upon seeing white plastic bundles piled haphazardly on the motel-room floor, crawled doggedly to, and whizzed gleefully on, twenty thousand dollars' worth of methamphetamine. To Grubb, the bundles looked like Pampers, a fine and private place to pee.

"Jesus Christ, Cheryl," Lonnie yelled. "He crawled out of his diaper. Can't you keep an eye on him for a fucking minute?"

"Fuck you. You watch him, stud. He's your kid." Cheryl threw a pillow at Lonnie as she stormed naked into the bathroom.

"You were the one that said you'd make a good mother. Throw me a towel."

Cheryl stood in front of the mirror working her jaw back and forth. "Get your own towel. I think you fucked up my jaw."

"I did? I didn't do shit."

"That's the problem, isn't it?"

Cheryl had been lolling Lonnie's limpness around in her mouth for an hour, trying to get a reaction out of him, when she heard a sharp crack in her right ear and felt a painful grating in the back of her jaw.

Lonnie grabbed a towel off the rack and went to where Grubb was happily splashing away on the drugs. Lonnie picked up the baby and put him on the bed, then went back to clean off the packages.

"Oh, Christ. Cheryl, clean up the kid, will you?"

"Fuck off."

Lonnie stormed into the bathroom and grabbed her by the hair, yanking her head back until she was staring up at him. He spoke to her through gritted teeth. "You clean up the kid now or I'll snap your fucking neck. You understand?" He yanked her head back further. "I've got to turn this shit early in the morning and then ride to South Dakota, and I need to get some fucking sleep. If I have to kill you to get it I will. You understand?" He relaxed his grip on her hair and she nodded. Tears welled up in her eyes.

He dragged her out of the bathroom and threw her on the bed with Grubb, then threw the towel in her face. "Now clean up the kid."

Lonnie took another towel and wiped each of the packages before packing them into Grubb's diaper bag.

Cheryl rolled Grubb over and dried his bottom. "Last time I take a vacation with you," she said. "No gambling, no shows, no fucking. I *said* . . ." She looked at him. "No fu—" The word caught in her throat.

He was aiming his pistol at her head.

Until he saw the orange 280Z rocket by him, the cop thought that the worst thing he was going to have to deal with on this shift was not smoking. He was wearing a patch on his left shoulder that was supposed to feed nicotine into his blood to keep him from craving cigarettes, but the urge to smoke was still there, so he fought it by eating donuts. He'd gained ten pounds in a week, and he was musing over the idea of inventing a donut patch when the sports car roared by him.

Out of habit, he butted a half-eaten cruller in the ashtray, hit the lights and siren, and pulled out in pursuit. The Z already had about eight blocks on him and he estimated it was doing about a hundred. He was reaching for the radio to call ahead for help when a black Mercedes pulled out from a side street in front of him. He slammed on the brakes and threw the cruiser sideways, bringing it to a stop not ten feet from impact. The Mercedes was at a dead stop, blocking both lanes. The cop watched the Z's tail-lights fade in the distance on the other side.

He killed the siren and switched the radio to the public address system. "Get out of the car, now!" He waited but no one got out of the car. In fact, he couldn't see a driver at all, yet the Mercedes was still running. He considered calling for backup, then decided to handle it himself. He stepped out of the cruiser with his gun drawn, careful to stay behind the car door.

"You, in the Mercedes, get out slowly." He saw something move in the car, but it didn't look like a person. Holding his revolver at ready, he shined his flashlight at the car. Movement, but no driver.

He saw three possibilities. The driver was unconscious, or was waiting to peel away when he moved away from the cruiser, or was lying in wait with a shotgun to blow his head off. He decided it would be safest to assume the last, and without further warning he crept to a spot just under the open driver's-side window. He heard a scratching sound just above his head and came up, gun first, to catch a glimpse of the back end of the skunk just as it sprayed him in the face.

As he wiped his eyes he heard laughing and the Mercedes pulling away.

Clyde, owner of Clyde's Cash for Your Car, said, "No offense, chief, but you don't see many Indians in Mercedes." He kicked a tire and bent down to look at the lines of the paint job for signs of bodywork, keeping a hand on his head to steady his toupee. "Looks clean."

"It's a good car," Coyote said.

Clyde narrowed his eyes and smiled. Clyde had seen a little too much sun in his sixty years and this sly smile, what he used to call his "gotcha" look, made him look like an old Chinese woman. "And you have the title, right, chief?"

"Title?"

"That's what I thought." Clyde stepped up to Coyote, his head about level with the trickster's sternum. "Are you a policeman, or are you working in the service of any law-enforcement agency?"

"Nope."

"Well then, let's do some business." Clyde grinned. "Now, you and I know that we could fry eggs on this car, am I right? Of course I am. And you're not from around here, or you'd have your own connections and wouldn't be here, am I right? Of course I am. And you don't want to take this car out on the interstate where the state patrol would spot it as hot in a second? No, you don't." He paused for effect, just to make sure everyone knew he was in control. "I'll give you five thousand dollars for it."

"Not enough," said Coyote. "Look, this car has a machine that tells you where you are."

Clyde glanced inside the Mercedes at the navigation system, then shrugged. "Chief, you see all these cars?" Clyde gestured to a dozen cars on his lot. Coyote looked around and nodded. "Well, all these cars got something that'll tell you where you're at. I call them windows. You look out of 'em. Now, do you want to sell a car?"

"Six thousand," Coyote said.

Clyde crossed his arms and waited, tapped his foot, smiled into the night sky.

"Five," Coyote said.

"I'll be right back with your money, chief. Can I have my boy give you a lift somewhere?"

"Sure," Coyote said.

Clyde went into his office, a mobile home whose entire side functioned as Clyde's sign. In a moment he returned with a stack of hundreds. He counted them into Coyote's hand. A greasy teenager pulled up in an old Chevy. "This is Clyde junior," Clyde said. "He'll take you wherever you need to go."

"It's a good car," Coyote said. He handed the keys to Clyde and climbed into the Chevy. As they pulled away Coyote dug into his medicine pouch and pulled out a small plastic box that had once been on Sam's key ring. He pushed the red button once, and a chirping sound came from under the hood of the Mercedes to signal that the alarm was armed.

Kiro Yashamoto stood in the corner of the treatment room watching two doctors battle for a man's life. One doctor was young, white, and wore a stethoscope around his neck. He was fighting death with electronic monitors, oxygen, a battery of injected drugs, and a degree from Michigan State. The other doctor was an old Indian man, as wrinkled and weathered as the patient, who fought with prayers, songs, and by blowing on the patient through a mouthful of charcoal. He held no degree, but had been called to healing by the trumpeting of a white elk in the Spirit World. Despite the difference in their methods, the two worked as a team. Kiro could see that they respected each other, and he wished that his children were here to see these two cultures working together not for profit, but out of a common compassion. Alas, he had left them outside in the clinic's small waiting room, and neither of the doctors would allow more people in here.

A tall, lanky Indian man dressed in denim stood in the corner opposite Kiro. His hair was cut short and shot with gray. Kiro guessed he was in his sixties, but it was hard to tell with these people. He saw Kiro watching and quietly crossed the room.

"My name is Harlan Hunts Alone," he said, extending his hand.

"How do you do," Kiro said. He took Harlan's hand and bowed slightly, then caught himself in the inappropriate gesture and felt embarrassed.

Harlan patted Kiro's shoulder. "Pokey is my brother. I wanted to thank you for bringing him here. The doctor said he would have died without your help."

"It was nothing," Kiro said.

"Just the same," Harlan smiled. The medicine man stopped singing and Harlan quickly turned to him.

"He's gone," the medicine man said.

The white doctor looked at the monitor. A steady blip played across the screen. "He's fine. His blood pressure's coming up."

"Not dead," said the medicine man. "Gone."

Pokey began mumbling, then speaking. Kiro could not hear what he was saying through the oxygen mask.

"That's not Crow. What is that?" asked the white doctor.

"Navaho," said the medicine man.

"He doesn't speak Navaho," Harlan said. "He doesn't even speak Crow."

"He doesn't *here*," the medicine man said. "He's not here."

· · ·

On a stone wall: carvings of dead gods and the shadow of a man with the head of a dog. Pokey looks, but there is no figure casting the shadow. He turns to run.

"Stop," the shadow says.

Pokey stops but does not look back. "Who are you?"

"Tell him there is death where he goes."

"Tell who?"

"The trickster. Tell him. And tell him I am coming back."

"Who are you?"

The shade and the wall are gone. Ahead lie prairies. Pokey runs, calls, "Old Man Coyote!"

"What? I'm busy. Twice in a few days is too much. Don't talk to me for another forty years."

"A shadow said to tell you that there is death where you are going."

"A shadow?"

"A man with the head of a dog. I thought it was you playing a trick on me."

"Nope. So he said that there is death where I am going. He ought to know. Anything else?"

"He said to tell you that he is coming back."

"Well, no shit. You have to go, old man. You're dying again."

"I am?"

"Yeah. Didn't you drink that Kool-Aid I left you?"

"There was no water. Who was—"

"Go now."

The green line went flat. The monitor screeched out an alarm.

"We're losing him," the doctor said. He grabbed a syringe, filled it with epinephrine, and drove it into Pokey's chest. The medicine man began to sing a death song.

CHAPTER TWENTY-SIX

HANG WITH A HORSE THIEF, WAKE UP WALKING

LAS VEGAS

Minty Fresh was staring at nothing and thinking "Zip-A-Dee-Doo-Dah" when the girl behind the desk grabbed his arm, startling him.

"Are you all right?" she said.

"Fine, what is it?"

"God, on the phone, for you."

"Thank you." Minty picked up the phone and tried to drive "Zip-A-Dee-Doo-Dah" out of his head. "M.F. here," he said.

"Your Indian is back in the building, main entrance. Keep an eye on him."

"Right." Minty hung up. He checked his watch and realized that he must have been staring for ten minutes before the call. Why couldn't he shake that song? He hadn't heard it since his grandmother had taken him to see *Song of the South* when he was a child. Grandma had heard the Uncle Remus stories of Br'er Fox and Br'er Rabbit from her own grandmother, who had been a slave. She said that the stories came with the slaves from West Africa. There, Br'er Rabbit was known as Esau, the trickster. Maybe it was the Indian talking about tricking people that had set it off.

Since the Indian had come into the casino, Minty had felt uneasy. It was as if the Indian could look into his soul and see secrets that he himself did not know. He looked up to see the Indian coming through the lobby.

Minty smiled. "Mr. Coyote, you're back."

"How do you know my name?"

Minty was spun by the question. He felt his shell of cool detachment cracking and dropping off like old paint. "I . . . I don't know. . . ."

"It's okay," Coyote said. "I want everyone to know my name. Not like you. You carry your name like a man with a knife hidden in his boot. You should wear your name like a red bow tie."

"I'll try to remember that," Minty said, trying to sound patronizing. If the casino knew his real name they'd have him greeting people in clown shoes and a purple wig within the hour. A red bow tie indeed.

Coyote fanned a handful of hundreds and waved them under Minty's nose. "Did you save my place at the table?"

"I'm sure we can find you a suitable place. Follow me."

Minty led Coyote to an out-of-the-way crap table where only a few players were gathered. One of them, a lanky middle-aged man in a cowboy hat and jeans, turned and looked Coyote up and down, then scoffed and turned to the stickman, shaking his head in disgust. "Prairie niggers," he said under his breath.

Minty moved up behind the cowboy and bent over until his mouth was even with the cowboy's ear. "I beg your pardon?"

The cowboy spun around and stumbled back against the table, his eyes wide. "Nothin'," he said. Minty remained crouched over, his face almost touching the cowboy's."

"Is there a problem, sir?"

"No. No problem," the cowboy said. He turned and scraped his chips off the table and quickly walked away.

Minty stood slowly and caught the stickman glaring at him. A wave of embarrassment burned over him. That sort of direct intimidation was completely out of line: bad form, bad judgment.

He imagined that there would be a call from God waiting for him when he returned to the desk. He turned to Coyote, who was staring down the front of a cocktail waitress's dress.

Minty said, "Can we get you something to drink?"

"Umbrellas and swords, lots of them."

"Very good." Minty nodded to the cocktail waitress. "Mai tai, extra fruit."

Coyote handed his cash to the dealer. "Black ones."

The dealer counted the money and handed it to the supervisor. "Changing five thousand." The other players looked up at Coyote, then Minty, then quickly looked down to avoid eye contact.

A pair of fresh-faced newlyweds stood at the head of the table, exchanging kisses and whispers. The stickman pushed the dice to the woman, who giggled as she picked them up. "That's my lucky girl," her husband said, kissing her ear.

"New shooter coming out," the stickman said.

"Is she lucky?" Coyote asked.

"She's made me the luckiest man in the world," the young husband said. The girl blushed and buried her face in her husband's shoulder.

Minty found that he was irritated by the couple's fawning and wondered why. He saw it ten times a day: newlyweds at the tables acting like they were the first to discover love, glued together for a few days of starry-eyed public foreplay between bouts in a hotel bed. And they'd be back in twenty years, separating when they hit the door, her locking onto a slot machine while he played blackjack and dreamed of sneaking off to a jiggle show. Minty wanted to warn them that time would make hypocrites of them. *One day you'll wake up and find that you're married to a husband and a father, a wife and a mother, and you'll wonder whatever happened to the lover that you swapped spit and sweetness with over a craps table.* But why did it matter? It never had before. *It's this Indian,* Minty thought. *He's making me lose it.*

Coyote placed all his chips on the pass line. "Are you lucky?" he said to the bride.

She smiled and nodded. Her husband placed a two-dollar chip on the pass line. "Go ahead, honey." He held her shoulders, bracing her against the weight of the dice, and the girl let fly.

"Two! Snake eyes! No pass!" The stickman raked in the bets. Coyote dove over the table and caught the woman by the throat, riding her to the floor. The husband stepped aside as the light of his life went down.

"You are not lucky!" Coyote screeched. "You lost all my money! You are not lucky!" The girl clawed at his face with lace-gloved hands.

Minty Fresh caught Coyote by the back of the neck and pulled him off the girl with one hand, waving away the security jesters who had appeared with the other. "I've got this handled." He nodded to the girl on the floor and the jesters helped her to her feet.

Minty dragged Coyote away from the table.

"She lied. She lied."

"Perhaps you'd like to rest for a while," Minty said, as if he was taking Coyote's hat rather than dragging him across the floor. "Can we get you something to eat? The dining room is closed, but our snack bar is open." Minty was acutely aware that he was in the process of losing his job. He should have turned the Indian over to security. After years as the officer of order, he was falling apart.

"I need to get more money," Coyote said, calming down now.

Minty set Coyote on his feet, keeping a restraining hand on the trickster's neck. "You're sharing a room with Mr. Hunter, aren't you? I'll have the bellman take you up to the room."

Coyote thought for a moment. "No, my money is at another hotel and I don't have a car."

"That's not a problem, sir. I'll call around a limo and drive you myself."

Minty steered Coyote out a side exit of the casino and walked him to the valet booth, where he ordered a limo from the attendant. In a moment a stretch Lincoln pulled up to the curb and an eager squire held the door while Coyote climbed in.

Minty adjusted the seat before climbing in; still, his knees were up around the wheel. As he drove he tried to form some sort of rationalization for his mistakes—something to wash him clean with the management. Perhaps the Indian would lose enough money to justify the lapses of judgment.

"Where are you staying, sir?"

"The Frontier."

Minty nodded and pulled out onto the strip. "Call Camelot," he said.

A series of beeps sounded in the car and a woman's voice came on the speaker. "Camelot."

"Desk, please."

"Thank you."

A series of clicks and a different voice. "Camelot, reservations."

"This is M.F.," Minty said. "I'm taking a customer to the Frontier. I'll return in a few minutes."

"Very good, sir. There's a message for you from upstairs. Do you want me to put you through?"

"No. Thank you." There was no sense in rushing to the mailbox if you knew there was a letter bomb waiting for you. "Off," Minty said. There was a click.

Coyote was hanging on the back of the seat, looking down at the cellular phone. "You can talk to machines?"

"Just this one. Voice activated so you can keep your hands on the wheel."

"I can talk to animals. Can you take other forms?"

Minty smiled. The Indian was a nut case, but at least he was an amusing nut case. "Actually," he said. "This *is* another form. In real life I'm a short Jewish woman."

"I wouldn't have known," Coyote said. "It must be the sunglasses." He looked at the dashboard. "Does this car tell you where you are?"

"No."

"Ha! Mine is better."

"Pardon me?"

"Follow that car," Coyote said, pointing ahead to a 280Z with a shattered back window turning off the strip.

For a second, Minty was tempted to follow the car, then he caught himself. "I can't do that, sir." What was it about this Indian that he could twist the world? If he wasn't fired when he got back to the casino, Minty decided he would hire a hooker to rub his temples and tell him that everything was okay until he believed it or ran out of money, whichever came first. Maybe the Indian was right about people wanting to be tricked.

"I need cigarettes," Coyote said.

"We have complimentary cigarettes at the casino, sir."

"No. I need some now. At that store." Coyote pointed to a minimart across the strip.

"As you wish," Minty said. He pulled the limo into the minimart and turned off the engine.

Coyote said, "I'm out of money until we go to my motel."

"Allow me, sir," Minty opened the car door and unfolded himself onto the curb.

"I'll pay you back."

"Not necessary, sir. Camelot will take care of it."

"Salems," Coyote said. "A carton."

Minty closed the door and walked into the minimart. He found the cigarettes, then grabbed a package of Twinkies off the shelf for himself. He checked the date on the Twinkies: July 1956. Good. They had another thirty years of guaranteed freshness.

He fell in line behind a drunk man who was waving a gas card at the clerk. "Look, man, it's this simple. You charge my card for forty bucks' worth of gas and give me twenty in cash. You get a hundred-percent profit."

Minty listened to the clerk try to explain why this couldn't be done and smiled in sympathy, as if to say, "They lose their money, then they lose their minds." The clerk rolled his eyes as if to say, "This might take a while."

Minty looked outside to check on his passenger and saw the limo backing away from the curb. He tossed the cigarettes and

Twinkies on the counter and ran out, losing his glasses as he ducked to get through the doors. He reached the street as the limo accelerated out of reach, then stopped and stared down the strip, watching the Lincoln's taillights until they blended into a million other lights. Acid panic rose in his throat, then subsided, replaced by the resolved calm of the doomed.

He turned and walked slowly back to the minimart to find his glasses. As he reached the door, the drunk, his gas card still in hand, stumbled through and Minty caught him by the shoulders to avoid a collision. The drunk looked up, then tore himself away and stepped back. "Jesus Christ, boy! What happened to your eyes? You been sittin' too close to the TV?"

Minty raised his hand to cover his golden eyes, then dropped it and shrugged. "Zip-A-Dee-Doo-Dah," he said with a grin.

Dawn was starting to break and the sky was turning from red to blue. Coyote sat in the limo, which was parked a block behind Calliope's orange Z, which was parked a block away from Nardonne's Harley-Davidson Shop. Lonnie's bike was parked outside.

"Call Sam," Coyote said. Nothing happened. He pounded on the car phone. "I said, call Sam." Nothing happened.

"Call Sam's room," Coyote said to the phone. Nothing happened and the trickster yipped with anger. "Call Sam's room or I'll rip your cord off." He picked up the receiver and beat it on the dashboard, then he saw a sticker with the casino's logo stuck to the receiver. "Call Camelot," he said. The phone lit up and beeped through some numbers.

The phone rang once and a woman answered. "Camelot."

"I want to talk to Sam."

"Do you have a last name, sir?"

"No, just Coyote."

"I'm sorry, sir, we have no guest listed under Coyote."

"Not me, I'm here. His name is Hunter."

"We have no Coyote Hunter. There's a Samuel Hunter."

"That's him."

"One minute while I connect you."

"I'll bet you're ugly in person."

"What?" Sam's sleepy voice came over the phone.

"Sam, I found the girl."

"Where? Where are you? What time is it? Who's ugly?"

"Morning. You have to come here. I'm at a place called Nardonne's Harley-Davidson Shop. The girl is here, and the motorcycle with her picture on it is parked outside."

"Give me directions. I'll be there in a few minutes. Keep Calliope there. I have to check out and get the car."

"Take a cab."

"You didn't take my car?"

"No, this car is better. You can talk to the phone. Your car is gone. I sold it."

"You what?"

"Take a cab. I'm in a big black car. Off."

The phone clicked, cutting Sam off in the middle of a tirade. Coyote didn't know whether the girl had a phone in her car, but he decided to try. "Call the girl," he said to the phone.

The phone beeped through the numbers. "This is Carla," a sexy woman's voice said. "Would you like this on your phone bill or your credit card?"

"Phone bill," Coyote said.

"If you like leather, press one," Carla said. "Twins, press two. For California blondes, press three. Big bottoms, press—" Coyote picked up the handset and pressed three.

Another sexy voice came on, "Hi, I'm Brandy, who are you?"

"Coyote."

"Would you like to know what I'm wearing, Coyote?"

"No, I have to tell the girl to stay here until Sam comes."

"We'll take as long as Sam needs. Is Sam getting hard?"

"No, he's pissed off about his car."

There was a pause and the sound of her lighting a cigarette. Brandy said, "Okay. Let's start over."

• • •

Minty waited for the second limo at the pay phone outside the minimart. He flipped through his address book until he found the detective's number, then dialed.

The phone rang twice, then there was the sound of the receiver rattling and falling. Finally a sleepy, hostile man's voice said, "What?"

Minty said, "Jake, this is M.F., at Camelot."

"Fuck that. This is harassment. It's ... it's five thirty in the morning. You said I could have all the time I needed to pay."

"I'm not calling about that, Jake. I need a favor. One of the limos has been stolen."

"Why call me at home? You guys have LoJack beacons in those limos, don't you? Call the station. They'll track it and have it back in half an hour."

"I can't call the station, Jake. This is delicate. I need to get it back without bringing the police into it."

"You're fucked. The LoJack trackers are installed in the cruisers."

"Can you put one in one of our limos? Just until I find the stolen one."

"No way. The tracking system takes hours to install."

"Jake, I need a favor. Just a favor. I haven't mentioned what you owe us."

"This strong-arm shit isn't your style, M.F."

"But you *can* get use of a unit with the LoJack tracker in it?"

"Meet me at the station in a half hour."

"What's the range on the tracker?"

"About a mile, depending on the terrain. Farther in the desert. You're not going to be able to cover much area with only one car."

"Then make it fifteen minutes. And Jake—"

"What?"

"Thank you." Minty hung up. *So much for the police,* he thought. *Now if I can get it back before the casino finds out. If not, I guess it's time to go shopping for a red bow tie.*

·   ·   ·

Calliope was sure she could do it: if Grubb was trapped under a Chrysler she could lift the car and pull him out. You heard about it all the time: *Hundred-Pound Mom Lifts Two-Ton Car to Save Trapped Tot.* It seemed to happen often enough that it should be part of Lamaze training. "Okay, now breathe, focus, grab the bumper . . . now lift!" Yep, she could do it—a Chrysler on each arm if she had to. She wasn't so sure about getting Grubb back from Lonnie. Maybe if that other woman wasn't with him, being so hostile and negative.

She was feeling a little better now that the sun was coming up. She'd been shivering since the punks had broken her back window, from nerves and the cold. And she didn't have enough gas money to leave the Z running with the heater on while she waited for Lonnie to come out of the Harley shop. She might not have enough to make it home as it was. Besides, something was wrong with the car; she'd tached it too high while running from the police and something had given way in clatter and smoke.

As she watched, Lonnie came through the front door of the shop carrying Grubb's diaper bag. Calliope swallowed hard, trying to push down her fear—fear of failure. She got out of the Z. The woman followed Lonnie holding Grubb in her arms. Calliope ran toward them, then stopped when she saw the woman's face. It was like one painful purple bruise with eyes.

"Lonnie," Calliope called.

Lonnie and the woman turned. Grubb saw his mother and reached out. Lonnie pushed down Grubb's hand. "What are you doing here?"

"I came to get Grubb. You shouldn't have taken him."

"Talk to the judge. He's mine half the time."

He was right. Calliope had gone to Social Services once before when Lonnie took Grubb on a road trip. Her caseworker told her that the law couldn't do anything to help.

"You don't want him. You just want to hurt me."

Lonnie laughed, threw his head back, and shook with laughter. For all the times he had postured and threatened and screamed and pounded, he had never really scared her. She was scared now.

"You shouldn't take him on a run like this, Lonnie. What if you get busted?"

"Run? What run? We're just on a little family camping trip, aren't we, Cheryl?" The woman tucked her face behind Grubb.

"Give him to me, please," Calliope pleaded.

Lonnie climbed onto his bike grinning and hit the starter. The bike fired up and Lonnie shouted over the engine, "Go home. I'll bring him back in a few days." Cheryl climbed on behind him and he dropped the bike into gear.

"No!" Calliope started to run after them. Lonnie gunned the bike and roared off.

She shuffled to a stop and saw Grubb reaching out over Cheryl's shoulder. Her eyes blurred with tears. She turned and ran to her car, wiped her eyes, and saw the limo parked down the street. Someone was sitting in it, just watching her. "What are you looking at?" she screamed.

Sam made the chambermaid help him search the hotel room for his wallet for fifteen minutes before giving up and leaving her with a promise of a tip on the credit card. He was thinking *This is like being stuck in some Kafkaesque Roadrunner cartoon* when the taxi from the Acme Cab Company pulled up, the driver wearing a fez. *Animated by Hieronymus Bosch,* Sam thought.

In the cab, he said, "Do you know a Harley-Davidson shop called Nardonne's?"

"Bad part of town. Cost you double."

"It's broad daylight."

"Oh, it is. My shift is over. Sorry."

"Okay, double," Sam said. Why quibble? He couldn't pay the guy anyway.

When they pulled in behind the limo, Sam said, "Wait here, I'll get your money." He got out and looked down the street to the Harley shop, then went up to the limo and pounded on the blacked-out window. The window whirred down. Coyote grinned.

"Where is she?"

"Took off. Just now."

"Why didn't you stop her?"

"She didn't want to be stopped. We'll find her—she's following the biker, and we know where he's going."

The cabdriver beeped his horn. "Give me my wallet," Sam said. Coyote handed the wallet out the window. Sam rifled through it and came up empty. "There's no money left."

"Nope," Coyote said.

The cabdriver leaned on the horn. Sam signaled for him to wait, ran around to the other side of the limo, and got in.

"Go," Sam said.

"What about the cabdriver?"

"Fuck him."

"That's the spirit." Coyote started the limo and peeled away. He checked the rearview mirror. "He's not following."

"Good."

"He's talking to his radio. Got a smoke?"

Sam dug a pack of cigarettes out of his jacket pocket, tapped one out, and lit it. "Where's my car?"

"I sold it."

"You can't sell it without the title."

"I got a good deal, five thousand."

"Are you nuts? Five thousand wouldn't buy the stereo."

"I needed to win my money back. I won a lot of money on the machine you put the cards in, but a shaman with a stick won it back from me."

Sam butted his cigarette in the ashtray and hung his head in his hands, trying to let it all sink in. "So you sold my car for five grand?"

"Yep." Coyote snatched the mashed cigarette and relit it.

"And where is that money?"

"The shaman had strong cheating medicine."

"That's the kind of thinking that got Manhattan sold for a box of beads."

"So they still tell that story? It was one of my best tricks. They gave us many beads for that island. They didn't know that you can't own land."

Sam sighed and slouched in his seat, thinking he should be angry, or worried about his car, but strangely he was more concerned with catching Calliope. They were on the highway now. Sam glanced at the speedometer. "Slow down to the speed limit. We don't need cop trouble. I'm assuming you stole this car."

"I counted coup: stealing a tethered horse."

"Tell me," Sam said.

Coyote told the story of Minty and the limo, turning it into a fable full of danger and magic, making himself the hero. He was coming to the part about the car phone when it rang.

Sam reached for the answer button and pulled back his hand in disgust. "What's this gunk all over the phone? It looks like—"

"I'm not to that part of the story yet."

"Then you answer it."

"Speak," Coyote said, and the phone lit up and clicked. "Is that you, Brandy?"

A very deep, calm voice came over the speakerphone, "I want the car back, now. Pull over and stop. I'm a couple of minutes behind you. The police are—"

"Off," Coyote said. The phone hung up. Coyote turned to Sam. "This is a good car. You can talk to the phone. Her name is Brandy. She's very friendly."

"Uh-huh," Sam said.

"That wasn't her."

"Pull off at the next exit."

CHAPTER TWENTY-SEVEN

FOOD, GAS, ENLIGHTENMENT, NEXT RIGHT

KING'S LAKE, NEVADA

The exit sign said, KING'S LAKE, but when they pulled off and followed the ramp around the base of a mesa, there was no lake, no life at all, just a dirt road and a strip of gray wooden buildings with faded facades. A weathered wooden sign read, EMERGENCY, NEVADA. The population had been crossed out and repainted a dozen times until, finally, someone had painted a big zero at the bottom and the words *We gived up.* Coyote stopped the car.

"What do you want to do here?"

"I don't know, but we had to get off the highway before they caught up with us." Sam got out of the car and peered down the empty dirt street, shielding his eyes against the sun with his hand. A prairie dog scampered across the road and under the wooden sidewalk. "This road continues out of town. Maybe it joins up with another major road somewhere else. We need a map."

"No map in the car," Coyote said. "We can ask someone."

Sam looked around at the empty buildings. "Right, let's just stop in at the chamber of commerce and ask someone that's been dead for a hundred years."

"Can we do that?" Coyote asked, with complete sincerity.

"No, we can't do that! It's a ghost town. There's no one here."

"I was going to ask that prairie dog." Coyote walked to where the prairie dog had disappeared under the walkway. "Hey, little one, come out."

Sam stood behind the trickster, shaking his head. He heard a squeak from under the walk.

Coyote looked to Sam. "He doesn't trust you. He won't come out unless you go away."

"Tell him we're in a hurry." Sam couldn't believe he was being snubbed by a rodent.

"He knows that, but he says you have shifty eyes. Go over there and wait." Coyote pointed down the sidewalk.

Sam walked past a hitching post and sat on a bench in front of the abandoned saloon. He watched the road leading to the highway, waiting for the dust cloud from pursuing police cars. The road remained empty. He watched the prairie dog scamper out from under the sidewalk and stand on his hind legs as Coyote talked to him. Maybe he had been a little hasty in thinking Calliope nuts for talking to her kitchen pals. They probably thought he had shifty eyes as well.

After a few moments of talking and chattering Coyote threw his head back and laughed, then left the prairie dog in the street and came to where Sam was sitting.

"You've got to hear this one," Coyote said. "This farmer has a pig with a wooden leg—"

"Hey," Sam interrupted. "Does he know where the road goes?"

"Oh, yeah. But this is a really good joke. You see—"

"Coyote!" Sam shouted.

Coyote looked hurt. "You're nasty. No wonder he doesn't trust you. He says that he saw an orange sports car go by a while ago. He says that there's a repair place down the road."

"Tell him thanks," Sam said. Coyote headed back toward the

prairie dog. Sam dug into his windbreaker for his cigarettes and found a chocolate mint he had taken from the hotel room pillow the night before. "Wait," Sam called. He ran to Coyote's side. The prairie dog bolted under the sidewalk. "Let me talk to him."

Sam bent down and placed the mint in the dirt by the sidewalk. "Look, we really appreciate your help."

The prairie dog didn't answer. "I'm not a bad guy once you get to know me," Sam said. He waited, wondering what exactly he was waiting for. After a minute he started feeling really stupid. "Okay then, have a nice day."

He went back to where Coyote stood looking at a sign on the saloon door. *NO INDIANS OR DOGS ALLOWED.*

Coyote said, "What do they have against dogs?"

"What about the Indians part?"

Coyote shrugged.

"It pisses me off." Sam yanked the sign off the door and threw it into the street.

"Good, you're still alive. Let's go." Coyote turned and headed for the car.

"I'll drive," Sam said.

Coyote threw the keys over his shoulder. Sam snatched them out of the air. As they pulled away the prairie dog dashed into the street and grabbed the mint thinking, *That pig joke works every time.*

They drove for twenty minutes, bouncing the big Lincoln over ruts and rocks, and pushing it through washed-out, wind-eroded terrain where the road was reduced to the mere suggestion of tire tracks. The cellular phone rang twice more, but they did not answer it. Sam was suspecting that, once again, Coyote was playing some sort of trick when he spotted the corrugated steel building sticking up out of the desert. The building consisted of one story, roughly the size of a two-car garage. The steel walls were striped with rust and pulling away from the frame in places. The area around the building was littered with abandoned vehicles, some dating back fifty years. Above the doorway, a ragged hole that had been cut with a torch, hung an elegantly hand-lettered sign that read, SATORI JAPANESE AUTO REPAIR. In the doorway stood a slightly built Oriental man in saffron robes, grinning as they pulled up. Calliope's Z was parked in front.

Sam stopped the car and got out. The Oriental man folded his hands and bowed. Sam nodded in return and approached the man. "Do you know where the girl is that was driving that car?"

"What is the sound of one hand clapping?" the monk said.

Sam said, "Excuse me?"

The monk ran to Sam and jumped up, screaming in Sam's face, "Don't think. Act!"

Thinking he was being attacked, Sam raised his arms to cover his face and inadvertently hit the monk in the mouth with his elbow, knocking the little man to the ground.

The monk looked up at Sam and smiled. "That was the right answer." His teeth were red with blood.

"I'm sorry," Sam said, offering his hand to help the monk up. "I didn't know what you were doing."

The monk waved Sam away, climbed to his feet, and began to dust himself off. "The first step to knowledge is not knowing. The girl is inside with the Master."

"Thanks," Sam said. He motioned for Coyote to follow and went into the building. It was one room, dimly lit from the doorway and by sunlight filtering through the gaps in the walls. Around the edges, workbenches were stacked with greasy car parts and tools. In the center of the room, on a grass mat, Calliope sat with another monk, this one ancient, drinking tea from tiny cups. She looked up and saw Sam, then without a word ran into his arms.

"I lost him, Sam. The car started making this horrible noise and I had to pull off the highway. Lonnie took Grubb and he's gone."

Sam held her and patted her head, telling her it would be okay, not really believing it, but knowing that was what you were supposed to say. She was soft and warm against him and a musky smell of girl sweat and jasmine was coming off her hair. He felt himself getting aroused and hated himself for the inappropriateness of the feeling, thinking, *You sick bastard.*

Almost as in answer, Calliope said, "You feel too good," and buried her face in his chest. She was crying.

Behind them, still standing in the doorway, Coyote said, "Let's go."

Calliope looked around at him, then to Sam. Sam said, "A friend. Calliope, this is Coyote. Coyote, Calliope."

"Howdy," Coyote said. Calliope smiled.

"The Master will now fix the car," the younger monk said. Sam looked to the tatami mat; the old monk was gone. The young monk turned and went out into the sun.

Outside, the Z's hood was open and the old monk was bent over the engine, running his hands over the hoses and wires, but staring off into the distance. Sam realized that he was blind, and noticed that there were fingers missing from each of his hands.

"What's he doing?" Coyote asked.

"Quiet," the young monk said. "He is finding the problem."

"We really have to get going," Sam said. "Can we leave the car here and pick it up later?"

The monk said, "Does a dog have a Buddha nature?"

"Does a fish have a watertight asshole?" said Coyote.

The young monk turned to the trickster and bowed. "You are wise," he said.

"This is nuts," Sam said. "We've got another car. Let's go."

"We've lost them," Calliope said.

"No, we haven't. We know where they're going, Cal."

"How do you know?"

"It's a long story. Coyote helped."

"Not enough," Coyote said. He pointed to the police cruiser that was bouncing across the desert toward them. Sam looked to the limo and realized that they had run out of time, and, more important, places to run. The cruiser slid to a stop by the limo and they were all engulfed by a cloud of dust. When it cleared, a seven-foot black man stood beside the limo. A bald man in a sport coat was leveling a riot shotgun over the hood at them.

"I'd like the keys to the limousine, please," Minty said.

Calliope looked at Sam. "Are we in trouble?"

"This is not good," Sam said.

The monk said, "Life is suffering."

"You need to get laid," Coyote said.

Sam dug into his pocket for the keys. "Careful," said the man with the gun.

Minty Fresh approached Sam. "Relax, Jake," he said. Then to Sam, "Mr. Hunter, the police are not really involved in this. I just want two things. I want the keys to the car, and I want to know what the hell is going on here."

"Quiet!" the monk said. "The Master is finished." They looked to the Z, where the old monk was staring blankly in their direction.

"Disharmony in the cam chakra," he announced. The young monk bowed. Sam wondered about the Master's missing fingers.

"Well?" Minty said.

Sam said, "Do you have a little time?"

Minty Fresh sat on the tatami mat with Sam while the young monk, who they had found out was named Steve, served them tea. He'd sent Jake back to town and the others were outside fiddling with the broken sports car. Minty wanted some answers.

"Mr. Hunter," he began. "There is something very strange about your friend."

"Really? He seems fine to me. Tell me, though. Do you think I have shifty eyes?" Sam affected his best innocent look.

Oh, no, two of them, Minty thought. "They look normal to me." They didn't look normal at all—they were golden. Minty hadn't noticed before.

Sam said, "I mean, do I look untrustworthy to you?"

"Mr. Hunter, you stole my employer's car."

"I'm really sorry about that. Besides that, though. Do I look shifty?"

Minty sighed. "No, not particularly."

"How about if you were shorter, say, eight inches tall."

"Mr. Hunter, what is this all about?"

"We really needed the car. It doesn't justify taking it, but we would have brought it back."

"Look, I'm not going to involve the police in this. Just tell me."

Sam took Minty through the story of Lonnie taking Grubb and the chase, leaving out as many details about Coyote as he could, making their destination in South Dakota seem close, easy. The story was slanted, however; Sam told it with a purpose in mind, thinking as he spoke, *You can't sell if you don't pitch.*

Sam closed, "If we don't have the limo we won't be able to find Lonnie and get Calliope's baby back. You have a mother, don't you?" Sam waited.

"I'm sorry, Mr. Hunter, I can't let you have it. It's not mine. I'd lose my job."

"We'll bring it back after we get Grubb."

"I'm sorry," Minty said. He climbed to his feet and walked to the door, then turned. "I'm really sorry." He pushed his sunglasses up on his face and ducked through the hole in the steel. Sam followed him out.

"Mr. F.," Sam called.

Minty looked up as he reached the car. "Yes?"

"Thanks for not going to the cops. I understand your position."

Minty nodded and got in the Lincoln.

Calliope came up beside Sam and stood with him watching Minty drive away. She said, "Grubb is all I have."

Sam reached out and took her hand, not knowing what to say, having failed at the only thing he was really good at, talking people into doing things they didn't want to do.

The young monk came out of the door behind them. "The

Master is fixing your car," he said. He was stirring some green tea into an earthenware bowl with a bamboo whisk. "More tea?"

They stood together in the sun, watching the old man work. He fingered each bolt carefully before fitting a wrench to it, then removed the bolt so quickly that his hands blurred with the movement.

Sam said, "How long . . ."

"Don't talk to him when he works," Steve cautioned. "He will finish when he finishes. But don't talk to him. When you work, work. When you talk, talk."

"Do you get many customers? I mean, you are pretty far out here."

"Three," Steve said. He was wearing a straw hat to protect his shaved head.

"Three today?"

"No, just three."

"Then what do you do in the meantime?"

"We wait."

"That's all?"

Steve said, "Is that all the patriarch Daruma did at the wall for nine years?" There was no anger in his voice. "We wait."

"But how do you pay your rent, buy food?"

"There is no rent. The owner of King's Lake, Augustus Brine, brings us food. He is a fisherman."

"King's Lake is up the road, right? What is it, a resort?"

"A house of pleasure."

"A whorehouse that supports Buddhist monks?"

"How sweet," Calliope said.

"He's got it," Coyote said, pointing to the Master, who was holding up a rod of polished metal.

"A bent push rod," Steve said. The Master carried the push rod into the shop. They all followed and watched as the old man tightened the rod into a vise. He picked up a hammer and stood over the vise, his free hand feeling the rod. Without warning the old man screamed and delivered a clanging blow to the push rod, then bowed and set the hammer on the bench.

"Fixed," Steve said, bowing.

"Is that how he lost his fingers?"

"To achieve enlightenment, one must give up the things of this world."

"Like piano lessons," Coyote said.

CHAPTER TWENTY-EIGHT

HOPE IS BULLETPROOF, TRUTH JUST HARD TO HIT

As Minty Fresh drove back to Las Vegas he thought about what Sam had said: *"You have a mother, don't you?"* And the question set Minty Fresh to thinking about a phone call from his mother that had changed his life.

"You're the only one left can do something, baby. The others are too far or too far gone. Please come home, baby, I need you." (Even when he had to duck to pass through her front door she still called him "baby.") That tone: he'd heard it in her voice before, when she was tugging at her husband to get him to stop strapping her youngest. But he hadn't gone back for her, had he? It was a call deep with duty and silent pride that brought him home. He went back for Nathan.

Nathan Fresh had never been home when any of his nine children were born. He was a sailor, and as far as he knew, when you came home from sea a new child would be waiting for you. The others grew an inch or two at a time, and the shoes that one was wearing when you left would be on the next one down when you got home. He loved his children, foreign creatures that they were, and trusted his wife to raise them—as long as they could line up, snap to, and pass inspection when he came home. And although he was gone most of the time, making the high seas safe for democracy, he was a presence in the house: photographs in crisp dress whites and blues stared down from the walls; commendations and medals; a letter once a week, read out loud at the supper table; and a thousand warnings of what Papa would do to a doomed misbehaver when he got home. To the Fresh children, Papa was only a little bit more real than Santa Claus, and only a bit more conspicuous.

On the ship, Chief Petty Officer Nathan Fresh was known only as the Chief: feared and respected, tough and fair, starched, razor-creased, and polished, always in trim and intolerant of anyone who wasn't. The Chief: did you notice that he was black? only five foot five? barely 130 pounds? No, but did you see his eyes, like smiles, when he was showing the pictures of his kids—when he was telling tales of lobbing shells the size of refrigerators into the hills of Korea? Did you ever mention retirement to him? That's a frost, that's a chill.

Minty Fresh, the youngest of nine, the one born with golden eyes, knew the chill. "He's not mine," Papa said—said it only once. Minty stayed out of Papa's way when he could, wore dark glasses when he couldn't. At age ten he stood six feet tall and no amount of slouching would roll Papa's resentment off his back. His place in the family was a single line at the bottom of a letter—"Baby's fine too"—far enough from "Love, Momma" to deny the association. At night, by flashlight, he wrote his own letters: "My team is going to the state championships. I was voted all-conference. The press calls me M.F. Cool, because I wear tinted goggles when I play, and sunglasses during interviews. The colleges are calling already and sending recruiters to the games. You'd be proud. Momma swears you're wrong." In the bathroom he watched the letters go, in tiny pieces, around the bowl, down, and out to sea.

Minty Fresh left for the University of Nevada at Las Vegas the week after high school graduation, the same week that Nathan Fresh took his mandatory retirement from the navy and came home, to San Diego, for good. The coach at UNLV wanted Minty to lift weights all summer, beef up for the big boys. The coach gave Momma Fresh a new washer and dryer. Nathan Fresh put them out on the porch.

The day before the first game, when UNLV was going to unleash its secret weapon on the unsuspecting NCAA—a seven-foot center with a three-foot vertical leap who could bench-press four hundred pounds and shoot ninety percent from the free-throw line—M.F. Cool got the call. "I'm on my way, Momma," he said.

"My father needs me," he said to the coach.

"When we brought you up from nothing, gave you a full scholarship, put up with the goggles and the shades and the silly name? Gave your mother a washer and dryer? No. You won't miss the season opener. You're mine."

"How touching," Minty said. "No one has ever said that to me before." Perhaps, he thought later, stuffing the coach in that locker had been a mistake, but at the time a few hours in seclusion, among socks and jocks, seemed just what the coach needed to gain some perspective. He broke the key off in the padlock, tore the M.F. Cool label off the locker, and went home.

"He's been gone four days now," Momma said. "He drinks and gambles, hangs out at the pool hall 'til all hours. But he always came home before. Since he retired, he's changed. I don't know him."

"Neither do I."

"Bring him home, baby."

Minty took a cab to the waterfront and ducked in and out of a dozen bars and pool halls before he realized that Nathan would go anywhere but the waterfront. There were sailors there, reminders. After two days of searching he found Nathan, barely able to stand, shooting pool with a fat Mexican in a cantina outside of Tijuana.

"Chief, let's go. Momma's waiting."

"I ain't no chief. Go away. I got a game going."

Minty put his hand on his father's shoulder, cringing at the smell of tequila and vomit coming off him. "Papa, she's worried."

The fat Mexican moved around the table to where Minty stood and pushed him away with a cue stick. "My friend, this one goes nowhere until we get what he owes us." Two other Mexicans moved off their barstools. "Now you go." He poked Minty in the chest with the cue stick and Nathan Fresh wheeled on him and bellowed in finest chief petty officer form.

"Don't you touch my son, you fucking greaseball."

The Mexican's cue caught Nathan on the bridge of the nose and Nathan went down, limp. Minty palmed the Mexican's head and slammed his face into the pool table, then turned in time to catch each of the two coming off the bar with a fist in the throat. Another with a knife went airborne into a Corona mirror, which broke louder than his neck. Two more went down, one with a skull fractured by a billiard ball; one, his shoulder wrenched from its socket, went into shock. There were seven in all, broken or unconscious, before the cantina cleared and Minty, dripping blood from a cut on his arm, carried his father out.

Momma met them at the hospital and stood with Minty as Nathan came around. "What are you doing here, you yellow-eyed freak?" Minty walked out of the room. Momma followed.

"He don't mean it, baby. He really don't."

"I know, Momma."

"Where you going?"

"Back to Vegas."

"You call when he sobers up. He'll want to talk to you."

"Call me if you need me, Momma," he said. He kissed her on the forehead and walked out.

She called him every week, and he could tell by her whisper that Nathan was home, was fine. It made him fine too—not M. F. Cool, just M.F., the one who handled things. All that was missing was the feeling of being needed, essential, bound to duty.

Sam had said, "You have a mother, don't you?"

Minty steered the limo off at the next exit, across the overpass, and back on the highway, headed back to King's Lake.

It had taken Steve, the Buddhist monk, only a half hour to put the car back together. When Sam tried to figure out a way to pay for the repairs, Steve said, "All misery comes from desire and connection to the material. Go." Sam said thanks.

Now he was driving the Z into Utah. Calliope was asleep on Coyote's lap. Coyote snored. Sam passed the time trying to figure out how long it would take to get to Sturgis, South Dakota, the location of the rally that the Guild was going to. About twenty hours, he thought, if the car held together. From time to time he looked over at Calliope and felt a twinge of jealousy toward Coyote. She looked like a child when she slept. He wanted to protect her, hold her. But it was that childlike quality that frightened him as well. Her ability to dismiss facts, deny the negative, to see things so clearly, but so clearly wrong. It was as if she refused to accept what any reasonable adult knew: the world was a dangerous, hostile place.

He brushed a strand of hair out of her face before looking back to the road. She murmured, and came awake with a yawn. "I was dreaming about sea turtles—that they were really dinosaur angels."

"And?"

"That's all. It was a dream."

Sam had been thinking about it too long, so there was anger in his voice when he asked her, "Why didn't you call me before you went after Lonnie?"

"I don't know."

"I was worried. If it weren't for Coyote, I would have never found you."

"Are you two related?" She seemed to be ignoring his anger. "You look a lot alike. He has the same eyes and skin."

"No, I just know him." Sam didn't want to explain, he wanted an answer. "Why didn't you call me?"

Calliope recoiled at his harshness. "I had to go get Grubb."

"I could have gone with you."

"Would you have? Is that what you wanted?"

"I'm here, aren't I? It would have been a hell of a lot easier if I didn't have to chase you across two states."

"And maybe you wouldn't have done it if it was a hell of a lot easier. Would you?"

The question, and her tone, threw him. He thought for a minute, looking at the road. "I don't know."

"I know," she said softly. "I don't know much, but I know about that. You're not the only man that ever wanted me or wanted to rescue me. They all do, Sam. Men are addicted to the wanting. You like the idea of having me, and the idea of rescuing me. That's what attracted you to me in the first place, remember."

"That's not true."

"It is true. That's why I had sex with you so soon."

"I don't get it." This was not at all how Sam had expected her to react. His brief moment of self-righteousness had degraded into self-doubt.

"I did it to see if you could get past the fantasy of wanting me and rescuing me, to the reality of me. Me, with a baby, and no education, and a lousy job. Me, with no idea what I'm going to do next. I can't stand the wanting coming at me all the time. I have to get past it, like I did with you, or ignore it."

"So you were testing me?" Sam said. "That's why you took off without telling me?"

"No, it wasn't a test. I liked you, but I have Grubb to take care of now. I can't afford to hope." She was starting to tear up. Sam felt as if he'd just been caught stomping a litter of kittens. She took Grubb's blanket from behind the seat and wiped her eyes.

"You okay?" Sam asked.

She nodded. "Sometimes I want to be touched and I pretend that I'm in love—and that someone loves me. I just take my moments and forget about hope. You were going to be a moment, Sam. But I started to have hope. If I'd called you and you had said no, then I would have lost my hope again."

"That's not how I am," Sam said.

"How are you, then?"

Sam drove in silence for a while, trying to think of something to say—the right thing to say. But that wasn't the answer either.

He always knew the right thing to say to get what he wanted, or had until Coyote showed up. But now he didn't know what he wanted. Calliope had declared wanting a mortal sin. Talking to a woman, to anyone, without having an agenda was completely foreign to him. Where was he supposed to speak from? What point of view? Who was he supposed to be?

He was afraid to look at her, felt heat rise in his face when he thought about her looking at him, waiting. Maybe the truth? Where do you go to find the truth? She had found it, let it go at him. She had laid her hope in his hands and she was waiting to see what he would do with it.

Finally he said, "I'm a full-blooded Crow Indian. I was raised on a reservation in Montana. When I was fifteen I killed a man and I ran away and I've spent my life pretending to be someone I'm not. I've never been married and I've never been in love and that's not something I know how to pretend. I'm not even sure why I'm here, except that you woke something up in me and it seemed to make sense to run after something instead of away for a change. If that's the horrible act of wanting, then so be it. And by the way, you are sitting on the lap of an ancient Indian god."

Now he looked at her. He was a little out of breath and his mind was racing, but he felt incredibly relieved. He felt like he needed a cigarette and a towel—and maybe a shower and breakfast.

Calliope looked from Sam to Coyote, and then to Sam again. Her eyes were wider each time she looked back. Coyote stopped his snoring and languidly opened one eye. "Hi," he said. He closed his eye and resumed snoring.

Calliope bent over and kissed Sam's cheek. "I think that went well, don't you?"

Sam laughed and grabbed her knee. "Look, we've still got twenty hours on the road and I'm going to need you to drive. So get some sleep, okay? I don't trust him at the wheel." Sam nodded toward Coyote.

"But he's a god," Calliope said.

"'As flies to wanton boys, are we to the gods; / They kill us for their sport.'"

"What an icky thing to say."

"Sorry. Shakespeare wrote it. I can't get it out of my mind this week. It's like an old song that gets stuck."

"That happened to me once with 'Rocky Raccoon.'"

"Right," Sam said. "It's exactly like that."

CHAPTER TWENTY-NINE

SHIFTING

Sam drove through the day and into the night and finally stopped at a truck stop outside of Salt Lake City. Calliope and Coyote had been awake for the last few hours, but neither had spoken very much. Calliope seemed embarrassed about talking to the trickster, now that she knew he was a god, and Coyote just stared out the window, either lost in his own thoughts or (Sam thought this more likely) absorbed in some new scheme to throw people's lives into chaos. From time to time someone would break the silence by saying, "Pretty rock"—a statement which covered the complete observational spectrum for Utah's landscape—then they would lapse into silence for a half hour or so.

Sam led them into the truck stop and they all took stools at a carousel counter among truckers and a couple of grungy hitchhikers who were hoping to cadge a ride. A barrel-shaped woman in an orange polyester uniform approached and poured them coffee without asking if they wanted it. Her name tag read, *Arlene.* "You want something to eat, honey?" she asked Calliope with an accent warm with Southern hospitality. Sam wondered about this: no matter where you go, truck-stop waitresses have a Southern accent.

"Do you have oatmeal?" Calliope asked.

"How 'bout a little brown sugar on that?" Arlene asked. She looked over rhinestone-framed reading glasses.

Calliope smiled. "That would be nice."

"How 'bout you, darlin'?" she said to Coyote.

"Drinks. Umbrellas and swords."

"Now you know better'n that—come into Mormon country and order drinks." She shamed him with a wave of her finger.

Coyote turned to Sam. "Mormon country?"

"They settled in this area. They believe that Jesus visited the Indian people after he rose from the dead."

"Oh him. I remember him. Hairy face, made a big deal about dying and coming back to life—one time. Ha. He was funny. He tried to teach me how to walk on water. I can do it pretty good in the wintertime."

Arlene giggled girlishly. "I don't think you need any more to drink, hon. How 'bout some ham and eggs?"

Sam said, "That'll be fine, two of those, over easy."

Sam watched Arlene move around the counter, flirting with some of the truckers like a saloon girl, clucking over others like a mother hen. She snuck a cinnamon roll to a scruffy teenage hitchhiker with no money and asked after him like an older sister, then moved across the counter and found the kid a ride with a gruff cowboy trucker. One minute she was swearing like a sailor, the next she was blushing like a virgin, and all the customers who sat at her counter got what they needed. Sam realized that he was watching a shape-shifter: a kind and giving creature. Perhaps he was meant to notice. Perhaps that was what *he* needed. She was good. Maybe he was too.

He turned to Calliope and caught her in the middle of losing a bite of oatmeal down her chin. "We can do this," he said. "We'll get him back."

"I know," she said.

"You do?"

She nodded, wiping oatmeal off her chin with a napkin. "That's the scary thing about hope," she said. "If you let it go too long it turns into faith." She scooped another bite of cereal.

Sam smiled. He wished that he shared her confidence. "Did you ever go to South Dakota with Lonnie? Will we be able to find them?"

"I went to the big summer rally, not this time of year. They don't camp with the other bikers. They rent land from a farmer in the hills. All the Guild chapters stay together there."

"Could you find it again?"

"I think so. But there's only one dirt road leading in there. How will we get Grubb out?"

"Well, I guess just walking in and asking for him isn't going to work."

"They usually have guns. They get drunk and play shooting games."

Coyote said, "Wait for them to go to sleep, then sneak in and count coup."

"They don't really sleep," Calliope said. "They do crank and drink all weekend."

"Then we will have to trick them."

"I was afraid you'd say that," Sam said. He spun on his stool and looked out the windows of the truck stop to the gas pumps, where a black stretch Lincoln was just pulling away.

Sam woke up in the passenger seat. The Z was parked sideways on the side of the road, the headlights trained over a pasture. The driver's seat was empty. Coyote, who was curled up in the tiny space behind the seat, growled and popped his head out between the seat. "What's going on?"

"I don't know." Sam looked around for Calliope. It was raining out. "Maybe she stopped to take a leak."

"There she is." Coyote pointed to a spot by the barbed-wire fence where Calliope was standing by a young calf, working furiously on something at the fence. A mother cow stood by watching.

"The calf's tail is stuck on the barbed wire," Coyote said.

Sam opened the car door and stepped out into the rain just as Calliope finished untangling the calf, which scampered to its mother.

"It's okay," she called. "I got him." She waved for him to get back into the car. She ran to the car and got in.

"Sorry, I had to stop. He looked so sad."

"It's okay. Pasture pals, right?" Sam said.

She grinned as she started the car. "I thought we could use the karma balance."

Sam looked for a road sign. "Where are we?"

"Almost there. We have to get going. There's been a car behind us for a while. I got way ahead of it, but I felt like it was following us."

She pulled onto the road, ramming through the gears like a grand prix driver. Sam was peeking at the speedometer when he saw a colored light blow by in the corner of his eye. "What was that?"

"The only stoplight in Sturgis," Calliope said. "I'm sorry, guys, it sort of snuck up on me. The Z goes better than it stops."

"We're here already?" Sam said. "But it's still dark out."

"It's a few more miles to the farm," Calliope said. "Sam, if a cop saw me go through that light can you take the wheel? My license is suspended."

Sam checked his watch, amazed at their progress. "You must have averaged ninety the whole way."

"I had to go to jail the last time they caught me. Three months. They taught me to do nails for vocational training."

"You did three months for a traffic violation?"

"There were a few of them," Calliope said. "It wasn't bad; I got a degree. I'm a certified nail technician now. In jail it was mostly LOVE/HATE nails, but I was good at it. I would have had a career except the polish fumes give me a headache."

Coyote pulled Grubb's blanket out of the hole in the back window and looked through. "It's clear. There's a car behind us but it's not a cop."

The sleeping town was only a block long—a stoplight with accessories. Calliope drove them through town and turned south on a county road that wound into the Black Hills. "It's a couple of minutes up this road to the turnoff, then about a mile in on a dirt road."

Sam said, "Turn off the lights when you make the turn. We'll drive halfway in and walk the rest of the way."

Calliope made the turn onto a single-lane dirt road that led

through a thick stand of lodgepole pines. The road was deeply
rutted, the ruts filled with water. The Z bucked and bottomed out
in several places.

"Keep it moving steady," Sam said. "Don't hit the gas or the
wheels will dig into the mud. Christ, it's dark."

"It's the trees," Calliope said. "There's a clearing ahead where
they camp."

Sam was trying to peer into the darkness. To his right he
thought he saw something. "Stop." Calliope let the Z roll to a stop.
"Okay," Sam said. "Hit the parking lights, just for a second." Calliope clicked the parking lights on and off.

"That's what I thought," Sam said. "There's a cattle gate back
there to the right. Back the Z in there so we can turn it around."

"Giving up?" Coyote said.

"If we have to get out of here fast I don't want to have to back
down this road." He got out of the car and directed Calliope as she
backed the Z in and turned it off. "We walk from here."

They got out of the car and started down the road, stepping between the puddles. The air was damp and cold, and smelled faintly
of wood smoke and pine. When the moonlight broke through the
trees they could see their breath.

Calliope said, "Wait." She turned and ran back to the car, then
returned in a moment with Grubb's blanket in hand. "He'll want
his wubby."

Sam smiled in spite of himself, knowing the girl couldn't see his
face in the dark. *Never face heavily armed bikers without your wubby.*

COYOTE AND COTTONTAIL

*It's an old story. Coyote and his friend Cottontail were
hiding on a wooded hill above a camp, watching some girls
dance around the fire.*

Coyote said, "I'd sure like to get close to some of them."

*"You won't get near them," Cottontail said. "They know
who you are."*

"Maybe not, little one. Maybe not," Coyote said. "I'll go down there in disguise."

"They won't let any man get close to them," Cottontail said.

"I won't be a man," Coyote said. "Here, hold this." Coyote took off his penis and handed it to Cottontail. "Now, when I come back into the woods I will call to you and you can bring me my penis." Then Coyote changed into an old woman and went down to the camp.

He danced with the girls and pinched them and slapped their bottoms. "Oh, Grandmother," the girls said, "you are wicked. You must be that old trickster Coyote."

"I'm just an old woman," Coyote said. "Here, feel under my dress."

One of the girls felt under Coyote's dress and said, "She is just an old woman."

Coyote pointed to two of the prettiest girls. "Let's dance in the trees," he said. He danced with the girls into the woods and tickled them and made them roll around with him laughing. He touched them under their dresses until they said, "Oh, Grandmother, you are wicked."

"Cottontail, come here!" Coyote called. But there was no answer. "Wait here for your old grandmother to return," Coyote told the girls. He ran all over the woods calling for Cottontail, but could not find him. He went over that hill to the next one and still no Cottontail. He was excited and wanted very much to have sex with the girls, but alas, he could not find his penis.

Finally the sun started coming up and the girls called, "Old Grandmother, we can't wait for you any longer. We have to go home."

Coyote stalked the hills cursing. "That Cottontail, I will kill him for stealing my penis."

As he walked he passed three other girls coming out of the woods. They were giggling and one of them was saying, "He was so little, but he had such a big thing I thought I would split."

Coyote ran in the direction the girls had come from and found Cottontail sitting under a tree having a smoke. "I'll kill you, you little thief," Coyote cried.

"But Coyote, I pleasured the three many times and four times I made each of them cry out."

Coyote was too tired from tickling and dancing all night to stay mad. "Really, four times each?"

"Yep," Cottontail said, handing Coyote his member.

"I feel like I was there," Coyote said. "You got a smoke?"

"Sure," said Cottontail. "Are you going to need your penis tonight?" Coyote laughed and smoked with Cottontail while his little friend told the story of his long night of pleasuring.

CHAPTER THIRTY

LIKE FLIES

They heard the bikers before they saw them: raucous laughter and Lynyrd Skynyrd from a boom box. They followed the road around a long, gradual curve that descended into a valley, stepping carefully to avoid the deep puddles. The trees were thinning out now and Sam could make out the light of a huge bonfire below them in the valley, and figures moving around the fire, a lot of them. Someone fired a pistol into the air and the report echoed around the valley.

"Do they have sentries or something?" Sam whispered to Calliope.

"I don't remember. I was pretty drunk when I was here before."

"Well, we can't just walk in."

"This way," Coyote said, pointing to a path that led away from the road. They followed the trickster up the path, through thick undergrowth, and up onto a ridge that looked down on the clearing.

From the top of the ridge they could see the entire camp. The fire was burning in the center of the camp with perhaps a hundred bikers and women gathered around it, drinking and dancing. The bikes were parked by the road leading in. There was a stand of tents and smaller campfires on the opposite side of the camp, with two pickup trucks parked nearby. Lynyrd Skynyrd sang "Gimme Back My Bullets."

"I don't see Grubb," Calliope said.

"Or the woman," Coyote said.

"Wait," Calliope said. "Listen." Amid the din of rock and roll, laughter, shouts, screams, and gunfire, they heard the sound of a baby crying.

"It's coming from the tents," Coyote said. "Follow, me."

Coyote led them farther down the ridge until they were about fifty yards from the tents and could see four women sitting around a campfire drinking and talking. One of them was holding Grubb.

"There he is," Calliope said. She started down the ridge and Sam caught her arm.

"If you go down there that woman will call for Lonnie and the others."

"What can I do? We have to get him."

"Take off your clothes," Coyote said.

Sam sneered at the trickster, "I don't think so."

"Here, take this," Coyote said, handing something to Sam. Sam couldn't make out what it was in the dark, but it felt warm and soft. He recoiled and dropped it.

"Ouch," Coyote said, his voice soft now, feminine. "Is that any way to treat a lady?"

Sam looked, moved closer to the trickster, and saw that he was no longer a he. Still in his black buckskins, he had changed into a woman.

"I don't believe it," Sam said.

"You're lovely," Calliope said.

"Thanks," Coyote said. "Give me your clothes. These don't fit me now." He started undressing.

In the dim moonlight that filtered through the trees, Sam watched the women undress. Calliope was right, the trickster was gorgeous, a perfect female mirror of the male Coyote, an Indian goddess. Sam felt a little sick at the thought and looked away.

Coyote said, "I'll go down and get the child. Be ready to run. And pick that up, I'll need it." He pointed to the ground where

Sam had dropped his penis. Sam picked up the member in two fingers and held it out as if it would bite him.

"I'm not comfortable with this."

"I'll hold it," Calliope said, now dressed in the black buckskins.

"No you won't!" Sam said.

"Well." She cocked a hip and waited for him to make a decision.

Sam put the penis in his jacket pocket. "I'm not comfortable with this, I want you to know."

"Men are such babies," Coyote said. He hugged Calliope, girl to girl, and made his way down the hill.

Sam watched the trickster move away from them toward the fire. Unable to look away, he became nervous with his own thoughts. Calliope patted his shoulder. "It's okay," she said. "In my jeans he really does have a great ass."

Tinker lay in the bed of the pickup sulking, listening to the nearby women going on about how badly they were treated by their men and how cute the baby was. The little bastard had been crying for an hour. What the fuck had Lonnie been thinking, bringing a crumb-snatcher to a rally? From time to time Tinker sat up and looked over the edge of the pickup to pick out which of the women he would fantasize about getting a blow job from. Fat chance, stuck here in the truck. Fucking Bonner and his military discipline.

"This is a business trip," Bonner had said. "A business trip we wouldn't be taking if Tinker would have taken care of business. So Tink, you guard the truck. No partying."

What was the point rallying with your bros if you couldn't get fucked up and start a few fights? Fuck this action. At least it had stopped raining.

Tinker peeked over the edge of the truck to see a new chick coming up to the fire. What a piece she was! Right out of *Penthouse* or something. She looked Indian, long blue-black hair. What a fucking body. He watched her fawn over the baby and touch

Cheryl's face. Lonnie had fucked her up, bad. Tink wondered what it was like to hit a chick. He was getting hard thinking about it.

The Indian chick was holding the baby now, walking around the fire rocking it. She walked behind one of the tents, then ducked down. Tinker saw her shoot out the other side in a crouch, headed up the hill with the baby. Two people were coming down to meet her.

"Hey, bitch!" Cheryl yelled. The other women were on their feet, yelling—going after the Indian chick. Tinker jumped out of the truck and started to circle around and up the hill to head off the Indian chick. As he ran he drew his Magnum from his shoulder holster. He slipped, fell to one knee, and drew down on the Indian chick. No, fuck it. If he hit the rugrat, Bonner would have his ass.

He climbed to his feet and lumbered across the hill, watching the Indian chick hand the rugrat to a blond chick. They were on the path at the top of the ridge. *Gotcha!* He'd take the lower path and be waiting for them. They had to come out at the road.

As Tinker made his way up the dark path he heard scooters firing up below him. Good. Bonner would get there and he would already have it handled. He'd be out of the doghouse. He reached the spot where the two paths intersected and stopped. He could hear them coming up the path, the baby still crying. He leveled his Magnum down the path and waited. If the dude showed first he'd waste him without a word.

He saw a shadow, then a foot. Tinker cocked the Magnum, put the sight where the chest would appear. A rush went through him, waiting, waiting. Now!

A vise clamped down over the gun and he felt it wrenched out of his hand, taking skin with it. Another clamp locked down on his neck and he looked up into the eyes of his deepest fear. He felt his face come down on something hard and the bones of his nose crush. His head was wrenched back and slammed down again, then it went dark.

"Shade!" Coyote said.

Minty Fresh threw Tinker's unconscious body aside and looked up at the Indian woman. "Who are you?"

Sam said, "M.F., what are you doing here?"

"The name is Minty Fresh." He held Tinker's Magnum out to Sam, then let it drop. "I'm learning how to sneak up on people." He saw the baby and smiled. "You got him."

"It was a fine trick," Coyote said.

"Who are you?" Minty insisted.

"It's your old buddy Coyote." Coyote cupped his breasts.

Minty stepped back from the woman to get a better look. "Something's different, right? Haircut?"

"We have to go," Calliope said.

"To where?" Minty said.

Calliope looked at Sam, panicked, confused. Sam had no answer.

Coyote said, "Montana. The Crow res. Come with us, shade. It'll be fun."

Minty turned to the roar of bikes behind him. "They're coming up the road," he said. "I'll block them as long as I can with the limo."

They made their way down the path to where the Z was parked. The limo was parked in front.

"I'll drive," Sam instructed. "Cal, you and Grubb in the back." They got in the car as lights from the Harleys broke through the woods. Minty got in the limo, started it, and pulled it forward to make way for the Z.

Sam pulled the Z into the road, careful not to spin the wheels in the mud. You guys okay?" he said to Calliope, who had curled herself around Grubb.

"Go," she said.

The bikers broke into view, Lonnie Ray in front. Minty hit the brights on the limo, hoping to blind them. He checked the mirror to see the Z pulling away, then started to back the limo up, careful to keep it in the middle of the road to block the bikes.

As Lonnie approached the limo he drew a pistol from his jacket and leveled it at Minty through the windshield. Minty ducked and hit the gas. The limo revved and stopped, the back wheels of the heavy car buried in the mud. Lonnie jumped off his bike onto the hood of the limo and braced himself on the roof as he aimed and fired at the Z.

At the sound of the shot Minty looked up to see the barrel of Lonnie's pistol pointing at him through the windshield. The other bikers, unable to get past, moved up around the limo.

"You're finished, spook," Lonnie hissed. He cocked the pistol. "Move the car out of the road."

"I don't think so," Minty said.

Lonnie jumped off the hood of the Lincoln and stuck the pistol through the window into Minty's temple. "I said move it."

"You move it," Minty said. He pushed the limo door open, knocking Lonnie to the ground. Two bikers yanked him from the car and rode him to the ground. Minty felt a boot in his kidney, then a fist in the stomach, then the blows fell on him like rain.

He heard Calliope's Z downshifting in the distance and smiled.

Sam pulled the Z back onto the pavement and floored it. "Everyone okay?" Grubb was still crying. Sam shouted, "Calliope, are you okay?"

Coyote turned in the passenger seat and reached back. "She's hit. There's blood."

"Oh fuck, is she—"

"She's dead, Sam," Coyote said.

PART FOUR

HOME

COYOTE HEARS HIS HEART

It is an old story, from the time of the animal people. Coyote was in his canoe, and had paddled all day and all night, only to find that he didn't know where he wanted to go. He sat in his canoe, drifting for a while, thinking that something was wrong. He wanted to do something, but he didn't know what it was, so he made some mountains and gave them names. But that didn't make him happy. He tried to think, but he wasn't very good at it, and he kept hearing a thumping noise that bothered him.

"Where should I go? What should I do? How can I think with all this noise?"

Coyote was becoming sad because he could not think, so he called out to the Old Mother, who was the Earth. "Old Mother," he said. "Can you stop this thumping noise so I can figure out where I am supposed to be?"

Old Mother heard Coyote and laughed at him. "Silly Coyote," she said. "That thumping noise is the sound of your own heart beating. Listen to it. It is the sound of the drums. When you hear your heart you must think of the drums—the sound of home."

"I knew that," Coyote said.

CHAPTER THIRTY-ONE

THERE ARE NO ORPHANS AMONG THE CROW

It was five hours from Sturgis to Crow Agency, and Coyote, back in his black buckskins, drove the whole way. Sam sat in the passenger seat, dazed, staring but seeing nothing, holding Grubb, rocking the baby in a rhythm to a pulsing emptiness in his chest and trying not to look at Calliope's lifeless body in the back. Mercifully, there was no thinking or remembering—his mind had shut down to protect him. Coyote was quiet.

As they drove through town an old warning sounded deep in Sam's mind and he mumbled, "I shouldn't be here. I'm in trouble."

"You have to go home," Coyote said.

"Okay," Sam said. He thought he should protest but he couldn't think clearly enough to remember why. "When we get there, no tricks, okay? Act human for a while, please."

"For a while," Coyote said.

A mile out of town Coyote pulled the Z into the muddy driveway of the Hunts Alone house. "Stay here," Coyote said. He got out of the car and went up the cement steps to the door. Sam looked around, seeing the house like a memory. It hadn't changed much. The house had been painted and peeled a couple of times and there were two horses, a paint and a buckskin, in the back field. An old Airstream trailer was parked by the sweat lodge and there were a couple more abandoned cars rusting in the side lot.

It all felt wrong, to have run so long to end up back where he had started—the danger that he had run from was still here, and now, with Calliope dead, he felt even weaker than the fifteen-year-old who had left so many years ago. As frightening as it had been to leave, it had been a beginning, full of hope and possibility. This felt like the end.

Coyote knocked on the door and waited. A Crow woman in jeans and a sweatshirt, about thirty, answered. She was holding a baby. "Yes?"

Coyote said, "I've brought your cousin home. We need help."

"Come in," she said. Coyote went into the house and came back to the car a few minutes later. He opened the door, startling Sam.

"Let's go inside," Coyote said. "I told the woman inside what happened." He helped Sam out of the car and pointed him to the door where the woman waited. Sam walked stiffly up the steps and past the woman into the house. He stood in the center of the living room, rocking Grubb. Coyote came in the door behind him. "Can I bring her in?" he asked the woman.

The woman looked horrified at the thought of a dead body in the house.

Sam turned suddenly. "No, not in the house. No."

Coyote waited. The woman looked uncomfortable. "You could put her in the trailer out back."

Coyote went back out. The woman came to Sam and pulled the blanket away from Grubb's face. "Has he eaten?"

"I—I don't know. Not for a while."

"He needs a change. C'mon, give." She put her own baby on the couch and coaxed Grubb out of Sam's arms. She spread the blanket on the coffee table and laid Grubb down on his back.

"I've heard about you," she said. "I'm Cindy. Festus is my husband."

Sam didn't answer. She took Grubb's dirty diaper off him and set it aside. "He's at work now, with his dad. They have their own shop in Hardin. Harry works with them too."

"Grandma?" Sam said.

She looked up and shook her head. "Years ago, before I met Festus." She brightened, trying to change the subject and the mood. "We have three other kids. Two other boys and a girl. They're in school—the little one in Head Start."

Sam stared over her head at the elkhorn hat rack hung with baseball caps, an old Stetson, and a ceremonial headdress. An obsidian-point buffalo lance hung beside it, next to an old Winchester and a *Sports Illustrated* swimsuit calendar.

"He's a strong baby," Cindy said, grabbing Grubb's fidgeting fists.

Sam looked back at her. "Pokey?" He looked down and away, a wave of grief washing over him. He walked to the kitchen doorway and stared at the ceiling, the first tears stinging as they welled up.

"Pokey's okay," Cindy said. "He went into the clinic last week. He almost— He was real sick. They wanted to move him to the hospital in Billings but Harlan wouldn't let them."

Cindy finished diapering Grubb and propped him up on the couch next to her own baby. "I'll fix him a bottle." She walked past Sam into the kitchen. He turned away from her as she went by. "Do you want some food? Coffee?"

Sam turned to her. "She never hurt anybody. She just wanted her baby back." He covered his face. Cindy moved to him and put her arms around him.

Coyote came in the front door. "Sam, we have to go."

Sam took Cindy by the shoulders and gently pushed her away, then turned and looked at Grubb, who was dozing on the couch. "He'll be okay," Cindy said. "I'll watch him." Sam didn't move.

"Sam," Coyote said, "let's go see Pokey."

Heading back through Crow Agency to the clinic, Sam noticed the new, modern tribal building and the new stadium behind it. Wiley's Food and Gas was still across the highway, just as it had been before. Kids were still hanging around outside the burger stand. Two old men shared a bottle outside the tobacco store. A mother led a pack of kids out of the general store, each carrying a bag of groceries.

"I shouldn't be here," Sam said. Coyote ignored him and kept driving.

The clinic was housed in an old two-story house at the far end of town. A line of people—mostly women and kids—waited outside. Coyote pulled into the muddy parking lot next to a rusted-out Buick. They crawled out of the car and walked up to the door. Some of the kids whispered and giggled, pointing at Coyote. An old man who was wheeling an oxygen cylinder behind him said, "Crow Fair ain't 'til next summer, boy. Why you dressed for a powwow?"

"Be cool," Sam said to Coyote. "Don't scare him."

Coyote shrugged and followed Sam into the waiting room, a ten-by-ten parlor with a checked linoleum floor and mint-green walls hung with racks of pamphlets. Twenty people sat in folding chairs along the walls, reading old copies of *People* or just staring at their shoes. Sam approached a window where a Crow woman was absorbed in scribbling on index cards, intent on not looking at those who waited.

"Excuse me," Sam said.

The woman didn't look up. "Fill this out." She handed a form and a stick pen over the counter. "When you hand it in—with the pen—I'll give you a number."

"I'm not here for treatment," Sam said, and the woman looked up for the first time. "I'm here to see Pokey Medicine Wing."

The woman seemed annoyed. "Just a minute." She got up and walked through the door into the back. In a moment a door into the waiting room opened and everyone looked up. A young, white doctor poked his head out, spotted Sam and Coyote, and signaled for them to come in. Everyone in the waiting room looked back down.

Inside the door the doctor looked them up and down, Sam in his dirty windbreaker and slacks, Coyote in his buckskins. "Are you family?"

"He's my clan uncle," Sam said.

The doctor nodded to Coyote. "And you?"

"Just a friend," Sam said.

"You'll have to wait outside," the doctor said.

Sam looked at Coyote. "Keep it under control, okay?"

"I said I would." The trickster went back into the waiting room.

"He should be in a real hospital," the doctor said. "He was technically dead, twice. We brought him back with the defibrillator. He's stable now, but we don't have the staff here to watch him. He should be in an ICU."

Sam hadn't heard a word of it. "Can I see him?"

"Follow me." The doctor turned and led Sam down a narrow hallway and up a flight of steps. "He was severely dehydrated and suffering from hypothermia. I think he'd been drinking even before he went on the fast. It leached all the fluids out of his body. His liver is shot and his heart sustained some damage."

The doctor stopped and opened a door. "Just a few minutes. He's very weak."

The doctor went in with Sam. Pokey was lying in a hospital bed, tubes and wires connecting him to bottles and machines. His skin was a brown-gray color. "Mr. Medicine Wing," the doctor said softly, "someone is here to see you."

Pokey's eyes opened slowly. "Hey, Samson," he said. He smiled and Sam noticed that he still hadn't gotten false teeth.

"Hey, Pokey," Sam said.

"You got bigger."

"Yeah," Sam said. Seeing Pokey was breaking through his fog, and he was starting to hurt again.

"You look like shit," Pokey said.

"So do you."

"Must run in the family." Pokey grinned. "You got a smoke?"

Sam shook his head. "I don't think that would be a good idea. I hear you're still drinking."

"Yeah. I went to some meetings. They said I needed to get a higher power if I wanted to quit. I told them that a higher power was why I was drinking in the first place."

"He's outside now. Waiting."

Pokey nodded and closed his eyes. "I had a couple of visions about you meeting up with him. All those years he's quiet, then I get a bunch of visions. I thought you was dead until I had the first one."

"I couldn't come home. I shouldn't have. . . ."

Pokey dismissed the thought with a weak wave of his hand. "You had to go. Enos would've killed you. He checked on us for years, lookin' in our mailbox for letters, watching the house. He drove himself plumb crazy. He give up on you when Grandma died and you didn't come home."

Sam had listened to the last part of the speech sitting on the edge of the bed with his back to Pokey. His knees had given out at the news that Enos was alive. He stared at the door. "I don't feel anything," he said.

"You okay?" Pokey said, trying to grab his nephew's arm.

"There's nothing. I'm not even afraid."

"What's wrong?"

Sam looked over his shoulder at Pokey. "I thought I killed him."

"You busted him up real good. Broke both his legs and an arm sliding down the face of the dam. Tub a lard didn't even have the manners to drown."

"I been running for nothing. I . . ."

"I should of never give you that Coyote medicine," Pokey said. His breath was starting to come in rasping gasps. "I thought if I got rid of it I wouldn't be crazy no more."

"It's okay." Sam patted Pokey's arm. "I don't think you had a choice."

Pokey continued to breathe heavily. "I saw a shadow that said you were going where there was death. I didn't know where to find you. I told Old Man Coyote. He said he knew." Pokey gripped Sam's arm. "He said he knew, Samson. You got to get away from him."

"Calm down, Pokey." Sam stood and put his hands on Pokey's shoulder. "It's okay, Pokey. It wasn't my death. Do you want the doctor?"

Pokey shook his head. His breathing started to calm. Sam took a pitcher of water from the bedside table and poured some into a paper cup. He held it while Pokey drank, then helped the old man lie back. "Whose death?" Pokey asked.

Sam put the cup down. "A girl." He looked away.

"You loved her?"

Sam nodded, still looking away. "She had a baby. Cindy's watching him."

"When did it happen?"

"This morning."

"Was Old Man Coyote with you when it happened?"

"Yes."

"Ask him to bring her back. He owes you that."

"She's dead, Pokey. She's gone."

"I been dead twice in the last two days. I ain't gone."

"She was shot, Pokey. A bullet went through her spine."

"Samson, look at me." Pokey pulled himself up on the bed so he could look Sam in the eye. "He owes you. There's a story that Old Man Coyote invented death so there wouldn't be too many people. There's another story that his wife was killed and he went into the Underworld to get her. There was a shade there that let her go as long as Coyote promised not to look at her until he got back to the world, but he looked, so now no one can come back."

"Pokey, I can't do this right now. I can't listen to this."

"He stole your life, Samson."

Sam shook his head violently. "This just happened to me. I didn't make any of it happen."

"Then make it happen now!" Pokey shouted. Sam stopped. "In the buffalo days they said that a warrior who had counted coup and had an arrow bundle could move in and out of the Underworld. He could hide there from his enemies. Go, Samson. Old Man Coyote can help you find your girl."

"She's dead, Pokey. The Underworld is just old superstition."

"Mumbo jumbo?" Pokey said.

"Yes."

"Crazy talk?"

"That's right."

"Voodoo?"

"Exactly."

"Like Coyote medicine?"

"No."

"Well?"

Sam didn't answer. He was gritting his teeth, glaring at his uncle.

Pokey smiled. "You still hate it when I talk about the old ways. Try it, Samson. What do you have to lose?"

"Nothing," Sam said. "There's nothing at all."

The doctor opened the door and said, "That's enough. He needs to rest."

"Fuck off, paleface," Pokey said.

Sam said, "Just one more minute, please."

"One minute," the doctor said, holding up his finger as he backed out of the room.

Sam looked at Pokey. "'Fuck off, paleface'?" He laughed. It felt good.

"Be nice, Squats Behind the Bush. I'm sick."

Sam felt something moving through him as he grinned at Pokey—something warm, like hope. "Now, quick, before you die again, you old fuck. Where do I get an arrow bundle?"

Sam came striding out of the clinic and grabbed Coyote by the arm, pulling him away from a group of kids he was lying to. What had been a paralyzing grief had changed to purpose. Sam felt incredibly alive.

"Let's go. Give me the keys."

"What's going on?" Coyote said. "Why the hurry? Did the old man die?"

Sam climbed into the Z and fired it up. "I've got to get to a phone, and I've got to get some clothes."

"What happened in there?"

"You knew she was going to be killed, didn't you?"

"I knew someone would."

"Pokey says that you can go in and out of the land of the dead?"

"I can? Oh, the Underworld! Yeah, I can. I don't like to, though."

"We're going."

"It's depressing. You won't like it."

"Pokey thinks you can bring Calliope back."

"I tried that once; it didn't work. It's not up to me."

"Then we're going to talk to whoever it's up to."

"Aren't you afraid?"

"I'm a little past that."

"Why do you need clothes?"

"We're going to Billings first, to get something."

"It's depressing. You won't like it. There's a big cliff in Billings that was a buffalo jump, but our people never drove the herds over it. The buffalo used to go up to the edge and say, 'Oh, no, it's Billings,' then they'd just jump over out of depression. Nope, you don't want to go to Billings."

Sam pulled into the Hunts Alone driveway, shut off the car, and turned to Coyote. "What's in the Underworld? What are *you* so afraid of?"

CHAPTER THIRTY-TWO

A DOCTORATE IN DECEPTION

According to Pokey, at the time the white men came, there were seven sacred arrow bundles. Each had been made by four medicine men who had the same vision at the same time. Once the bundles were made, the medicine men vowed never to gather again, afraid that if their combined power were stolen by one, he would become invincible and abuse the power. These bundles contained the most powerful of warrior medicine, able to protect the carrier from an enemy's weapon, give him the ability to travel swiftly, and escape to the Underworld in an emergency, to return later, unharmed. Of the original seven bundles, two had been destroyed by fire, two by flood, two were locked away in museums in Washington, and the last to leave the reservation was in the hands of a private collector in Billings, who had bought it from a family who had been converted to Christianity and thought the bundle might jeopardize their salvation.

At first Sam suspected Pokey's story. His choice finally to believe it was based more on heart than logic. Whether the story of the bundles was true or not didn't matter as much as the hope it inspired. Action based on hope just felt better than the paralysis of certainty.

When Sam came through the door of the Hunts Alone house, Cindy hardly recognized him. When she had first met him he seemed weak, wasted, and without reason to live. Now he was moving and talking with purpose.

Sam said, "Cindy, I'm sorry about before. I don't want to impose."

"You're family," she said, and that was all the explanation needed.

"Thanks," Sam said. "We went to see Pokey. He's doing fine."

"Did they say when he can come home?"

"We're bringing him home tonight, if things go the way they should. Can I use the phone?"

Cindy waved toward the kitchen table, where the phone sat amid a stack of cereal boxes and bowls. Sam checked on Grubb, found him sleeping, and went to the phone.

The first call went out to the Museum of the West in Cody, Wyoming. Yes, they knew a serious collector of Indian artifacts in Billings; they had bought several pieces from him over the years. His name was Arnstead Houston.

The next call was to his office in Santa Barbara. "Gabriella, I need you to take the key I gave you and go to my house. In my closet there's a corduroy jacket with suede elbow patches. Load it in my garment bag with the khaki pants, a flannel shirt, and that goofy Indiana Jones hat that Aaron gave me for Christmas. Put in my blue pinstripe suit—shirt, shoes, and tie to match. Then grab my briefcase and get it all on the next plane to Billings, Montana. Buy a seat for it if you have to. Put it on the corporate card. And run the name Arnstead Houston through all our companies' client files—go to the Insurance Institute if you have to. It's a Billings address."

He waited while Gabriella put the name through the computer and came back with the name of Houston's homeowner's insurance carrier. "Give me the agent's number." Sam scribbled it down. "Call me back at this number as soon as you confirm the arrival time of my stuff in Billings." He gave her the Hunts Alone number.

He dialed the number of Houston's insurance agent in Billings and spoke in an Oklahoma accent. "Yes, I'm interested in insuring some valuable Indian artifacts. Arnie Houston recommended you." Sam waited. "I didn't figure you handled that sort of thing. Do you remember who you referred Arnie to? Boulder Casualty? You got a number for them? Thanks, pardner."

Sam hung up the phone and it rang immediately. "Hello. Five today? That's the earliest? Thanks, Gabriella. Oh, I forgot—call and reserve a car at the Billings airport. Something with four-wheel drive. A Blazer or a Bronco or something. White if they have it. I'll pick it up at five. Yes, the corporate card. Fuck Aaron. Tell him I'm on a hunting trip. And Gabby, you are incredible, you really are. I know I've never told you that before. Because it was time I did. Take care."

He disconnected and dialed another number, waited, then spoke with an English accent. "Yes, Boulder Casualty. This is Samuel Smythe-White with Sotheby's, London. So sorry to bother you, but we've a bit of a problem that you may be able to help us with. It seems we've recently acquired some Red Indian items—a bit unusual for us—and we're at a loss as for someone to authenticate them. The owner, who must remain anonymous I'm afraid, has suggested that you insure this sort of thing and might know of an appraiser. Yes, I'll wait."

Sam held the phone aside and lit a cigarette. "No, no, location is not a problem. Sotheby's will fly him to London." Sam scribbled something. "Jolly good. Yes, thank you."

He disconnected and dialed Arnstead Houston's number. "Hello, Mr. Houston. This is Bill Lanier. I'm the new head of Ethnic Studies at the University of Washington. Yes. The reason I'm calling is that I just got a call from Boulder Casualty. It seems that there is an item in your collection that has been severely undervalued and they'd like us to take a look at it to make sure the schedule of coverage is in line. Of course, the new appraisal would increase the price if you should ever want to sell it." Sam paused and listened.

He continued, "A Crow medicine bundle. Yes. This one's a cylinder, a hollowed-out cedar log. That's right. Well, sir, we'll need to take a look at it in person. We happen to have a tribal expert visiting the campus right now. We could be in Billings by five thirty tonight. No, I'm afraid he has to fly to a dig in Arizona tomorrow. It will have to be tonight. Yes, I have your address. Thank you, sir."

Sam hung up, sat back, and let out a long sigh. The whole process had taken less than five minutes. When he turned around both Cindy and Coyote were staring at him. Cindy's mouth was hanging open.

"What was that?" Coyote asked.

"You," Sam said, "are now working, indirectly, as an artifacts expert for the Boulder Casualty Insurance Company and I am now a professor of anthropology at the University of Washington."

"I've been looking for a job," Cindy said, shaking her head. "They always make *me* fill out an application."

Coyote looked at Cindy. "He has shifty eyes, don't you think?"

Arnie Houston sat in his den looking at the arrow bundle on the coffee table before him: a hollowed-out log full of junk. But there was nothing quite so exciting as turning junk into money, and he was so excited now he could have peed his Wranglers. God bless archaeology. God bless museums. God bless historic preservation. God bless America!

Where else could a piece of oil-field trash with a fourth-grade education be living in a twenty-room house with a new Corvette in the garage, wearing thousand-dollar sea-turtle-skin boots and two pounds of silver and turquoise jewelry? And all of it from buying and selling Indian junk. God bless every eggheaded, gopher-hearted anthropologist that ever wrote a paper or dug a hole. Damn!

Arnie got up and went over to his bar, where he poured himself a snifter of Patrón tequila—thirty bucks a bottle, but the finest cactus juice ever burned hair off your tongue. And it calms you down. Can't let them think you're in it for the money, the dumb shits: most of 'em could say howdy in thirty-seven dead languages, tell you the time a day a shaman shit two hundred years ago plus the ritual that went with it, but couldn't tell a nickel from a knothole when it came to money.

They always went to the tribal council or a medicine man when they wanted to buy something—that was their big mistake. You got to do your research. Find out what family's got something and then find the one in the family who drinks the most. When he's feeling his firewater, you be there with the cash. Presto, you got yourself a priceless Indian artifact for dirt cheap. Arnie had just picked up a whole basket of heirloom beadwork over at the Yakima res—a hundred bucks. The Yakima were just getting into crack cocaine and Arnie was in on the ground floor with investment capital. The beads had been in the families for hundreds of years and he'd already had an offer of ten thousand for them from the Museum of the West—upon authentication, of course.

Anthropologists, here's to 'em! Arnie thought. He toasted the fish in the aquarium by the bar and tossed back the Patrón, then took a gamble by looking out the front window. A white Blazer pulled into the circular driveway and two men got out, both of them tall—one, an Indian in a suit, and the other in a corduroy jacket and khakis: the anthropologist. The Indian must be the expert he talked about on the phone. City Indian: making a living off of being Indian, going on about exploitation and such. *Worthless troublemakers: wouldn't shoot one if I needed to unload my gun.*

Arnie stashed the snifter under the bar and went to the front door. He brushed back the sides of his hair with his fingers—careful not to disturb the five strands combed over the top—and opened the door.

"Mr. Houston, I'm Dr. Lanier from the University of Washington. This is Running Elk, the gentleman I mentioned on the phone." The Indian nodded.

"Come on in," Arnie said, waving them into the tiled foyer. "I took it out of the safe and put it on the table for you." He didn't really have a safe, but it sounded good.

He led them into the den and stood by the coffee table. "Here she is."

The Indian moved to the fish tank and peered in. The professor walked around the table looking at the log, as if he were afraid to pick it up. "Have you opened it?"

Arnie had to think. What was the best answer? These fellows liked playing detective, finding their own clues. "No, sir. The fella I got it from told me what was inside, though. Four arrows, an eagle skull, and some, er . . ." Damn, how do you describe it? It was just brown powdery shit. "And some sacred powder."

"And who did you get it from?"

"Fellow on the res. Old family, but he didn't want me to say. He's afraid of the Traditionals getting revenge on him."

"I'm going to have to open it to determine the value."

"Quite so," the Indian said, still looking in the fish tank. The anthropologist shot him a nasty look. What was up with these two? An Indian who talks like a Brit; if that didn't just beat the ugly off an ape.

"It's okay with me," Arnie said. "Looks like them ends just come off like bottle caps." That's exactly how they had come off when he opened it.

"Jolly good, old chap," the Indian said. "The fish say that it's been opened before."

"Thank you, Running Elk," said the professor. He seemed kinda ticked.

He set his briefcase on the table next to the bundle, snapped open the lid, and removed some white cotton gloves. "We don't want to disturb the integrity of the contents," he said, slipping on the gloves. "I'd prefer to do this in the lab, but I assure you I'll be careful."

You can blow the damn thing up for all I care, Arnie thought, *as long as the price is right.* But what was the deal with the Indian and the fish tank?

The professor removed the end of the wooden cylinder and placed it on the table. He removed one of the four arrows and studied its length. When he looked at the point his face lit up.

"My God, Running Elk, do you see what I see?"

"What? What?" Arnie said. Was this good or bad?

The Indian looked up from the fish tank. "Oh, capital! He's promised them one of those plastic bubbling scuba divers if he sells it."

"What?" Arnie said.

The professor scowled at the Indian and held the arrow up for Arnie to see. "Mr. Houston, you see this arrow point?"

"Uh-huh."

"This is a small-game point, and the flaking is not the pattern you find on Crow points from the buffalo days."

"So?"

"So, I think this bundle is from the time before the Crows split from the Hidatsa. If that's the case, this bundle may be priceless."

Arnie saw a swimming pool appearing in his backyard, with a whole shitpot of girls in bikinis sitting around it, rubbing oil on his back. "How can you be sure?"

"I'll have to take it back to the university to have it carbon-dated." The professor put the arrow back into the bundle. From his briefcase he pulled out a sheaf of forms. "I hope you'll understand, Mr. Houston, the university can't bond something like this for its full value, but I could write a guarantee of perhaps two hundred thousand until the return." The professor waited, his pen poised over the form.

Arnie pretended to think about it. In fact, he was thinking about the new swimming pool. Now it was indoors and had a big hot tub full of dollies. "I guess that will be all right," he said.

The professor began writing on the form. "We should have it back to you within the week. I'll see to it personally that it's handled carefully. If you'll just sign here." He pushed the form over to Arnie.

There it was, $200,000.00 in big black numbers. It was all he needed to see. Arnie signed and pushed the paper back to the professor.

The professor closed his briefcase and got up. "Well, I'd like to get this back to the lab by tonight and start the work on it. I'll call you as soon as we know for sure." He picked up the bundle and headed for the door.

"You take care now. Thanks," Arnie said, holding the door for them.

"No, thank you, Mr. Houston."

"Cheerio," the Indian said as they climbed into the Blazer. "Oh yes, your mates said they'd like a *Flipper* video and a bit of brine shrimp to eat."

Arnie watched the Blazer pulling away. Boy, the old professor was sure giving Running Elk hell for something. Eggheads. He wondered for a minute why the Blazer had mud on the license plates when it was so clean everywhere else. Hell with it, it was time to celebrate. A buddy had given him the number of a little dolly who for two hundred dollars would come over in her cheerleader outfit. He'd been saving it for a special occasion and it looked like it was time to dig out that ol' number and see if she really could suck the furniture out of a room through the keyhole.

As soon as they were out of sight of Arnie's house, Sam took the Indiana Jones hat off and smacked Coyote with it. "What were you thinking? You almost blew it."

"The fish said he tricked someone to get that bundle."

"And what did we just do?"

"That's different. It was a Crow bundle."

"You wanted to blow it, didn't you? Why didn't you just hump his couch or something? Why didn't you just tell him the truth?"

"Well," Coyote said, "if your trick worked it would make a good story."

"I'll take that as as compliment." Sam was no longer angry. They had the bundle; now it was time to think about the next part of the plan. He believed what Pokey had told him about the power of the bundle, and all Pokey had ever asked of him was to be believed. He said, "Coyote, will you help me get Pokey out of the clinic?"

"Another trick?" Coyote asked.

"Of sorts."

"I'll help, but I won't go to the Underworld with you."

CHAPTER THIRTY-THREE

DOORS

Some of the color had returned to Pokey's face and someone had taken the braids out of his hair and brushed it. He opened his eyes when Sam entered the room.

"You got it?" Pokey said.

"It's in the car," Sam said. Coyote came in behind him.

Pokey grinned. "Old Man Coyote."

"Howdy," Coyote said. "How many times you died now, old man?"

"A bunch. It's plumb wearing me out," Pokey said. "The medicine man got tired of singing the death song and went home. I think he got scared." Pokey pulled a cassette out from under his covers and held it up. "I got it on tape for the next time."

Sam said, "Pokey, we have the arrow bundle. What do we do now?"

"Ask him," Pokey said, pointing to Coyote.

"I ain't going," Coyote said. "He has to go alone."

"Samson needs a medicine man to sing the bundle song."

"That's why we're here," Sam said.

"You want me? I didn't think you believed I had medicine, Samson."

"Things change, Pokey. I need you."

"Well then, get me out of here." Pokey started to sit up.

Sam pushed him back. "I don't think you should be walking."

"Samson, I done told you, I had my death vision. I don't die in no hospital, I get shot. Now help me get up." He struggled to a sitting position and Sam helped him turn so his feet hung off the bed. "You're right, I don't think I can walk."

Sam turned to Coyote. "You promised to help."

The clinic was officially closed for the day, but the skeleton staff of two nurses was still on. Adeline Eats sat in the waiting room with her six children, who were all green with flu, insisting that she wasn't going anywhere until they got treatment, even if she had to wait all night.

For the twentieth time, the nurse at the window was explaining that the doctor had gone home for the night, when she heard the hoof beats on the stairs. She dropped her clipboard and ran out of the office to see a black horse coming down the stairs, an old, half-naked man bouncing on its back. She ducked back into her office to avoid being trampled and looked up in time to see a man in a corduroy jacket running behind the horse out the front door.

The nurse ran out into the waiting room to the front door, which dangled in pieces on its hinges. She watched the horse stop beside a white Blazer and rear up. The old man, his gray hair streaming in the wind, let out a war whoop and fell into the arms of the man in corduroy. Then, as she watched, the horse started bubbling and changing until it was a man in black buckskins. The nurse stumbled back in shock. Someone tapped her on the shoulder and she jumped a foot off the ground. She came down holding her chest. Adeline Eats said, "You got room for my kids now, or what?"

Riding in the Blazer, Pokey said, "Old Man Coyote, how do I send Samson to the Underworld?"

"Just open the bundle and sing the song. He will go."

Sam said, "What happens then? What do I do?"

"My medicine ends when you get there. You will see the one that weighs the souls. Don't be afraid of him. Just ask him if you can bring the girl back."

"That's it?"

"Don't worry about the monster. The Underworld is not what you think." Coyote rolled down the car window. "I have something that I want to do. I'll be there when you return." Coyote dove out the car window, changing instantly into a hawk and flying off into the night sky.

"Wait!" Sam said. "What monster?" He stopped the car.

Pokey giggled like a child. "A horse and a hawk in one night. Samson, do you know how lucky we are?"

Sam leaned forward and put his head against the wheel. "*Lucky* wasn't the world that came to mind, Pokey."

Pokey had called Harlan and the boys down from Hardin. While they prepared the sweat, Sam stood at the door of the Airstream trailer trying to make himself open it. For the first time in years he was aware of his childhood fear of the dead and unrevenged ghosts and he hesitated. Since Pokey had given him hope of bringing Calliope back, he hadn't really thought of her as dead. He wanted to see her before he went to the Underworld, but he was afraid. *Strange,* he thought, *after all these years of selling the fear of death, talking about it every day, now I'm afraid. She's not dead, not really.*

He threw the door open and stepped into the trailer. Calliope's body was lying on the built-in cot by the door amid camping equipment and fishing rods. Coyote had covered her with a blanket, leaving her face exposed. She could have been sleeping.

Sam sat on the cot by her and brushed a strand of hair away from her face. She was cold. He looked away.

"I wanted you to know . . ." He didn't know what to say. There was no face to put on to meet this face. If she would just open her eyes. He swallowed hard. "I wanted you to know that I would do anything for you. That all this craziness was—will be—worth it if I can bring you back. I've been hiding out for my whole life, and I don't want to live that way anymore. Anyway, I wanted you to know that Grubb will be okay. My family will take care of him. I'll be with you, one way or another."

Sam leaned over and kissed her. "Soon," he said. He got up and walked out of the trailer.

Across the yard, the fire crackled and licked the sky, heating the rocks for the sweat. Pokey sat on a lawn chair, the arrow bundle in his lap, his eyes glistening orange in the firelight. Harlan was carrying rocks from the fire to the pit inside the sweat lodge. Sam stood by with Harry and Festus, watching. After the initial surprise that Sam was still alive, Harry and Festus simply fell into their normal roles of listening to their father argue with Pokey. Sam noticed that they had the lean, muscular frame of their father, the same square-set jaw. Harlan was a little thinner now, and his hair had gone gray, but otherwise, to Sam, he seemed the same.

"The boys and me have to go to work in the morning," Harlan said. "We can't stay late, Pokey. No drinking."

"I ain't going to drink," Pokey said.

Harlan dropped a hot rock into the pit and wiped sweat from his forehead. "I can't believe that doctor let you come home. Just yesterday he was puttin' your death on my hands for not moving you to the hospital in Billings."

"He's a pissant," Pokey said. "How's it coming?"

Harlan scraped another rock out of the fire and scooped it up with the pitchfork. "This ought to do it." He unbuckled his pants and began to get undressed. The others followed his lead, hanging their clothes on Pokey's chair.

Sam took the bundle from Pokey and put it in the sweat lodge, then helped the old man out of his hospital gown. Pokey crawled into the sweat lodge, where the others sat in a semicircle facing him.

"Before I drop the door, I got to open this here bundle. It's a real old one, so no one knows the right song. I'm going to have to make it up as I go along. Okay?"

Pokey held up the bundle and sang a prayer song, thanking the spirits for the gift of the sweat. He laid out a square of buckskin for the objects in the medicine bundle. "I don't know what's going to happen here, but Harlan, you and the boys got to pray that Samson has a safe journey. He's going on a kind of vision quest, but he ain't going to the Spirit World." Pokey looked at Sam. "You've seen her since you got here, right?"

"Yes," Sam said.

"And she's still in the trailer?"

"Yes."

"Who?" Harry asked.

"Never mind," Pokey said. They hadn't told Harlan and the boys about Calliope or Coyote. "Here we go." He threw a handful of sage onto the stones. When the smoke rose he held the bundle in it, then took off the cap. He began singing as he took each object from the bundle and set it on the buckskin. Sam closed his eyes and concentrated on going to the Underworld and what he had to do there.

> "Heya, heya, heya, an arrow.
> Heya, heya, heya, another arrow.
> Heya, heya, heya, another arrow.
> Heya, heya, heya, the last arrow.
> Heya, heya, heya, an eagle skull.
> Heya, heya, heya, some brown stuff."

"Some brown stuff?" Harlan said.

"Well, I don't know what it is," Pokey said. "It looks like brown stuff to me."

"Whatever it is, it's working," Festus said, pointing to Sam, who was shivering, even in the heat of the sweat lodge. His eyes were open but rolled back in his head, showing no pupils.

"I'm dropping the door," Pokey said. "Now pray for his return like you never prayed before."

CHAPTER THIRTY-FOUR

LET SLIP THE DOGS
OF IRONY

The owl was still perched on the power pole.

Adeline Eats sat in her easy chair reading the Book of Job, trying to keep her dinner down. On the way back from the clinic the kids had elected to have pancakes for dinner and Adeline had eaten a mountainous stack and all the mistakes. Now the matriarchs of breakfast, Aunt Jemima and Mrs. Butterworth, were waging a bubbling battle in her stomach while her kids burned with fever and Job suffered boils.

Adeline admired Job for keeping his faith. All she had was a house full of sick kids, a husband with a peyote hangover, an owl out front, and a little difficulty reading small print through her sunglasses, and she was ready to pack it in to her reserved spot in Hell. Old Job was quite a guy, especially with God acting like such a prick. What was that about? When her sisters talked about the Bible it was all the Sermon on the Mount and the Song of Solomon, Proverbs and Psalms; never smitings and plagues. And her sisters had never mentioned that God was a racist. He sure hated those old Philistines. Adeline had a cousin in Philadelphia; she wore a little too much eye shadow, but that didn't seem a sin you should get smote and circumcised for. . . .

Adeline's religious reverie was interrupted by a tidal surge of acid in her stomach. She put the Bible down and went to the kitchen for some Pepto-Bismol. She found the bottle and wrestled with the child-guard cap for five minutes before deciding to smite its head off with the cleaver Milo used for hacking deer joints. She was raising the cleaver when the doorbell rang like a call from the governor.

She waddled to the door and threw it open. An enormously fat white man in a powder-blue suit was standing on the steps, hat in hand, sample case at his side, grinning like a possum eating shit. He looked vaguely familiar.

"Pardon me, ma'am," he said. "I was looking for a Mrs. Adeline Eats, but I have obviously stumbled onto the home of a movie star."

Adeline remembered that she was still wearing sunglasses and her hair was piled up on her head. She lifted her glasses. "I'm Adeline Eats," she said. She peeked over his shoulder and shuddered. The owl was still on the pole.

"Of course you are. And I'm Lloyd Commerce, purveyor of the world's finest vitamin supplement and herbal remedy: Miracle Medicine. May I come in?"

Adeline eyed him suspiciously. "Didn't you sell me a vacuum cleaner a long time ago?"

"You've got a heck of a memory, Mrs. Eats. I did have the privilege of bringing to people's lives that beam of brightness known as the Miracle. How's it working?"

"I don't know. I don't have any rugs."

"Very shrewd, Mrs. Eats. What better way to avoid dirty carpets than to avoid carpets altogether? The very reason that I have turned my efforts to a product that addresses the number one problem facing families today."

"What's that?"

Lloyd put his hat over his heart. "If you could just afford me a minute of your time, you will reap the benefit of years of research."

"Okay, come on in. But you got to be quiet. My kids are sick and my husband is resting." Adeline stepped out of the doorway and the salesman floated by her to the couch.

Adeline sat in her chair across from him. Her stomach gurgled and rolled. She stifled a belch. "Excuse me."

"Indigestion!" Lloyd exclaimed as if he had discovered the cure for cancer. "Fortune has smiled on you, Mrs. Eats. I have in my case the bee's knees of indigestion remedies." He pulled a brown bottle from his case and held it out reverentially. "Mrs. Eats, may I present Miracle Medicine."

Adeline fidgeted. "I don't know if I can afford it. I've been off work for a couple of days taking care of my kids."

"In that case, you can't afford to be without it. And with a house full of illness you can't afford to wait."

"Will this stuff cure the flu?"

"The flu? The flu?" Lloyd shook the bottle at Adeline. "The flu doesn't exist when you have Miracle Medicine. It makes them that's sick well, and them that's well better. This is no backward primitive remedy, ma'am, but the finest product that nature and modern science could come up with. Miracle Medicine cures croup, cramps, cankers, and the creeping crud."

"I don't know . . . ," Adeline said.

"And how could you know until you try it? Why, Miracle Medicine will even raise your self-confidence, as well as doing away with excess mucus, the embarrassment of bad breath, intestinal gas, dandruff, the heartbreak of psoriasis, most mental illness, and the post-peyote dry heaves."

"I don't think so," Adeline said.

"You don't think so? Mrs. Eats, may I see your medicine cabinet?" Lloyd pulled a plastic garbage bag out of his sample case.

"I suppose so," Adeline said. "The bathroom is in there."

"Come with me," Lloyd said. He got up and led Adeline into the bathroom, where he threw open the medicine cabinet. He took a bottle of aspirin from the shelf and held it up. "What is this for, Mrs. Eats?"

"Headaches."

"Don't need it." Lloyd threw the aspirin in the garbage bag."

"Hey," Adeline said.

"Miracle Medicine makes headaches a thing of the past." He grabbed the tube of Preparation H and tossed it in the garbage bag. "Hemorrhoids are behind you, Mrs. Eats." Next went the cough medicine, the Band-Aids, some Neosporin ointment, and an old prescription for bladder infections.

"Hey, I need that stuff."

"Not anymore," Lloyd said. "Not with Miracle Medicine."

Adeline was starting to get angry. "Put that stuff back."

Lloyd lifted Adeline's sunglasses and looked her in the eye. "Mrs. Eats, you say you have a house full of sick kids. What exactly have you done to make them better?"

"I took them to the clinic but we couldn't get in. I've been praying."

Lloyd nodded knowingly. "Well you can say good-bye to prayer." He stormed back into the living room, picked up the Bible, and threw it in the garbage bag. "You don't need prayer when you have a medicine that reduces swelling, increases sex drive, and directly addresses the national debt."

"No," Adeline said, following him. "I don't want any."

He went to the crucifix on the wall, tore it off, and threw it in the bag. "Quiets coughs, promotes regularity, increases energy . . ."

"No!" Adeline said.

Lloyd took the 3-D picture of Jesus off the television and threw it in the bag.

"Calms nerves."

"No!"

"Cures acne."

"No!"

"Cures crabs, spiritual indecision, poison sumac, rabies, and—"

"No!"

"Gets rid of unwanted owls."

"How much is it?" Adeline said.

"Cash or check?" Lloyd said. He sat back down on the couch.

Adeline heard the bedroom door open. She turned and saw Milo coming into the living room, wearing sunglasses. He couldn't tolerate bright light for a day or two after a peyote ceremony. "What in the hell is going on out here?"

"I was just talking to this salesman," Adeline said.

"What salesman?"

Adeline turned around. The salesman, his sample case, and the garbage bag full of over-the-counter icons were gone. The brown bottle of Miracle Medicine sat on the table.

"Here honey, take some of this," she said. "You'll feel better."

She felt better already.

Sam felt as if he were passing out, then the vertigo of falling. The sounds around him faded; Pokey's voice became distant, then silent. He felt his stomach lurch, as if he had just gone into the big drop of a roller coaster, then an impact that flattened him on the ground. He looked up, expecting to see the others around him in the sweat lodge. The lodge, and everyone in it, was gone. There was nothing but blackness and the sound of his own breathing.

A thousand questions raced through his brain, but he realized that each one led to another and the best strategy was to maintain a state of automatic action and remember why he was here. He stood and squinted into the darkness. Two golden eyes were floating in front of him. He heard the sound of an animal breathing.

Suddenly a stone platform started to glow. On it stood a figure: a man's body with a dog's head, wearing an Egyptian kilt. Except for the golden eyes, he was black, so black he appeared to absorb light. He carried a golden staff tipped with the effigy of a falcon. Beside him on the platform was the source of the breathing sounds: a beast the size of a hippo, with the jaws of a crocodile on the body of a lion. It snorted and snapped at the air, flicking foam from its jaws. Behind them both stood a giant balance scale.

Despite all he had been through, Sam felt a wave of mindblanking terror pass through him. He wanted to run, but couldn't move. With the light coming off the pedestal he could see human bones scattered around him. He realized that he was standing on his toes, every muscle in his body rigid.

The black dog man snapped his staff on the platform. "Okay, up on the scale," he said. Then he narrowed his gaze and stepped down from the platform. "Wait a minute, you're alive. Go away. We only do the dead. Out, out, out."

Of all the strange things Sam had seen in the last week, watching the dog mouth forming human speech was the strangest. It looked like the creature was trying to yak up a chicken bone. Suddenly the fear was gone. This was too goofy, like an Alpo commercial filmed in Hell.

"Are you the one I'm supposed to talk to about—about getting some help?"

"Look, I tried to warn you that my brother was going to cause you problems. I sent my agent to help you."

"Your brother?"

"Coyote is my brother. He didn't tell you?"

"No, he never mentioned a brother. He said I had to find the one that weighs the souls."

The dog man scoffed. "Well there's the scale. And here I am. Take a wild guess. Go ahead, Einstein, figure it out. I can't believe he didn't mention me." He sat down, hung his head and began scratching himself behind the ears. "He's an ingrate."

The monster growled and Sam jumped back.

"That's Ammut," the dog man said. "He wants to eat you."

Sam shuddered. "Maybe later. I'm here to ask a favor."

"You don't even know who I am, do you? That hurts. You think I don't have feelings?"

"I'm sorry," Sam said. "I'm a little preoccupied. I didn't mean to be rude." Preoccupied? Naked, in a supernatural world, talking to the dog-food god, trying to get back the woman he loved. *Excuse my manners,* he thought. "I'm Sam Hunter, and you are?"

"Anubis, son of Osiris. God of the Underworld." He scratched behind his ears harder and his leg began to bounce with pleasure.

"Osiris? You're Egyptian?"

"My people lived in the Nile Valley, yes."

"But you said that you were Coyote's brother."

"He didn't tell you that story either?" Anubis was irritated.

"No, sorry," Sam said. How could Calliope's life be in the hands of this neurotic canine? He decided to try to placate the god. "But I'd love to hear it."

Anubis pricked up his long ears. "It was long ago," he began. "And the god Osiris brought to the people of the Nile Valley the knowledge to plant grain, and he brought great floods to nourish the grains. With his queen, Isis, he ruled all of civilization, until his brother Set, the dark one, became jealous and killed Osiris, tearing his body into fourteen pieces and scattering them over the valley.

"But Osiris had consorted with Set's wife, Nephthys, and she gave birth to two dog-headed sons, Anubis and Aputet. When Set found the boys he put them into baskets and set them afloat in the Nile. Later, Isis found Anubis and adopted him. But Aputet floated out to sea and across the ocean to another land in the West."

Here the dog-headed god puffed himself up with pride. "Anubis was always the one bound to duty, the faithful. He found the pieces of our father and bound them together so that Osiris lived again. For that he was given the job of weighing human souls against truth, and taking people to the Underworld.

"And my brother," Anubis said, "grew up in a wild land, with the powers of a god and no sense of duty or justice. All he cares about is the stories people tell about him. And he never remembers his brother, who has saved him so many times. He never visits. You're sure Coyote never told you this?"

Sam didn't know what to say. He thought of the Coyote tales he had heard as a child, and how this seemed to fit. "No, I was told he brought my people the buffalo and taught us how to live off the land."

"He did those things to serve himself. Without a way to live, how could they tell stories about him? He has used me for years to make his stories. Now he has returned to Earth and used you."

It all fit. "He fucked up my life and got Calliope killed for the stories." Sam was trying to control his anger. "I'm here because he wants people to tell stories about him?"

"He had to or he would end up like me." Anubis lowered his voice. "Your people don't have a word in their language for 'computer' or 'VCR' or 'television.' The children are losing the old stories, the stories of hunting buffalo and counting coup. That's not their world. Coyote was afraid he would be forgotten, like me. With the new stories he's real again. You lived the stories that will bring him back. He doesn't care about the people, only that they are talking about him. I tried. I sent my agent to help you."

Sam looked at Anubis. "The big black guy, Minty? You sent him?"

"He's mine, a dutiful son, but he doesn't know it," Anubis said. "I can no longer walk in your world because I am a dead god. I died of change. So I sent the black one to help you. He is mine like you are Aputet's."

"I'm his? What does that mean?"

"You were born for his stories. To live them, to carry them on."

"He wants little kids to hear stories about killing innocent women? That's supposed to be good for a people?"

"He doesn't care. As long as the stories are told they will hold his people together. He says people need a good bad example. It gives them pride in doing the right thing. I have always done the right thing and my people are gone because of it, swallowed up by the Christian god."

"So how does the story end?" Sam asked. "Can I bring back Calliope? She didn't do anything wrong."

"I weigh the souls of the dead against truth. If there is balance, then the soul passes on. If not, I feed it to Ammut." The monster snarled at the mention of his name. "I'm stuck here doing this tedious work while my brother roams the world having fun. It's not fair."

Sam kept pressing. "Let me take the girl back. It's not her fault that Coyote is a jerk."

"No," Anubis said. "My brother needs to learn a lesson. He has never had to sacrifice anything."

"Let her live and I'll tell your story. You'll be remembered again. People will believe." Sam had to keep pressing.

"Like the other stories?" The god affected a whiny, mocking tone. "'Then along came Coyote's brother, who jumped over him four times, and he came back to life.'" I never even get my name mentioned."

"Please," Sam pleaded.

Anubis shook his head slowly. "No. Tell my brother he needs to learn to sacrifice for his people. I have done what I can do." The jackal-headed god stood and walked off the pedestal into the darkness, the monster at his heels.

"Wait!" Sam started to run after him. The pedestal went dark and he felt the loss of his love even as the ground dropped out from under him.

Just before dawn Coyote climbed into the sweat lodge and sat beside Pokey. Sam's body was shaking, his eyes still rolled back in his head. "Wait!" he screamed. He jerked, as if someone had applied a current to his body, and his eyes rolled down. The door flap of the sweat lodge was thrown open and the first light of dawn was spilling through.

"How's my brother?" Coyote asked.

Sam lunged for Coyote's throat. "You killed her for stories!" Pokey caught him from behind in a bear hug.

"No, Samson." Pokey struggled to hold Sam. "You were gone all night. Harlan and his boys left. Someone named Minty Fresh called the house for you. He said to tell you that some bikers are coming here to take the child. He said they would be here about dawn."

CHAPTER THIRTY-FIVE

CRAZY DOGS WISHING TO DIE

The Underworld made Calliope's death real, stripping Sam of the last of his hope, leaving him like a raw, screaming nerve. He ran naked out of the sweat lodge and dove into the cooling fire pit.

"Samson, stop it!" Pokey shouted.

Sam grabbed handfuls of ashes and rubbed them on his face and chest, then ran through the yard and into the house, Coyote and Pokey close behind him.

They found him in the living room, pulling the buffalo lance off the wall. The women had taken the children and retreated to the bedrooms. Pokey could hear them crying. Coyote grabbed Sam by the shoulder. "Stop this."

Sam shrieked and swung around with the lance, slashing Coyote across the chest with the long obsidian point. The trickster fell back bleeding. Sam ran out of the house.

"Go get him," Pokey said to Coyote.

Coyote got up and ran out the front door in time to see Sam vaulting the fence into the side field. Sam jumped on the back of a buckskin horse and wrapped a hand in its long mane, then dug his heels in and smacked the lance across its hindquarters. The horse shot forward and over the fence into the road, taking a line of barbed wire out with its front legs.

"Sam, wait!" Coyote shouted. Sam pulled the horse up and looked back at the trickster. Pokey joined Coyote on the porch.

"Samson, don't do this," Pokey said.

"I'm tired of being afraid, Pokey. This is a good day to die." Sam slapped the horse's flank with the lance and galloped down the road.

"Get the gate," Coyote shouted to Pokey. He ran to the field, scooping up a handful of mud from some tire tracks as he ran and rubbing it on his face and chest. He vaulted the fence and the paint horse, spooked by the commotion, ran to the other side of the pasture. "Come," Coyote commanded.

The paint horse stopped as if it had been jerked back by an invisible rope, then turned and galloped back to the trickster. Coyote calmed it, then climbed the fence and jumped on its back.

Pokey swung the gate open and Coyote rode the horse through, up the driveway, and down the road after Sam.

Rarely does one encounter a combination of human traits quite so frightening as a psychopath with a purpose. Yet, as dawn broke in Crow Agency, forty examples of that particular perversion cruised, in a double column of Harley-Davidsons, off the ramp from Highway 90, under the overpass by Wiley's Food and Gas, and down the main street of town. Lonnie Ray Inman rode at the head of the column, followed closely by Bonner Newton on one side and Tinker on the other. Behind them were the other members of the Guild's Santa Barbara chapter, and behind them joiners from other Guild chapters who, pumped with the mere idea of self-righteous vengeance, had volunteered to come along.

Pulling into town, they were losing some of their resolve, and confused glances passed from one biker to another. They knew they were coming to the Crow reservation to get a kid who had been stolen, but now that they were here, what were they supposed to do? No one was out on the street at this hour to observe their fierce show of unity and force. It was rapidly turning into an unsatisfying experience, especially for those who were not used to wearing shoulder holsters and were a little chafed under the arms.

Lonnie slowed the column to a creep as he looked down the side streets of Crow Agency for signs of the orange Z. At the edge of town, near the tobacco shop, he signaled the column to stop. It was obvious they were about to head into open ranchland. The big bikes thundered out iron flatulence as they idled, putting up a din that rattled the windows of Crow Agency. A few lights went on in town; a few faces appeared in windows. Lonnie Ray signaled Bonner to join him for a conference. Bonner Newton was moving to his side when they heard the war cry.

Lonnie and Bonner looked down the road to see two men on horses charging them, one waving a spear over his head and screaming. Bonner was the first to recover from the shock and started to draw his pistol when a shot went off to his left and the speedometer on his bike exploded, peppering him with splinters of glass and metal.

"I wouldn't draw that." The voice came from the rooftops. "I wouldn't fucking move." Bonner looked up to see someone holding a scoped hunting rifle on them. The horsemen were still bearing down on them. One of the bikers in the column started to draw and a shot came from the other direction, taking the light off his bike. There was another one on the roof across the street. The bikers looked around. There were four men with scoped high-powered rifles pointing down on them from different rooftops.

"I can take a flea off a gnat's ass at two hundred yards with this," Harlan shouted over his rifle. "You let them popguns stay where they are."

Sam screamed again, a long rasping wail.

"He's not fucking stopping," Tinker said. He drew his Magnum and fired before Harlan put a bullet in his shoulder, spinning him off his bike to the pavement. Coyote grabbed his chest and rolled off his horse, bouncing into the ditch. Seeing that Sam wasn't going to stop, Bonner Newton dropped his bike and dove into the gutter, covering his head.

Lonnie watched the crazed horseman, streaked with ashes and sweat, bearing down on him. Sam was only a few yards away, raising his lance for the kill, when Lonnie went for his gun. Sam yanked on the horse's mane, jumping it over the front of the bike. One hoof hit Lonnie in the chest; another took off a piece of his right ear before the horse stumbled into the bikers behind him. Sam rolled free and up to his feet. He ran back to where Lonnie lay and raised the lance above his head as Lonnie's eyes went wide and he screamed.

"Samson!" Harlan shouted.

Sam put all his weight behind the lance and came down with it, screaming at the top of his lungs. At the last second he spun the lance and touched Lonnie on the chest with the butt end. "Go away," he said.

Sam stumbled away and dropped the lance.

"That's it," Harlan shouted. "Everybody just turn your bikes around and go back the way you came. We'll drop the first one that looks like he's doing the wrong thing."

The bikers looked around in confusion. Festus, Harry, and Billy Two Irons kept their rifles shouldered and trained on the column. Bonner Newton climbed to his feet. "Turn around," he said, waving his hand in the air. He looked at Lonnie. "See if Tink can ride. Let's get the fuck out of here."

Sam walked back down the road to where Coyote had fallen. The trickster was lying naked in the ditch, covered with mud, his leg bent under him. Blood was coursing from a hole in his chest and he was breathing in short, rattling pants. Sam bent over him and held his head. Coyote's eyes slowly opened. "That's the last coup," Coyote said. "You counted the last coup. It's a new world now." The trickster coughed; foamy blood covered his lips.

Sam had no anger left, no thoughts, no words. A minute passed. He heard someone blowing a car horn somewhere, and Harlan saying, "Let him through."

Finally Sam said, "What can I do?"

"Tell the stories," Coyote said. He closed his eyes and stopped breathing. Sam gently lowered the trickster's head and lay down in the ditch beside him. He heard a car pull up on the road above, but did not look up. A car door, footsteps, and hands under his body, lifting him. He opened his eyes to see a battered black face with golden eyes.

"Are you okay?" Minty Fresh said. Sam didn't answer. He felt himself being put in a car. "I'll take you home," Minty said.

Sam sat in the limo, the car door open, staring at the dashboard. Someone walked up beside him and said, "Nice outfit, Hunts Alone." Sam looked up to see Billy Two Irons standing over him: older, and just as thin, but unmistakably Billy Two Irons.

Sam managed a weak smile. "Your face cleared up."

"Yeah," Billy said. "I got laid, too. Only last week, but who's counting after thirty-five years?"

Sam looked forward trying to squint back tears. Billy shuffled a bit with discomfort. "This guy's going to take you home. I'll stop by when things settle down a little."

Sam nodded. "It was a good day to die."

"You're always trying to cheer me up," Billy said. "Don't take off again, okay?" He patted Sam's shoulder and opened the back door of the limo for Minty Fresh, who laid Coyote's body on the backseat, then closed the door.

Minty closed Sam's door, then went around and got in on the driver's side. He put the key in the ignition and paused. Without looking at Sam he said, "I'm sorry. Your uncle told me about the girl. They beat on me pretty bad and I told them where you were going. I screwed up. I'm sorry. If I could make it up . . ."

Sam didn't look up. "How did you get away?"

"They found my casino ID. I think the rumors about the Mafia running the casinos is what stopped them. They were afraid of retribution. I called the casino and got your office number. Your secretary gave me the number here. I called as soon as I got away."

Sam didn't say anything. Minty started the limo and pulled slowly onto the road, headed out of town to the Hunts Alone place.

Sam said, "What are you going to do with his body?

"I don't know. I guess it will come to me, like everything else I've done in the last two days."

Sam looked at Minty, and for the first time saw the golden eyes, surrounded with bruises. "Do you know what's happened here? Do you know what we are?"

Minty shook his head, "What we are? No. I was a trouble-shooter in a casino until yesterday. Now I guess I'm a car thief."

"You didn't really have any choice. But I think it's over now. You're free now."

"Sure, throw that responsibility on me," Minty said. He grinned.

Sam reached deep down and found he had a smile left, like the last worm in the bait can. They were approaching the Hunts Alone place. Minty turned into the driveway and stopped. "Do you need any help?"

"No, I'll be okay," Sam said automatically, not knowing what he needed. He opened the car door. "Where will you go?"

"Like I said, I guess it will come to me. Maybe San Diego."

"You can stay here if you want."

"No, I don't think so. But thanks. I'm feeling like there's still something I have to do."

"When it comes to you, remember, the sacred number is four. You jump over the body four times."

"Am I supposed to know what that means?"

"You will," Sam said. "Good luck." He got out of the car and stood at the end of the driveway watching Minty drive away. What now? He hadn't died, and he didn't have a life to return to. Nothing. Empty. Dead inside.

He turned and started toward the house. Cindy and another woman appeared at the door, and waited. From the shocked look on their faces Sam realized how crazed he must look: naked, covered with soot, streaked with sweat and tears. He waved to them and headed around the house to wash himself in the barrel back by the sweat lodge.

As he walked by the Airstream he heard the door unlatch and looked up.

Calliope stepped out of the trailer. "Sam?" she said. "I had the strangest dream." She looked around the yard, then at the trailer. "I didn't just land on the Wicked Witch of the East, did I?"

Sam closed his eyes and took her in his arms. He held her there for a long time, laughing, then sobbing, then laughing again, feeling as if he had, at last, come home.

COYOTE AND THE COWBOY

One day, a long time ago, Coyote was coming along when he saw a cowboy sitting on his horse, rolling a cigarette. Coyote watched the cowboy take a little pouch of tobacco out of his shirt pocket, and then some rolling papers. He poured some tobacco into a paper, then pulled the strings of the pouch tight with his teeth and put it back in his pocket. Then he rolled up the paper, licked it, and stuck the cigarette in his mouth. He lit it with a match.

Coyote had smoked a pipe many times, but he had never seen anything quite so wonderful as rolling a cigarette. "I want to do that," Coyote said. "Let me do that."

"You can't," the cowboy said.

"Why not?"

"You ain't got a shirt, so you ain't got a shirt pocket for your tobacco pouch."

Coyote didn't wear a shirt in those days. He looked at his bare chest, then at the cowboy's shirt. "I can make a pocket in my chest."

"Well, why don't you do that." The cowboy unfolded his pocketknife and handed it to Coyote. Coyote looked one more time at the cowboy's pocket, to get the size right, then he made

a deep cut in his chest. He looked a little surprised, then he fell over dead. The cowboy got back his pocketknife and rode off.

A little while later. Coyote's brother came along and saw the trickster lying dead on the ground. He jumped over Coyote's body four times and Coyote sprang up, good as new.

"You did it again," Coyote's brother said.

"I really wanted to roll a cigarette like the cowboy."

Coyote's brother shook his head. He said, "If you're going to live around these white folks, Coyote, you got to learn. Just because you want something, it don't mean that it's good for you."

"I knew that," Coyote said.

CHAPTER THIRTY-SIX

THERE AIN'T NO CURE FOR COYOTE BLUE

There is a saying that goes back to the buffalo days: there are no orphans among the Crow. Even today, if someone stays for a time on the reservation, he will be adopted by a Crow family, regardless of his race. The idea of a person without family makes the Crow uncomfortable. So when Samuel Hunter became, once again, Samson Hunts Alone, he found that there was family waiting for him, as well as his new white wife and her son. Pokey said, "There ain't near enough blond Indians, if you ask me."

And even as he left his old name behind with his old life, Sam maintained his shape-shifter ways, putting on each face as it was needed. Sometimes he was quick and clever, and other times he was simple, when simple served his purpose. When he spoke for the Crow to the government he wore traditional tribal dress and an eagle feather in his hair. But when he reported to his own people he dug out one of his Armani suits and the Rolex (that had long since stopped running), because that is what *they* needed to see. He was given the honor of pouring for the sweat, and the responsibility to carry on the old ways, and he programmed a computer to speak Crow, and using it, at the age of eighty, Pokey Medicine Wing learned to speak his own language.

And Sam put on many faces when he told the stories. When he told the old stories, of how Old Man Coyote made the world, of how he got his power to change shapes, of Cottontail and Raven and the other animal people, Sam was like the trickster himself, grinning and laughing, making rude noises, his golden eyes shining like fire. When he told the new stories—of the Crow man who had forgotten who he was, of a Japanese businessman who saved the life of an old shaman, of a black man who helped rescue a white child from the enemy, of all the tricks and machines that Coyote used to bring the Crow man home, and of the last coup— his voice took on a melancholy sweetness and his eyes went wide and bright, as if life itself was a delightful surprise. And when he told the story of the journey into the Underworld, of how Coyote's brother let Calliope live again because the trickster gave his own life, Sam became grave and dark, and those who doubted were quickly convinced when they saw the scar on Calliope's back from the bullet that had killed her. But even as Sam put on these faces and wore these personalities, he knew exactly who he was. He was happy.

After a while Calliope became pregnant and Sam's peace was again thrown out of balance. He was jumpy and nervous until the day the little girl was born and he saw that she had Calliope's deep brown eyes, not the golden eyes of a trickster. And meanwhile, as Grubb grew, he found that he could frighten his adopted father by hiding and making the sound of a coyote howling, and for this he suffered long lectures from his old Uncle Pokey about respecting his elders.

When Grubb was nine, in the time of the new grass, Sam took him to the great medicine wheel for his first fast. During the ride, in Pokey's ancient pickup truck, Sam instructed Grubb on how to enter the Spirit World and prepared him for what to expect there. "And one last thing," Sam said as he left the boy on the mountain. "If a fat guy in a big blue car comes along and offers you a ride, don't get in."

What Grubb saw on his vision, and what happened when he

grew up, is a story for another time. But it should be noted here that over the years, as he grew into manhood, his eyes faded gradually from dark brown to a bright, shining gold.

"Coyote medicine will do them white folks some good," Pokey said with a grin.

ABOUT THE AUTHOR

CHRISTOPHER MOORE is the author of ten novels, including this one. He began writing at age six and became the oldest known child prodigy when, in his early thirties, he published his first novel. His turn-ons are the ocean, playing the toad lotto, and talking animals on TV. His turnoffs are salmonella, traffic, and rude people. Chris enjoys cheese crackers, acid jazz, and otter scrubbing. He divides his time between San Francisco and an inaccessible island fortress in the Pacific. You can email him at BSFiends@aol.com. Visit the official Christopher Moore website at www.chrismoore.com.

SIMON & SCHUSTER PAPERBACKS
READING GROUP GUIDE

COYOTE BLUE
A NOVEL

CHRISTOPHER MOORE

Part love story, part vision quest, and always somewhat wacky, *Coyote Blue* tells the story of Sam Hunter—born Samson Hunts Alone on a Crow Indian Reservation, but who reinvents himself as a successful insurance broker, until he is hit with the lightning bolt of love that goes by the name of Calliope. However, as with all Christopher Moore novels, there is something . . . weird . . . afoot, and that comes in the form of Old Man Coyote, an ancient Indian god famous for his abilities as a trickster, who leads Sam into more trouble than he can imagine, but also helps him find his way home.

Questions for Discussion:

1. Sam Hunter was initially known as Samson Hunts Alone. What does his name represent? What about the other names in the novel? Is Moore telling us more with the naming? What Indian/Native American name would you select for yourself and why? What do you think describes you best?

2. In ancient Greek and Roman mythology Calliope was the Muse that was associated with creativity, music, artistic expression, and epic poetry. Why name the main female character that name? In what ways did Calliope inspire Sam? How did she lead him on a journey?

3. "Old Man Coyote," or "Coyote," is also known as the Trickster, who can alternately be scandalous, disgusting, amusing, and disruptive, but can also be a creative force in people's lives, transforming their worlds in bizarre and outrageous ways. Why do you think the Coyote comes into Sam's life when he does, and are all the changes he makes for the better?

4. Discuss morality in the course of the book. After the Coyote has disrupted Sam's life, he goes about "making things right" in various ways—for instance, by getting Sam's home back by breaking Josh Spagnola's legs and helping to blackmail Aaron Aaron. Is he really doing right to Sam by doing wrong to others?

5. Sam doesn't drink because he fears the stereotype of the "drunken Indian" that he has left behind on the Crow Reservation. Discuss stereotypes and how grounded they are in reality. What other "stock" characters are represented in the book? How close are they to their stereotypes?

6. Religion and faith weave themselves into the book in many different ways from Indian/Native American mysticism, Egyptian mythology, to various eastern religions. Discuss faith as it relates to the characters in the book.

7. When Aaron is teaching Sam the various tricks of the insurance game, he tells him to "remember the three *m*'s: *mesmerize, motivate,* and *manipulate*" because you're not selling a

need, but rather a dream. How does Sam react to this? What does this say about his character?

8. Discuss the idea of communities serving as extended families, which is something stressed in the book about the Crow tribe. Discuss other examples of the "it takes a village" idea.

9. Chart Sam's course from denying his heritage to "finding his way home." Identify and discuss key points in the book that mark a turning point in Sam's journey.

10. Which main character did you get the most "attached" to in the book? Sam? Coyote? Why? What qualities of this character make them endearing to you?

Enhancing Your Book Club:

1. Imagine leaving the life that you grew up with and creating an entirely different persona for yourself, as Sam did. What would you change about yourself, where would you go? What new profession would you choose?

2. In many Native American cultures, when you enter the Spirit World, you can be reincarnated as some new being. Do you believe in reincarnation? If so, what would you like to return as? Why? Learn more about reincarnation at http://en.wikipedia.org/wiki/Reincarnation.

3. Learn more about Christopher Moore and his other works at www.chrismoore.com/.

Also available from *New York Times* bestselling author Christopher Moore

> "Bloody funny!
> Like a hip and youthful 'Abbott
> and Costello Meet the Lugosis.'
> His laugh-out-loud one-liners . . .
> make horror a hoot."
> —*San Francisco Chronicle*

A romance novel like none other, *Bloodsucking Fiends* is the bloodcurdlingly funny story of the relationship between Jody, a beautiful redheaded vampire, and Tommy, a supermarket night manager and would-be writer. A tale of passion, bloodlust, and blood loss, *Bloodsucking Fiends* is Moore at his best: achingly funny and filled with characters both memorable and real.

> "Moore's storytelling style is reminiscent of
> Vonnegut and Douglas Adams."
> —*The Philadelphia Inquirer*

> "The careers of the writers with even a quarter
> as much wit and joie de vivre as Moore are
> always worth following." —*USA TODAY*

> "The funniest writer of comic fantasy novels
> working today." —*The Washington Post Book World*